Fly Me

Fly Me

A NOVEL

Daniel Riley

Little, Brown and Company

New York Boston London

Little, Brown and Company
Hachette Book Group
1290 Avenue of the Americas, New York, NY 10104
littlebrown.com

First Edition: June 2017

Little, Brown and Company is a division of Hachette Book Group, Inc. The Little, Brown name and logo are trademarks of Hachette Book Group, Inc.

The publisher is not responsible for websites (or their content) that are not owned by the publisher.

The Hachette Speakers Bureau provides a wide range of authors for speaking events. To find out more, go to hachettespeakersbureau.com or call (866) 376-6591.

Excerpt on page vii from "Notes from a Native Daughter" by Joan Didion. Copyright © 1968, renewed 1996 by Joan Didion. Published in *Slouching Towards Bethlehem*. Reprinted by permission of the author. • Excerpt on page 227 from "The Double Standard of Aging" by Susan Sontag. Copyright © 1972 by Susan Sontag, used by permission of The Wylie Agency LLC. • Excerpt on pages 274–275 from "Castling" by Renata Adler. Published in *Speedboat*. Copyright © 1976 by Renata Adler. Used by permission of the author. • Excerpt on page 286 from *The Hunters* by James Salter. Copyright © 1956 by James Salter. Used by permission. All rights reserved. • Excerpt on page 326 Copyright © 1973 by Thomas Pynchon. From *Gravity's Rainbow* (Penguin Books). Reprinted with permission by Melanie Jackson Agency, LLC.

Library of Congress Cataloging-in-Publication Data
Names: Riley, Daniel, author.
Title: Fly me: a novel / Daniel Riley.
Description: First edition. | New York: Little, Brown and Company, 2017.
Identifiers: LCCN 2016033558 | ISBN 978-0-316-36213-9
Subjects: LCSH: Flight attendants—Fiction. | California—Social life and customs—20th century—Fiction.
Classification: LCC PS3618.I532735 F59 2017 | DDC 813/.6--dc23 LC record available at https://lccn.loc.gov/2016033558

10 9 8 7 6 5 4 3 2 1

LSC-C

Printed in the United States of America

To Patti, Penny, Peggy, June, Ethel, LeValley, and all the other founding mothers of Sela del Mar

"California is a place in which a boom mentality and a sense of Chekhovian loss meet in uneasy suspension; in which the mind is troubled by some buried but ineradicable suspicion that things better work here, because here, beneath the immense bleached sky, is where we run out of continent."

—Joan Didion, "Notes from a Native Daughter"

Part I

Fourth of July
Nineteen Seventy-Two

See it like Suzy sees it. The wide white beach, the blue carpet rolling out to the edge, the red bodies cinched around the courts at Nineteenth Street. The peninsula to the north and the peninsula to the south, bookends on the bay. Just imagine how that view might register in the body of someone still getting used to living at the ocean. How it might bleach her judgment, boost her nerve, and lead her to places she never meant to go. This is what it looks like from the top of Nineteenth, where the blacktop green-flags its tumble to the water. As she steers her eyes over the edge, her body follows.

Suzy carving. Suzy rolling the board with the arches of her feet, all heels to all toes, way out wide and again across the middle. Suzy skimming the yellow centerline and snapping back at the curb, hard rubber and asphalt pinging like a typewriter. Suzy upright but curved, like parentheses, shifting open and closed, tracing even switchbacks, leveling the grade.

Suzy's got a cotton dress over an American-flag bikini, striped bottoms knotted at her hip. Her light-red hair blows back behind her like a vinyl banner tailing a single-engine Cessna. Suzy keeps her eyes on the asphalt but senses the beach growing closer, the music sharpening from bass to melody. It's already packed, clusters buzzing over the radio. She should know some of them, these boys from here, those girls from nowhere. She should recognize the ones from work (six or seven of the stews she flies with live in town), and from Howlers (she chatted with some staff at a show last weekend), plus Grace and Mike. It's Tuesday, Independence Day, and according to the note Grace left her this morning, Grace has "all sorts bitchin' shit in store for the 4."

Suzy pulls up halfway down the hill to straighten her sandal. It is morning still, just before noon. It is cool and gray, but bright—soft and expansive, like when a high-watt bulb sieves through a lampshade. Suzy feels a sudden heat in her hair. There is an elevation all around. The houses lining the street, single story and quietly proportioned, show themselves to be painted not shades of charcoal but full-spectrum colors. The palms and elms and bougainvillea that edge the small yards plug in like strings of lights. White pickets, wet surfboards, neoprene bodysuits salted and drying on the property fences. Suzy lifts her sight line over the rooftops toward the sweep of the horizon and pushes her butterfly frames up the bridge of her nose. The water glints like a scattered handful of ground-up glass.

The bottom half of the hill flattens out, and Suzy picks a straight line toward the sand. She aims the nose of her board toward the courts at Nineteenth and pulls herself tall like a bowstring. There's a busy avenue to cross at the bottom, and she barrels through with a quick prayer to the intersection. As she steps into the sand, the clouds break.

To Suzy Whitman, that promise of gray to blue—the burning off of the clouds, on cue each day near noon—has become proof that Sela del Mar was the right place to land after all. The certain spot for her just now. It's happened each day since she arrived: thirty mornings of June Gloom, reliably shed into summer. It was the first thing Grace mentioned when Grace and Mike moved to Sela. Not the palms. Not the beach tar. Not Taco Tuesdays at Howlers. But that weird weather thing, how it just seemed to vibe with what all these people were about.

Suzy slides her flip-flops off and sinks her feet into the sand, tucks her board under arm, turns her face up into the naked light. She wades farther out onto the beach, watches a volleyball game to her right. Though she expected to be among plenty of strangers, she's surprised she doesn't recognize anyone at all. Just bodies thrown wide, lunging for passing shots. Or hinged open in beach chairs, stretched out but propped up, like square root signs flipped over. All but one or two sets of skin are darker than hers. Even after a month in the sun, she hasn't had much success jackhammering through the calcified layers of her upstate winters. She's just never cared this acutely before, never given it regular thought. But around her now: the toasted girls alight with their gumminess, the boys with their counterhandsome peeling noses and white eyelashes. Their rhythmless rubber flailing to the Hollies. What is missing for them, Suzy has come to realize, is a plain self-consciousness. Their confidence, their satisfaction — complete and uncomplicated. That, and they're wasted already. Suzy keeps her dress on and looks for something to drink.

She slips between adjacent volleyball courts. The tournament has already been running for three hours. She'd been told all about it by Grace and Mike. The Drunk 'n' Draw. Mixed pairs, two on two, a case of Coors for each team to split. She doesn't know the pair receiving serve to her left but recognizes the other couple from Howlers. The boy's body is long and wide at the top — surfer's torso, swimmer's shoulders — and it's the color of the grilled hot dogs on the Weber. He serves from the back line and drifts into position to receive an on-two dink around midcourt. The pass to his partner at the net draws her into a setter's squat, and her hands move into a steeple above her head. The ball trampolines off her fingers, high and still like a soap bubble, and he leaps to meet it with the base of his palm. But the timing's all wrong. He's way up out of the sand before the ball hits its crest, and he slaps it open-handed and side-armed, on a direct course for Suzy's face. Without processing it, she gets both arms up and blocks the ball right back into the court. It's more effective than if she'd had time to think it over. The point evidently ends the game, and both teams look relieved to settle back in with their cases.

The guy passes Suzy and smiles. He tries to say something, but it comes out as sound and saliva. Suzy waves him off and says, "No, no, *I'm* sorry." She finds a keg buried at the weathered post at the edge of the court. The post has names and dates carved into it. Hearts and initials. Phone numbers. A couple RIPs. The oldest date she sees is 1/1/61. New Year's on the beach.

Suzy finds a seat far enough from the court to avoid stray shots, but near enough to keep an eye out for Grace and Mike. She plants her board into the sand like a spade, crosses her ankles, and compresses into a tidy knot. She drinks half her beer and scans the horizon. It is hotter all at once, and she feels as though her head is floating perceptibly above her hairline.

A jet rises over the water. It's well off the runway and tracking, at fifteen degrees of ascent, above the white verticals of Santa Monica and then the big upper arm of Malibu. Suzy squints: United. Fifty-five seconds later: Western. Another fifty-five: Pan Am. IDing the paint job isn't a challenge—guessing where it's headed is the game. The United jet spirals deliberately before aiming itself back east toward the continent. United hubs: Chicago, Washington, Newark. She watches the plane swirl higher and perceives it to be pointing more northerly than not. O'Hare in four hours. Three flights a day, spread across the timetable, LAX–ORD. Next up: a red-and-white 727. Western. L.A.–Las Vegas, maybe. Grand Pacific's odds-on up next; they're zero for the last eight takeoffs. But instead: Pan Am again. Zero for nine. Then TWA. Zero for ten. Continental: eleven. Finally, there it goes: Grand Pacific. The aquamarine bullet, a tail Suzy's eyes read as lavender but that she knows to be striped red, white, and blue. It follows the others up the corkscrew and points it-self north. San Francisco, Portland, Seattle. Suzy wonders who might be working today—who among the other girls got stuck flying on the Fourth like she has.

It seizes her like a cramp: with no Grace and no Mike, with her strange presence at this beach party, she's only just recognizing the radical isolation of being here, in this new place, without anything or anyone. January had become July in the space of a sneeze. It felt that quick—she closed her eyes to brace for her final semester and opened them here. The return to school after Christmas, after Grace and Mike's wedding, was the last time she really breathed. Ever since: forward motion, momentum, speed—and on bearings set by autopi-lot override. The end of a whole bunch of things at school and the beginning of whatever this is. And yet for the first time in forever, Suzy feels herself stuck. Moving neither west nor east. Neither flee-ing nor glomming on. Not taking off, but not landing, either. What she feels is the nonpresence of seventy-two degrees, the lack of sensa-tion on her skin. It is weightless. It is seductive. The planes keep their rhythm, and Suzy pulls off her dress to keep from doing nothing at all. Which is when she is spotted.

"I know you." There's a body standing beside her, a backlit figure made fuzzy around the edges by the sun.

"You do?" Suzy says.

"You were in Mrs. Riddlehoover's class with me."

Tarred-up feet, floral swim trunks, and a white tank. Sun freckles and a pink nose, once broken maybe. A dumb mouth that's fixed in a grin, the suggestion of eyes squinting behind Vuarnets. Long face, pinched as it falls like a fit upper body. Neatly swept white hair and sideburns that give the effect of a winter hat with tassels.

"You sure?" Suzy says.

"Then you moved away."

"I think you've got the wrong girl."

"No, no, it was definitely you. I'm pretty sure. You used to wear pigtails. Twist them up and out with paper clips—like Pippi Long-stocking. Then you moved to Germany."

"That girl sounds pretty bitchin', but sadly, not me."

His face—its white mustache on charred skin—gives the impression of a photonegative.

"Do you have a sister?" he says.

"I do, but she's not from here, either, and doesn't much look like me."

"So you're not from here at all?"

"I barely feel here now. I...I moved a month ago."

"Lemme guess..."

"I'm sure you've got it."

"Which airline?"

"You *do* have it figured out, huh?"

"You're not Pan Am."

"Why is that?"

"You'd have told me already."

"Ha." She says it just like that. "Go on. Three guesses."

"Let me see your hand."

"Come on."

He grabs it anyway. "Hmm. No international routes."

"Where do you get that?"

"This line here. It means you're way into America."

"Yeah?"

"That and the bikini."

"It's the Fourth," she says. "Get to it, you're avoiding the task at hand: which airline?"

He closes his eyes and clasps both hands around hers. "No accent, so probably not Delta."

"No accent."

"A little everygirlish…American?"

She grits her teeth and sucks in air.

"Wait," he says, certain. "Grand Pacific—definitely."

"Wow," she says.

He crosses his arms and nods at the bull's-eye. He points at her palm again, to the answer there, and Suzy leans in to look closer. "I'm just bullshitting," he says. "Shelly told me."

Suzy smiles—the kind that fails to conceal much, her wide mouth opening up half her face. "Shelly, the Howlers bartender?"

"Yeah, she really *was* in Mrs. Riddlehoover's."

"Is she here now?"

"Yeah, over there. She said you were new. I love a new stew."

"She sold me out."

"Oh, she was being friendly. So, Suzy Stew…when's your next flight?"

"Oof, she told you my name, too?"

His face shows that the slip wasn't intentional. "Nothing more—name and airline. The important things."

"I don't know if I believe you." It's probably nothing but a breeze, but it's all at once cold beneath the nest of hair concealing the upper reach of her spine. "But since you seem to genuinely care: flying tonight actually."

"*Tonight?* No way."

"Red-eye to New York. Eleven forty-five."

"To New York? You're kidding."

"Not the weirdest thing."

"Tonight at eleven forty-five to New York?"

"Yeah, are you on the flight or something?"

"Nah. I've never been. Seems kinda rough out there. How 'bout you?"

She smiles again. "Yeah, I've been to New York," she says. "I just haven't flown this route yet. North-souths for the most part so far."

"Well, listen, the *real* reason I came over is to say you've got nice hands."

"You decided that before you even read my palm?"

"I mean, I saw you react to that shot. *Quick* hands. *Nice* hands. Crazy-good reflexes. Do you play?"

"I don't."

"Oh, c'mon, everybody plays."

"I've tried. I tried last week. I can't..." And she does the motion, overhead, searching for the word. "I can't set."

"Can you drink?"

"It's probably a relative answer."

"I'm looking for a partner if you're down...."

"I don't know about that."

"It's cool, I'll set."

"Aren't we a little behind?"

"They'll burn out."

"I've gotta get somewhere pretty soon, I think. I'm waiting for a couple people. But thanks."

"Who's that?"

"My sister and her husband...boyfriend."

"Her husband-boyfriend."

"Depends on the phone you're calling."

"Not following, but I dig the weirdness. Think I know 'em?"

"Oh, maybe. Grace Whitman and Mike Singer?"

"I bet I'd recognize them. They've lived here a month, too?"

"Six months. At least my sister has for six months."

"Any kids?"

"If she did, I wouldn't be able to say so."

"Still not following."

"She wears wings."

"And she's *married*. At *Grand Pacific?* Okay, I get it now. Secret's safe."

Suzy puts her finger to her lips: "Shhh."

"I'm into it."

"Better if you're not living with it, probably."

"You live with them?"

"For now. Right up..." And she throws her hand over the hill at Nineteenth.

He nods at the deck in the sand. "I've got the same board, by the way."

"Oh yeah? Where'd you stash it? I'm realizing now I probably shouldn't have skated down."

"Nah, it's fine, nobody'll touch it."

"What if it's taken by accident?"

"My name's carved on mine," he says.

"You're daring them to steal it."

In an easy conspiracy, everything goes silent—on the radio the needle falls off the edge of the Nilsson record; the conversations shutter; three separate games on three separate courts, and no balls in play. But in just the way the sound vanished, it returns.

"Well, let me know if you change your mind. I really do need a partner."

Suzy expects him to move on but finds herself faintly buoyant from the first beer and searching for a reason to keep him here.

"What about you? What do you do?" she says.

"Uh," he says, distracted by a pair of men walking through the sand wearing polyester suits and shoes. "I'm a pawn in a multinational outfit that specializes in drug running."

He says it so straight she has no choice but to mirror the affect.

"That sounds exhausting."

"It's a cool summer job, I guess."

"'America's public enemy number one'—that's the president's line, right?" she says.

"The *real* war," he says.

"Any chance of getting promoted?"

"Only if the guy above me gets arrested. Or killed."

"Not the most reliable pathway in the space of a summer, then."

"Maybe they'll let me stick around through the fall."

The dampness in her hair again, the heat and cool—it turns the strap of her bathing suit into a steel blade against the skin and bones and tubes in her neck.

"So, Su-*zy*—do people ever call you Z?" he says.

"Not once ever."

"I had a basketball coach who called me Z."

"We would've had that in common, then, if anyone had ever called me Z."

"I knew there was something."

"Zach? Zoro? Zurich?" she says.

"Billy."

"Ah."

"Billy *Zar.*"

Billy squats down to about her level. "Smoke?"

"Nah."

He caves his hand around a match to shield the breeze and strikes the tip with his thumbnail.

"That was pretty fancy," she says. He shrugs and pulls a joint out of his trunks pocket. "You're full of surprises."

He smiles with the paper between his lips. "'At's pro'lly true." He draws without making it a thing. Someone lifts a beach towel and shakes the sand into the air. The shadow passes across Billy's face.

"You know many other people here?" he says.

"Some, I guess," she lies.

"Want to meet the rest?"

"Maybe sometime. But seriously, I don't mind just waiting for—"

"See that couple over there?" He means the ones warming up—a heavy guy, not fat, just a lot of pounds, with long arms and a hairline pushed way back on his head; and then a petite brunette whose Tinker Bell cut is flush with the bottom of the net. "I've gotta tell you one about them from yesterday."

"All right."

"Stop me if you've heard it. Fifteen or twenty people were there firsthand, so ya know...maybe it's gotten around. Maybe you were even there."

"I'm pretty sure I wasn't."

"So that's Marty. Marty lives in the spot he grew up in. Nice place, small, supercool. His parents died in a car crash last year. The worst."

"Jesus."

"Right? So he has this great place all to himself. Marty's wife's name is Kim. They got married a month ago. Might be because she's pregnant, but it's hard to say."

"I don't see a baby."

"Hang on to that thought for a sec. So they got married all of a sudden. A month after he asked her. Did it in front of everyone at Howlers. Got up on the bar instead of down on his knee. Put a calamari ring on her finger, and whatever band it was started playing 'The End.' Funny dudes. So, righteous: they're married, newlyweds. Last night Marty has some people over for a little pre-Fourth thing. He lives on a corner. People ride by, stop in. That's how it's always gone. Things get going a little bit. Opens the windows, brings the record player out into the yard, fills up the kiddie pool with a couple inches of water. You know the scene."

"I don't totally, but you're painting a nice picture."

"So Marty's got this new neighbor. Just moved in. A few years older than you—I'm guessing you're, what, twenty-four?"

"Twenty-two."

"Twenty-two, so more than a few years, twenty-six or twenty-seven, works a real job, makes some scratch, rents this place. She comes over to the fence, asks Marty to turn the music down, she's got some work, whatever. On Fourth of July Eve? Doubtful. But they kinda keep going. He's full on pressing it. Tells her to hold tight and comes back from the house in a couple ticks with a fucking mai tai. Little umbrella and everything. Skip the needle forward an hour and she's grooving, dancing holes into her heels on the patio. People are lighting up. Someone finds some of Marty's dad's old rum locked in a cabinet, which makes Marty sad for a sec. But not too sad, ya know? He starts making drinks with it, communing, dancing, twirling the neighbor chick around. Before you know it, they disappear. Nowhere in sight, but doesn't take many guesses, right? Someone sneaks next door and peeks in the window. Just full on at it in her place. But guess who's coming home?"

Suzy nods over to the warm-up session.

"Again, hold that connection. But right, Kim's coming home. Kim's great. Likes to party. Gets down. But she's kinda tough, too, ya know? From Bakersfield, or somewhere up 5. Just gives people the wrong vibes sometimes. So most of the gang at this thing, they're in it for Marty. Kim comes walking up to the house, just off work, not a drink in her, looking a little haggard. And all these guys start blocking, running interference. Grabbing her hand for a dance. Bringing her shots they know she can't take. Keeping the party outside. Word bounces around back to the neighbor's bedroom, ya know? 'Marty, get your shit together, Kim's home.' 'kay? And he climbs out the window, hops the fence in the back, and comes bounding out onto the patio as though he's just been taking a dump. Kim's pissed about the party. Someone has the wise idea to move on to the next place, hit a bar or whatever. I meet up with that crew. But the last thing people see is Kim bent over in close, sniffing his shirt. Like she just smelled it on him, man."

"But he got away with it."

"No, this is what I'm trying to say: that little baby over there isn't Kim—it's the neighbor."

Suzy's lips crack and she takes her glasses off, all eye whites and pinpoint pupils dialing back into green.

"Teammates in the tourney just like that," Billy says. "But listen, I shouldn't be spreading that. I know they're not exactly hiding it, but just, you know, keep it tight."

"Guess we're even with discretion."

"Exactly, partners who can keep secrets," he says. "I'm gonna go say hey. Want me to introduce you?"

"Ha," she says it again. "I'm good. I'm so good. I'm just gonna hang here, I think."

"Cool, well, let me know if you change your mind about playing."

He seems to mean it, but his eyes have drifted back to those two suited men on the beach.

"You betcha," Suzy says.

"Oh, and listen," Billy says as he's walking away. "Find me sometime later today. There's something I want to give you."

"Something you want to give me?"

"Super important. A little later. You'll see me again." And then that's that. Billy Zar is gone and Suzy is alone. The five minutes of conversation only serve to highlight the fact that Mike and Grace have stranded her here. She rolled in late last night after a full day of flying, double up-and-backs to Seattle, went straight to bed, woke up to the note: "Nineteenth at noon." Would they really no-show? She draws herself a second beer and then halves it. *C'mon, Gracie.* It was Grace all over again.

*   *   *

Grace is three years older, three years earlier, the difference of a generation. In Schuyler Glen they shared a room. Straight through till Grace graduated and moved out. The changing faces on the walls were Grace's selections—John and Paul, then Brian Jones, then, by '65, her senior year, Dylan and Van Ronk. Grace would shut the door after school and wear deep grooves into her vinyl, records on repeat. She had transitioned, in a short space, from dinners scored by *Bandstand* to late-night sessions restitching dresses at the Singer. She hitched her wagon to the music, and it was a simple thing to do.

First from Schuyler to Ithaca, where the satellite folk scene welcomed all stray kindling. Weekends in the beginning, then weeknights in summer—Midwestern guitarists and professors her parents' age and freshman lit students who talked just the right proportions about Russians she hadn't read and records she knew intimately. Really, Grace probably had no business going to school in the first place. But a couple of generous letters from her prof friends and a handful of passing grades at the JC in Ithaca landed her a spot at the state university in Westchester. It was more useful for its Metro-North stop than it was for any consecrated erudition—four hours closer to the Village than Schuyler Glen. Grace's first year at the university was her last.

Though it was in evidence throughout high school and those fleeting years of college, Grace's reputation for chronic tardiness was fixed in junior high when their mother, Edith, introduced Grace to makeup. Even today, alone on the beach, Suzy can readily transport herself to Schuyler and inhabit her ten-year-old body—slouching impatiently, plain-face freckled and ponytailed, while their father, Wayne, watched the long hand on the kitchen clock slip past the hour of their intended departure; Grace, pleading from the top of the stairs for just one more minute to work out her raccoon eyes and candy-coated mouth.

For years Suzy felt like Grace was playing a game no one else—in the family, at school, in town—knew they were consigned to. Playing toward a scoreboard Suzy couldn't see. And yet Grace had the ability, too, to erase the pencil lines of her efforts, to beat back the impatience of her parents, teachers, and friends, with a smart joke and a low laugh. When Grace finally shows at the beach today—*if* Grace finally shows—Suzy's sure it'll play out the same as ever: Grace will float in on a pink Glinda bubble, pass out hugs, kisses, and chewing gum, and break up whatever knots of resentment have taken to material-izing on account of the lateness, the too-chillness, the casual cool. Everything important so unimportant to Grace.

It was different for Suzy. In Schuyler, Suzy learned about speed.

Blame it on Wayne. Wayne blew glass at the Schuyler Glen Glass-works for ten hours a day and fixed up European sports cars at a specialist body shop in his downtime. Alfa Romeos. Austin-Healeys. Triumphs and Bugattis. When Wayne's brother, an Albany prosecu-tor, died of a heart attack at forty-five, Wayne inherited his Fiat 8V, a silver roadster with curves like Wayne's glass and a grill like grit-ted teeth. He tweaked it toward improvement until he got an offer in the post office parking lot one day to swap it for two cars Wayne regarded as being of greater value. A new hobby was born. Wayne started volunteering at the local shop, began proliferating an arsenal from Italian and German catalogs. Whether with engines or glass, Wayne scratched two itches with one paw—what he was doing was both essential and artistic.

Wayne brought new glassworks home each week. The vase for Edith's summer tulips. The living room table for a fanned-out season of *Saturday Evening Post*s. Highballs for the G and Ts Wayne and Edith would drink in August as the lightning bugs flipped their switches. Wayne was a sculptor. That most of what he made had util-itarian value, his girls knew, diminished his art zero. But the cars were different—the cars were not rested upon or sipped from. The cars were made to go.

Both girls were trained in the garage. They play-baked with tire irons and ratchets. They raced across the cool concrete on dollies. As they got older, Grace peeled off but Suzy stuck it out as first mate. She ruled over the tool bins. On bored weekends she'd empty the drawers into a pile on the workbench and restock them from the bottom up. As she grew more comfortable in the garage she made greater claims to her place there. At eight, she pinned a handmade sign to the wall: I AM SUZY! At ten, she helped build her first go-kart. By twelve, thanks to a tractor license, she was racing on the upstate junior circuit. It was no surprise, then, that by noon on her sixteenth birthday she was halfway through her first lap at the Watkins Glen racetrack, running full-tilt.

Despite his interest in sports cars, Wayne had never raced. He liked tuning cars like a piano, not thrashing them like a drum set. Suzy felt differently. At Watkins Glen, Suzy chased personal records. She accelerated with ease through the stages of karting, competing up, and counting down the summers till she could race open wheel. Wayne coached her in driving and he coached her in cars. He loved her love, loved nothing more.

That first summer at the Glen—summer of '66—there was a bird's nest of paranoia tangling up Suzy's head at the track. She'd never thought twice about her own shortcomings, but as the speeds increased and the cars grew to be powerful extensions of one's reflexes, she grew concerned about the twitchiness of other drivers. She didn't like to race against boys her age. She was frantic about their mistakes. But at seven in the morning or eight at night, when the track was all but empty, she carved seconds off her lap times, alone in the sounds of acceleration and upshifting. Come November they'd clean the engine and suspend the go-kart from the rafters in the garage, using sailing ropes and a simple system of pulleys, and Suzy would slow down and take care of school. As had been the case for years, she glided by on her big brain—prolific reading, precise writing, fastidious test taking. She approached her language arts and history courses as though they were mechanical. Concepts were things to be understood not by memorization, but by interrogating the way they worked. School was something to master with efficiency. There were always ways to shave off tenths.

The summer before senior year, summer of '67, she broke her personal record nine times. Now that they were a little older, in possession of at least some self-control, she ran with the boys. Every once in a while she'd get out front from pole and complete entire races clear of the pack—at least until she started lapping the stragglers. She wasn't where you needed to be to race the big ones in Virginia and North Carolina, but she won a bunch upstate, and in Pennsylvania and western Mass, which for Suzy constituted the whole world anyway. Not much in her life had suggested borders extending beyond the Northeast—no exotic family travel, no transfer students into school from Oregon or Louisiana, no built-in family mythmaking about lives lived in a different place. Just Wayne and Edith and two sets of grandparents, all of whom seemed to regard the claw marks of the Finger Lakes and the tightly sealed slate lid of winter to be preordained conditions of life as all and any knew it.

For Suzy, though, there was one keyhole through which she could glimpse the wider universe: every October the big boys came to town to race.

Wayne went by himself the first year Formula One brought the United States Grand Prix to Watkins Glen. It was the furthest extension of Wayne's interest in cars, the sleekness of a body and the adeptness of an engine made manifest in speed, in competition. He caught the bug and brought Suzy along thereafter. He'd write

Suzy a note for the Friday—not that she ever really needed it, her grades bought her space—and they'd hit practice, followed by Saturday's qualifying and Sunday's grand prix. The first time she went, Suzy was thirteen and midmorph, Picasso-proportioned facial features and a mouth full of wires. She sat quietly in the stands, silent in her shell, while Wayne narrated the biographies of each of the drivers—these were the best of Italy and Germany and England, of Japan and South Africa. Wayne summarized the season to that point, the lead changes, the chases for not just first- but fifth-place points, ninth-place points. The crashes, the team management tussles, the impossible expectations of Scuderia Ferrari. Wayne said the words of the racetracks, words satisfying in and of themselves—Monza, Zandvoort, Spa—but then transformed them into places Suzy felt she'd been, described the elevation changes, the famous turns, the colors the tunneling trees made when they blurred together in a straightaway. The drivers passed into the pits, one by one, year after year, and by the time she was racing herself, by the time she was winning on that very track, they were her most fundamental bearings on the world beyond her world. Not just to the simpler locales of Italy and Germany and England, but to that big, borderless existence in the sky, that world of highest-class racing, in which all those racers had more in common with one another than anyone from their own countries anyway. Matching trailers, matching wives, matching turtlenecks and hair parts and crystal-faced watches. The extranational luxury of Formula One.

Her senior year of high school, Suzy raced and Suzy read. She read history and literature and biology. She read novels about New England and Old England, books she'd seen on the shelves in the living room all her life, books she suspected had pages glued together, untouched as they were, perfect and rigid in their set. She cross-pollinated geraniums and she unlocked derivatives. She wrote a newspaper column and swam long-distance—hours on end with the lane line. She applied physics and calculus to the weekend runs at the track, learned the names for forces she'd intuited and internalized for years. She was friends with more boys than girls, boys from the neighborhood, boys from elementary school, boys from the swim team. She dated one of them for a while, a long, dumb sprinter, hair like Mick's and eyes like a Jersey cow's, kissed him 'cause she should, screwed him for the first time at Halloween when he got her drunk in a milkmaid costume. She made money working at the track, working the pits, staining her hands, hanging with the men. But she still went to dances and wore minis, showed her limbs in shorts and tank tops in the heat. It was a residual effect of her sister. Gracie had been girl concentrate, girl enough to leave a mark, her perfume still clinging to the walls of their room, her foundation still dusting the surfaces of their shared shelves and desk.

That fall of her senior year, Suzy's English teacher encouraged her to apply to her alma mater. Suzy had planned to race after graduation, to take classes at a JC, maybe transfer somewhere farther away like Grace had. But never somewhere private like Vassar. Mrs. Meyers considered this to be a preposterous plan. What did her parents think? Suzy and Grace had grown up in the comfortable chasm of having not nearly enough money but being ignorant of the fact. Their parents didn't buy anything; Wayne only swapped cars. He was a lifer at the glassworks and Edith taught sixth-grade English. They read the paper and watched the news and traveled not at all. Suzy said they were fine with the prospect of junior college, that money from the track, from semipro races, would cover the costs, take the pressure off them financially. "Have you even taken the tests?" Mrs. Meyers said. Suzy hadn't but still could, certainly planned to before Christmas. "You have all the things they want," Mrs. Meyers said, "and in such abundance that they'll likely pay for most of your tuition." This was news to Suzy. "And I'll help you with your applications," Mrs. Meyers said—to Vassar, to Radcliffe, to Bryn Mawr. "They're all girls," Suzy said. And Mrs. Meyers mistook her meaning: "There are plenty of functions with the boys." Vassar did things with Yale, for example. But Suzy had meant, *So many fucking girls, so many girls and so little racing.* Suzy took the tests, wrote her statements, and in the end she had her pick. Vassar was just four hours from the track, four hours from home. And they would pay for everything.

Vassar meant closer to Grace, too. Not that it was much of a contributing factor. Grace was in New York by then. She lived in the Village with a girl named Tess and then a girl named Rose. Or at least that's what she told Suzy and their folks. For money she served coffee and sandwiches at a diner on lower Sixth Avenue, and for fun she smoked grass with guitarists. She followed Creedence through the South for a couple weeks. She sent a Polaroid from Florida of her head between the jaws of a stuffed gator. She sent a postcard of Charlotte Motor Speedway with an arrow pointing from a ballpoint-scripted "Suzy" to Richard Petty's car. Grace was good at staying brightly in the periphery without requiring of Suzy any real time or attention.

The Christmas of Suzy's sophomore year at Vassar, Grace mentioned that she was thinking about becoming a stewardess. That she'd applied and might be hearing in the spring. Until then she'd keep waitressing—"doing basically all the shit I'd do on an airplane, only without getting to go anywhere." Suzy couldn't really imagine her sister in a Roman café or on a Tokyo city street but had no trouble picturing her in the uniform.

That spring, while she was interviewing with recruiters, Grace met a guy in a bar in New York. Grace has this big, sticky red mouth—all through growing up, it looked as though she'd been sneaking time with a lollipop—and Mike Singer had watched it move for hours one night. Grace talked to a couple of Mike's friends while he tried some lines on a couple of hers. When the pairings in the bar broke down and someone moved to the bathroom, Mike mentioned to Grace that there was a secret Gram Parsons show that night. A solo thing of the new Flying Burrito Brothers record straight through at this art guy's loft. Would she maybe...? This was the right thing for Mike Singer to say, even though he couldn't find the show in the end.

He'd heard about it—the rumor, at least—because he was a magazine guy. Wrote for *New York* and *Esquire*. Small things—but stuff that put him on their lists. If Wolfe or Mailer or Halberstam couldn't make it, and the twenty guys after them were tied up, then Mike Singer might get a call. It didn't kill Mike, being number twenty-four. Limited work meant more time to write his novels. There were three when Grace met him. He'd rotate around: when he felt hopeless about one, he'd comfort himself with the presence of two and three, especially three, the real deal—the haymaker-in-waiting.

Mike was from a Big Ten town—Madison, Bloomington, Ann Arbor (Grace used them interchangeably at first)—and he'd come to New York for college at Columbia. He felt in New York that it was possible to project his whole life forward, to see the full picture, the wunderkind spoils, the humble deflection of praise, the Village loft with its modern furniture pieces, the way the elegant lines might look with a fancy-blooded graduate student pressed against them. He pictured his books along the shelves, his magazines stacked in boxes, gray coming at the temples like a sign of ascension. He'd look like his father, the economics professor, who'd died of a heart attack when Mike was twenty-two. By then there was no one left: Mike was an only child and his mother had abandoned him when he was a boy. Mike might return to the Big Ten town, but only in body, never in spirit. He planned not to have a reason to live anywhere but New York ever again.

Mike was a little older than Grace and off on what might be called a trajectory. The sort of early calculations where small ticks upward presumed large dividends down the road. The summer before Suzy's senior year, Mike came into a pipeline of assignments, writing extensively about the upstart candidate Shirley Chisholm for *New York*. Mike wrote the straight stuff; Gloria Steinem said what it meant. Mike had a little money and wanted to trade up to a bigger apartment. By that time he and Grace had moved in together. They were all wrong on paper but seemed to fill in each other's gaps, to double their strength in composite. He was locked in, reliant upon her. She, less so. She'd been picked up by a new airline called Grand Pacific. She worked out of Kennedy, one of just a few, flying New York–L.A. a couple times a week. But after the first year the opportunities for Grace were growing limited, both professionally and socially. Mike wanted to move into that larger apartment. Grace wanted to move to Southern California. There was this little beach town she'd heard about during stew school, a place where half the girls ended up. It was her intention to get there. That Mike come was requested but not required.

At the start of Suzy's final year at Vassar, Mike and Grace agreed that they'd move out to Sela del Mar. This was Mike's sacrifice, his proof of commitment. In exchange he wanted Grace to marry him. This was tricky: Grace would have to quit her job with Grand Pacific if she said yes—it was a cardinal rule of the airline that stews be single. There was no way she would, but Grace was committed to fairness. So when they got hitched at Christmas in Schuyler Glen, they swore the family to secrecy. Suzy thought it was all pretty dumb, but she did duties as the maid of honor, gave a toast about sharing a bathroom, about fistfights and psychological warfare. About the warmth and closeness they'd feel in the dial-down after a good tilt, how they'd fall asleep together in one or the other's bed. When they got out to

Sela, Mike and Grace installed a second, secret phone in their kitchen to take the airline's calls.

"I saw that!" It is a voice in the present. It is a voice at the Fourth of July Drunk 'n' Draw. It is a voice that floats in distorted, piercing and low. And then a laugh that is an even lower roll, so self-amused, so illiterate sounding, it makes Suzy laugh, too. Her beer is finished all over again. Grace is late and somehow it is exactly the right timing.

"I didn't know you played back row!" The voice grows deeper as she gets closer. Like every woman but Suzy, Grace has color. Raw-sugar skin, lemon-meringue hair, plus a peach dress and pearls. "We saw you from the top of the hill, we saw you block that shot."

"That was thirty minutes ago," Suzy says.

"We bumped into some friends."

"You've been around for thirty minutes?"

"No," she says. "I dunno. It's gonna be a long day. Speaking of, we have to go."

"You two aren't signed up for the Drunk 'n' Draw?" Suzy says.

It's a joke, but Mike is eyeing the scene with a thin grimace: "I thought Updike's cuckolds were the only men who played volleyball."

It's something Mike would say to Suzy and not Grace, but Grace says, "I even know what that means," before quickly getting to business: "Let's go, we're late, we're meeting people and heading to a party."

Suzy grabs her board and follows Grace and Mike to the Strand, the walkway that stretches for miles along the beach. She watches her sister clop along. How does she take up so much *space*? She moves in and around an entire little zone of her own, Grace in three fully occupied dimensions—her steps, whether in sandals or heels, walking this elegant fine line between high composure and a drunk stumble.

"Mom called again," Grace says, smiling over her shoulder. "Left another message."

"Hiiiii, guuyyys, it's meeee...."

"We'd reeeally like to heeeear your voiiiices, pleeease. Or even beeetter—see your faaaaces...."

They both smile at their shared skill.

"I just...," Suzy says, warm with the attention of her mother but irritated, too, "I've been here *a month*. We each call once a week."

"That's a message a day for the past four days," Grace says.

"This is probably just a holiday call—before heading to the lake or whatever."

"Maybe we really should try to go home soon. I mean, if we're going anyway."

"I just got here! They can wait a *little* longer."

"And how is it, then, that I'm still the only one catching flack for being a deserter?" Grace says.

"You were first to the reputation," Suzy says. "Reputations are tough to transfer."

When they reach Twelfth Street, they ninety up the hill and hit a set of concrete terraces, where a restaurant called Huevos sits on the corner. It's a stucco-and-tile shoe box that brings to mind the adobe outhouse of a Spanish mission. On the sidewalk out front they hitch up with a train of strangers Grace and Mike evidently just ate brunch with.

As they pass through town, Suzy's pulled by the pack of the shirtless and champagne-high as though strapped to someone else's legs. She's near the fat part of the pack's tail, right beside Mike and Grace, and she keeps her board tucked tightly under her arm. The route is an easy one—down a lolling decline into the center of town, the water to the right, the steeper amphitheater seating of the hillside houses on their left.

The sidewalks are crowded with men and women who love America. Cars roll by with flags pinned to the windows. Old people shout patriotic non sequiturs from balconies. They move through downtown—an all-night diner and a pair of competing sunglasses shops, an Italian restaurant and a French restaurant for birthdays and anniversaries. The buildings are cream stucco and the roofs are Spanish-tile orange. Every now and then there's a building with a second floor, a bed and a toilet for a shopkeeper. It's warming up. The ocean blows rotting seaweed up the hill. On typical summer weekends the downtown is crowded, bright and erect. But today it sags even heavier, oversaturated, a fallen cake.

They track up the hill and onto a carless, roadless pedestrian walk-street. A strip of communal concrete yards sprawled from picket fence to picket fence. Spillover planters, tricycles, and abandoned lemonade stands chime sweetly. It feels the way a street does in the aftermath of a block party, only one run by children.

Halfway down the block they hear the three-note bass progression of a Who chorus. A shirtless hulk with a beard to his Adam's apple waves a long wooden rod with an American flag on the end. He shouts, "A-mer-i-ca!" and, "Fuck Canada!" A pair of dark men with mirror-image mustaches are doubled over, laughing, tearing from beneath their shades, and they're still laughing as the first of the pack unlatches the little white gate to the tiny bricked yard and heads into the house.

"There's Bethany," Grace says when they reach the property line. Suzy notices an unexpected quiver, a vocal reluctance. Most of the girls here are sitting out in bikini tops and shorts. Grace, in even a casual peach dress, is dressed like someone's aunt.

Bethany titters over like a windup toy and throws her arms around Grace, hinging a lower leg so that her heel presses against her ass. Grace introduces her to Suzy and Mike, and Bethany hugs them, too.

"The boyfriend and the sister—it's all making sense!" Bethany says. And then she leads them into the party and gives a speedy roll call. The names sound friendly to Suzy but drift away on the breeze, unhitched to faces. Each person is kinder than the last, adamant that Suzy's time at the party be the greatest time ever. During her month in town they've worked collectively to make sure her opinion of Sela is as faultless as their own. They make sure she never has two empty hands.

In the corner there is a half-length vanity mirror laid on its back, dusted in a light snowfall. She hasn't seen coke since Vassar—and even then it was rare. She figures she's closer to South America now. The kids around the table, younger than Suzy, siblings of someone probably, take turns leaning in. After nosing up the lines, they take a rapid second lap and sniff at the crumbs. Then they stretch their arms above their heads, lean back—each makes the identical move—and sink into the understuffed couch.

What the girls party-wide seem to have most in common is interest in cheap champagne, the sort they've apparently not stopped drinking since the night before. They tell jokes punctuated by nicknames, the intimacy impenetrable. Grace stands with some of Bethany's friends, whose hair and teeth and pinched waists Suzy recognizes as belonging to stews. But most of the others seem to have been friends since elementary school—and friends all over again at the post–high school, post-college beach. These women of Sela: half stews, half homegrown. Suzy gets rolled by a wave of skin-prickling curiosity. What were *her* high school friends doing just now? The boys from swimming? The girls from newspaper? When did she even see them last? Were they still technically friends, with all the time and distance? And what about the Vassar girls—that last class to miss the liberation parade? Does the ocean look different from their parties on Martha's Vineyard and Block Island? How does she not know the answer to that—how has she never been invited?

No matter, this is it now: *Look around, Suzy, you're home.* What she sees is hair. Hair and sunglasses. Uncountable center parts and golden frames. Hair and sunglasses, and in deep, dark, grotesque slomo, wide mouths and heavy chests of uncomplicated laughter, the big knee-slapper of the in-joke, tan tits heaving with the fun, a part of Suzy's body she's never desired to turn another color until this very moment. Some better shade of translucence.

Suzy finds Mike standing in line for the keg, nodding politely to a conversation about the waves that morning. Suzy wonders where his head's at, whether he's back in a life left behind in New York. She taps him on the shoulder and he gives her flirty eyebrows, which she's never misunderstood to be anything more than *This, huh?*

"Thing is," Mike says to her as they pair off together, "I even know my sports. That's what I talk about with guys I've just met. 'Hey, Lakers, Knicks, blah, blah, blah.' I've got the language, the passion for my teams...." He pauses, then moves to a place of greater frustration. "But here we are, in July, and they don't even know *baseball*."

Suzy thinks this is a very funny thing to say and starts laughing and clapping her hands. But it's not so funny, and she realizes that she's teetering. She does the fingertips test—thumb to index, middle, ring, pinkie, and back—with both hands, quicker in each succession. But she still hasn't said anything, and Mike keeps moving his head around, trying to find her eyes, peering into a window whose curtains keep shifting.

"Hey," he says, "you're starting to make me think I'm not the only one who can't quite piece together how I got here."

Suzy rode the bus to New Haven the day after Mike and Grace's wedding. She'd been offered a chance to do her final semester at Yale. Not a full transfer but an experimental step toward a better exchange between brother and sister schools. Suzy had taken a course that fall with a visiting graduate student from Yale who'd advocated for the experiment. The grad student, Camille, had been pushing to thread older coeds into the campus fabric now that Yale had younger female students of its own. Yale, after all, had opened itself to women the year after Suzy graduated from high school. It hadn't bothered Suzy then, but the longer she spent at Vassar in the sea of two thousand girls, the more she simmered beneath the surface. She'd visited Yale's libraries to borrow books on several occasions and, while in New Haven, watched the female admits float on the privilege. The experiment hadn't been her idea, but she didn't hesitate to accept the offer, either. It was something she needed without knowing why.

Suzy thought about just driving back and forth but instead arranged last-minute for an apartment nearest to the library as she could find. Rather than grip tighter as the world came knocking, she felt that an exit—graduation, like death (she'd read the confessional poets with Camille)—was that much more welcome. Before Christmas, she packed up most of her belongings in Poughkeepsie, ready for New Haven and the strange island of unbelonging.

That first Monday in January, HAPPY 1972 hats still gumming up the gutters on York Street, Suzy left Sterling Library with a couple slim volumes of poetry tucked under her arm and a dramatic angle of attack on the headwind. Her apartment was on Lake, on the other side of the gym. She'd taken a step over a bank of slush onto the sidewalk beside Mory's when she saw a young man in a jacket and pom hat failing to turn over the engine of a '68 Camaro. She almost missed it. Silver, it didn't pop much off the filthy snow. She'd never seen one up close before. She'd have to call Wayne.

He pushed it again and again—it gargled at that high register without a release. She could make out his shape through the frosty windshield, could hear Badfinger on the radio. She watched his body slide down in his seat. Suzy knocked at the glass. He flashed her his eyes and sat tall, as though embarrassed to have been caught giving up. He rolled down the window.

"Yeah?" he said.

"You good?" she said.

"Good, not great."

"I can help you start it if you want," she said.

"How's that?"

"I know a few things to try."

He was disarmingly handsome. She recognized him from her previous visits to campus—not the libraries but a sandwich shop or something. She'd never met him, but she'd seen him, as in really seen him, remembered the contour lines of his face. He had a big head with thick hair pouring out from under his hat. He had a long, scalene nose and stubble and a Christmas-in-the-Caribbean tan. He had gray eyes that were wet from the wind, lashes that were longer and curlier than hers.

But the moment Suzy said it, those eyes did this pitying narrowing. His forehead creased. It was a face practiced in patronizing women.

"All right, good luck," she said, and started back toward the walkway beside Mory's.

"Hold up," he said. "Do you know magic or something?"

It took Suzy sixty seconds to start the car and she hit it on the first turn of the key.

"What the hell was that?" he said.

"Foreplay," she said. He was in the passenger seat now. "Five pumps on the accelerator. Wait fifteen seconds. Five more pumps. Wait. Five. Wait. Gold. Gotta get the juices flowing."

"Foreplay," he said.

"I'm gonna drive myself home," Suzy said. And before he responded, she pulled off the curb and down York toward Grove.

"Your dad fix cars or something?"

In the steering wheel she could feel the gale whipping off the cemetery.

"He can fix cars, I can fix cars," she said. "Where'd you get it?"

"Graduation gift."

"You're not a grad student, are you?"

"Nah, '72, senior."

"Isn't that bad luck to get your gift before May?"

"It was, uh, high school graduation."

"Ah."

"My parents can be generous."

"And this is a . . . '68? Which would've made it a *brand-new* one?"

"Very generous, kind to their kids."

He had forty-fived in his seat and shaded his body toward her. She could feel his eyes.

"What?" Suzy said.

"What what?" he said.

"You're staring at me."

"Just looking at your face. I recognize you from something."

"I go to the same school as you." She tried it out.

"You're a singer."

"Not a singer."

"Not choral—I mean I saw you sing somewhere some night."

"I don't think so, I'm pretty new here."

"I remember—you were at a table with friends near mine. You were hammered and you were singing some fancy melody to an Allman Brothers song."

Suzy was silent. This was possible. There *was* one night. She had come over to pick up some books and ended up getting drunk with Camille, too drunk to drive home. They'd made a night of it—pizza, music, harmonizing in public, evidently.

"Ha, I knew it!" he said, slapping her thigh. He had overlarge hands, and now that she locked that idea into place, it was clear that the handsomeness came from the scale: a big face, big hair. He didn't seem any taller than tall men, but it was a head for television. All the features clear and defined, glowing before a blue screen.

"My sister just saw them in Philadelphia," she said. "Her honeymoon to herself, pretty much."

"You see them here last April?"

"I didn't."

"At the Palace. So good. You should try out your pipes onstage there."

"Bars only, thanks."

"Well, at least let's maybe go to a show there, then. I work all the events."

"Oh yeah? At the Palace?"

"Pick a show. Or come over to my place and we can jam."

"Ha." She said the word like she does. "Are you in a band?"

"Nobody can really cut it here. When I move to the city this summer, things'll be different."

"What do you play?"

"Rhythm. Wanna come?"

"That sorta thing works better on my sister."

"Never too late to develop a new taste. Sure you don't want to come along?"

"Yeah... I dunno," she said, pulling up to her apartment building. "Welp, here's my place."

"Think I can get your number?"

"What for?"

He smiled, big as his face. "Least you can do since I drove you home," he said.

"To set the record straight for all time," Suzy said, "I drove *you* home; you owe me *your* number." And so Dave wrote it on the library card on the inside cover of the Yeats.

As more students returned to school, Suzy enrolled in her final courses. The thesis was what mattered most, the reason she was here. And rather than write it with one of the white-haired eminences caught up in the "Yale school" thing, she devised a project with Camille.

Camille had this breaking wave of dyed-gray hair—like a surfer could shoot the tube off her forehead—and she was interested in weird sex in Western art and lit. All Suzy heard from people who knew was how good Camille was at weird sex in Western art and lit. Suzy saw her out at bars with men but wasn't really that surprised when she propositioned Suzy in her office one afternoon. "Don't take this any way but how I mean it," she said. "I'd like to have you over for dinner at my apartment. If you're interested, let's set a date. If you're not, I take no offense, and I hope you don't make the mistake of letting this affect our relationship."

Suzy politely declined and Camille convinced her to write her thesis on Led Zeppelin. An interrogation of the poetics. A "Sailing to Byzantium" = "Ramble On" sort of thing. In many ways English made better use of the auto mechanic's toolbox than physics or engineering did. Especially with all the cool tricks passing through the department right then. The ways to take apart a sentence like a carburetor and build it back out into a box with better airflow. Camille helped Suzy with her writing. Told her to read Sontag before she wrote each day. "You want to get to the point where you can parody her," she said. "To parody her at half skill will only have the effect of making your own writing twice as good." Suzy had a surgeon's confidence in her ability to write a term paper. Its order, its argument, its repeatability. How to say one novel thing, and say it clearly and convincingly—smothering and defensible. It had worked for her without exception.

But the thesis was just one credit. In order to legitimize the experiment, Suzy had been asked to carry a full load. And in order to complete her degree, she'd have to enroll in the core roadblocks she'd put off for three and a half years. Suzy had done well at Vassar, exceptionally well. She'd competed with herself, chased personal records. She'd formulated this idea of her collective efforts there as this work of sculpture—built of stellar marks, superlative praise, girlfriends, professors, and useful lifelong advocates. A pristine record of high achievement that might suggest to whoever looked upon it that the person responsible could've cut it with the very best anywhere, even at a place with boys. In preserving that sleek academic record, though, she'd deferred some science. And during the week before spring break, she failed three exams in three days. Physics was the shock. Racing was physics, after all. She could visualize the lines, she could ride the language of acceleration and force. Physics wasn't supposed to be an issue. The exam took the form of just one problem. Rudimentary components of a Saturn V rocket launch. She miscalculated the first derivative and it brought down the whole project. It was like pouring a crooked foundation for the pad at Cape Canaveral. It was a failed attempt for the moon.

The results of the exams reached her the day she left for spring break. She was visiting Grace in Sela del Mar—Suzy's first time west. The afternoon she arrived, Mike picked her up at the airport in his new blue Karmann Ghia and drove her along the water to the small house he and Grace rented on the back side of the hill at Nineteenth Street. Grace teased Suzy and wouldn't let her in the door until she smiled. But Suzy wasn't in the mood. She'd spent the duration of the flight reading and rereading and failing to register meaning in any article of the in-flight magazine. She found herself muttering dramatic fatalisms about "it" being over. She welled up and exploded in a single sob before gaining composure and cursing herself out. The stew brought her a free cocktail and then a couple others. Now Suzy was hungry and tired and just wanted to sleep.

In an attempt to cheer her up, Grace forced Suzy to follow her through a neighbor's yard and down a path along the side of their house. A surfboard leaned against the wall, and wet sand was piled up near a coiled hose. Grace was wearing cowboy boots and hoop earrings, and when she came out from the shade of the yard's palms, her ears cast round globes of gold like candle flames.

The view west: sky, water, sand—three distinct pastels, stacked like an ice cream sandwich. On the way in from the airport, she'd caught glimpses of pretty-looking things, standing bright and alive as though it were already advanced spring. Everything had had a straightforward beauty—a dumb pretty. But Suzy had passed back into her problems at school and failed to be moved by the moment.

She put on a good show, acting unimpressed and committed to her request just to go home and take a nap. Ignoring her, Grace narrated the markers—the peninsula to the left, the peninsula to the right, the island, the Strand, the pier, the volleyball courts. And then she held her arms wide above her head, as if to say it emphatically: *All this!*

Suzy noticed the temperature only in its absence. No discernible register of hot or cold. In a moment without breeze she felt without weight and without time. Like a child on a swing at the height of its arc. This was an option, Suzy thought. This was proof that there was an alternative. That no matter the corners she might paint herself into at school, there could be a reasonable thing like this, the way it felt on your skin. But then a breeze washed up the hill on the back of a wave. The ocean presented itself as a frozen body of water, and the enormity of the beach seemed suddenly desolate. That sort of easy made her restless, like the anxiety of deserts or the silence of space. All the jangly stresses of the semester surged through her body at once. "I'm cold," Suzy said, shivering. Grace dropped her arms and frowned. They watched the sun go behind a cloud and, before long, the lights went out.

The rest of that week Suzy did a lot of apologizing. Sorries and sorries. Grace said she understood—that bad grades on tests could do that to you. Only, Suzy knew Grace *didn't* understand. Grace was a stewardess. Suzy sometimes wondered if she'd studied for an exam even once in her life, stew school included. Grace didn't comprehend the stakes. Not just that good grades might lead to a fulfilling job and life. But that there was something that needed to be proven. Suzy had been *kept out*—the wrong side of history by a year, born one spring too soon. She might not have even known to care if the opportunity had presented itself to her in high school, if she'd been a year younger. But it hadn't and she wasn't. She'd been fatefully passed over, the last class of women tied to the old way.

"Give me a fucking break," Grace said when Suzy tried to explain. "That's the most self-important bullshit I've ever heard. Get a job. Get any job. Better: get a job stewing."

Suzy knew Grace was right. She'd been coasting along, playing to her strengths, working to prove something and steeping in the indignation of being lumped together with the girls. And yet, when confronted with a little big-boy math and science, the only thing she'd proven was that she couldn't hang.

"I don't think I'm going to get a job stewing," Suzy said anyway.

"Well, we'd be happy to have you if you ever sink so low."

"Hey! You guys! Come here!" Suzy and Mike smirk at each other, caught. Though there are fewer lines at the party dividing lifelong friends and first-time guests, they've been standing together at the edge of the patio anyway. They move toward Grace and are introduced to a new wave of acquaintances. They drink more. Mostly beer, but every once in a while this one friendly, red-faced phantom—the host, Flipper—comes by and demands, "This is my palace, every last one of you girlies *must* take a pull." Suzy is granted exemption when she invokes the loosely enforced twenty-four-hour booze ban for stews.

Important conversations are tracking out, about movies and cars and sandwiches, but mostly about music. There's only one record player, but the speakers fill the small house—about the size of Grace and Mike's—so that each new song precipitates a new conversation. "Holloway Jail" opens wide.

The recording features a corroded guitar. It throws its sound into the corners of the house, and Suzy gets rushed up into a good memory. She dances slowly with her head down and her eyes closed, and starts giggling to herself. Mike elbows her and she opens her eyes sleepily. "I've always wondered whether you were capable of some Graceness," he says. Suzy flushes and bends way over, head to the floor, before popping up, hair fallen in front like drapes.

A new boy Suzy finds herself talking to says no way, he saw them this spring, too, at the Troubadour—if she ever needs a lift, ever needs someone to go to shows with, he'd be happy, she seems like a cool chick, knows her music, where does she come from, anyway?

And while she's explaining, this sensation of dread bowls through the house and out onto the patio. The second keg is finished and the refrigerator has blown out. There's disbelief. How could it have happened on this of all days, in the goodness of this place? To Suzy's surprise, Mike crosses the room to discuss something with Flipper. Flipper seems to welcome any prospect of salvation and tilts his ear, a full-bodied gesture, toward Mike's mouth.

Suzy watches Flipper's face change, a blank field of rapt attention that suddenly comprehends what Mike has said, what he's offered. Flipper kisses Mike on the forehead and pulls a loose ten from his pocket—and before Mike knows it, there's change springing from swimsuit pockets in all corners of the room.

Grace is at Suzy's side: "What the hell is going on?"

"I think Mike volunteered to go buy more beer."

Grace's mouth is a squiggle. "Really…"

Mike shouts from across the patio: "I'm gonna take one of their strand cruisers—the one with the basket—and bring a few cases back."

"Can you really ride with that much?" Grace says.

"They assured me I could."

"What market are you going to?"

"Just down the block, and then over a few…"

"Just remember the water's always west," Grace says.

"Yes," Mike says.

As Mike pulls the strand cruiser from the side of the house, Grace and Flipper and the cluster of friends smoking grass in the yard wave at him, as though he's departing on a steamer. Mike is wobbly at first push, but he levels out and floats toward the ocean.

"So weird," Grace says.

"He's trying!" Suzy says.

"I'm just already pretty beat. Drank too much at brunch. Before he pulled that move, I was gonna see if you two wanted to get out of here."

"If you can't wait till Mike gets back, I could go with you—"

"Hey, I know you," a voice says over the cackling in the yard.

Billy is shirtless, with a backpack double-strapped on his shoulders. He has a gob of zinc covering his nose, and it looks like he's combed his hair in the interim, maybe even showered.

"Mrs. Riddlehoover's class," Suzy says.

"*Riiighht,*" Billy says. Grace has a waxy, fixed grin as she watches Suzy slip into rhythm with this stranger.

"Uh?" Grace says.

"This is my sister, Grace—that I told you about."

"Right. Pleased to meet you," he says. "Billy Zar."

Grace squints. "I've heard about you."

"All good things?" he says as Grace turns her narrowing eyes to Suzy. "I dig your street, by the way," he says. "How high up are you?"

"Hmm?" Grace says, turning back. "Uh, 400 block."

"Back side of the hill."

"You grew up here."

"Yeah, yeah," he says, and scans the crowd, "like a lot of these."

"And when did you two meet?"

"Suzy was gonna be my Drunk 'n' Draw partner."

"Is that right?" Grace says. "She's not much of a setter."

"That's what I hear," he says.

Billy lifts a hand and offers Grace what's left of a lit joint Suzy hasn't noticed till now. Grace flips her lower lip out as a pass.

Suzy hasn't smoked since school and didn't come close to considering it during training. But she's just taken her final drug test, received the all clear. And Billy does this thing, this *Please, no pressure* shrug-and-wink that makes certain she knows it's totally cool if she isn't cool with it—which only convinces Suzy it's the right thing to do. And so she plucks the paper from his fingers, grazing his knuckle fuzz, and pulls it to her lips. Not too much, no coughing, she thinks—and so she inhales as slowly as her lungs allow, those swim-team lungs stretched for the first time in months. She lets it swirl inside her before she slips the smoke from her nostrils, her eyes fixed on a hedge. Hardly any smoke, but she's done it without embarrassment, and now it's in his mouth, drawn deeply, his lips pressed smack flush to the pale lipstick she's left behind. Now there's hardly anything remaining, and Billy asks if she and Grace want to sit in the shade of a tangerine tree.

"I have to go to the bathroom," Grace says, uncrossing her arms. But Suzy collapses in a cheap mesh beach chair next to his, her legs crossed extra tightly as the cotton dress rides up in the strange angle of the seat.

"She's kinda dressed up," Billy says.

"Well, *brunch.*"

Billy opens his eyes big, as if this were a call-back to some joke he already made.

Billy hums something she can't quite place. He saw the Eagles the night before at the Santa Monica Civic Auditorium, says he's been oooing "Witchy Woman" all day. He's fixed in his seat, but everyone seems to acknowledge him. They nod his way, swing by for quick hellos and brief updates about mutual friends. His value to the network seems to have been acquired by never not being around.

"See that guy over there?"

"Sure," Suzy says.

"He started a bumper sticker business."

"Is that really a thing?"

"Well, apparently, you only need one to really hit. Especially something Sela del Mar–related." He frames it in the air with his hands: "'Sela Vie.'"

Suzy giggles.

"Like the French thing," he says.

"Oh, I got the reference," she says, laughing a little harder.

"Can't print enough of them."

Suzy laughs again and, for the first time since the first hit, hears its warm mettle externally. There is a voice in her head, speech mechanics happening with her throat and tongue, and then a laugh — a thing not whole but made of distinct parts of sound; it was all science…hard science, Cs in each. And the whole two-shot with this saltwater towhead, and even that silly mustache, a separate entity in itself; the picture seems to dim at the edges, a Vaseline lens, the effect of motion blur. There's something missing in Billy's face, and it's only now in their shared cocoon that she's placed it: his eyelashes are blond, too, blond like pound cake. And they do this thing to his eyes that has the inverse effect of mascara. Is it even handsome? Here are these little lakes on a face—edgeless, though—contained not by shoreline, but by these high-walled, shale-cut cheek- and brow bones. She's seen pictures like this, from the continental ranges of Italy and Switzerland. Lakes you'd walk *into,* not just *up* to. Hike for days toward a moonscape of heaven-stretching rocks that puddled black eyes depthless at their base....All this inside the silence in their conversation, Suzy wrapping a long strand of her own orange hair around her index and middle fingers and popping her lips to the backbeat like a goldfish in a tank.

"You're feeling pretty good," Billy says.

She nods and smiles.

"You know who you look like?"

She ticks her head low to high, like, *Who?*

"Sissy Spacek."

"Ugh. Really? Try again."

He smiles and inhales: "You know who you look like?"

Nods upward again.

"Mia Farrow."

"Better."

"Mia Farrow on *Peyton Place.* Mia Farrow with hair."

"Mia Farrow and..." She gestures to him. "Robert Redford?"

"Sure, that's it," he says.

"*Peyton Place* Farrow and *Butch Cassidy* Redford."

"You've got it, good."

A while on, she's moving her head around with her eyes closed, and the silence summons an onset of strings. "E-L-Ohhh!" she says. There's a clatter of silverware somewhere, the foamy choke of the keg. The sounds flip Suzy's lights on. And then there's Mike, a case over each shoulder, stepping onto the patio, looking both more propped up *and* more destructed than Suzy has ever imagined he could. His shoulders pull in on themselves and collect in big fists in his upper arms. But then there's his leg—torn open below the knee and spilling a black, sandy flow down his shin, dammed, firebroken, at the edge of his sock.

"Oh God, what happened?" Suzy says, leaping up to meet Mike.

He unloads the cases on a wooden table, and a few guests sidle up to grab a longneck.

"Well, uh, I kinda got lost—was riding up and down PCH, cutting up one block and then down another. All the walkstreets look the same to me." Mike didn't move with Grace in January. He took two months in New York to tie up loose ends. The place really is still new to him. "Anyway, I found a market and bought the beer, and on the way home I was no-hands-ing it, until right at the base of the hill when I hit this slick of sand and the bike crumpled beneath me." Suzy looks again at the gash. It has clotted, but it's stuffed with grit—crushed shells as old as the first fish that lay out on Sela Beach, that came up for air and got tan instead. *Fish with suntan,* Suzy thinks. *Fish with sunglasses!* She's smiling even though Mike's in pain.

"And I didn't think it'd be such a good first impression," Mike goes on, squinting at her cinched-off giggle, "to toss the beer to save myself, so I kinda held on and let my legs and shoulder take the—*what?*"

"Nothing, sorry, that's horrible." Suzy pulls it together. "Does your back look like that, too?" she says, flipping him around. His seafoam button-down is sliced into a clean flap along the spine. It's strange to see him like this—Mike, whom, until she moved, she pictured mostly dressed up for dinner in Schuyler Glen or suited for a wedding. And yet here he is torn to pieces like an eight-year-old who's fallen out of a tree and into a rosebush. It has always sped a small sense of shame through Suzy seeing adults outfitted in corrective plaster or gauze. A pretty Vassar girl in a cast; a white-shoe attorney in a neck brace; a mother of three with molar-to-molar braces. They are extrafashion trends people are supposed to grow out of. Now Mike has his own—bloody as a little kid launched from his basketed bike.

And yet Mike seems better fit for the party than he was forty minutes ago. In ragged bones and blood comes a looseness. And having it implemented unwittingly makes him simpler, freer.

"Holy shit, amigo, what happened to you?" Flipper says to Mike.

"I fell," Mike says. "The beer's fine, though. And here's this...." Mike hands Flipper a handful of coins.

"You are *fucked up!*" Flipper says. He grabs a beer. "I can't believe you didn't break any bottles." Flipper grabs another beer and pops the caps on the edge of the patio table. The foam draws up the necks like blood in a syringe and Flipper lifts his bottle to his mouth to cut the surge. He cheerses Mike and pats him wide-palmed on the back.

Mike has passed.

Now Grace is at Mike's side with a wash of horror in her face.

"What *happened?!*" He tells the story again while Grace's fingers drift over the raspberries beneath his shirt. Suzy moves back toward Billy, and they sit in their chairs, and Suzy explains.

"Whoops," Billy says, running his tongue along the edge of some rolling paper. He's somehow wearing her sunglasses, so she grabs his.

He describes several places around town, the spots she has to try this very week. The streets that correspond to the best parts of the beach. The totally good guys who throw better parties than the other guys whose parties are still pretty great. As far as Suzy can see (through the honey-colored lenses of Billy's Vuarnets), there isn't a place or person or idea in Sela deserving of a critical word. At some point, after Suzy opens another beer, Grace decides she can't look at Mike's blood any longer.

"We're gonna head home and clean up," Grace says. "You good?"

"Mm-hmm."

"Airport by ten forty-five."

"I've got all the time."

"Ehhh," Grace says.

Suzy puddles up right there in her chair for another couple hours—four o'clock, five o'clock—and experiences an encouraging coming-into-focus. The restaurants Billy described earlier float in her mind at first as islands in a black void—El Guincho, the Mexican joint with the tripe tacos and the parrot on the sign... it's just a Billy story, tagged with a detail. But when she learns that Tuna, the bar that's best on Wednesdays, is not only across the street from El Guincho, but also run by the same family as Howlers, the web touches. The darkness on the map, cast in new light, bridges with connective tissue. Billy even untacks a real-life map from a wall inside the house and brings it to Suzy to show her: there it is, Sela del Mar, and all its referents. She is beginning to see it. And just as brightly as she sees it, the answers appearing in relief, the Big Idea starts coming into focus, too—the meaning of the interconnectivity and infinity of it all starts to organize itself in an elegant and obvious solution to the great puzzle, the key to comprehension right over the edge there, just beyond that last wave, one deep dive, deeper than the last, down down down...

When she wakes up—having drifted, for how long she can't tell—she feels like she's slept with a sock in her mouth. The sun still hasn't set, but she's beat. Someone has covered her in a serape, and with the exception of a burn-stained couple smoking cigarettes near the bougainvillea, everyone else has left or moved inside.

Suzy stands, embarrassed, and the blood rushes to her toes. She sits again, white in the head, and folds up the map with her eyes closed. She collects some drained beer bottles into an empty box. She toes up to the front door and tries to locate Billy before stepping inside.

"You're awake!" Flipper says. The "Starman" 45 is moving in circles at low volume, and smoke hangs from the ceiling like a thunderhead. There are eight of them, no women, stretched out around the coffee table. Flipper's leaned over a bowl of reds and blues, deliberating like a child selecting a jelly bean. When he picks one, he bends himself back, and shakes it down his throat. Suzy finds it improbable that she shares a generation with them. Flipper offers Suzy the bowl and an orange Frisbee coated with the peach fuzz of unlined blow. She declines, there's a flushing, and then a door opens. Billy emerges from the bathroom looking oddly put together. His hair is wet and freshly tilled. No matter what, the crisp part. He slips a purple comb into the front pocket of a fresh lavender tank top, and Flipper extends his arm toward him.

"No thanks, good bros," Billy says.

He's midmorning-weekday alert, smelling like soap and lotion up close. Did he have toiletries and a change of clothes in his backpack? Suzy becomes instantly self-conscious, tasting her mouth as he might, a wet cave of champagne and malt and char. She brushes her hair with her fingers and finds it fried.

"Sorry for checking out like that. I don't normally just, you know, collapse midconversation."

"I saw it coming quick," Billy says. "You started talking about your final-semester grades with your eyes closed."

"Oh God."

"Last thing you said was how you sensed between us an accelerated gravitational pull. A potential energy. No, an undeniable potential energy."

"Oh my God, no I didn't."

"No you didn't. But you did talk about physics. And you did tell me about Dave."

She covers her face with her hands. "That's bad, too."

"Nah, he sounded like an all right guy," he says. "You hungry?"

Suzy hasn't thought of it, but she is murderously empty. She feels hard and hollowed out, like a seashell. Growing up, Suzy would sometimes imagine the color and texture of the contents in her stomach. A healthy green bed of lawn mower clippings after a salad; cartoon-strip toxic lava after a day of fried eggs and booze. She needs salt, she needs starch. "Yes," she says.

"Cool, I've got an idea."

Just a minute to clean up, she tells him. She steps into the bathroom and flips the switch. She wets her fingers and streaks her hair—darkening with the dampness. Her eye whites harbor little lightning bolts, and a pair of heavily shadowed half-moons lie on their sides beneath her lower lids. She's taken in just enough sun to wake up her freckles, to roust the red in her hair. It's latent but there—an all-out redhead deep on one side of the family, responsible for a sixteenth share of the makeup, just enough to taint the family blond the color of a grapefruit. She surveys the medicine cabinet for a tube of toothpaste and squeezes a segment onto her tongue. She runs her tongue over her teeth, and with a ring of mint hanging around her mouth, she walks back into the living room and says some nice things to Flipper, before Billy cracks a joke she barely hears and pulls her from the room on the laugh line.

It's maybe thirty minutes out from sunset, and there's a buoyant glow hovering above the rooftops. The sky peels back shades and the light grows richer. When Suzy looks up, there's this thing that happens, where she can see through the light but also detect the faintest reflection. It's like a glass ceiling, a sky of mirrors—each talking to another, all color moving together from warm to cool, to cream-colored and then white.

Down the hill, down toward the water, they find the Strand. Pressing north, they pass house after house, about which Billy shares intel: This stretch of four homes is where the Sela del Mar Club hosted Hollywood types for a while, before they moved on to the Jonathan Club in Santa Monica. That Tudor with the sloped roof attracted bad news—a few years ago, three teens fell from way up on a big, breathy Santa Ana afternoon and cracked their heads right there. This bungalow is where one of the Manson girls lived, one of the ones wrapped up with Sharon Tate. Winkel-something. And then that lot next door—no house, just ice plant and dog shit—is where a Dodger infielder was all set to build a mansion before they traded him away to Kansas City, or somewhere else in the middle.

"Tough luck," Suzy says, getting a feel for the POV.

"Incomprehensible."

As they scoot along, a few kids fire off some Piccolo Petes, comet-tail screeches that fail to resolve in explosions.

"I'm always waiting for the bomb," Billy says.

"That's 'cause you were in elementary school in the fifties. Sirens and drills."

"I like the stuff that explodes."

"You should enlist, then."

"Not that much."

"We were only ever given sparklers," Suzy says.

"That's probably the pro-peace thing to do."

A sizzle and a bang this time. Suzy jumps, still a little light in the brain.

"Jesus, they're everywhere," she says.

"And this is *illegal*. You should've heard it when anyone could be on the beach."

Pretty soon they're there, a stucco block like a lump of clay: El Guincho. The Tow Truck. Its insides are unstuffed, walls hand carved, seemingly by the scoops of a sculptor at one end and, at the other, by the greedy paws of a child gutting a pumpkin. An overweight server with long black hair and smudgy tattoos counts cash in the register. The counter looks to seat about a dozen, and the honkings of a mariachi record leak from the speakers. A leather pipe of a man with golden hair and golden nails swallows the fat end of a burrito and skims the front page of the *Sela del Mar Sounder.*

"Memo! Qué tal, migo?" the server says.

"Bien, bien. Qué pasa?" Billy reaches over the counter with both hands, and they grip each other's forearms. The cook turns over his shoulder and flashes a shaka. "Pablo, this is my friend Suzy. She's just moved here. I told her this is the only place to eat. *El primero, el mejor.*"

Pablo wipes his hand on a stained dishrag he keeps tucked in the front of his apron and offers it to Suzy. Suzy shakes but can't stop eyeing the burrito being double-palmed by the little golden man. She can't remember ever having been this hungry. If she doesn't eat soon, she might throw up—and in her cursory survey of the facility, there wasn't any certain indication that a bathroom existed.

Pablo reaches into a steel bin beneath the counter and emerges with a basket of tortilla chips and a Styrofoam cup of salsa. Suzy waits for Billy to take the first chip and then dives in two at a time. Billy walks her through the menu, his favorites—which, like his opinions of most things and people, are not terribly discriminating. "It's all the best, each as good as the next," he says. "But maybe since it's the first time, it's not such a bad idea to start with the Number One."

Suzy asks for the One and Pablo writes down Billy's usual without his asking for it. Instead Billy says, *"Escuchame, Pablo: Jack está aquí?"* Pablo hands their ticket to the cook, who disappears behind a tin wall that's cluttered with concert flyers and stickers of what look to be surf brands and skateboarding companies and, how 'bout that, front and center: SELA VIE. The infamous bumper sticker. Pablo doesn't glance up at Billy but nods toward the ceiling.

"I'm gonna go say hi to the owner for a second," Billy says. "He's upstairs, I'll be right back."

Suzy shrugs happily. While she waits, she swivels in her stool from ten o'clock to two o'clock, in rhythm with the schlock-plod of "Mary Had a Little Lamb" on the radio. It triggers flashbacks to the war she waged with Dave in defense of Wings. But here was a gift for the opposition—a miserable single that choked the stereo at stew school. She stands and steps just outside the door onto the sidewalk and watches the moon slip behind some thin, low-hanging clouds, and it is suddenly a bright dusk—an unnatural glow that reminds her of the seedy flashings of Times Square. Pablo waves a brown bag at her and Billy emerges from the staircase.

"Want to take it to the beach?" he says. "They usually start up the fireworks right after sunset."

Something has changed in Billy. Something in the backpack. He went upstairs light; he returned with the leafy-green JanSport nice and bulky.

Suzy is happy to go along. Fireworks are never something she goes out of her way to find, but the protracted show—the heavy presentness of sitting and watching, neck craned—is always better than she expects. *"Hasta luego, Pablo! Hasta, Chuy!"*

They clatter down the steep hill—long, loud steps—and they're suddenly on the Strand with the twilight walkers and dogs without leashes. Suzy orients herself by proximity to the pier. The pier is closer than when she tracks to the beach from Mike and Grace's house, but not much. Six blocks nearer, she figures—and then glimpses a street sign that confirms it. Six blocks, on the money.

"I'm getting it," Suzy says.

"What's that?"

"I know where we are, and where I go from here. It's making sense."

"It's easy, right? Complicated elsewhere; easy here."

"I'm having a tough time resisting that idea."

"Goddamn!" Billy says, swallowing the first bite. "You've gotta just take it to the face. All at once."

They chew in silence.

"People from San Diego say it's better there," Billy says. "The closer to Mexico, the more Mexicans and all."

"I suppose that's logical."

"Well, they're wrong."

Suzy eats as quickly as she's ever allowed herself, and then it's all gone and she's ready to sleep again.

"I guess my timing was off," Billy says. The clouds just hang there, no explosions yet. Families gather on the sand. People move to the balconies in the Strand-front homes. It is growing dark enough to detect television sets in some of the ocean-facing windows.

"I feel like it should be daybreak," Suzy says.

"What do you mean?! Things are just getting going. Plus, you've got work in a few hours."

Suzy has worried all afternoon about this moment—the one from which she must fill the sails and push forward or just head home and level out before reporting to the airport.

"I don't know if I'm gonna make it," she says. "I do know that *that* was unbelievable, though." She balls up the tinfoil that had wrapped her Number One, scraps and droppings and all, shapes it into a perfect sphere, drops her wrist back over her shoulder, and flicks it, high arcing, into the trash can.

Billy flames the tip of a joint he's pulled from behind his ear and offers Suzy a hit. She squints at the joke. "So that doesn't just bomb you out for the rest of the night?"

Billy shrugs and focuses on something out in the darkness. Admiring the way his hair sprouts from his head, from near his ears, the lightness so convincingly embedded in each strand, she wonders if she'd ever have met someone, upstate or in New Haven or in New York, with a physical property like this one—the brown skin licked with a swirl of white up top, a composition so reserved to children that it seems certain to bleed out. Baby teeth vanish and platinum blonds go brown. But with Billy—and here is when her eyes begin to wander, administering a mapping from those translucent lashes to the fine cotton of his arms and legs and toes...She loses the thought. Snipped. If he feels her eyes, he doesn't flinch.

"So there are three parties tonight," he says. "They're all starting at roughly the same time and likely going until neighbors complain. It's a lot."

"And here I thought you were Mr. *Chillerzz*"—she throws up a misconstructed shaka, pinkie and index, hook 'em horns instead of hang loose. "Mr. I Just Flow With It. Who wouldn't *possibly* care about where the night is taking him, so long as it takes him there."

Billy pulls deeply from between his fingers. He peaks his eyebrows as though he's never considered this. He fixes her hand, replacing her extended index finger with an extended thumb.

"That's not an unfair thing to say." It's a concession. "But you know, I'm not *totally* like the others. I like to know what's happening, what I'm experiencing and what I'm missing. There's an order to it all that I like to follow. I like to show up when I tell friends I'll be there. I promise things to lots of people."

"An overpromiser..."

"Well, it's not overpromising if you always come through. I'm reliable, even if I'm not a lot of other things. I'm never not there," he says. He smiles: discovery. "I like that....Let's make that the motto. Like on a business card: 'Billy Zar: Never Not There.'"

Suzy pushes her hair off her forehead and fixes herself still in the dim light. She hears a pair of sandals clapping down the walk-street behind them. Not worth turning over her shoulder. But they're louder than the others, don't pass like the others. The steps cut off heavy and deliberate at their backs.

"Billy, it's Dan Francis."

Suzy turns. It's already getting too dark for faces.

"What's up, Danny! I haven't seen you in months. Grab a seat."

Dan Francis is a head taller than Billy, with hair like a hulled walnut shell. He's closer to seven feet than six, and his body curls over. He keeps his hands stuffed in his jeans pockets.

"Danny, this is my new friend Suzy. She's from New York and just moved to Sela. I'm showin' her the ropes."

"Hey," Danny says, just real enough to be polite.

"Danny," Billy says, "was an all-state middle blocker. Then all-Pac-8 at 'SC. With the right setter, like he had our senior year, Danny gets that ball down inside the eight-foot line every time, am I right? A little butter off the fingertips on two?"

Danny squints painfully, his cover in greater threat with each bio line.

"That sounds super impressive," Suzy says. "I'm sorry, though, that I don't know all that much about volleyball."

"No, no," Danny says, looking across Billy toward Suzy and putting his enormous hands up toward her. "I don't...So, I'm here 'cause, you know, Mark and Greg told me you were the one, if I found you..."

"Yeah, Danny, yeah. You did good. We're gonna go somewhere else, though. Let's talk about volleyball for now."

And so Billy asks Danny about life after USC, the six months in

Europe when Danny played for a pro team in Sweden. And how after that it was either try to pick up some paychecks hustling on the beach or else give it up. The talk is pleasant enough but strained. Billy wasn't like this with anyone at the party. It is the least accommodating she's seen him. And Danny still looks itchy, impatient—a reluctant interview subject.

The twilight extinguishes while they're talking. The sodium lights on the Strand flicker to life and cast cones of orange once per block. Billy signals to Suzy like it's time to go. No fireworks here, then. The three of them move north, in the direction of Mike and Grace's place. Danny doesn't say much, but Billy continues to narrate stories about the houses along the waterfront.

When they get to Mike and Grace's street, Billy stops and thumbhooks the straps of his backpack.

"Well, cool," he says to Suzy. "You're for sure making it out tonight, right? I still have to give you that thing."

He hasn't mentioned it since the beach at noon.

"All right, maybe," Suzy says. She's still catching up to the fact that they're parting.

"No maybes, it's important. It's an important thing."

He's weirdly grave as he says it.

"*We'll see . . . ,*" she says, hoping he'll smile.

"I'll be home till nine or so," he says, looking around, distracted. "Number's 545-1089. Hit me up, okay?" Suzy rests on her heels. She kinda can't believe it. No fireworks together. Billy offers a waist-high low five, and after a distended beat she swings in with an exaggerated slap of his palm. Danny stands to the side, squinting up the alley and shifting his weight around. "Seriously: I'm counting on you tonight, Z."

"Talk soon, *dude,*" she says, and Danny follows Billy along the Strand.

Suzy starts up the incline to the house but then turns back toward the beach and then again back toward the house. She lets herself believe it's nice to be heading home with plenty of time to spare.

Suzy keys in through the front door. She prepares herself for Mike and Grace's line of questioning, for their double-person presence in the cramped living room. But she can tell right away that the house is empty. Everything is visible from the front door: the living room–slash–dining room, the island counter and cupboards, the kitchen with the Hotpoint fridge, the table surfaces spread with magazines. The black holes spinning off the corpus of the living room: Mike and Grace's bedroom; the shared closet; the bathroom; and Mike's office, where Suzy sleeps. She should really start looking into finding her own place. This house is big enough for no more than two and a quarter full-time residents. The lights are off and she keeps them off. It is so still. There are two notes on the counter:

Mom and Dad called AGAIN

and

Walked to the market to pick up chicken and veggies to grill tonight. We'll get enough for you if you're around. xoxo, G.

It makes her feel better — not so suddenly alone.

Suzy kicks her shoes into the corner of the room and arranges herself in the nook at the end of the couch. She pulls her legs up so that they stretch the length. She forgot to turn on the television but is reluctant to lift herself right back up. A heavy silence pours into the curves of her ear like plaster into a cast. She knows she's not going back out. She feels guilty. But this is fine, this is all she can expect from herself anyway.

Evenings at home aren't so bad. Holiday evenings especially. She has to work; it's not a waste of a night. Plus, Mike and Grace will be back soon. She looks for something within arm's reach. A crossword puzzle, but no pen. A sleeve of photos from a road trip Mike and Grace took in May to the central coast. And under a cushion, an issue of *New York* magazine—the cover a full-framed blonde with roller-coaster hips, pressing out toward Suzy, nude or bikinied except for a pair of triple-scoop vanilla ice cream cones she holds in front of her tits. Her mascara is so thick it seems applied by a stew school instructor. It is a summer special issue. A hundred and ninety things to do before the season passes—swimming topless at Fire Island, a sex show on East Broadway, a private booze cruise on the Hudson. There's a big story by Gail Sheehy about prostitutes in Times Square. A piece of a series. Suzy starts to read. Sheehy pulled on a leotard and a leather skirt and sat in the corners of motel bedrooms while the girls went about their work.

Suzy moves through the issue until she's out of pages. A hundred and ninety things no one who is anyone could miss that summer. On the table, on a neat stack beneath the crossword puzzle, she finds three other issues. Mike has them everywhere. *New York*s and *Rolling Stone*s and *Esquire*s, *Time, Sports Illustrated, Fortune.* Inspiration for his own writing, for his own magazine. Envy, too. Inspiration, envy—twin fuel sources.

She reads these ones right through as well—Jack Nicklaus on the cover of *SI*; Groucho Marx on *Esquire,* THE GOOD LIFE OF A DIRTY OLD MAN. She hears the first bang of fireworks at the pier. She considers hopping to her feet. But she's fixed in place.

She knows this feeling and the fluid in her nerves goes cold.

During the spring term Suzy grew addicted to Dave. She grew addicted to his scale. To his left part and his gray eyes. To a face that was not yet famous, but that would be one day, it had to be, it was preordained. A face and a voice, a voice a Keats might call mellifluous. Lowish and pure. She worked in the library and he worked at the Palace. On busy nights she'd help deliver drinks—for big ones like Carly Simon, Billy Joel, Steve Miller, Pink Floyd. She started picking up tips, and the theater hired her as a cocktail waitress. They'd see movies together, too—*Cabaret* in a March blizzard, *The Godfather* downtown during a week of April rain. Or they'd sit for hours in front of Dave's record player while he squeezed long runs of improvisation from the pentatonic scale, practicing little phrases five, ten, twenty times through before moving on to the next.

It was a good arrangement. He was an embodiment of ambition seen through. Dave who was supposed to be at Yale. He was, back in her senior year in high school, precisely who she felt like she'd be missing the opportunity to meet by going to an all-girls school. He was the young man mothers said existed at most colleges even though they only really existed in New Haven. He studied history and politics and planned to work at the Pentagon or Langley. At least, if the band didn't work out, if they could get him to give up the New York music thing, which at that point he was already thinning on. He'd missed the boat on law school for the fall, but he seemed to be relieved that elbowing around for gigs on the Bowery, that life, would only be temporary, a capsule of youth to crack open at future dinner parties.

The real plan, the blood ambition, was familiar pedigree—the kind that seemed administered by a rubber stamp at Yale. On paper, Dave's father worked for DOD, but Dave knew he was CIA. He'd spent long stretches of Dave's childhood abroad, leaving him and his brothers to two-v.-two lacrosse in the fenceless backyard in McLean. The line was always London or Paris, but Dave would snoop through his father's cash when he got back and find bills from Eastern Europe and Africa. His mother worked at the National Gallery as a curator. She specialized in portraits of Colonial and early-American statesmen, Founding Fathers and their wives. She was a social chair at the Sulgrave Club, and she and the other members were proud of Dave for supporting the introduction of women (by dating one) to his university. Dave was good for Suzy.

Still, though, all winter she'd been dealing with this strange new physical ailment: a waking paralysis. She'd be lying in bed, somewhere between sleep and consciousness, and her foot would fail to respond to her command, the signal cut off. She'd try the other leg, her fingers, her arms—nothing but fuzz. She'd attempt to speak and the sound would be smothered. And then she'd see it—the specter in the room, the visitation, moving about at the periphery of her frozen gaze. Sometimes it would be a family member, other times a friend. Any attempt to move would prove futile, and she learned that the only way out was through sleep, drifting her mind down a dark staircase until she returned via a natural snapping-to of consciousness.

Suzy spoke to someone at Yale and learned that it was a diagnosable condition, related to anxiety, something that dated back thousands of years. It was the condition, her doctor told her, of the actual "night mare"—the visiting demon to the subconscious. The doctor asked her to identify any overlaps among the episodes, and the best she could come up with was that in each case she'd opted out of something frivolous—coffee with a classmate at the Rock, a reading by a young novelist Camille admired, a Stevie Wonder show in Hartford—only to be seized by regret shortly thereafter.

She was never exactly where she was convinced she should be. The whole thing, it seemed, was wrapped up in an anxiety of mislocation.

All semester, while she sat in her apartment writing perfect little meaningless chapters for Camille, she'd been growing overwhelmed by a sense of uncertainty. For four years there had been no cause greater than herself and her studies, no intention beyond the pleasure of completism—turning the last font-blocked page of a novel to the blank one beneath the back cover; reading till the end of the Revolution; safely plagiarizing Susan Sontag and Elizabeth Hardwick; submitting a blue book with one, small, safe original idea. She'd raced to this juncture without much thought. But with graduation fast approaching, there was, for the first time, true freedom of choice—and it froze her up.

One evening, late and drunk, after a night of big, leisurely B sides and wire-tight radio singles colored by the red and blue gel filters of the Palace, Suzy indulged a monologue of concerns to Dave. There was no one around to tell her that, say, October 1972 would be a month where it was critical to be present in Philadelphia. That during that month she'd meet the man or woman who would turn her on to the thing that would finally help her figure out what she was truly after—that would set the moving parts into motion to arrange job and spouse and ultimately home. That there would be a place and a time where it wouldn't feel like it was all happening elsewhere.

Dave pointed out, with aggravating reasonableness, that it might not be the exact right answer for Suzy or Dave or any one person specifically, but that New York seemed as hedged a bet as any.

He was right. And for a little while that conviction served as an antidote to the specter that had been plaguing her. There was a new calm. And when Dave changed his mind about law school and got back-doored into Columbia, following him to New York seemed fully actionable for the first time. They could spend June at his parents' summer place in Narragansett—one last month, Dave kept saying, of clean air and open windows—and then ultimately move into his uncle's spare studio near the river on the Upper West Side. An apartment his uncle sold as "close to the classroom, closer to Gristedes."

Middle of April, Grace came to visit. She'd worked a flight into Kennedy and trained up for a night. The Eagles were in town, playing the Palace, which Grace defined as irony to several people who asked where she was visiting from. Fly across the country to see the local boys. Watching Suzy shuttle drinks back and forth across the room reminded Grace of her very finest idea.

"What are you doing after May?" she said.

"I still don't know. But I want to go to New York."

"For Dave."

"*With* Dave, *for* me."

"And what are you gonna do for money?"

"I could work at a club or something. Start talking to some alumni."

"New York is disgusting."

"What are you talking about?"

"It's the most dangerous place in America!" Grace finished her drink, and Suzy moved to get her another one, to signal to her manager that she'd taken an order, that she'd been working, not chatting. "Thank you. But it really is the pits. How often have you even been there without me or Mom and Dad?"

"Plenty of times."

"Like once a year?"

"No! Once a *semester.*"

Grace smiled. "And?"

"I love it."

"How come you've never mentioned it before? How come you hardly ever visited when I lived there, if you love it so much?"

"I didn't love it then, I didn't know yet."

"But you know now."

"Maybe I can work for a magazine. My thesis adviser says I should go and do that, try to think about writing, even."

"How come you've never said anything about writing before?"

"This is what professors do, this is the point of college."

"There are magazines in Los Angeles."

"Mike's magazine doesn't count."

"Mike's magazine *does* count. What does New York have that Mike's magazine doesn't have?"

"Mike's magazine doesn't exist yet."

"You could be in on the ground floor."

"*Rolling Stone. New York. The Village Voice.* All the stuff Mike did. That's not even what I'm talking about, though. I want to work from the bottom. Opportunity from the feet up."

"You're moving because of Dave."

"Dave will be there, so what?"

"Well, listen, you don't really have a plan—and that's fine, seriously. But what if you signed up for stew school?"

"I'm not going to stew school."

"It's not fancy enough."

"It's not fanciness, it's just—it's your thing."

"Listen, you don't have to tiptoe. I know how things are. I know what I am and I know what you are. But this is a short-term thing. No one does it their whole life. As much as I'd love to try..."

"I just—where would I live?"

"That's not your concern yet."

"I'd miss Dave."

"And," Grace said, "what else..."

"And I feel like I'd be letting myself down. Or something. Doing a job that didn't require *this place.*"

"Thank you. I just wanted to hear you say it. But again, sweetie, this is not a lifetime. It's a thing to do while you're young and pretty, when you have time to see things, to buy yourself a little gap to figure it out."

Suzy didn't respond, tuned into the guitar solo instead. Grace hadn't called her pretty since they shared a roof. The discrepancy between the two ("She's a nine and you're a seven," their mother had told Suzy her junior year of high school) had always irritated her, and the fact of her irritation only irritated her more. Grace wouldn't acknowledge it outright, but she'd know the use of the *p* word was a clever appeal.

"Just do this for me," Grace said, picking up again. "As a contingency. The best possible contingency. Something you and I could have in common. A thing for us to share..."

Still nothing—the same solo.

"It's the most important decision I've made in my life," Grace said. "Do it for a year. It's a year in a lifetime."

"I'm just gonna race cars," Suzy said finally.

"And you'll be bitchin' at it," Grace said, content to finally drop it.

Grace left town early the next morning and didn't mention it again. But she smiled at Suzy on her way out the door—a smile that summed up the entirety of the previous night's conversation: *Whatever the fuck, just don't relinquish momentum.*

Four weeks later the experiment was over. Suzy turned in her thesis and squeaked through her other courses, and then, overnight, the Old Campus quad was transformed into an amphitheater for a ceremony. Suzy would, of course, not be graduating with Yale's Class of '72, but after drinking all morning with Dave and his family—and after bumping into Camille, who'd been encouraging a stunt like this for weeks—Suzy decided to borrow a gown and sit with Dave in the last row. "Every act is political," Camille had said, "and every occasion like this one is an opportunity to act."

The politics of her generation were complicated for Suzy. She wanted things—race wins, entrance into the locked rooms of Yale—not for the benefit of womankind but for the benefit of herself. For Suzy. She suspected some of the women her age would ride the language of their cultural moment all their lives, fighting for liberation without ever reaping the sorts of benefits that were much more interesting to Suzy. She'd always been less into living as a liberated woman than just skipping the line and living as a man. There's a difference. When she was the only girl racing, it was a novelty, news—until it wasn't. She didn't change, and yet they all gradually grew to unsee the ponytail. She transitioned from being a girl who'd been granted exception, to a driver with the birthright of boys.

As she filed in to her seat next to Dave, an imposter among this new set of old boys, Suzy's indignation heated all over again: Mom and Dad had jumped the gun, and on account, she'd been one year too early for this place, one year too early for the rest of her life.

Parents ringed the seated graduates on Old Campus. With her hair pinned beneath her cap and her dress concealed by the androgynous gown, hardly anyone noticed that Suzy didn't belong. Even those in their row dismissed her, she could tell, as merely a girlfriend who wanted in on the action. Dave had brought a flask with him and he passed it around their section. They'd already had several Bloody Marys and mimosas and Cups at Mory's with Dave's parents and brothers. Dave's father had showed them where his name was engraved on the wall, from when he was a student. Suzy loved it—it aggravated her how much she'd grown to love this place—but she could tell Dave had seen the engraving a hundred times too many.

Dave joked loudly as the president spoke, and he stopped paying attention altogether while they awarded the honorary doctorates. Suzy reached for Dave's hand and he quieted down. He unlocked his fingers from hers and let his hand fall off her lap. His fingers began to crawl up her leg, beneath her gown. He did it skillfully, without ruffling the gown. It felt nice to have a hand on her thigh. His hand slid up her leg, freshly shaved, to the hem of her dress, a cream-colored scoop-neck with green vines and petals of roses. His hand was concealed by the gown, and it slipped over the edge of her thigh between her legs. "Dave," she said. He moved his hand farther up her dress. She pinched her legs shut, trapping his hand. "Dave," she said as tersely as she could without drawing eyes. His hand was held in place by friction, but she felt the tip of his longest finger extend between her thighs and trace the edges of the elastic on both sides and the cotton in between. "I'm gonna fucking slap you," she whispered. He traced his finger like he was writing something. "All evidence I'm experiencing suggests that you won't," he breathed back. The words from the stage registered as muffled thunder. She was going to hit him unless she tied her hands back with her mind. "Five, four..." She started counting down like a kindergarten teacher. And he snickered and let the clock meet the buzzer. He'd called her bluff. She started again, "Seriously this time: five, four..." His finger traced the cotton and she kept counting. The speech ended and there was applause and Suzy shifted. And seizing the opportunity, Dave's finger lunged for the elastic, tugged at it, and she felt a cool, uncut fingernail crawl inside her. Her elbow flew from her lap in the upward arc of a backstroke. She caught him in the cheek with such force that it knocked him silently out of his seat and into the aisle. The applause had dissipated, but the sight lines were such that no one but the boys in immediate proximity noticed. All those boys who'd been handed everything she hadn't. There was a decision to be made—the very kind of decision that had physically locked her in place all winter and spring. But by the time she'd processed the choice she'd made, her feet had already carried her up one of the grass aisles toward College Street, and stew school, and Sela del Mar—the picture, Grace would assure Suzy once she arrived in California, of momentum unrelinquished, of her advice seen through.

*   *   *

The paralysis returned around the time she signed up for stew school. Suzy had missed the deadline, but Grace made a call, found a slot due to a dropout. They were happy to accommodate Suzy, to add her degree to their promo materials—a win-win. She packed up in New Haven, walked with the women in Poughkeepsie, stopped by home, and flew to Chicago in the space of a few days. Grand Pacific hadn't developed its own training school in Los Angeles yet, and so shared facilities in Chicago with some other smaller airlines. Three weeks of instruction, then preferential placement in L.A. She'd been getting locked up with greater frequency ever since—and she's stuck on the couch in the living room now.

It is hot in the house. The ceiling fan is still. Silence fills the room like water. Her mind drifts into the same soup her body seems to be submerged in—a warm bath that obscures the line between awake and asleep, between an anxiety over inaction and a resignation toward surrender. She would not be much of a fighter on the edge of death. And yet, right now, it's the same pairing of sight and sensation that has snapped her out of the stickiness lately. This strange recurring image: Suzy facing forward, a color field of rich light and simple lines, like a window looking out on an infinite sky. A force greater than jet propulsion at her back, a force greater than fear driving her forward. This wide-open window and the need beyond any other need to double-hand the wheel and steer toward it. That's what gets the feeling back, that's what lifts her to her feet.

She feels the air rushing back into her body, as though a vent in her skin has been cracked. She feels her body tingling still, each surface, like a foot that's coming out of sleep. She breathes. She swims her arms. She touches her toes and does jumping jacks. She is awake now, present, filled with a cleaner oxygen than she's been all day—and she feels it in her head, a lightness, a sense of morning.

She pulls the chain on the ceiling fan and picks up the telephone.

The 545 she remembers. Just like Mike and Grace's. But why didn't she write down the last four digits? She repeated it to herself on the Strand; why didn't she jot it on a piece of paper when she got inside the house? It's 10 something—545-1043. She dials, and an old woman picks up.

"I'm sorry, wrong number. Sorry, sorry."

She hangs up and starts second-guessing herself. Is it even a 10? Is it 545-2043?

She's lost the number to the ocean of all numbers. But she has one other idea. On an evening like this one, now that the fireworks are wrapping up and the kids are heading home, how hard could it be to hear a party from a few blocks off? Even a small one? She has two hours before check-in.

She scoots to the bathroom, pulls off her dress, and steps out of her bikini for the first time since morning. She touches up her makeup in the mirror. But before she flips off the light and moves to put on clothes, she shuts the door. She considers her body in the mirror. A freckled stomach and shoulders and arms. Some burn lines, like she's never encountered, framing her breasts high on her chest. Some elastic impressions strung hip to hip like a rope bridge, above which her stomach swells from the burrito. She pulls her neck high off her shoulders into the posture of the exemplary stew. She turns sideways and her eyes trace the line from her neck, down her back, around the S of her pigment-free ass and upper legs. She zooms farther into the mirror and begins to objectify her body, so much so that she starts to get turned on by her own nudity. Nobody has seen her like this since graduation. The shared bunks during training and the immediate dissolve to sharing a wall with her sister and her husband. Seven weeks without sex, after four months without a break. And yet even as she tries to focus on Dave, the concreteness of the physical is difficult to conjure. The memory is like something that happened to someone else, to two other people. Images in playback, bodies on a screen. Linda Lovelace in a white baby doll.

She holds her hand out and blocks her face at the surface of the mirror. A body and no head. She imagines herself being seen this way. She bends at her waist and through a veil of hair watches her breasts commit to staying pointed forward. She stands tall again, spreads her legs slightly, and feels her sunburn on her thighs and chest and back. She shifts the weight from foot to foot until she's evenly distributed and her knees are bent, like when she skates. . . .

Holy shit, she left her board at Flipper's. *Goddammit.* No chance she sees it again. No way she can afford a replacement. It's just another end to going fast.

She's lost the line on whatever she was seeing in the mirror. She must still be a little high. She smells her cover-up and rolls it and her bathing suit into a dense ball of pretty fabric. She moves to Mike's office, where she pulls on a pair of tight, faded bell-bottoms and a silky white blouse Grace bought her for graduation. She combs her hair in the office and gathers her things to leave. She checks the contents of her carry-on and zips it up, to save her the extra moment should she need it later. She'll be in New York in the morning—where she'll be even closer to all those things the magazine told her she couldn't miss this summer. She finds her keys and some cash and steps outside. On her way back down toward the Strand, she hears Mike and Grace's voices approaching from close by. But instead of stalling to bump into them, she slips into the dark of the alley and pushes north, aimlessly toward where Billy Zar might be.

Suzy glides across the sand slicks of the Strand, ears trained as if on a hunt. She'll feel so foolish if after thirty minutes she turns right back around and joins Mike and Grace for their dinner. Stragglers from the fireworks pass her on their way back home. She moves past the narrow three-story houses on the beachfront, railed balconies at each level. On one a couple share a cigarette and watch the darkness together. How unexceptional the western view is at night—nothing to distinguish it from a cornfield or a latticed backwoods. All black. She can make out a single oil rig on the water, an ugly sight during the day, but at night the only light, a proleptic sign.

Farther on, Suzy hears a mellow big-band standard, Duke Ellington, maybe—the stuff of Sunday-evening scotch. A couple blocks later, a conversation and cigarettes; competing opinions about the Rams and their new running back. It was a bad idea, she decides. She loops up off the Strand, taking the grade of the incline in little pickax steps, and crosses Ocean Drive, whose name suggests a boulevard with an unobstructed panorama, but that is in fact a narrow alley, cracked at its center by seasonal storms and poor drainage. She turns back toward Mike and Grace's and makes peace with the benefits of an evening stroll just for nothing.

And that is, of course, when she hears it: the unmistakable tin of drunk bunnies speaking over one another. Bass from a record player, and laughter. Just east up the hill. It is a geometrically depressing split-level—half the house plugged atop a squat garage, the other half built on a foundation that meets the garage at shoulder height. The siding has been painted once before, but not so recently, and the heavy blue door is open an inch. Suzy digs her nails into her part and combs her hair to her shoulders. She knocks twice and then throws some weight behind it so that the door creeps open. A couple girls are drinking red cocktails near what appears to be the kitchen. Suzy enters and moves her hand in a long wave that announces her presence as inoffensive.

"Hey, I'm sorry," Suzy says.

A girl with daisies strung into her braid turns and says: "For what! Happy Fourth!"

"Happy Fourth to you. I just…am looking for someone: do you know Billy Zar?"

She puckers her face and turns over her shoulder to her friends. "Billy Zar?"

A guy behind them approaches the cluster and says: "Billy?"

"You know him?" the girl says.

"Yeah, he was just here." .

"Oh, *Billy!*" the girl says.

Suzy isn't sure what this means. "Any idea where he went?"

"Actually, yeah," the guy says. "Paul Miller's house. You lookin' for him?"

"Yeah, he's a friend. He said he might be here."

"Miller's house is on Thirtieth and Mirabell."

"Thirtieth and Mirabell. Thanks. Really, thanks."

The girls smile at her, and the guy makes a show of jogging to the kitchen counter to offer her a drink.

"No, no thanks, I should try to catch up with Billy."

"Right on, right on."

Suzy hits the street and orients herself again without trouble—it really is getting easier. She isn't sure where Mirabell is, but she figures once she bumps into Thirtieth on Ocean and starts walking east, it will find her. And sure enough, within ten minutes she's trudging across the yard of a deliberate little bungalow down in the hollow beneath the sand dune. It sounds the way she imagined—the fading wails of Joe Walsh trailing off into harmonica and cymbals and dancing fingers way up the fretboard.

As she finds herself facing another party door, it springs open and out pops Billy. It's stupidly straightforward. A new song, the slow, lyricless funk of something she's never heard before, maybe Earth, Wind & Fire because of the brass. Billy's back is turned toward the entryway, and he sort of dances his way across the threshold, shutting the door slowly until the lock clicks, attempting, it seems, to leave without jangling the entry bells. He is still wearing his sunglasses, but he's changed out of his tank and into a wide-collared maroon-and-gold shirt, dark-brown cords, and a pair of worn-to-holes sky-blue Vans. The backpack is slung over his shoulder.

He spins suddenly, a little one-eighty twirl on the ball of his foot in time with the music, and nearly slams into Suzy. She squeaks and throws her hands up.

"Jesus!" Billy says. He doubles over with a honk that owes its origin to somewhere beneath his lungs. Once he catches his breath, he says: "This is really good."

"I found you."

"Seriously. After you didn't call me at home..."

"I couldn't remember your number, so I just started walking around down by the Strand and found the last party you were at."

"Max's?"

"I guess? Busted little split-level?"

"Get out."

"And they told me you might be here."

"And they were right!" he says. He's lit up. Suzy isn't familiar enough with Billy to know which substances manifest themselves which ways, but this is different from the afternoon. This is grass, pills, maybe mescaline. "You have no idea how huge this is."

"I can't believe it worked," Suzy says, smiling with the full realization. "But you're leaving."

"I am. Done here. One more stop. We can hang out there if you'd like to come along."

"Sure, yeah. How far?"

"Ten minutes that way," he says.

"You don't ever drive?"

"They let you off for just about everything in Sela. Everyone's a friend of a brother of a cop, you know? But I used up the last bit of my juju a couple weeks ago."

"How's that?"

"Too much fun, dude!"

"Now you walk."

"I usually skate. *But*...I broke my rear truck on my way to Flipper's."

"Ah, right."

"Yeah, you knew that. I mentioned it three times at his house, huh?"

"No, no—only once. But it seems...debilitating."

"Unsettling," he adds. "To rely so heavily on something, to take it *for granted.*"

"I think I left my board at Flipper's."

"No shit. I was wondering where it went. Why you didn't have it when we got food."

"I can't lose that thing."

"How's stew insurance?"

"Only good when it comes to plane crashes," she says.

During the walk Billy pulls up short at a hedge planted on a property line.

"Here, hold this, I'm gonna go take a leak."

He presses the backpack into her arms and disappears into the shadows.

The backpack is light but far from empty; it holds its shape. Her finger inadvertently grazes a zipper, and her hand springs from it as though the zipper's hot. Still, she tries to ignore what is no longer ignorable—that she's accompanying Billy on dealing rounds. She's never really known a dealer—was never the one, at least, among her friends in college who went to the corner to meet the guy. Never had to give out an address or phone number. She starts thinking about it and realizes she's never even been in possession of what she might call her own personal supply. It's pretty selfish. She's always accepted a hit but never risked even so much as the direct purchase of her ten-dollar share.

And yet here she is: Suzy Whitman, Billy Zar, *the backpack*. A small part of her wants to put a stop to whatever this is. It will end up somewhere not good. And yet this is action. This is what got her out of the house in the first place. This is the accelerator.

The house is farther east than she's walked in town. They cross the highway—the big, six-lane thoroughfare that gets you to the freeways in a hurry, and to the airport and the neighboring beach towns. The house is on a corner, the low stucco walls of its backyard exposed to the sidewalk traffic. The yard is stuffed with a hundred people—a blurry Xerox of the scene at the Drunk 'n' Draw—dancing around a fire, whose flames are lunging for the lowest branches of a magnolia tree.

"They're gonna burn that tree down," Suzy says.

"Very possible but unlikely," Billy says. "I think the tree's kinda bored with the fire pit. Been there so long. If it was gonna go up, it would've happened by now."

It doesn't take long for Billy to be recognized. He hugs friends and laughs at jokes that Suzy can't hear. He shouts her name to other guests, and they body-nod as though they've never been more pleased to meet someone. As she and Billy pass the fire, Suzy can't help but worry for its scale. It's expansive and growing steadily. She couldn't vocalize a concern if she wanted to, though, so she figures it might be worth grabbing a drink. When she draws her attention back toward Billy, he's gone. Business, she figures, and so she finds the cooler and drinks a beer in the corner quickly while she watches the flames grow taller.

A sliding glass door—smudged around the handle from what Suzy guesses were late-night, pitch-dark attempts to get inside—leads to a sparsely decorated office. One plush chair, an orange rug, and a small television propped up on a book. The TV has a ball game on,

Dodgers and Expos, international. Over Vin Scully's stat lines, the A side of a Three Dog Night album carries her through the house. Down a narrow hallway she hears a toilet flush and a small pack of women producing the noise of their number squared. She finds Billy in the kitchen with two other guys his age, each, like Billy, with swimmer's hair the color of white oil.

"Suzy, come here, come here," Billy says. "This is Kermit. And this is Chester." Suzy shakes their hands, and Billy goes on: "Suzy moved to Sela recently and tonight I'm her guide."

"I'll bet," Kermit says. Chester ducks his head into his chest to hide a smile from Suzy. The light in Billy's face dims. It isn't that Suzy doubts the attraction, or even the possibility of her needling its effect someday later. It's just that she's chalked up his accommodating spirit to compatibility (what her mother insufferably calls "peapodding")—not purely sex. For the first time her mind begins to identify a familiar plot element, the gracious host with an ulterior motive. Something recognized, she is certain now, by everyone she's met all day—longtime friends of his and coconspirators, whose willing compliance in stringing her up suddenly stings.

"Suzy, check this out," Billy says, changing the subject. "Chester's got a pig."

Suzy figures that's the nickname for a bulldog or a bong. She keeps her reaction neutral, not wanting to draw more attention to her waifish gullibility, her willingness to be told anything.

But in the living room, right there, in a cage meant for a large dog, is a potbellied pig no longer than her forearm and hand.

"He's a baby," Billy says. "His name is Hamlet."

Suzy sips her beer. "The mad prince."

"Hmm?" Chester says.

She kneels and offers Hamlet her hand. "I like the allusion, the name."

"You know Hamburger Hamlet?"

"Nah, I meant—just..."

Chester is distracted by a crash in the corner. A head-high indoor rubber tree, balanced in its black plastic basin and decorated with red-white-and-blue streamers, has been tipped onto the hardwood, spilling black soil to their feet.

Hamlet pinballs from one end of the cage to the other, his miniature hooves occupying all space at once, nostrils dilating with fright. He shakes like he's freezing. Billy bends down and extends his fingers tenderly. He presses his palm to the side of the cage and hushes Hamlet, even though the pig is silent. Hamlet sniffs his palm, distracted from the commotion in the room, focused on this single point of interest.

Suzy crouches down beside Billy. "It's none of my business, but he doesn't seem to like this much."

"No, he doesn't," Billy says. "I love these guys, but Chester shouldn't have gotten the pig. It was a terrible idea. This isn't the first time I've seen him like this."

"Where did they even find him?"

"At the pound."

"Really?"

"They went to pick out a dog and got Ham instead."

"Won't he get big?"

"Hundred and fifty pounds within a year, Chester says."

"Jeez."

"I don't know what they'll do then. In three months he'll be too big for the cage. And besides, it's illegal. Anyone who wants to could turn them in."

"Doesn't that bother them?"

"Look around," Billy says. Kermit and Chester are sweeping up the wet soil off the floorboards, each taking turns running out the front door to toss a panful into the yard. Beside them, pulling long double gulps from plastic cups, are the girls who knocked the tree over, scrunching their faces with inconsequence as they admire Hamlet from a distance. "They walk him on the Strand. He's getting to be known. Chester and Kermit are instantly spottable, notorious for lots of things. I don't know why they feel the need to draw so much attention to themselves."

This could mean anything, but Suzy takes it to mean something about whatever business they had in the kitchen.

"Let's bring Hamlet out to the yard," Billy says.

"'Kay."

"Chester, Suzy and me are gonna take Hamlet out front, let him run around some, yeah?"

"Careful, brother, that little bastard's greasy."

"Quick, slick!" Billy says to the pig. "He thinks we'll lose you." Billy latches the screen door behind them. "It probably wouldn't be such a bad thing. . . ."

Chester and Kermit's front yard is one of the few on the block with a picket fence. The fence is a muddied green, like too many drops of black got in the paint can. Billy wraps Hamlet in a wrestler's half nelson to carry him, but as they move down the front steps, Billy calmly tells Suzy he's losing his grip. Suzy rushes ahead and locks the gate, and Hamlet falls to the lawn and starts booking laps.

The yard is surprisingly well manicured, uniform in length, and consistent in color. Rich and well watered, spongy like bundles of wire. At the far end of the yard is a small rose garden that was no doubt planted well before Kermit and Chester arrived. Hamlet digs at the base of the bush nearest the street.

"He's looking for truffles," Suzy says.

"Hmm?" Billy says. He pulls two beers from concealed pockets.

"In parts of the South and in Europe, they use pigs to sniff out these fancy mushrooms—"

"A Yale thing," he says.

"Nope."

"Fancy mushrooms?"

"They're not *that* uncommon. But they are stupid expensive."

"How expensive?"

"Don't know. A lot, though. Worth more than their weight in gold."

"Sounds like something worth getting involved in," he says.

She wants to ask but knows it's not the right time: why the dealing when he could make money any other way?

"How long till you need to be at the airport?" he says.

"You have a watch?"

"It's five to ten."

"I should probably get going, then."

The pig is still digging.

"How does it work once you land in New York? Will you be there for a while?"

"I'm turning around and flying back tomorrow afternoon. After another few weeks or so, I guess they start to give you days wherever you go. My sister will sit on a beach in Miami for forty-eight hours while she waits to fly back. She might even get to go to Europe one day, too. Though it's tough to picture her parading around *les boulevards*."

"How come?"

"She's just very...American. I would've lost a bet about who might be the first one to get to Europe."

"Seems like something you could do soon, right?"

"We'll see if I stick around as long as her."

"Who would bail before the perks kick in? I'd do the work till they sent me to Australia. Then I'd walk off the plane, buy a board, figure it out on another continent for a while."

"Didn't you tell me at the party that you've never even left California?"

"A guy I know spent nine months down there doing construction. Said the day he showed up, he walked out to this beach above Brisbane and it was just this massive swell, cheap beer, topless women. He grew up here—says that beach town there is like it was here when his folks were young. Thirty years behind, but with all the goods for the taking. Things are getting a little crazy here, ya know?"

"I'll take your word for it. It seems pretty mellow to me."

"Yeah, I just wonder sometimes if it's over, if we missed it or something."

"I thought you were the mayor of Sela," she says. "Director of public relations."

She smiles, but Billy's eyes are fixed on the yard. He squints at Hamlet.

"I dunno—maybe it's that fucking pig. He's wigging me out."

A breeze shakes the fronds in the towering palms across the street. Hamlet stands on two legs and presses his front hooves against a picket, peering out at the street. He circles to the middle of the yard and then, with a running start, leaps at the fence, slamming hard into the waist of the picket. Both Suzy and Billy fix their posture upright.

Hamlet returns to the middle of the yard. He rushes toward the same mark again, this time leaping a little higher but hitting the fence with greater force. A whine slips from Hamlet, floating. He trots back to the center of the yard. He's cut his shoulder. Suzy can see the blood, wet against his coat.

"What the hell is he doing?" Billy says, moving quickly across the yard.

The final attempt, he springs at a greater distance from the fence and his forelegs reach above the crossbeam, his lower half swinging into a picket belly-first. For a moment he hangs there, halfway free, but then he drops backward with a piercing squeal, landing on his side and resting steady there. He breathes slowly, widely. Billy and Suzy kneel beside him and touch his skin. His inky eyes are fixed forward, but the pig seems pained and distant. His open mouth pulls back into a misleading grin.

"Let's get out of here," Billy says.

"What do we do about him?" Suzy says.

"Nah, I mean *with* him. I know this place we can take him. This big house with some acreage up on the Peninsula. They'll take him for now and we'll figure it out later."

"With what car? I've gotta get to the airport."

"What's the latest you can be there?"

"Eleven, I guess."

"We can make that. Whose car were you gonna use?"

"I was gonna take a cab."

"Is there any other option?"

"I can drive my brother-in-law's, I guess."

"Is that really a possibility?" She knows this is a bad idea. She's already cut it close and needs to start making moves to get to check-in. "We're not actually that far from where you said you're living, right?"

Suzy tries to conjure the cross streets but decides to take his word for it instead.

"All right, you pick him up, and walk down to the end of the block. I'll tell Chester and Kermit that he got out and ran away. They might care, but they've got a party going. I doubt they'll go looking for him tonight."

It seems reasonable enough. Suzy approaches Hamlet slowly and crouches beside him. He doesn't move, and so she cradles him along her forearm, hoists him onto her hip. Suzy has held a baby just once, but this comes easily. He's lighter than she figured. A hundred and fifty pounds is a long way off. He squirms, but only halfheartedly, instinctively, and soon he's breathing quiet in her arms. In the shadows at the edge of the neighbor's house, Suzy listens to Billy and Chester.

"What?! How the fuck did he get out?!"

"I don't know, dude. He was digging over by the rosebush, and then he just...leapt."

"He *leapt?*"

"You should've seen it. He just trotted over to the edge of the grass near the steps and got a running start and *leapt.*"

"You're shitting me."

"Not shitting you."

"That little fucker."

"I know."

"What do I do?" Chester says.

"I mean, he tore out of here. Right up the hill. He wanted the fuck *out.*"

"Jeez."

"I'm sorry, hombre."

"Me too. It's been some of the best weeks of my life."

"Yeah...," Billy says. "So listen, I'm gonna take off. We cool?"

"Yeah, brother, thanks for stopping by."

"Cool, cool, I'll see you next time."

Suzy carries Hamlet down to the corner, where Billy told her to wait. He takes the pig and they make their way through the dark grid. It's even hillier in this part of town than the others she's explored. High-rolling waves of asphalt, gullies and precipices. One block is lined on both sides with palms. Another with magnolias. Their street eventually dead-ends at a sand dune that rises like a quarter pipe. A railroad-tie staircase carves its way by switchback up its side, two hundred steps. At the top of the dune Suzy recognizes the black horizon of the water, and the map in her mind defogs: they're five minutes from the house.

Billy waits outside and Suzy rushes in. Mike is mixing drinks on the countertop, reading the *Times* (New York). The shower is running. When Mike notices Suzy, he peeks his head through the gap made by the cupboards and the island.

"You got time for dessert or are you heading out?"

"I've gotta hit it," Suzy says. "But listen, huge favor..."

She says she'll have the car back in the afternoon, she'll fill up the tank. Just needs to run an errand before the flight. Mike offers to drop her off, and she squirms out of that, too. She grabs her prepacked carry-on bag, and two minutes, tops, she's out in the alley with keys to the Karmann Ghia.

Suzy drives. Billy holds the pig in his lap. They make greens like downhill skiers split gates. Everything is A-OK. Where they're heading is the private property of some guy Billy met once. A guy with horses who has permits for weird animals, too. The house is gated, but Billy knows a dirt service road off the side street—a way to get up to the edge of the property.

"How do you know this person, again?" Suzy says.

"I made a house call once. There were explicit instructions. They had me use this road."

The house sits atop the Peninsula, the land mass that cups the southern end of the bay. As they pull to the side of the road, Billy thumbs over his shoulder, indicating that Suzy should turn around and look. The black bay like a D. The beachline stretching north from the Peninsula through the South Bay towns, past Sela, and then the airport, and, beyond that, through the smog layer to Venice, Santa Monica, Malibu. A bleating light pitching up from LAX vanishes into the ceiling of clouds.

There are five-story eucalyptuses everywhere in sight. The house is farther up the hill, but the property has an iron fence robed in olean-der bushes. The pig is nestled in a towel on the floorboard.

"Apparently, this guy even has a lion and a panther."

"That's not real," Suzy says.

Billy raises his hands, just the messenger.

"Can Hamlet cut it with a lion and a panther?" Suzy says.

"I dunno, man. But we're sort of out of options."

"Are you just gonna...ring the doorbell?"

"I don't think we can do that, either. National holiday and all."

"So, we're..."

"Listen, he wanted out of that situation. And this is a better one. He might have to fend for himself tonight, but it'll be fine by the morning."

"Is this a good idea?"

"Listen," Billy says, "I didn't mention it before 'cause it's pretty fucked up, but I've seen this little guy eat bacon. Just rolled right up to the living room table the morning after a party and cleared people's plates of fucking *bacon*. This will be an improvement."

Suzy frowns in the radio light.

Billy bends back into the car, looking for something in the glove compartment, and when he emerges, he bites the cap off of a dark felt marker.

"Is that shirt expensive?" he says, gesturing toward hers.

"What? It was a gift."

"I'd write it out on mine, but dark on dark's not gonna work, ya know?"

"I don't get what you're saying."

"We'll write a note to the guy, so that when Hamlet turns up in the morning, he'll have an idea what's going on. His name's Mr. Honey-well, I remember. He'll figure it's from someone worth helping if we add the note. I just don't have any paper."

"I'd really rather not...," Suzy says.

"Well, how 'bout this: you give me the shirt, or I leave you out here to find your way back alone."

She waits for him to break his expression, but it holds fixed. It's as though the whole frame has warped to uncanny colors, a TV screen with screwy reception. In the instant, she fears for her decency and then her job and then her life, in that order, an ascending scale. His face has hardened, a quiet waxiness, and it hangs there distended. Right up until he doubles over, grinning. He laughs and she frowns. She pulls her arms in tight across her chest.

"Sorry, not funny," he says. "We could always just toss him over the fence."

"No, no," Suzy says. "Take my shirt...I have to change into my uniform anyway." She crisscrosses her arms over her torso and tugs at the hem at her hips, so that the blouse comes off in one motion, long and fluid as she can muster, the light fabric up over her eyes, and the cool air all around her stomach and shoulders and breasts, like fingertips. She looks at Billy to see if she's caught his attention, but he's turned the other way, Mr. Manners.

He carefully flattens Suzy's blouse on the hood of the car and then tears it in half. He takes the larger piece and carefully arranges the message in block letters:

MR. HONEYWELL,
THIS PIG NEEDS HELP. HOPEFULLY YOU CAN TAKE HIM IN. HIS NAME IS HAMLET AND HE'S A KEEPER. PLEASE DON'T FEED HIM TO LARRY THE LION.

Billy ties the blouse around Hamlet's neck, tucks him under his arm like a running back, like the Juice, and climbs the fence. He whispers something Suzy can't hear, kisses the pig on its brow, and drops him over the edge. Hamlet lands on his feet, handsome in his cape. "It's okay to run," Billy says.

She knows she's cutting it too close, but Suzy's convinced she's gonna be okay timing-wise. They just did the right thing. Someone will look out for her. Drop Billy off, change into her uniform, ten minutes on to the airport—check-in, boarding, vodka sodas for the red-eye.

On the way down the hill, off the Peninsula, Billy pushes the heat lever to max red, and the skin between Suzy's exposed cups flushes pink. She catches a peek in the rearview: like she's wearing a bathing suit at night. She's beginning to belong.

They park in the alley; Billy lives in a back house. The view of his apartment from the street is obscured by bowing fronds that seem not to have been thinned since Spanish settlement.

"I'm gonna change fast and then jam," she says.

A tropical dampness hangs like moss from the alley to the door. The inside is orderly and adult-seeming, subject to mixed taste and accumulation. Not clutter, but just the comforting gravity of fixedness, intransience.

She leaves her bag near the door, grabs her uniform, and gets herself dressed without much thinking. Stockings, heels, wings. She pins her hair beneath her aquamarine hat. The bathroom mirror presents someone defying one of the only true imperatives of stewing: *Glow, honey, glow.*

"This isn't what I expected," she says on her way to the door.

"You didn't expect the dealer to live in his parents' garage?" he says. He hands her the freshly laundered Beefy-T he's retrieved as consolation for the blouse. "This isn't quite a fair trade, but I'll make it up to you."

Suzy takes the shirt from him and holds it in her hand, but she's drawn to a bookshelf with picture frames. Several of the same white Labrador.

"I have one of those," Suzy says. "Is it one dog, or two different dogs?"

"That's Zuma and that's Rincon," Billy says. "Zuma's dead. And same could be said for her namesake...."

Suzy looks at him blankly.

"Surf joke!"

She frowns and turns back to the photos. In the rest, the three: Billy, whose physical transformation from toddler to present seems to have played out in the most predictable sequence possible, looking the same at every age. Then a narrow man with round glasses and light suits, midproclamation, it seems, in each image, mouth moving always. And a short, blond-haired woman with puffy eye flesh that provides a sort of makeupless definition for her smiley slits, and a smart mouth turned up at one corner that seems eternally amused with whatever her husband is saying at the flash.

"I should really go," Suzy says.

"You know, she died a little after that," Billy says, as though tracking Suzy's observations.

"Oh my God," Suzy says, elevated by the rush. "I'm so, so sorry."

She halts her movement to the door. Almost leans back toward Billy.

"You've gotta go," he says. "Let's go."

Billy walks her to the car and she gets behind the wheel. They hang there in a disparity of height, and then before she throws the transmission into gear, he bends down and kisses her on the cheek. "Well, I bet I see you tomorrow," he says, and she chuckles at the presumption and pushes out, his hand tracing the curves of the car the way it would a body swimming underwater.

Suzy parks in short-term and hustles over to check-in. She's technically under the wire, so the ladies in charge at flight ops state their disapproval with their eyes only. She carries her bag into the office. She's weighed and told to "give your makeup another go," which makes Suzy snort. She's the last one to arrive but heads straight aboard without any of the other girls pausing to comment. She's flown with one before. Meredith. She recognizes another from training in Chicago.

They board a half-full flight, run protocol, pour drinks for first-class businessmen whose midweek holiday is now over. Suzy brews coffee for herself and lets it cool while she hands out headsets.

This is how you buckle a seat belt. This is where you go when you survive a crash in a cornfield. This is when the lights will go out. We'll be arriving at eight-ish in the morning, East Coast daylight, Wednesday the fifth of July. One final time: Happy Fourth, everyone.

She's seated right up front, next to the boarding doors, back to the cockpit. Before she's really had time to overthink any of the moves of preflight, she's buckled in with a heavy click. Meredith asks her if she has a copy of the new *Cosmo,* and sad-seeming, Suzy says, "No, sweetie, I'm sorry."

She closes her eyes, a knot of dehydration nestled right up top in the crack between the two hemispheres of her brain. She begins to drift as the plane makes the sweeping ascent she observed, one after another, half a day ago on the beach. Really, what just happened? She left the house, watched the planes, then something was followed by another thing. And now she is at work. It all happened right there, too—on the beach below them now, beneath the canopy of the flight path. She'd been looking for something in Sela del Mar she could grasp concretely, something besides just the breaking of the clouds to convince her she'd landed in the right place after all. She's spent the last month circling Sela without certainty, skating from this end to the other, slipping past strangers, wrapping the place with a loose string of comprehension. And today, it seems, she finally pulled on

the free end of that string and cinched it up—all at once tightly conceived, knowable. She's finally gotten a grip.

Before long the plane levels, and Suzy prepares fresh drinks for the
passengers in first. She looks for something to cut the edge off the
coffee in her blood. All they have in the cabin is unheated breakfast—egg sandwiches, dry oatmeal—so she digs into her carry-on
bag to look for the PB&J she made in the morning. As she feels
around for the sandwich, her hand grazes a familiar light fabric she
couldn't have packed. She pliers it out with her index and thumb and
knows it—the half of her shirt that wasn't left with Hamlet. This,
too, has writing on it now:

Z,

NEED AN ASSIST, POR FAVOR. WON'T REQUIRE MUCH. PLEASE SAY
HELLO TO A FRIEND OF MINE WHO HANGS AT THE AIRPORT.
MIGHT BE A GUY, MIGHT BE A GAL—POSS. ONE OF EACH.
THEY'LL MEET YOU WHEN YOU GET OFF THE PLANE AND THEY'LL
KNOW WHAT'S UP. THEY JUST WANT TO SAY HEY. I KNOW YOU
DIDN'T ASK TO BE A PART OF THIS, BUT IT MEANS A LOT, AND YOU
JUST MIGHT DIG IT.

YOU'RE BITCHIN', FOR REAL,

Z

She fishes around in the bag and finds it without trouble. A brown
paper sack, sizeable. The top is rolled over into a handle. She unfolds
it and looks inside. A one-gallon Ziploc bag, stretched tight like a
pillowcase around a five-pound sack of Gold Medal flour. Suzy crumples the paper bag shut with a swift sealing-off, like trapping a bat in
a bedsheet. *Motherfucking fucker.* Her eyes are on the passengers. She
swallows and stands and stuffs the paper bag into a deep corner of her
carry-on. She assured herself it was a casual gig, Billy making scratch

for burritos in a seventy-two-and-sunny zona of limited consequence. Nothing real. But what were her grounds for dismissal? She'd known him for twelve hours. Meredith clicks in next to her again and triumphantly presents the new *Cosmo*.

An overweight man with leather-cream skin throws his arm into the aisle to get their attention. Meredith sighs.

"I've got him...," Suzy says, and zips up her carry-on and buries it deep in the crew compartment, beneath all the other luggage. And for the next five hours, without a break in the night, she stays on her feet, pacing extra-attentive, casting vectors with her eyes from all points of the service aisle, up toward the front of the plane and the bag within the bag within the bag within the bag.

Part II

The Glen

On final descent into Los Angeles, the man in 1B starts breathing faster. He's in a suit with wide lapels, a slack white shirt, and a loosened paisley tie. He has a thin neck and a large, bald head that's wet the way balloons get in the rain. The flight has been rough, but it has passed for Suzy like a movie in a dark theater—Suzy physically fixed in place while her mind engages with the images she's just encountered. That there should be any threat to the safety of this flight, any concern beyond the implications of the handoff in New York, catches up with her only now, as the man in the suit, alone in 1B, with no wife or child or business partner to grab hold of, reaches out his hand, beckoning for Suzy's comfort. She is buckled in and stays upright, high shoulders and crossed legs. He closes his eyes and leans back but keeps his mitt extended. Suzy glances at Meredith, who's consumed by her magazine, and then turns back to find the man's fingers dancing pathetically in the space between them.

Suzy unbuckles and gives the man her hand. He squeezes it sexlessly and then regrips. His eyes are still closed and his hand is chilled. The plane rattles on its way through the clouds and then stills five thousand feet above Pomona. Out the window: the soundless rivers of the Santa Ana and Golden State Freeways; the green thumbprints of the county golf courses; the eastern developments, all dug clay and fresh lumber, dark against the peach-colored dust, singeing the edge of the desert—a new line in the sand. The cabin drops and Suzy's planted foot leaps. The man opens his eyes, which seem to plead for a countdown.

"Just a few more minutes," Suzy says.

It breaks the spell. He releases her hand and swallows. He removes his jacket and folds it in half and then in half again. The Pacific appears like a tube of neon out the window, and then there's the Peninsula, scrunched into topographical relief like a comforter badly slept in. A ring on the man's hand has impressed a little slot near Suzy's knuckle, deep enough to balance a nickel in. The ground comes fast, and when they hit, there's applause from the way back. The seat belts click and Suzy's man is the first one up. As he makes his way toward the exit, Suzy forces a smile and he pats her on the head.

The primary thing Suzy's thought about all day was getting back here. This touchdown was the curtain. She and the girls count headsets and spray the washrooms and discuss vague leisure plans with the pilots, and when she's finally out, the new mission is a straight line: right to the curb, to a cab, and back into town to find that Q-tip shit Billy Zar.

The cabdriver doesn't hide his frustration that Suzy's only going to Sela. It's a short trip and a cheap fare, and then, for him, it's back to the end of the line at Terminal 2. He slams his door and turns up the radio to eliminate the opportunity to give new directions. But back from a chocolate-milk commercial, it's the first chilled-out *fwang-fwang* Gs of "Take It Easy," which seems to wind the driver into an even more compressed coil in his seat.

He cuts west on Imperial, the scenic roundabout that threads the narrows between the oil refinery and the airport. When he's facing down the cliffs above the fire-pit-pocked beaches between Sela del Mar and Venice, he can't divert any longer: there's only one road and it heads for home. Sela, from the north, reveals itself like a time-lapse sequence, a compressed self-history. It looks, at the northernmost edge, as it did during the twenties—electricless, heat-free second homes for Los Angeles doctors. Then there came a bar. Followed by a motel. Another bar. A Laundromat. And finally a taco stand. They're all still there, beside the refinery, in the same order in which they appeared, first fifty, then forty, then thirty years ago—the war. It is a cruise through regional history, oil to tacos, the story of all Southern California beach towns. And the cabdriver takes it fast. So fast that when they appear at the only stoplight on the north end, they collapse into the present, and they're back where Suzy and Mike and Grace are improbably living their lives on the edge of the ocean. She pays the cabdriver at the curb, and he races off without a word, back to the queue at LAX. Suzy finds Mike in the office writing something important.

"Hey, wow," he says. "Can't believe you've already been there and back. We're barely awake."

"Totally," she says, "went by in a blur."

"Lemme get out of here."

"No, no, I've gotta run some errands anyway. I'll just change in the bathroom."

"Anything cool happen?"

"I thought a bald guy in first was gonna piss himself on approach. Begged me to hold his hand."

"Was it rough?"

"Not especially. It took two passes, though—had to pull out the first time because the Dodgers' plane was in the way. Then had a couple drops, I guess."

"I always felt like it'd be better to go on takeoff than landing—like, if you had to pick one. I'm always doing a pulse check on my life when I'm making that climb. Thinking about what I've been up to, things I *should* be up to. But on approach, to L.A. especially, once you see the little buttons of the Forum and Hollywood Park, it's like you're already on the ground running around. To crash *then?*"

"I think this guy was just drunk," Suzy says. "But if I was choosing, I'd rather it happen at altitude—max out the fall."

"I don't think Grace would much enjoy this conversation."

"I think you're right."

"Speaking of which—she wants to go to Howlers Friday night. The StrandDogs are doing a thing. And she says you should come if you can."

"I don't know the StrandDogs."

"Band she likes."

"Okay, sure."

"You hungry? You need any lunch? Grace left half a turkey sandwich in the fridge from last night."

"Nah, maybe in a little bit. Have to take care of this thing and then I'll probably eat."

"Car run okay?"

Suzy freezes. She's left the car in overnight parking. She's forgotten altogether. It was that kind of trauma—the package obscured the simplest things, the details of the handoff searing sunspots in her brain.

"I...I left it in short-term. I'll go back and get it now."

"No problem. I don't need it till tomorrow."

"I'm gonna get it this afternoon. I promise."

"Really, it's nothing."

"I don't mistreat cars."

"I know."

"Three hours."

First she needs her board, though. The other thing she lost yesterday. She moves through town, makes the turn onto Flipper's walk-street, sees it leaning against the fence, exactly where she must've placed it as she passed through the gate. Too easy. She plucks it from the yard, hears groaning from inside, and then starts skating toward the intersection Billy led her to the night before. Blue jean shorts, a peach cotton blouse, rubber flip-flops. Weatherwise, it's a mimeograph of yesterday. One could be fooled into imagining it as a do-over, as though none of the events of the Fourth transpired.

Suzy plays it again: the moment she discovered the package. The heat she felt it giving off during the flight, while she poured drinks and repelled sleep. She'd buried it underneath the carry-ons of the other stews, as deep into their shared compartment as it would go. No one would know until the drug dogs rushed onto the plane in New York. But at the gate: no drug dogs. The passengers exited, morning in New York. Eighty degrees at eight a.m. They had two hours at the airport before the turnaround. Another mission with a straight line: cabin, jet bridge, concourse, ladies' restroom. She walked slowly in her pumps, mentally restraining herself from running. There was a Union News serving coffee and hash browns and then a restroom next door. She would flush the contents, no matter the bulk. But then: a hand on her shoulder.

"Excuse me, miss? What kind of mascara is that?"

The woman reached Suzy's shoulders, five feet in a modest heel. Her hair was black enough to be blue, eyes brown enough to be black. Jacket and shift, a uniform of the office, invisible in its averageness. Suzy said she didn't know offhand and began digging in the side pocket of her carry-on to check.

"Mind if I see?"

"I'm grabbing it if you'll—"

"Show me in the bathroom. We're gonna end up there anyway, let's just head in now." So it was happening like this. "See those two over there?" the woman said. "They're not gonna let you get much farther

95

than the bathroom anyway, so might as well come let me try on your mascara."

On the way the woman called herself Cassidy. Suzy watched Cassidy in the bathroom as she muddied up her eyelashes in silence. "Think they'd let me fly?" she said.

"Too short," Suzy said.

"Well, fuck me."

The only other woman in the bathroom flushed and washed her hands and said something about the heat melting her rouge. While Suzy watched Cassidy work the applicator through her lashes, the bathroom walls seemed to slowly compress, the way the stage set would break apart whenever Suzy recognized herself in a dream. It wasn't possible to be in this place because she'd taken none of the natural steps that could've led her here. She couldn't recall walking from the gate to the Union News, or even off the plane. She couldn't recall taking the flight, meeting Billy Zar, moving to Sela, signing on for stew school—she hadn't been in control for any of it. The present moment made no sense unless you strung together two months of semiconscious incident. Not so much decision-making as forces that had been allowed to work on her, forces that upon closer reflection—like, if she really thought about it—had pushed her straight to this place. A crime, a criminal.

She'll be gone, Suzy thought, *and your bag, after all this hallucinating, will be filled with nothing but clean clothes.* Suzy and Cassidy were suddenly alone.

"You seem kinda dull to the process here, and there's nothing I can really do about it but give you the options: either head into the stall and leave the package on the lid, or hand over your bag and I split with everything else, 'kay?"

This was relief, really. Straightforward instructions. Suzy didn't even think about resisting. She latched the door behind her, dug to the bottom of her carry-on, and pulled out the Gold Medal bag. It hadn't dusted the Ziploc the way even unopened bags of flour do. She reemerged and closed the door behind her.

Suzy asked Cassidy what next.

"You can do whatever the fuck you want."

Suzy clopped out into the concourse. She'd lost her bearings and squinted at signs to see if she could find the stew lounge to go vomit in private. She pulled off her heels and started hustling. But she hadn't made it a gate before she felt another hand, this one at her elbow, so forceful it nearly spun her.

"Whoa, whoa, easy," he said, "I think you dropped a bag."

The man was wearing a charcoal-gray suit and a repp tie and smelled like he had an expense account. He was clean-shaven, with midlength sideburns, and his hair was slicked back for the office. He handed Suzy a small green purse.

"Now, don't go dropping this anywhere else except where it's meant to be dropped." It was an easy smile and he winked. He seemed like a person who'd decided one day to be a winker. "Tell Billy he picked a cutie."

He glanced toward the adjacent gate area, and another suited man stood and walked in the direction of the baggage claim. Cassidy traced his line at following distance, and then this man sandwiched her from behind. Suzy collapsed the distance between the concourse and the lounge and didn't feel her feet beneath her until she'd made it through the door, turned on a shower, and screamed into a towel.

As she lifted her face, another woman in a robe looked at her, eye lines all torn up from crying about her own problems. Suzy hung up her uniform beside the stall so that it could take steam before the turn-around. She stepped into the hot shower and, running her fingers through her greasy hair, fixated on the sequence she'd just been subjected to. The absence of information. The humiliating depletion of strength. Most especially, though, the failing that had followed: Suzy wasn't a screamer. Who was it who'd screamed? Who'd let it all happen? Who was this woman who'd been puppeted for all these sleepless hours?

She felt her pulse fading from her wrists as it would at the end of a race, in the pits at the Glen. She held her hands out before her, rolled them so that her fingers hovered parallel to the floor. They were long and still and red at the tips. They were hairless and veinless and whiter than she would've liked. On the palms of those hands were some gnarly calluses, the vestiges of racing—she felt them with her thumb. "Step it the fuck up," she mouthed aloud beneath that brass rain cloud in the shower. "He's a fucking *skater.*"

In daylight Billy's parents' house shows itself: a squat little cake box of yellow clapboard, a concrete slab of a porch, a window near the front door, and a porthole, eye high, that permits whoever's doing the kitchen dishes a look out onto the street. A white Lab—this must be Rincon—moves not at all and watches Suzy walk herself along the narrow side yard of crabgrass, past the cream Volvo and the lemon Bug and the oleander bushes, through the yellow wooden gate. She heads toward the converted garage in the back, where something Bowie she doesn't know is playing. She knocks at the screen door. Nada. She knocks again and then flips around: Billy in a chaise lounge in the yard in the concealing shade of a magnolia tree, bare and burned waist up, reading an issue of *Rolling Stone* with Mick on the cover, and sipping a drink with a straw.

He doesn't say anything, but he's smiling and sucks at the ice.

"I was about to come see you," he says.

"Let's go inside."

"Nah, pull up a chair."

"I don't want to do this out here," Suzy says, opening the screen door and moving into the back house.

"Look, I know I should've said something...," he says from the chaise.

"I can't hear you," she says, pushing deeper inside and turning the volume knob on the record player. She sees Billy smile and stand and move toward the door. The back house presents more details during the day—brown shag, a crisply made bed covered in a Mexican blanket, the shelves with high school novels and seashells, matching teak dresser and desk, a table and chairs with an unlit candle. There's a disconcerting tidiness.

"I said, I should've said something, but if I'd *asked,* I think you probably would've said no."

"Oh yeah? What gives you that impression? You don't think I would've been hot to trot to traffic blow?"

"It's an acquired taste, so I dunno, I just assumed."

"I mean, *what the fuck?* What was gonna keep me from going straight to the police when I landed?"

"You noticed it before you landed?"

"You put a fucking *five-pound bag* in my carry-on."

"*Did* you go to the police?"

"What if I did? What if I gave you up and I'm wearing a wire and I just needed you to acknowledge that you planted that shit on me?"

"I didn't say anything about it being me...," Billy says, squinting. "Look, we're talking about baked goods, if you really want to know the truth." He pulls on a linen shirt and moves toward her. She grabs her board by the trucks, ready to swing. He stops short and bends forward at the waist, leaning into the alleged microphone she has beneath her shirt. "For a bakery me and a couple guys are starting up in New York. Nothing but premix for cookies and shit. Thanks for your help, *Suuz.*"

He giggles and stands up straight again. This is so much fun for him. He's sucking at the straw in his tumbler and he's got his hand on his hip, his whole body arranged in the shape of a beer stein.

"Listen, I get why you're a little steamed about this, but let me spell it out some. I mean, you know what's what anyway, so it doesn't really matter what more you know, so long as you don't know stuff they can get you for, right?" Suzy's in a room with one way out, and that one way is blocked by a giggling drug smuggler in burgundy dolphin shorts. She could walk out, but she'd want more answers in an hour anyway. She's forfeited her free will all over again.

"You want some grass?" he says.

Billy sits at the desk, opens the top drawer, pulls out an Altoids tin and rolling paper.

"Just tell me what happened," Suzy says.

And while he methodically works through the steps of fashioning his joint, he paints in the lines.

"There's a guy around here who gets stuff straight from a plane once every couple weeks. The guy I know gives me stuff to keep the parties going in town, plus a couple bricks to get to New York whenever he asks. There used to be a girl in Sela who'd make the runs, but she got knocked up on the road—by a Giants middle reliever or something. And so she had to clip her wings. I've been sitting on some bulk for a while now. Tried out one girl who was so upset she transferred home to Pittsburgh and moved back in with her folks. It's not for everyone. And I certainly didn't expect you to *love* it or anything. But you got me out of a bind. A lot of people were putting the screws to me. And I'm gonna do you good for all that."

"You're going to *do me good?*"

"I mean moneywise—you're getting fair, plus some, outta what they gave you."

He lifts the work in progress to his mouth and seals the seam, offering Suzy first light.

"They didn't give me anything. A little, dark-haired pixie pulled me into a bathroom, swapped the package out of my bag and into hers, and that was that."

"They didn't give you a bag with cash?"

"Nothin'. They were supposed to?"

Billy rises to his feet and runs his fingers through his hair, tempering the flood of distress by watching his reaction in the mirror. "Well, that's a wrinkle," he says. "People aren't gonna like that."

"Sorry, dude, guess you picked the wrong girl."

"Thing is, it's not me, really, but the guy who has me do this, who put me onto this little thing—they're not gonna believe me. They're gonna call the folks in New York and those guys are gonna say they gave you fifty grand in a manila envelope, folded once over and stapled, in a green purse, with a used hairbrush, a pack of Juicy Fruit, and a bottle of L'Air du Temps. And everyone's gonna wanna know where it went. They'll come over here and tear up my room. But, as you can see, it won't take 'em long. And then they'll be off to visit you and your sister and your sister's husband, and they'll fuck things up there until they're satisfied that *you* don't have it, either. And maybe you don't. Maybe, if they look everywhere, they still won't find it—*totally* possible. But if that's the case, they'll probably pull you—actually, probably more like you *and* me—out of bed in the middle of the night, throw us in a van, tie us up in a warehouse in one of those industrial cities along the river, Vernon or Boyle Heights. And they'll ask us whether we're *still* sure we don't know where the money is."

"All because some jerk didn't give me a green purse."

"Right. So lemme know if it turns up. These guys are pretty chill when they don't have to work too hard. They make things very cool for everyone. But they *hate* chasing down what's theirs."

"What do you get out of each of these?"

"I get two thousand; girl gets two thousand."

"So why not just take the full fifty and split?"

As he inhales, his eyes acknowledge this as an interesting question: "Where would I go?"

"What?"

"Where would I go? Nowhere to be but here. 'Sela Vie,' sister..."

"Right, of course," she says. "So how long have you been doing it?"

"Nine months."

"So twice a month, nine months...thirty-six grand."

"That's some game-show speed."

"What do you do with it?"

"Gonna help buy a house."

"Won't that seem a little weird—you being able to buy a house?"

"Don't have anything else to spend money on. I mean, might get a new Bug once I get my license back. Otherwise all I buy is cheap beer. I grow my own grass out in that little garden. Maybe I go see the Stones again, but what else? I'm gonna buy my parents out."

"You're gonna live here."

"Buy them out, get them somewhere better, make it look like they just handed it down—pretty clean."

"This is your dad and your...stepmom?"

"Nah."

"You said last night your mom had died."

"Yeah, I say things sometimes."

"So she's not dead."

"Want to meet her?"

Suzy's face fails to conceal her disgust.

"My dad wants to move closer to the beach. It's always been a big deal to him that they're on the wrong side of the hill. He's worked at North American Aviation for twenty-seven years, right there on the edge of the airport. Built an airframe for the X-15. And the astronaut parts of the Saturn V. That's how the surf thing started getting big here, ya know? All the fiberglass and poly-whatever foam left hanging around from the aviation and space stuff. Turned the scraps into decks and skegs." There's that word—Suzy's heard it before and it imprinted. *Skeg.* The crudeness of the sound subsumed by the elegance of the function: that fin slipping through waves like a scalpel through fat. "But all the old man wants, all he seems to have ever wanted, is to live on the west side of the hill. Hang some stars and stripes off a balcony that looks out over the ocean."

"Your parents know your plans?"

"They know I'm busy and that it'll only upset them if they ask too much. And so maybe it'll be a nice surprise one day."

"Noble son."

"Look at it the right way, 'kay? We're all in this on behalf of the space race. Helping the guys who put men on the moon get the houses near the beach they deserve."

Suzy snorts. "What about your mom?"

"She likes it here."

"I can't believe she's not dead—what an awful thing to say."

"She's making cookies right now."

"And you're not doing this on her behalf? Just your dad's?"

"She doesn't need any help."

"She's content to be provided for?"

"Oh, no, she takes care of herself. She teaches chemistry at the high school. They met at 'SC. Smart lady, so-so baker. Not as good as she thinks. Maybe that's what they'll use the money for—hire a Guatemalan or something." Billy stretches out on his bed and puts his hands behind his head. "Wanna lie down?"

"I'm leaving."

The music has gone silent.

"Can you flip it?" he says.

For some reason Suzy moves to the record player and places the needle at the edge of the B side. She hasn't listened this deep in. *"People stared at the makeup on his face…"* She grabs her board and moves toward the door. The light has leveled itself so that it slides through the trees and bites the screen like a razor.

"If that bag turns up, it's twenty-five hundred for me, fifteen hundred for you," Suzy says on her way out.

"That's not really how it works."

"And that four's coming out off the top. I'm not handing it over for them to cut off a piece."

"That's not really for you to decide, either. You hand over the bag, they cash you out."

"I really don't care. I don't. You can explain to them that on this one it's working like that. Let 'em know it's okay 'cause this will be the only one, ever, with this particular girl—they don't have anything else to worry about. If you're so concerned, cover the difference out of your piggy bank."

"Two and two," Billy says, grinning on his back.

"Three and one. And I'm keeping the French perfume."

The StrandDogs get to keep their time slot, but they're relegated to a midbill act when Jackson Browne calls the bar's owner and asks if he can work out some new stuff after whomever, which is why there's a crowd at the bar and it's tough to catch anyone's eye, even if you're Suzy after a shower and you're wearing new French perfume. She pays for the first round by breaking a twenty from her haul. They settled on a $2,500/$1,500 split—her penalty assessment to Billy. She wonders if he'll be here tonight, seeing as most everyone she's pardoning her way past was at the beach on the Fourth, or if not there, then that brunch at Huevos or the party at Flipper's. She holds the cocktails high above her head, doing better not to spill than she does in a turbulent aisle in coach. She keeps her bearings on Mike's head, which is on the horizon, beneath an indoor rubber plant, screaming about something with Grace.

"Okay!" Suzy says as she pulls up to the argument. Grace smiles prettily and sucks from her straw.

Onstage a three-piece cover band called The Cover Band shifts capably from Three Dog Night to Stevie Wonder to a big, taffy-stretched eight- or nine-minute version of "Rocket Man," for which somebody's girlfriend climbs onstage to sing harmonies.

"Have you seen these guys before?" Grace says.

"I don't think so," Suzy says.

"They're one of the good true local ones. J.P., the one playing rhythm and singing, he's from right around the corner. Both main guys, they're songwriters for Warner Brothers, like, they've written hundreds of songs for the label that go into the pot for any of the artists to play. J.P.'s a good guy, I like him."

When she finishes her drink, she shakes her ice at Mike.

"I don't even know what it is," he says.

She narrows her eyes.

"Vodka pineapple," he says.

Mike throws the rest of his own drink into his mouth and bobs toward the bar.

"Everything all right?" Suzy says.

"He can be such a little bitch at these things. I don't say anything about how he spends his time, don't question whatever he's doing when I'm flying. But he gets so weird at these shows. He'll never say it, but he just looks at me with this pure disdain when I start talking about bands. The fact that I read about them in the paper, or talk to the bartenders, or, God forbid, meet some of the musicians, like J.P., and chat with them about what they do."

"He's jealous?"

"I'm not totally convinced he even likes listening to the music.

Which is the main offense. If he's gonna come just to babysit, he can go ahead and treat me like a kid and pick up the tab."

Howlers is the last building at the south edge of Sela, a yellow-green snail shell that swirls upward on the inside like the Guggenheim, a three-story atrium with two bars, a stage, and a roof with a view of the water. From the outside it looks as though it's made of the same two ingredients as most structures in town—brick and chipped stucco. A large wooden sign, salt bitten, hangs from chains off the roof. But after The Cover Band set, when it's sufficiently dark, someone in management invites whoever outside for a jokey little unveiling of the *new* sign: hot-green neon, wide as the second-story balcony, bathing the otherwise unlit block in light, like it's Sunset.

The light gives the hallway from the front door the feeling of a sci-fi portal—a bridge from an outside world of sea smell and ceaseless mellow and broken-muffler Bugs to something a little higher oxygen. From where they're standing in the corner near the stage, Suzy and Grace watch the StrandDogs unload and plug in, three cousins and some friends from Sela, experimental, but conceived by the stencil of the Beach Boys. Harmonies and surf guitar, but more brass. They work through each mike—tongue twisters and "oooh-ahhhs" and an impression of Chick Hearn ("Chamberlain, baseline, fourteen-foot jumper...Good!")—before the guy in the middle snaps his fingers and they hit a five-part harmony on: *"Don't talk, take my hand and listen to my hea-art beat.... Lis-ten...lis-ten...lis-ten..."*

Pet Sounds was a thing in the Whitman house. Something, for reasons never really articulated, that made both girls and parents feel feelings. It came out the spring of Suzy's sophomore year of high school, that first year Grace was away—the first stretch that Suzy had really missed her. While hitching home for the summer, Grace had stopped at the record store in Schuyler Glen and picked it up. Day after day they sat in their room, Grace on the bed and Suzy on the floor, with the windows wide and new blooms wending their way in. That touch of the outdoors on the skin and those pantry-locked sentiments were soldered in Suzy's mind, recalled involuntarily whenever she smelled honeysuckle or heard those "Lis-ten … lis-ten … lis-tens."

At Howlers, Grace is maybe already on her way to that place, too—she has that kind of purposeful look to her. Sticky sentimental. But she seems also to be moving down a road that leads from those sounds to boogying on a tabletop. She's loose. Whereas Suzy is fastened still in that bedroom in Schuyler, growing damp in a mist of memory, watching this present rather than acting in it. Mike hands Grace her drink and gives Suzy a beer, too. Both of Suzy's hands are full, and so she sort of offers up her hip pocket with its wet bar cash, but Mike shakes his head—*Let me at least have this one dignity.*

The set is mostly quick little originals, radio bait with big-wall brass, and then a couple pieces of wordless jazz that opens space for solos and intros. On the second-to-last song Jackson comes out and sings the lead of "Spill the Wine" in a spot-on mock. And then sticks around to play the piano outro on a "Layla" cover.

"Don't know about you guys," the StrandDogs' singer says, "but we sometimes play the Death Song game—name the one you wanna go out to. This is mine."

Jackson reaches for the bassist's mike and says: "Mine's *Rhapsody in Blue.*"

"Rock 'n' roll," the singer says.

Grace orders another vodka piña and then another, and in between sets she argues with Mike about Dylan songs and threatens to separate their record collection to emphasize an aesthetic principle. Or at least that's what Suzy imagines, judging by the haughty leg posture and head nods. As Suzy begins to lose the line on the conversation, she moves back to the bar herself to stand on the rung of a stool and get a better look at the crowd. With the lights up she can see back to the green glow of the front door, and toward the hallway with the bathrooms, where they keep all the photos of past performers like they do up in Hollywood, groups who come through to try new stuff and work out timing. Linda Ronstadt was here last week. Gram Parsons comes down on Mondays. Suzy takes a loop, acts as though she's looking for someone, a sister or a boyfriend. And as she's about to head up the stairs to the roof, she hears laughter and the name "Zar." She turns expectantly but sees it's only someone hawking a loogie in the corner.

Mike gives Grace a piggyback home, her sandals in her hand and her big toes hooked into the belt loops of Mike's dungarees. Every couple blocks along the Strand, Suzy wrestles Grace's dress down below her underwear, even though it's dark except for the lamps.

"Well, that was fun," Mike says once he's dumped Grace into bed.

"I always get super bummed out listening to Jackson," Suzy says. "He's, like, the most depressing musician in California masquerading as its most fun with his radio hits."

"'Song for Adam,'" Mike says.

"*Ugh.*"

"I liked him singing covers better than anything else he did."

"I didn't know the story about 'Take It Easy,'" Suzy says. "Whoops."

"I only caught part of it, I was coming out of the bathroom."

"He wrote the whole thing, music and lyrics, *except*—"

"*Except* the only lines most people know. Oh, I did hear that part."

"He said Glenn came up with the 'It's a girl, my lord, in a flatbed Ford, slowin' down to take a look at me...' bit."

"I love how he talks about that lyric writing like it's some revelation," Mike says. "A solution that unsticks the universe."

"They're good lines."

"But *music* writing, man, it's not like—"

"*Real* writing…"

"Didn't you do your thesis on this? Rock lyrics as poetry?"

"Exactly, so I may not quite be in your corner on this one," Suzy says.

Mike moves to the kitchen sink to wash his hands.

"Hey," Suzy says, "everything cool with you two?"

"Eh, we've been going at each other since the Fourth. Weird day. Fought in the morning about some bullshit—that's why we were late meeting you at the beach. Argued on the way home from that party, too. She was pissed I was *bleeding*. And she thought I was hitting on people."

"What's the issue, though?"

"I dunno, hard to say. Mostly things are good. We're both a little stressed about money. I really do need to get this magazine off the ground. Or get a job in the meantime."

"Flip burgers. Pound some nails. Fix engines."

"I'm not the multitalented Suzy Whitman."

"You can find something."

"The bigger issue, the thing that's killing me, is she's more tweaked than ever that the airline's gonna find out about us and ax her. And then there'll be no money whatsoever. She just thinks we see too many stews in Sela. She worries too many of them know about the wedding and that someone's bound to blab."

"You don't even wear rings."

"She invokes it outta nowhere and a little too often," Mike says, popping the top of a Coors. "Sorry, don't mean to dump this all at once."

"I mean, I asked," Suzy says. "I'm a little drunk, so, you know, don't take it the wrong way, but I've wondered awhile: what *was* the rush? She said she wanted to wait—isn't that a guy's dream?"

"Well, I hope you'll remember, she wasn't *that* resistant. She was all about it after I asked."

"But you could've just hung out, right?"

"I wanted to punch my ticket. Coolest, best-looking chick I ever met."

"That's reasonable enough."

"I mean, if not me, it was gonna be someone fast. You know how she puts it out there. She acts all prim, all upstate Episc-y, when certain people are around. But it's a validation switch stuck in the on position. 'Oh my God, that vodka pineapple is so *interesting.* It's the best drink I've ever had, and you make it so *well.*'"

"She had a grip like that at thirteen. 'You made a *volcano.* How did you *do* it? Wanna be *partners?* You play *cello,* too, that's *amay*-zing.'"

"With the musicians it's a whole other level," Mike says.

"I've never understood that."

"With Grace?"

"With anyone, really."

"You don't get the appeal of musicians?"

"I mean, we seem to forget that it's only been cool for, what, *ten years?*" Suzy says. "All these nerds were forced into classical lessons by their parents, with the widow at the end of the block or whatever, and spent their entire childhood in their basement practicing. And so you emerge as an adult male who never went to a school dance or got to second base, and yet the Age has confirmed you as the man. All 'cause Dad would've beat you with a belt if you'd skipped out on piano."

"Jeez, what'd they do to you?"

"I just don't buy it. Once a nerd, always a nerd. Ignored by girls like Grace until the end of high school, maybe even in college, and it's all still there, that resentment. They just lick their chops looking down from the stage on a sea of pussy, ready for revenge."

"Dave was a guitarist, wasn't he?"

"Weird, hadn't considered the connection," Suzy says, caught.

"Duane Allman never learned to read music," Mike says, steering wide of Suzy's acid.

"Oh yeah, and *that*," Suzy says, reminded. "That's an even *better* reason for me to be pissed. 'Jeez, what'd they do to' me? All these guys, these guys my sister followed around on tour—they took her away from me right when I was finally starting to like her."

"But here we are now," Mike says.

"Yup," Suzy says. "The band's back together."

Suzy has nine round-trips in ten days. They're mostly out-and-backs to places like Denver and Houston and Seattle. The routine of those shorties—airplanes and airports—smothers the novelty of flying. She's numb to it that fast. It doesn't help her feeling of sameness that no matter when she lands, the Dodgers are playing: Vin Scully's voice narrating the fraught cab rides home from LAX, a stream of play-by-play and biographical "wouldn'tchaknowits" that's possible to follow without interruption from the taxi radio to the stereos in neighbors' open windows to the on-screen television commentary when she steps through the front door.

On a Tuesday in mid-July, after working the shuttle from San Francisco, Suzy meets Grace on the beach. It's afternoon and the beach is deserted. There is a single surfer, a lifeguard in his station at Nineteenth, and a pair of towels—belonging to two people—that overlap with each other at their edges. It takes her longer than she can quite believe to cover the sprawl between the Strand and their spot in the sun. The sand is boiling, and she's forced to keep her flip-flops on the whole way.

Grace is wearing a new yellow bikini and, confirming her hunch, Suzy sees that the man with Grace is not Mike. He is tan and he is long, but he is familiar. The Howlers show. The Cover Band guitarist. His mustache is thicker up close, and though it turns down his mouth at the corners, he seems to smile at all times.

"Suz, you got my note!" Grace says.

"I did," Suzy says, dropping her towel and Mike's new issue of *New York* on the available side of Grace.

"Did you meet J.P. when we saw them?"

"I don't think so," Suzy says. "Hi."

J.P. lunges over to shake her hand. "Heya," he says, collapsing onto his stomach. "How was the flight? Where to?"

"Fine. Just San Francisco. I can't recall a single thing."

"You're too green for that," Grace says. And, turning to J.P., smiling: "This is, what, start of the seventh week?"

"It wasn't a *bad* flight. I mean, you know. You're up, you pour some soda and juice, and then you're down. I think Warren Beatty was supposed to be on the flight but then didn't show. That cast a shadow. All the girls were glum."

"He made a pass at me once," Grace says, sitting up, messing with her hair—clumped and fried, salt drying from an earlier dip.

"Beatty?" J.P. says.

"It was pretty lazy. He asked me if I'd ever seen the northern lights. I said I preferred warm weather. He asked if I wanted to screw in the bathroom."

"So...did you?" J.P. says.

"I told him to try again later if he was still interested. He had another couple drinks and passed out, and by the time we landed, he had his eye on someone else."

"That's a sad story," J.P. says.

"I disagree. When you think about it, it's one where everybody wins."

"Speaking of stories," Suzy says, "where's Mike? I wanted to talk to him about the last book he gave me."

Grace acknowledges Suzy's crude transition by pressuring her lips together. "He's driving around. Went to talk to some publishers about money. *Playboy*'s ad guys."

"That's good."

"It's something. I guess they're gonna move the magazine from Chicago to Los Angeles, or at least part of it, maybe."

"Everybody's coming, one by one," J.P. says. "Hey, he should write for *Playboy*."

"You a subscriber?" Grace says.

"As a matter of fact..."

"For the record reviews," Grace says.

"And the interviews."

"The interviews *are* pretty great," Suzy says.

"Thank you, Suzy," J.P. says.

The silence that follows demands that J.P. search the pocket of his trunks for a joint.

"Ladies?" he says, surfacing one. Suzy waves him off and expects Grace to as well, just as she did on the Fourth. But she allows J.P. to place the joint in her mouth and shelter the flame from the breeze.

"Out of curiosity," Suzy says to J.P., "what's the name of your guy?"

"What guy?"

"Who do you buy your grass from?"

"You know Billy Zar?"

"Yeah," she says, "met him a couple weeks ago. That's what I was guessing."

"Look at you," Grace says, light in the head.

"He was the one I was talking to at the party on the Fourth."

"I know, I remember. Does it make me a bad big sister that I'm proud of you for knowing the town weed dealer on your own?"

"Not just weed," Suzy says.

"Oh great, even better," Grace says.

"He's good for pretty much anything," J.P. says. "People say it goes up pretty high. Like, not that he's flying to Colombia or anything, but that he knows the guy who does."

"Shut up," Grace says. "That kid collects on ten- and twenty-dollar tabs. No way he's tied up in more than you or me."

"He's a smart guy," J.P. says.

"What does that matter?"

"He was second or third in his class at SDM," J.P. says. "He and my brother were in school together. He gave a speech at graduation and everything."

"Billy Zar?" Grace says.

"Why didn't he go to college?" Suzy says.

"You'd have to ask him. I always just figured it was 'cause he was dealing already. Had a gig, was ready to go."

"Weird dude," Suzy says.

"I like him," J.P. says. "Everybody likes him. He's reliable and he's fun. Supports a lot of people. Knows everyone and is a one hundred percent genuine hombre. He's like, I dunno, a town mascot or something."

Grace and J.P. lie flat on their backs and watch the clouds drift by, describing the animals and countries their shapes resemble. Suzy reads the cover story in *New York*: FIRE ISLAND BEHAVIOR—WILL IT SPREAD TO THE MAINLAND?

"'As California is to the rest of the nation,'" Suzy reads to Grace, "'Fire Island is to New York: the place where everyone's rosiest dream of a future Utopia bears fruit in a somewhat unreal present....'"

Suzy smiles and hands the issue to Grace, who gets caught instead on a story about New York's abortion clinics.

"So where do you guys go next?" J.P. says.

"Uh, I know I have Denver twice in a row," Grace says, "and then New York, I think."

"When are you going to New York?" he says. Suzy hasn't been to New York since the Fourth. She wonders if J.P. is wrapped up in it, too, and braces herself for the ask. "'Cause the Stones are closing out their North American tour there with a few dates middle of next week."

"Oh yeah, what days?" Grace says. "I was flying when they came through here in June."

"Twenty-something. Midtwenties. Four shows, I think."

"J.P. is a walking concert calendar," Grace says. "Any band, any venue."

"I think I'm scheduled for New York next week, too," Suzy says.

"Any chance we're on the same flight?"

"Don't know, I can call when we get home."

"Well, listen, if we're not, we should be," Grace says. "We can ask to move it around." Suzy recognizes that Grace must be feeling body-warm by now, velvety all over, but Suzy appreciates the suggestion anyway. "We can finally see Mom and Dad."

"They do seem desperate," Suzy says. "Fly in, drive up, come back into the city for the concert?"

"Do you think we could still get tickets?" Grace says to J.P.

"If you have any trouble, give me a ring and I'll hook you up with my man out there."

"The Billy Zar of New York."

"Lucky for us and unlucky for New York, there's only the Billy Zar of Sela del Mar."

While she keeps one ear in the conversation, Suzy reads and rereads the same sentence from a Nicholas Pileggi story about the mob. She reads it until it's devoid of information.

"Sisters, man," J.P. says. "People on flights must flip."

"Oh, and Hawaii in a few days, too," Suzy says.

"Man, jackpot."

"First time," Suzy says.

"How long will you be there?"

"Half a day and a night."

"Still, half a day and a night on Oahu?" he says, wistful on the beach.

"Hawaii plus sister flight to New York…," Grace says. "Both a little more memorable than San Francisco?"

"Sure," Suzy says. "But don't you ever get a *little* bored?"

"Listen to you," Grace says. "Always and will ever be: Special Suzy."

"You *do* know what I mean.…"

"Suzy: racing high. Grace: *high* high."

Suzy's mouth twists up at the corner.

"Racing couldn't have been *that* great," Grace says. "Don't forget that I had to take care of you after some crashes."

"I know," Suzy says, "and somehow that made it seem all the *cooler*. So beat up and center-spotlight that you had to fetch me OJ. While Mom hovered in the hallway, begging me to take up ceramics instead."

"Ugh, so weird. I'm already stressed about this trip."

"So many *questions*," Suzy says.

"Get ready to answer for all of your life choices."

"Man," Suzy says, "I just need to figure my shit out."

"How's that?" It's J.P. Suzy thought he'd drifted off.

"I just need to maybe start figuring out what else I want to do."

J.P., oblivious to the fact that she doesn't expect to find the answer on the beach today, begins to list a number of activities he supposes Suzy might be interested in. For J.P., as with Billy and so many others who grew up here, the web of connections is robust. He knows some great girls who just started a bakery. And these roommates who used to be his neighbors who got certified last year to teach kindergarten. Plus, obviously, he knows bands in need of better musicians—does she play anything? She doesn't, but Suzy says things like "Really?" and "Interesting" as the list ticks on and on.

"Or how 'bout taking flight lessons with me?" he says eventually.

"What?" Suzy says. It jolts her in a manner she's not prepared for.

"You used to race cars, right? That was your thing? There's at least some things in common. A couple months in the classroom, a couple months up in the air, fifty hours of logged flight, and then they give you a pilot's license. I just started, but so far so good."

"You just sign up and they give you a pilot's license?" Suzy says.

"I mean, after you do the course work and put in the hours. It takes a little wad of cash, but think of what you get for it."

"You don't need to be military?"

"Nah, but it's interesting you mention that part. So: I got super lucky in the draft—I was three eleven. I didn't want any part of it, and so I was obviously relieved. But the more time goes by, I feel like I'm really missing something, you know? Just the feeling of having been a part of a big thing. The band's not getting any more popular. But I figured here's some skill I might've picked up if I'd served. Some skill I might've been able to put to good use down the road."

Suzy's heard a version of this all her life. Their father only ever wanted one thing and that was to fly planes. At the outset of the war Wayne enlisted with the navy, but his physical revealed his eyes were too poor to fly jets. He became an engineer on a navy carrier in the Pacific, a charge that ultimately led to the career in glass at Schuyler Glen. But there was nothing that ever softened the sting of that initial rejection. All their lives he'd told the girls there was nothing he could do about it, nothing but buy Airfix models for the garage. But here, on a deserted beach in Southern California, a rhythm guitarist whom Suzy perceived until this moment to have no further ambition beyond nailing a thirty-bar harmony is telling her the only hurdle she faces in flying airplanes is some pay-to-play training.

"Okay," Suzy says.

"Okay?" J.P. says.

"I'm in. I'll do it."

"Okay!" J.P. says.

"Wait, what are you doing?" Grace says, returning from wherever her head's been.

"Suzy's gonna do flight school, too."

"What?" Grace says.

"I'll give Grace the number," J.P. says, "so you can see when it makes sense to start."

Grace gets this look in her face—a sharp edge of competitiveness, but one that's dulled by the high. She's in a place beyond jealousy, and so it comes out mellow and round: "All right, then. Just *do* it, Suz. Just be so, so good."

"Okay," Suzy says, smiling at the pride she perceives in her sister's voice. "Cool. Cool cool cool cool..."

Everything on board is as ever, with the exception of the POG juice. By the time they're taxiing, cartons are in the hands of not just the first-class passengers, but all one hundred and fifty aboard the 707 back from Honolulu.

This trip has been filled with the most straightforward enjoyments yet, the greatest quotient of pleasure to effort. Suzy had simply stepped off the plane and into the three-dimensional heat, and there was this van that had the look and smell of a plumeria lei on wheels, at the ready to whisk them directly to the water, no stop at the room even, hope you wore a bikini beneath your uniform. It was late afternoon when she and the others arrived, but peak humidity, and the finite hours of sun suited Suzy fine. They were stuffed into doubles at

the Royal Hawaiian, and it was not till well after dark—after the little island boy lit the trail of torches—that the luau got under way and
Suzy made a move to her room for the first time. When Suzy walked
across the lawn in the fading light, it occurred to her that nothing in
her life had ever felt quite so right as the grass on her feet did then,
the grass of the grounds of a Hawaiian hotel.

Just after noon the next day they're up and out of sight of Diamond Head and Pearl Harbor and the last look at land, embroidered
at its edge by the chalky swirl of a shallow reef—nothing, for six
hours, but that flat face of the tanzanite Pacific and the occasional
black shadow of an orphan cloud. They work the aisles collecting the
empty four-ounce pop-top cartons, and when they're back in the gal-
ley, Suzy puts on a pot of coffee (special request from 17D) and pulls
her book from her bag. Three of the four girls are back there now, all
except Marion, who's on her way. But there's something uncomprehending about the way Marion moves. Her eyes hum and her body
seems to trail her legs. She looks like a boxer who's been jabbed in the
nose after the bell.

"There's a man," Marion says to the compartment. "There's a man
with a note asking to speak with the captain."

They know what this is, the four of them—Marion, Belle, Ruth,
and Suzy—and they look at one another with unchanging expressions.
In the seven weeks since Suzy started, there have been six hijackings. It
has been going on for years, to no great resolution, and after slowing
some, things have begun to sizzle again. Grand Pacific provides a weekly
update of hijackings in a black box in the airline newsletter. There's
probably been a hundred attempts in the last few years—dozens of
flights to Cuba, demands for millions in cash. The skyjackings were covered feverishly, and the feverish coverage inspired copycats. It is a rarer
and rarer thing to have a flight staffed with stews who haven't experienced one firsthand, but such is the case here with these four.

"I didn't want to bother Captain Mulaney," Marion finally says, "if it's, you know, not that big—"

"Do you have the note?" Ruth says. Ruth is the senior stew, the head of the crew.

Marion pulls the note from the pocket of her uniform. It's a bar napkin, still damp. Circumscribed by the wet ring of a cocktail glass is the logo for the Aloha Grill, a hula dancer in silhouette. In full-cap black ink:

ID LIKE TO SPEAK TO THE CAPTAIN PLEASE. TELL HIM THIS IS AN IMPORTENT MATTER OF SAFETEY AND FREEDOM. I HAVE A GUN AND I DONT WANT TO KILL PEOPLE BUT IF I HAVE TO I WILL, EVERYONE, IF MY SIMPL DEMANDS ARENT MET. ALL I WANT IS TO HAVE A CONVERSASION GO TELL HIM NOW IN 10 MINUTES OR I PRECEED TO SHOOT ONE PERSON.

Added to the back side:

(DONT TALK TO ME JUST GO AND COME GET ME WHEN THE CAPTAIN IS AMENNABLE TO MY DEMANDS)

"Oh God," Ruth says, "which one is he?"

"22B. There on the aisle with the black hair." All Suzy sees is the back of his head and the bright line of a red-and-tan Hawaiian shirt peeking around the edge of the seat. Short sleeves, a hairy forearm. Everything about him is still.

"Did he seem serious?" Suzy says.

"Gosh, I don't know. He was like anyone else. He didn't smile or nothing, but he didn't seem overly this way or that. He was like every other passenger. He said, 'Take this and give it to the captain.'"

"We can't risk it," Ruth says. "I'll take it up if you want."

"Do you think he'll get mad?" Marion says. "Since he gave it to me."

The girls look at one another again.

"You go," Ruth says. "I'll take another pass to collect trash, just to be up there with you, without making more suspicions."

"Okay," Marion says, smiling feebly and rolling the note over into the cup of her hand.

"We can keep watch over him," Suzy says. "In case he gets up or something. Just to have, you know, extra eyes or whatever."

"I knew this would happen," Belle says, speaking up for the first time, her face squinching toward tears. "It said so this morning in the paper at the hotel. 'An unsettling surprise at work' is what it said."

"C'mon, sweetheart," Ruth says. "Nothing's happened, and we just need to be helpful now."

"You'd better go," Suzy says to Marion. "I'll take the coffee with me, just in case I need to use it or whatever." Belle shows Suzy a morbid face. "Stay here," Suzy says to her, "and maybe get lunch going, 'kay?"

They roll out in sequence—Marion, Ruth, and then Suzy. Suzy takes the aisle slowly, as though she's making a standard pass, but without offering anyone anything. She watches Marion knock at the door to the cockpit, and though she can't hear the exchange, she can see Captain Mulaney's hat and the handover of the note. After reading the napkin, Captain Mulaney holds still in his seat. Suzy sees him turn toward Marion, imagines his eyes moving quietly over Marion's shoulder, twenty-two rows aft, and quickly sizing up B on the aisle. Marion steps back out of the cockpit and the captain shuts the door. She passes Ruth and then stops short of where Suzy's standing with the coffee to communicate a message to the man.

"Sir, if you'll please follow me...," she says softly. The man unclips his seat belt and stands. He's no taller than Marion. Looks

Hawaiian. Tropical shirt and corduroy shorts, Reebok tennis shoes, striped tube socks that stretch halfway up his brambled legs. As he shuffles behind Marion, Suzy notices he's got a fanny pack on his hip and a hand buried inside. Suzy finds herself swallowing hard, not out of fear but as an involuntary response to a flush of envy—impressed, even, with the man's conviction, the single-mindedness of the pursuit, the hunger and willingness and ability to steer a moment belonging not just to himself but to a hundred and fifty others. It is a shameful lump, and she shoves it back down her throat.

Ruth asks loudly for empty cartons of POG juice, insisting that passengers not shove them into the backs of the seats. Marion passes Ruth, followed by 22B. Ruth resists glancing up to look at his face and makes another call for garbage instead. Marion knocks lightly at the captain's door and then steps aside.

In less time than eats up a frame of film, the man in the Hawaiian shirt crumples to the floor of the airplane, his two hands gripping his face.

Captain Mulaney is through the door and on top of him, pinning the man's wrists beneath his knees while searching for a gun. The man is bucking his body, kicking the doors to the cockpit and the bathroom. A woman in first class screams, cueing the rest of the plane to unbuckle and peer toward the tussle.

"Everybody stay seated," Suzy shouts as she rushes forward with Ruth. Marion stands near the boarding door with her hands over her face, and nearly backpedals into the laps of the passengers in the first row. The man is shouting and gargling, resisting the frisk of the captain, who suddenly, exhausted by the inconvenience, lands a hook that quiets the man's body.

The woman up front screams again. The captain slides off and unzips the fanny pack. He removes a handgun, a Colt sidearm.

"You dumb, dumb bastard," the captain mutters as he rolls onto his heels and up to his feet. Mulaney's hat has fallen to the floor, revealing the standard-issue gray crew cut of former military. He has a retiree's tan, Phoenix by way of Fort Collins by way of somewhere else. He has long legs and high-hitched trousers and the arms and chest of a man who does his hundreds—push-ups, sit-ups, chin-ups—every day still. He looks less boiled by adrenaline than just personally offended by the situation. "God *damn*, what were you thinking?"

"Jack?" It's the copilot through the crack in the door.

"He's out. I got his gun."

"What should I tell the tower?"

"Tell 'em we'll keep him up here, keep on going."

"You sure you don't want to turn around?" the copilot says.

"Ladies," Mulaney says. "How many extra seats do we have?"

"Six, Captain," Ruth says.

"Perfect, let's shift some folks around and clear out that last row, if you don't mind."

"Jack," the copilot says, "they just want to confirm that we're okay to proceed as planned. If not, they're ready for us in Honolulu."

"We're not inconveniencing a hundred and fifty passengers because of this asshole."

"Yes, sir."

"Ladies, would you please make sure everyone knows we've just opened the bar."

"Yes, Captain," Ruth says.

"Bill, will you let folks know what's goin' on?" The copilot clicks into the PA.

The captain rummages through a compartment behind his seat. He emerges with a pair of bungee cords, cords that might typically be used to strap down a service cart. He asks a suited man with sun-bleached hair to lend a hand, and together they carry 22B to the last row, where Belle kindly asks passengers to gather their belongings and stand by for relocation to new seats. Captain Mulaney and the blond businessman unload 22B into the last row, and Mulaney fixes him to the aisle seat, double-wrapping the bungee cords around his chest. The man's head, masked by a soft brown face, lolls forward. Mulaney unthreads the shoelaces from the man's trainers and ties each wrist to the armrest. He binds the man's ankles together with a third cord and fixes them to the seat.

Mulaney gathers up the four stews.

"I am so goddamned fed up with this shit," he says, glancing back at the man. "This is my third this year."

"Oh my God," Belle says, hot in the cheeks.

"Sorry, ladies, pardon my French. It's just, they see it on TV, think they can do it themselves, and all the airlines do is give in to the demands—making it a more attractive proposition than ever."

"What happened with the other two?" Suzy says.

"First time there were three guys. Said they had a bomb in a briefcase. Denver to Miami, they wanted to go to Cuba. It was on our way, we had enough fuel, had no reason to believe they were bluffing."

"They didn't want any money?" Suzy says.

"Didn't say. Just said they wanted to get to Cuba."

"And so you went."

"We let Havana know we were coming, got cleared to land, and handed them over. Let Castro deal with them. Took off and had everyone else at the gate in Miami an hour after they were due in...."

The captain trails off as the body of 22B begins listing toward the window seat, only to be caught in suspension by the cords.

"Then, a couple weeks ago," he says, turning back, "there was a guy who said he had a whole crew on board. Chicago to Seattle, started making demands over Montana. Asked for half a million from the Treasury, plus a helicopter. Said he was military, recent discharge from

'Nam, wanted it delivered upon arrival and that he was going to divvy it out among the families of the guys in his platoon who were killed. Had dynamite strapped to his chest and a detonator in his hand. The guy was calm enough, said he'd been planning things for a year. So the airline and the FBI are scrambling—I mean, there's been so many they're starting to get tapped out on these ransoms.

"As we get closer, the guy's gettin' a little edgy. Asks to talk to our folks on the ground directly. Starts saying 'I' instead of 'we'—makes me think he's lying about there being others. Makes me wonder what else he's lying about. People on board aren't terribly wise to what's up. We're still landing where we're meant to and he's not making a big scene. We actually get on the ground. That's when the feds say they were only able to scrounge up forty-two grand. I mean, fuck them, right? No mention of it the entire time. The guy coulda ended us right there.

"So he starts freaking out, says he wants us to take off again. I don't really have much of a choice, so I tell ground control what's gonna happen. We start to taxi and the SOBs shoot our goddamned tires out. Can you believe that? There's this big lurch. We drop. People are screaming, oxygen masks are flying around, and a couple sticks of the kid's dynamite fall to the ground. And wouldn't you know? They're road flares. Road flares with little fake fuses on the ends. Before I can tell anyone what's even going on, a couple of the passengers sitting up front, they somehow get the boarding door open and—get this—*push the kid out the door.* These guys must've been listening in the whole time. Saw the same thing I did with the flares. After the fact, we learned that they'd been going through his carry-on, found the packaging for the flares, figured he was full of it and didn't really know what he was doing. Turns out they were coming back from a hunting trip in Wisconsin and still had their blood runnin' a little red.

"Anyway," the captain says, "the guy broke a leg falling out of the plane, and the feds were right there to pick him up."

"That's the craziest story I've ever heard," Belle says.

"How'd you know our guy didn't have a bomb?" Suzy says.

"He would've said so in the note."

"And what if he'd shot you first?"

"I was just gonna make sure he didn't. Besides, nobody wants to be pilotless over the ocean. He wasn't gonna be that dumb."

"But seriously," Belle says, "you're a hero."

Mulaney watches for the man's movement, impervious to the heat radiating from beneath Belle's uniform. "I'm just sick of these guys. I'm sick of the way the airlines deal with them. I'm sick of the way the papers and TV news are always talking about it. These guys are not original thinkers, they're not creators. They're imitators, they're pathetic little copycats. One flight: *nobody to somebody*—that's what they've got in their heads. And I'm tired of this idea that we're supposed to give in to them. I don't know, I'm gonna deal with it my own way from here on out."

Belle and Marion nod, but Suzy looks to Ruth to see if this is something they're supposed to go along with.

"We're gonna get these people to L.A. safe," Mulaney continues. "And we're gonna hand this motherfucker over. After that, they're gonna ask you ladies some questions. Do a whole thing with you. All I can say is remember that you were scared and remember that this is a bad guy."

The captain finds himself a carton of POG in the back, and Ruth leads the girls out to start taking drink orders. Open bar, captain's call. Ruth, Marion, and Belle hit the aisle, while Suzy starts stocking a service cart.

"Appreciate your help, sweetheart," Mulaney says, and he throws back the rest of his juice.

"Thanks for making that go away so fast," Suzy says. "Could've been bad."

Mulaney squints up the aisle and then turns back to Suzy. "You know," he says to her privately, "I could get in big trouble for what just happened. I broke protocol. I didn't know the situation—I guessed." He tilts back his head and tries for juice that he knows isn't there. "And they're gonna fry me for it."

"You saved a planeful of people."

"That's not how they're gonna see it. They're gonna see it as me *endangering* a planeful of people."

"You said we'll be asked some questions," Suzy says.

"Yeah, but realistically, it won't matter. This might be it for me. Things are dicey right now. Every airline's had its bad day. They don't love me, the big bosses on the ground. And this is a good way to make an example of me."

"It's bad PR, though. Punishing the pilot who saved a plane from a hijacker."

"When I assessed the situation and saw the guy sitting there, I was convinced that he was some hippie burnout on acid, or whatever it is now. That he didn't pose a serious threat to me or you girls or the passengers. But you know what? You ever seen that kind of gun before?"

"No."

"It's a Colt M1911. Same handgun they gave me in Korea and same handgun they give everyone in Vietnam. Standard-issue sidearm of the armed forces. Means he either served or bought it from someone who did. In any case, it's a real gun with real bullets. Seven rounds in the magazine. And that fact there—that I made a call based on what the guy *looked* like, when I was actually dealing with a loaded gun and someone who might know how to use it—that'll cost me my career."

He shakes his head and smiles weakly at Suzy, before turning back toward the cockpit.

He passes the man tied up in the last row and, without glancing down or slowing his stride, elbows him swiftly in the face, so that any signs of stirring consciousness are extinguished. Then he's carried the rest of the way to the cockpit by the mounting shapely-bodied wave of approbation, equal parts whooping and applause.

Suzy skates to the southern tip of the Strand and, at Mike's suggestion, takes a brand-new book he's bought, *Fear and Loathing in Las Vegas.* She spreads herself out in a tractor-combed, footprint-free brushstroke of empty beach, but she pinks too quickly and so rides to the next beach town, turns over her only singles at a taco stand, and, by early evening, winds up skating back past Howlers. The marquee seems to suggest that it's a real concert tonight, a leg of a tour. In fact, it's the last leg of a tour, she learns from the curly-blond manager smoking near the door. They've just returned from Europe, a homecoming, Los Sandcrabs hot off a plane from Paris.

"What was your favorite city?" Suzy says.

"In Europe?"

"Right, you can't answer 'Sela.'"

"I don't know, they all kinda seemed the same. We'd travel eight, nine hours a day and get to the new place when it was dark. Every city looks the same in the basement of a music hall with the lights off."

"So...Rome," Suzy says.

"Huh?"

He offers her a cigarette, and when she declines, he smokes two simultaneously.

"That's a little sad isn't it?" she says.

"I don't know," he says. "We enjoyed it. They enjoyed it." He pulls a straw hat from the ticket booth and fixes it over his curls. "Maybe Amsterdam. Amsterdam was better than the rest. But we're happy to be back."

"Well, that's good. Welcome home."

She drops her board to the sidewalk and, in evidence of a great betrayal, he says: "Are you not coming to the show?"

"Nah, I was just cruising by. Don't have any money on me anyway."

"You're on the list."

"You don't have to do that."

"Come in for a few songs, and go whenever you want. Comped drinks, too."

Suzy has always been susceptible to a free thing.

The band looks like they've been fending off cholera. Three of the four are pale and gaunt, their faces, in the colored stage lights, looking like old fruit. The bassist and drummer must be twins—imagine how nice that must've been for the parents, Suzy thinks, to harbor a complete rhythm section in their garage growing up. The lead guitarist is Giacometti shaped, his nipple-length, center-parted, bead-curtain hair playing an optic trick that makes him look seven and a half feet tall. And then the singer, three stacked circles, like an Intro to Drawing Humans exercise: a round head on a rounder torso on the roundest base, a Baskin-Robbins triple. He's got a mustache and prominent buckteeth, like photos of the Queen front man she's seen in *Rolling Stone*. And yet somehow together they look undeniable on-stage. Utterly sore-thumb-ish in the normal world, but perfectly cast in performance.

They bow and then start in, a jangly surf guitar that sounds like it's being run about in a cathedral; a Dick Dale surf-rock drumbeat; and then the feeble nasalings of one long, happy-sounding complaint—what it would be like if Neil Young drank enough to find his way west and face-plant off the pier. The music is simple and ubiquitous; the voice is closer to discrete. But still, Suzy thinks, it'll never quite break through at home, here in the South Bay, where everyone knows this kind of beach music and anyone can play it. It takes leaving, exporting that ordinary local sound, in order to find its audience. Where the mundane arrives packaged as the exotic. The accents, the beat, and that uplifting nasal. "We're going to Asia next," the manager said. "We seem to do all right everywhere else, but all the guys want is to stay at home."

They play four or five songs before Suzy realizes they're different songs—the drums don't stop, no break for whiskey or cigarettes. Her own drink is gone and she side-shuffles to drop her glass at the bar, but before she makes it, she feels a pinch on the numb point of her elbow.

"You stoked they're back, or *what?*"

Look at that face: total indifference to any line she's drawn in the dirt. And then it curls right around the eyes and mouth, an expectant smile, as though this run-in is both the most probable occurrence and also the most preposterous.

"Super stoked, brah," she says, slow and half-dead of enthusiasm.

"Your sister here?" Billy says.

"Just me. But I'm heading out. The manager or something, I was passing by and he invited me in."

"Owen?"

"I didn't catch his name."

"Overalls?"

"Overalls and a straw hat."

"Owen."

"Owen didn't seem to love Europe," Suzy says.

"He's just bummed 'cause his girlfriend left him while he was gone."

"Sorry to hear that."

"It was kinda brutal. He got home and saw all the unopened letters he'd sent from the road. She left him a note that said: 'I don't know where this is going, but I need to do some things before it's too late.' And then she actually made a list of those things."

"What did the list say?"

"I don't remember all of them. 'Swim with dolphins in Baja.' 'Live in a cool house.' 'Fuck a world-class athlete.' Owen was hung up on the dolphins thing because it was something that *he'd* always wanted to do. Something he'd figured they'd do together."

"But he was on the road. And she wanted to get to Baja."

"Exactly. I guess he couldn't do much about the other two, either."

" 'Fuck a world-class athlete' is tough to take," Suzy says.

"I asked him what she might mean by 'world-class.' "

"An NBA player?"

"No, I think it was more that she'd been watching a lot of the Olympic trials. You know, track and swimming and stuff like that."

"An Olympian," Suzy says.

"Yeah, not one of the Rams or the Dodgers. Not one of the US Open surfers."

"Does an archer count?"

"I think it's probably about the muscles."

"A fencer?" Suzy says.

"Some dude who's six three with stomach muscles."

"Dressage?"

"I don't know that word."

"Oh, come on."

"Sounds Yale-y," he says.

"One semester only, remember," she says.

"Yale word."

"It's horses, has to do with horses."

"I think she probably just saw a photo of Mark Spitz on the starting block."

"'Not Owen' is the point of her note."

"I think it's just bad luck with the Olympic year. Gets the mind going, you know?"

"I always like the Olympics."

"My favorite thing in sports. Well, Trojans up here, Lakers here," Billy says. "Olympics right here, above all the rest."

"You should go. I'll get you a discount on tickets to Germany."

"Is that right?"

"Actually, I don't give a shit—and no, I'm not helping you. But you should go somewhere. Go to Arizona. Go to Minnesota."

"I've waited this long, it can't just be *anywhere*."

"Why have you *never* left?" she says. "What's the *real* reason?"

He shrugs with his lower lip. "My folks didn't take vacations anywhere else. I mean, we'd go to Lake Arrowhead and Mammoth most years. But their big idea would be to go see Old Sacramento or where the Russians settled California, their little colony."

"I thought it was the Spanish."

"*Exactly.* People don't realize the Russians were here, too. Right up above San Francisco."

"Is your family Russian?"

"Don't think so. Even though it sort of sounds like it.... They're just all about deep, old California stuff, like how their families came. These places, you get there, spend a couple hours walking around—and then you're out of things to do besides drive more."

"I'm surprised Nixon hasn't blown it up."

"Maybe he has. But I'd bet it's still there. Fort Something. Think about that: if it'd been the Russians instead of the Spanish."

"Then they'd be simply Sandcrabs."

"How do you say *the?*"

"That's what I mean, they don't really do *the*s."

"*Sandcrabs* in all caps with a backward *R*."

"Totally," Suzy says.

"But see what I mean? That's the *thing: so much in C.A.* Big state. Big history. You know that in fourth grade when we did California history, they told us most other states' histories weren't interesting enough and so those kids got taught California stuff to fill in the gaps?"

"That's not remotely true."

"Well, that's what they said."

"I love that that's your reason for never going anywhere."

"*Plus:* whatever's not here to begin with, there's new people bringing it every day. I prefer to just kinda sit here and let it come to me."

"The more you talk, the more I'm convinced I want to go back east immediately."

"But everything you need in the world is right here."

Even Billy's face seems to lose enthusiasm for the bullshit he's shoveling. Suzy shifts her bag to the shoulder closer to the door. Billy registers her impatience.

"Maybe," he says, "it's more like I just never imagined myself to be the kind of person who got to go to a bunch of different places."

"Why's that?" she says.

"It just seemed like a thing meant for other people."

Suzy frowns. There's a shadow of familiarity, an imprecise familiarity: "That makes sense."

"You might be mocking me and I might deserve it—"

"No, I mean I understand that feeling, I've felt that feeling."

"And now you fly around the world."

"And now I pour cocktails and clean up vomit."

"Next chance I get, I'll do it," he says.

"Yeah, where to?"

"Somewhere with a beach, somewhere chill."

"Of all the places in the world, your first trip is somewhere with the same super-bitchin' kicked-back lifestyle as Sela."

"Just 'cause you've been more places than anyone here doesn't mean you get to condescend...," he says. "How 'bout we ask a Ouija board?"

"You want to check with the bartender to see if they have one?"

"Actually, you know what?" Billy says. "Let's settle it now, for real. There's a map of the world in the men's pisser. Follow me."

"I'm not going to the bathroom with you."

"Jesus, Z, I'll leave the door open."

"Please don't call me that," she says, but he's moving now and he's got her firm around the wrist. Los Sandcrabs keep bouncing from one song to the next; it happens quicker than an album moves through tracks. The leanest one feints like he's going to dive into the crowd, his guitar case serving as a surfboard. But the fans are thinly dispersed and he thinks better of plunging in. Suzy bets it worked in Brussels.

Billy grabs a dart out of the bull's-eye near the entrance to the bathroom, and together they wait for the men's room to vacate. Suzy's suddenly very aware of the time, that she should really be going.

A muffled flush and then the door's open, and there inside on the wall, a tattered world map drafted in double-barreled hemispheres, looking like when a movie spy glimpses a target through binoculars.

"All right," Billy says, "no matter what, this is the first place I go, deal?"

"Whatever," Suzy says.

He toes his right foot up to the threshold, and Suzy apologizes with her eyes to the woman waiting for the ladies' room. He warms up and fires the dart on a course that's as tight as a drying line. Its tip pricks a spot in the middle of the Pacific Ocean, then clatters off the cinder block wall and into the toilet bowl.

"Welp, Minnesota it is," he says.

"Wow."

"World-class athlete right there."

"Go to Munich," she says. "Just pull the trigger and go to the Olympics."

"Owen said Europe wasn't much anyway."

"Owen told me all he saw was highways and the basements of music venues."

"Oh, he likes that line. The 'Every city looks the same...' line. He said that to you?"

"He said that."

"We'll have to try again," Billy says, meaning the map.

"I've gotta go. Flying in the morning."

"Always off to fly."

"Yes, it's a job."

"Where are you going this week?"

"Couple places."

"That's cool. Anywhere good?"

"Going to New York."

"Oh, I do love New York," Billy says, his face on a trip of imaginary nostalgia.

"Mm-hmm," she says.

"If you're at all interested..."

"I'm not."

"I'm not talking about this week. I wouldn't dream of talking about this week. I mean if ever in the *future*."

"See ya."

"If ever in the future you change your mind, just know...," he says as she covers the distance to the door. And she can't really hear anything else he says over the *mmmm pop-pop mm-pop, mmmm pop-pop mm-pop* and the saxophone solo.

*   *   *

The flight is the morning's first, six sharp, the line leader on the tarmac. Each evening, after the midnight red-eyes to Boston Atlanta Miami, the airport contracts into its black window of low hours, receiving stragglers from the burning colonial capitals of Latin America but sending no new flights out into the night. That blackness is like the space between a heartbeat: that another day will come isn't absolutely certain, but worth betting on all the same. When the morning arrives, each muscle in the system shows up for work, puts the machinery into motion, catapults its blood to the outermost extremities—those first airplanes out over the water.

Suzy and Grace are backlit on takeoff, a proximate deep-summer sun washing up over the curve of the plains and down toward the second coast, the pitch of the light and the engines of the 707 whining higher, in concert. The sky and sea are a Lakers-colored Rothko out the window. They're up and out, banking over the water with the patient spiral of a wheelchair ramp, until they're riding an antsy jet stream back to New York.

The other girls find the whole idea adorable, though they keep guessing Suzy's the older one 'cause of the worry lines on her forehead. Grace wins a ro-sham-bo for the business cabin, and so Suzy takes care of drinks in the back. It's a packed flight, the kind that could go down and reset the lives of a hundred and eighty families. Why is this the thought each time Suzy's up? *What is the Worst Thing?* she's always wondering, in order to establish an edge, a margin of possibility. After all, to come to terms with the Worst Thing is to live in a pretty satisfied space of Not That.

The plane doesn't go down—not until it means to. They're a little late, but there's still plenty of daylight to cover the drive up to Schuyler Glen. They rent a Gremlin, toss the bags in the back, and change out of the tops of their uniforms in the parking lot. Traffic's bad getting out of Queens, but once they're through Harlem and over the George Washington, the highways open up and New York collapses around them like a big top during the load out. It is inescapable: the curtains of pitch pine and scarlet oak lining the highway, the scent of a rain shower in the process of steaming back out of the soil, the summer stereo of insects like electric wires. They keep the windows down and the radio off for at least the first few dozen miles through Rockland and Orange Counties. It hasn't been *that* long—they've been away only since Suzy's graduation in May—but it feels for Suzy as though she's transitioned back from the imaginary world into the real. The hyperpresent clarity of these sights and sounds makes Suzy feel as though Sela life might just be a movie they're caught up in, simultaneously making and watching, an occupation of the mind, a dream drifted into while waiting to return to this very moment, to the uncurving highway to the center of their home state.

When Grace catches a glimpse of her swept hair in the side mirror, she cries out in mock horror and rolls up the window. They're within range to catch the FM rock station out of Poughkeepsie playing some tracks off *Harvest*. With the gaps of an organic four count and the natural album order of the songs, Suzy recognizes that they're just playing the record straight through. Which starts Grace singing without a thought.

During a track she's bored with, she says, "This goes right with the drive."

"The right amount of glumness," Suzy says.

"I barely even know what they're saying except that Ontario sounds worse than upstate New York."

"I think that's basically what he's saying."

"I do miss summers," Grace says. "I miss camp. I miss Dad in summer—ditching work to take us to the lake."

"Mom still maintains she prefers winter. She prefers the clothes."

"That about sums it up, right?"

"Labor Days, piled up in the yard, leaning on Dad as he let us just bask in our sadness about the start of school, him sadder than us, just *dying* that it was the last night, that there were already fewer bugs," Suzy says. "How he'd call that heat in September, he'd say it had a 'cold edge'—that just *bummed me out.* And Mom would be in the house putting up the winter candles in the windows already."

"Next track's a little groovier."

"We need something stupid," Suzy says. "We need 'The lime in the coconut...'. We're getting sucked into the Sad Canada vibes."

The sun's still putting out heat as they pass Binghamton, and Grace tells Suzy a story about a boy she went on some dates with but never brought home, a boy a year younger than Suzy is now, twenty-one at the time, who'd already been to Vietnam and was back after six months with a leg broken in all these places that wouldn't heal fast enough for him to stick around the war. Who seemed pretty all right, hadn't had any buddies who'd died or anything, but spent his free afternoons calling for the kill sheets out of Saigon.

"It wasn't anything crazy," Grace says. "He'd just do it when he got home like you and I check the mail. And there was nothing for a while, I guess, but one night we were on a date, and that afternoon he'd found out that basically every guy he'd lived with had been killed in some sort of ambush, confirmed deaths for almost everyone, except two, who were missing but almost certainly dead or worse. He just told me the score and then started jabbing into this chicken parm he'd ordered. But he did it that way where you hold the fork like you're strangling it—like the guy grips the knife in *Pyscho.* Anyway, he just carved his dinner up into about a hundred pieces and then switched the fork over into his other hand and ate away like it was how he did it every time. And all I could fucking think of was what Mom would do if she was sitting at dinner across from him, her horror at the way he was holding his knife and cutting his meat."

"You weren't thinking about the massacre?"

"I mean, Suz, I was thinking about seriously dating this guy, and yeah, it was this awful day—but bad manners to boot. Anyway, the reason I thought of it was he was from Binghamton, that restaurant was in Binghamton. Only saw him a couple times after that."

"What do you think happened to him?"

"Don't know. But he's one of the three or four boys I keep expecting to see on a flight. Just, like, the ones where I wouldn't be surprised in the least if I leaned over with a napkin and pretzels and there he was."

"The ones that got away . . ."

"Exactly."

"I was kidding."

"Well, I mean, he was a fox. So were the others. Foxy and lucky, apparently. That night, after he told me, after we'd barely ordered our first drink, I said, 'Jesus, why didn't you just cancel, I would've understood, I'm not a monster.' And he said, 'Ya know, why would I let it affect tonight when it happened ten days ago? *That* was the night to let it ruin things, the night it happened. They've been dead ten days, who am I to cry about it now?' I wonder if he went back, if he re-upped once his leg healed."

"I don't know about you," Suzy says, "but for some reason I never run into vets in Sela."

"I think they're there, they're just maybe content with other things?"

"It's true—but I mean, how could that be, that you just *never* see them?"

"No uniform," Grace says. "Shirtless at the beach."

"I guess. Just seems like nobody even *talks* about it. Like, vague allusions to the body count, to Nixon. But there's hardly ever a brother or a cousin or a best friend."

"J.P. had a superhigh draft number," Grace says.

"He told me," Suzy says. "Maybe everyone's charmed."

"I don't know."

"But it's the same with Watergate. Maybe, *maybe* somebody reads a newspaper in the morning, but no one's exactly losing their mind about it in the streets."

"You sound like Mike."

"He must feel a little lost," Suzy says.

"Oh please, how can you sit around all day moaning about the absence of that sort of thing when that sort of thing is so *shitty,* when New York is so *rotten,* when Washington is *investigating itself,* and everything near our house is nice to look at? He doesn't have grounds to feel sorry for himself."

They cross stone bridges over rivers that flow from gorges.

"You've been on him a little lately."

"He's been on me."

"Well, regardless, I feel a little too in it," Suzy says. "I'm crowding you guys."

"Please, again: if you weren't there, we'd be screaming at each other instead of whispering in our bedroom. It's nice when you're around for dinner. It's chiller."

"What's the issue, though?"

"He needs a job."

"But he's working every day."

"And if the magazine happens, great, but if it doesn't, what else?"

"What would he want to do?"

"There's a lot he *wants* to do. What *could* he do? is more like it. There are things. He could sell insurance. He could write defense grants. Something with some money and some hours. I don't know how long it'll be till they make me stop flying. But even if—and it's a big if—I get away with this for another year, then in a year we will have *no* money, aside from, you know, the money left behind by his dad. But let's be real. I'd love nothing more than for Mike to write a nice big moneymaking book or run a nice big moneymaking magazine. But he's just been acting so *attacked*, so beaten up over the whole thing. I go out with the girls, or we go to hear music, and it's the same thing over and over—he tries a little and then starts playing with his drink. Oil and water with all the people we meet in Sela. Even when he drives around during the day, up to Pasadena or out to Riverside, doing whatever he's doing, looking for stories, I dunno, I just get the sense he's desperately trying to get away from the beach. Which is something I can't handle."

"You have to acknowledge that you fit in easily anywhere. You have friends who are flying. It's the place you're meant to be—even if there are lots of places you might be meant to be."

"What's he been saying to you?"

"I just mean—he's trying, he tried at the party on the Fourth."

"And then he ate shit and scraped his knees like a five-year-old."

"It can be hard to be alone in a new place."

"Most places, *yes*. Not there."

"Mike's a good guy. He's a better guy than almost all the guys, certainly the ones I've known."

"You're right. And he's good in most of the major ways. I'm just not one to sacrifice the present whatever for the future."

"I know," Suzy says.

"I'm not one to sweat that sort of thing."

"I know."

"But I'm just . . . I've just been thinking more than ever in the last couple months."

"Thinking what?"

"Listen, you're not gonna like this. For a number of reasons. But it's been something I've been meaning to tell you since my trip to visit you in New Haven. It was just always the wrong moment. Even on the beach, just the two of us, it felt wrong. And we're not alone elsewhere *that* often. So now seems right, I guess, unless you don't—"

"Grace."

"In March, I found out I was pregnant."

"Oh my God."

"And I got an abortion."

"What?"

"In Mexico."

"How—how did you not tell me?"

"It was super early, seven weeks in, is all. . . ."

"Are you okay?"

"Yeah, of course, it's history, all right? But here's the thing. Mike doesn't know."

"Grace."

"I never told him."

"Was it his?"

"Jesus, yes, of course. I just—if he had known, there's no way. I mean, he doesn't really buy in anymore, but with the way he was raised, and just wanting children—we've talked about it since we first started dating."

"But they would've made you stop flying. . . ."

The radio has found the song Suzy was looking for during the Neil marathon. *"You put de lime in de coconut, you drank 'em bot' up."* Grace laughs—a pistol report, Suzy's "ha"—before she frowns and her cheeks start reflecting light in streaks.

"I wasn't ready. I want to be a mom. I could be a mom now. But I wasn't ready to stop. This job is the only thing I've *ever* loved doing. I wasn't like you. I didn't have racing and reading and college. I loved *listening* to music, but that was others doing the thing and me admiring it. This is something *I* do. This is the thing *I'm* good at. Nobody flies forever. But once it's over, I'm never going to do anything this *me* again."

"That's not true at all," Suzy says, though she's worried it might be. She's as uncertain about Grace's future as she is about her own. Nothing beyond their stints of stewing besides the whole infinite world. . . . But also the limitations that come with that world. Grace has picked her lane, but it has the capacity to vanish as easily as she found it.

"It is," Grace says. "Or whatever, maybe it isn't, but it's what I feel. And I just couldn't bear to give that up yet. So I went with a couple girls down to Tijuana."

"I can't fucking believe that part."

"It wasn't an issue. It was easy. It was clean. Walked over the border—the border's a turnstile there. It cost a hundred bucks and the guy spoke English and the nurses were nice and we were on the beach in Encinitas by the afternoon."

"And then what?"

"What do you mean? We stayed the night at somebody's friend's house and we drove back in the morning and Mike was none the wiser. I told him I was on the rag and that he should switch his brand of rubbers."

Grace's face is drying. She's sitting upright, glancing out the window with complete composure.

"You seem remarkably cool about it," Suzy says.

"It was something that happened four months ago. That was the time to be upset. Nothing left to deal with now. Just hang on to the job for as long as I can."

"You're allowed to talk about it, you know."

"I'm sorry I didn't tell you. But please don't give me that look."

"It's just...Grace, you're allowed to be upset now, even if it *did* happen four months ago."

"Funny thing, thinking back again, about that dinner and that guy and what happened afterward. I moved to New York, dated some, met Mike. It feels like it happened fast even though it didn't, like there was almost a straight line from him to Mike."

"And *that* one you brought home to Mom and Dad," Suzy says.

"Mike Singer was born to be brought home to Mom and Dad."

The turnoff from Route 17 comes fast but familiar, and before Suzy's tapped the brakes, they're downtown, on Market, the Victorian-Gothic brick corridor awash in last light, the Eckerd Drug Store and Arbor Theater and Borelli's Pizza, where both girls worked as waitresses. It's only another minute before they've crossed the bridge over the Chemung and rolled up to the curb at 56 Cherry, but already the shadows have faded, screeded over the green yard and the pink trees and the blue house in such a manner that the onset of a full-force nostalgia flood is muted by the darkness.

Edith's into the yard before the trunk is shut, kissing her palms and throwing those palms to her daughters at the curb. Grace is wrapped up first, in a big storm of cooking apron and limbs, while Suzy braces for her turn.

"Where's Palmer?" Suzy says. Palmer has been first out the door since she can remember, the hundred-pound streak of white Lab skiing the porch and stairs like a downhill racer out of the gate. Mom moves on to Suzy and double-kisses her, something she's never done except when showing off to dinner party guests. She tells Suzy she looks remarkably radiant in spite of the drive.

"Mom, where's Palmer?"

Edith juts out her lower lip. "Girls, I'm sorry I'm telling you like this, but we had to put Palmer down."

They stand in silence. It hangs there the way a sliced finger does, flapped open in that dead moment before the blood comes, a moment just long enough to believe there might not be any blood at all.

"*What?!*" It's Grace. And then some new, warm tears. "What are you talking about?"

"He was *fourteen,*" Edith says. "And he couldn't get himself outside to go to the bathroom anymore." She's hugging Grace again.

"How long ago?" Suzy says. Edith pats Grace's head, caught up in the mothering duty, one at a time. Suzy's getting frustrated. "How long ago did the dog die, Mom?"

"The week after you left."

"That was almost three months ago!"

"You don't call us back, you don't come home enough, so we—"

"We've called since May!"

"I can't believe he's *gone,*" Grace says into Edith's hair.

"You don't have a new one, do you?" Suzy says.

"Of course not, sweetie," Edith says. "But your father may finally let me get a cat."

Wayne's standing on the porch with the screen door propped wide, drying his hands with a dishtowel. Suzy skips up the lawn, drops her weekender in the entryway, and hugs him hard. They're the same height—head, shoulders, waist, legs—which made it easy for Wayne to pass along sports equipment to Suzy as she grew.

"How was the drive?"

"Oh, fine, easy, average time."

"How 'bout the flight? What's it like to get paid instead of paying?"

"It's good, Dad. It's just like Grace described it—some dickhead passengers but otherwise an adventure, and for money."

"Need me to get in anyone's face for you?"

"Don't insult me."

Wayne shows a wide, yellow, crooked smile with a gap between 8 and 9 you could drive a station wagon through.

"I'm gonna run this to my room and then I'll catch you up."

"Mom told you about Palmer?" Wayne says as Suzy takes the stairs.

"She wouldn't have if we hadn't forced her to."

"It's been hard."

"Why didn't you tell us?"

"You've got your things out there. You're living your life."

"That dog's been a family member for over half that life!"

"It was better for you to keep on. It was a long run. As far as those things go, it was okay."

"I did get a proper good-bye in May."

"See, that's good."

"Fed him the entirety of my leftover moussaka the morning I left."

"Mom was wondering where it went."

"I needed to make sure I made weight at stew school."

"Maybe that's what killed him."

"What a terrible thing to say."

"You can take it. You didn't kill him. Fourteen winters killed him."

"Mom says there's gonna be a cat?"

"Don't even start."

"That'd be disgusting."

"You will learn one day that not all things are worth fighting for."

"But that should be one of them."

"Trust me, there are other things."

"We haven't eaten since the plane."

"Good thing we're almost up."

Suzy hears Edith narrating the garden's new flowers to Grace. Peruvian lilies. Zinnias. Orange and yellow tulips. Suzy carries her bag upstairs to her room, second on the right, above the kitchen—the room she made her own once Grace was long gone. It's just as she left it—not just in May, but in August four years ago, August '68, August freshman year. A couple vestigial stuffed animals. The quilt Grandma Whitman overstitched in anticipation of an early teenage winter. The movie poster for *Grand Prix,* James Garner and Eva Marie Saint. The black-and-white photos of the real-life racers—Graham Hill, Jim Clark, Jackie Stewart, and the American champ, Dan "The Man" Gurney, son of Port Jefferson, the home-state hero when Formula One rolled through Watkins Glen for the Grand Prix. The fact of their presence—their world-class-ness and cosmopolitanism—just up the road from Suzy's home always seemed a received privilege. But since she's been gone, it strikes her as closer to astonishing. That these racing champions (the finest, fastest, most self-sure legends of international motorsports) would come to the Glen each year (after Monaco and Monza and Spa) and sign ticket stubs for Suzy, their royally glamorous English wives cowering in face of the upstate enthusiasm—it made no sense. And yet it had been built into the logic of her life.

Dinner is a dinner they've shared hundreds of times growing up: four rib eyes from Mel Forman's butcher shop, summer vegetables out of the garden, and the rice pilaf recipe that was handed down from an uncle of Wayne's who'd been to the Middle East during the Great War. Grace sees the cuts of beef seasoned on the counter and informs her parents that she's become a vegetarian. They regard her blankly, careful that the first reaction doesn't spoil an opportunity to bring her back from the edge. But before they get in a word, Grace snorts and smiles: "Just kidding, not even me, guys—bridge too far."

After throwing the steaks on the Weber and dishing up the sides while they cook through, the four arrange themselves in their usual spots in the orange kitchen, beneath the cuckoo clock and the family of ficuses suspended from the ceiling.

"We haven't done this since graduation," Wayne says. "The grill always looked sad with three, and sadder with two."

"Don't you have the Morrisons over anymore?" Suzy says.

"They've been in Maine most of the summer."

"Do you cook every night?"

"We go into town more than we used to."

"You wouldn't believe how many restaurants have opened up," Edith says.

"Three?" Grace says.

"Yes, three, exactly."

"Oriental, Mediterranean, and Barbecue," Wayne says.

"We have a nice little rotation," Edith says.

"How does Sam feel about it?" Suzy says, meaning their old boss at Borelli's.

"It's been ages since we've been in," Edith says.

"We should stop by and pay our respects," Suzy says.

"Enough of this—tell me where you've been," Edith says. "I can hardly keep up."

The girls look at each other, neither eager to lead off. "Well," Grace says, "I went to San Francisco twice last week, Seattle on Saturday, Honolulu at some point."

"You went to *Hawaii* again?" Edith says.

"Suzy went, too. Last week."

"Oh my God, how did you not tell us? We've always wanted to go," Edith says. She has a long face and the same butter-colored hair as Grace, and she keeps it shoulder length still. She's running her fingers down to the ends, like she tends to after a big meal. "It was never in the cards with Dad's work. But we've got to make it. Maybe this winter." Edith looks at Wayne for a nod of team accordance, but he only offers a tight smile and cuts a slice of rib eye thin enough to serve as a microscope slide.

"We can probably get you something," Grace says. "Maybe if you're flying standby. Maybe even standby on both legs, New York–L.A.–Honolulu, something funky."

"I thought Honolulu was only for senior girls," Edith says.

"Someone called in sick," Suzy says. "Fill-in. Night in the Royal Hawaiian."

"It's pink like a cake, isn't it?"

"Some cakes, I guess," Suzy says. "Pink like a pink hotel."

"How magnificent. Did you swim?"

"I swam, I sat on the beach, I read a book and drank a drink with an umbrella."

"Did you meet any men?"

"I meet men every day," Suzy says.

"Go on...."

"I met dozens of men on my way to Hawaii and dozens of men on my way back. Some of them are married and some are single, most of them are employed, and all seem to have robust self-confidence. At least on the surface. Oh, and they feel their coach ticket entitles them to a share of any woman's ass."

"Suz, c'mon," Grace says.

"Girls, how's your steak?" Wayne says, acting as though there are fingers in his ears.

Grace, stuck chewing, shows an A-OK with her free hand.

"I'm not dating anyone, if that's what you mean," Suzy says.

"But she's getting on just fine," Grace says. "Slipped right into the groove out there."

"I still can't believe we haven't been out to see you. It can't truly be the way you say it is."

"Come for Christmas," Grace says.

"We couldn't."

"Why not?" Grace says.

"You know why—Nana and Pop and Jack and Mary and your cousins, what—"

"They can do one without you," Grace says.

"I'm sure we'd love it, but I don't know if this is the year."

"Well, how 'bout if Suzy and I make a pact not to come home?"

"You can't do that."

"Suz?"

"You should come out," Suzy says.

"We've never not done Christmas here," Edith says.

"Start of a new tradition," Grace says.

"You're not meaning to suggest this is the first of many...."

"I'm not going anywhere," Grace says.

"But you won't fly forever," Edith says.

"See if they can stop me."

"But when you and Mike decide..."

"We're not having children."

"Don't even joke about that."

"I'm serving Jack and soda till my skin's sagging off my face. I'm going down with the ship."

"Why do you *enjoy* this so much?" Edith says to both of them.

"'Cause it's so *easy*," Suzy says.

Edith drifts, staring at the wallpaper as though mentally testing out a change of color. Her skin is so white and so soft, her lipstick is playing-card red. She makes herself up like the women in *Yankee* magazine.

"You don't mean the thing about the babies," Edith says.

"How 'bout we reconsider if you come to Sela for Christmas?" Grace says.

"This is cruel."

"I'll come," Wayne says.

The girls rap their cutlery on the table in victory.

"Is that right?" Edith says, frowning.

"I'm in."

"You won't be able to come back here," Grace says. "The first taste is free...."

"The first taste of what?" Edith says.

"Freedom from an upstate winter," Suzy says.

"I love Christmas in the snow," Edith says.

Grace tosses her vegetables with her fork and knife. "That's a sure sign of denial."

The next morning Wayne and Suzy head to the racetrack. Wayne is fuzzy. After three or four glasses of scotch, he played the piano till midnight, around which point he slumped on the bench into the shape of a croissant and bowed out midsonata. Still, he rose early, picked blackberries off the bushes in the yard, made pancakes and eggs, and brewed black coffee, and they sat around the dining room table and did it all over again, the four in harmony in a way that was beginning to make Suzy anxious.

"You and Mom seem particularly even keeled. Not a single tiff last night about work hours, the television, drinking…"

"I've been cutting back to a pretty reasonable nine-to-five," Wayne says. "And I've been taking the sailboat out a little more. It's been a nice summer. Lovely weather."

"Does Mom go with?"

"Sometimes."

"Which lake?"

"Keuka usually. We've even stopped by a couple of the vineyards up on the hills above the lake. At Cayuga and Seneca, too. It's been a funny summer—with you wrapping things up at school and taking the job you did, Mom and me not having terribly firm plans. And work being pretty regular."

"What do you mean, me taking the job I did?"

"Just you starting work."

"You didn't mean '*that* job that you took'?"

"All I meant was, your mom and me, we never thought it through this far. It was the war, then a wedding, then one girl, then a second girl, then planning to just keep those two plates spinning for as long as we possibly could. Then suddenly you had a diploma and that was that."

"But this job *is* very weird."

"It sounds like you like it."

"But you couldn't have imagined me..."

"Is that what you want me to say?"

"I certainly couldn't have."

"I guess I'd never really thought of what it would be. You weren't interested in being a doctor or engineer, so I suppose I wrote those off—but nothing else would've surprised me. You were endlessly capable."

"But this is a little weird."

"I don't know."

"No, I'm saying it: it's a little weird. Especially being back here—it slams everything into context. Everything that had built to whatever. The good grades and the books and the racing—that was building toward something. And then one day it wasn't. And I was in training and then at the beach and everything's sort of reset its frame of reference. I'm sure it happened with Grace, too, but that's one of her defining qualities: she can wake up each morning in a new situation and immediately adopt its sights and smells and standards of practice as though they're her own...."

"Mm-hmm."

"I don't know what I'm saying. I guess what I mean is being here all of a sudden makes me realize how strange it is that I've started to regard all that ridiculousness out there as totally normal."

"Maybe for someone like Grace and someone like you—and I don't mean to suggest that that's the same person—but maybe for girls like you it *is* normal to make it work wherever you end up. I couldn't have done it, your mother couldn't have done it. But what's so strange about it being possible for you? I mean, what're we even talking about that's so strange?"

"I don't know. It's not, like, 'surfing' or 'burritos' or something like that. It's that so many of them have only known the one thing. It's like they don't realize how different they are. How alien the entire mise-en-scène is..."

"The what?"

"The arrangement of everything. The setting, the characters, the dialogue, the *ambitions*. So many of them have only Sela. Apparently, they grew up only learning California history—and *bad* California history at that. They have no sense of what's going on anywhere else. What the rest of the country and the world are about—some of them haven't even ever left California before."

"There are people here who haven't been on an airplane, Suzy."

"But we'd at least driven to Pennsylvania! I just mean, they were born into this bright, quiet little world and never even had to be convinced of their exceptional good fortune. They're just like, '*Duh*, we know, dude.'"

"It sounds charming," Wayne says. "And I want you to know I'm serious about Christmas."

"Oh, I can tell you are. You said it twenty times at the piano last night. Good luck with Mom."

"Nothing would make me happier than to be outside in the sun on Christmas."

"It's not just 'be outside,'" Suzy says. "It's actually *go to the beach*, from what I'm told."

"I take that back: nothing would make me happier than missing one year of coq au vin with Nana and Pop and the greater Rochelles."

"I feel like it'd be breaking the law or something."

"Oh, it will definitely be a thing. It will be an irrevocable statement. A breaking apart into Before and After. And it is something that I'm happy to engage in. More doing, less talking—that's what we're after."

"This is what I mean—there's something up with you."

He considers this for a moment and then starts, quietly: "Your mother and I started trying... The Weed."

"Stop it."

"It's very, very groovy, if you ask me."

"Stop."

"Us and the Morrisons. Saturday nights in the basement. We *groove out.*"

"You don't say that anymore."

"What's the word, then?"

"I don't know anything about drugs."

At the racetrack they head halfway up the bleachers near the finish line, where they used to sit among the eighty thousand during the Grands Prix. Suzy drifts her eyes from the starting grid across the bobbing asphalt to the hard uphill right of turn one, from which the cars disappear onto the far side of the course. She moves, in her mind, through the languorous esses of turns two, three, and four, out onto the back straight, kicking up through the chicane and into the heavy Gs of the Loop, downhill through the Chute and into the downshifting speed trap of the Big Bend, and finally into the final ninety and the sprint to the line. She relishes the way the track feels to her eyes, the natural flow. Suzy could race with a blindfold. She could picture the track from a hundred vantages at once. From up high, to a bird, she always imagined it looking like a discarded garden hose.

Seeing the track for the first time in a year, she is reminded of something she read during the spring semester, something Camille had given her to look at. Rodin, it said, had regarded sculpture as the incantation by which the soul of man was brought down into stone, the awakening of stones. To capture a man's soul in stone, to imprison it there for centuries—that was the point. Or, in the case of someone like Michelangelo, the point was to strip away excess stone to reveal the figure that had been enclosed therein all along.

Suzy considers the track here—this site of her adolescence, the endless circuitry of one long race stitched across several summers—to be a sort of sculpture. She always felt this way, she realizes now; she just didn't have the language. Whether she ever articulated it to her parents or her sister or her friends, it felt as though she was, on a daily basis, in communion with something very much alive, something living but trapped in asphalt. She had always regarded the track as the variable—the dynamic thing. She, Suzy Whitman, stayed the same, while the track changed, in near-missable ways, each day. The same chemical elements, the same order of turns, the same pitch and roll—but shifting ever so slightly in the light, in the rain, in the heat and cold. Just barely breathing: a prone body rising and falling in sleep.

A pair of race cars, a red 3 and a blue 6, turn onto the flat and sprint across the start line, accelerating into the next lap, where the intention is not to beat the other but to beat the course, a victory defined by besting one's own top time. As the cars pass—two years sleeker than they looked her last run on the track, with shaved wings, a longer nose, a narrower cockpit—Suzy keeps the inquiry alive: is it really the track that possesses the soul, or is it the car? Those sculptures of physical dynamics. Modulating each year, applying the trickle-down advancements of the Formula One engineers. Maybe the Glen twitches in subtle ways—but the cars really are altered. The cars move in a modern direction. They *advance*. And they push the envelope until someone dies. Bandini at Monaco. Schlesser at Rouen-les-Essarts. Death on the racetrack defined the end of one avenue of progress and forced man and his mechanic to explore another.

Suzy hears Red and Blue on the backstretch, the faint racing drone of cicadas, and then they appear over the grid again, another loop, as fast as Suzy's ever seen a lap clocked outside of the Grand Prix. How was Suzy never afraid of dying?

"These guys are *moving*," she says.

"I think they're the kids from Connecticut that the guys in the garage have been talking about. Live way out on the sound but come over here to stretch out."

As they vanish again out of turn one, the track quivers. She can barely detect it but knows it's there, finds it by looking through it—like the fluttering gas from a stovetop. Like a guitar string that seems to have stopped making sound but hasn't. The track moves with the fescue of the infield and the pines at the edges.

"You gonna come home for the Grand Prix this year?" Wayne says.

"I dunno," Suzy says. "I mean, I wasn't planning on it, but maybe if I'm here with work. Getting home's just that much farther than convenient, ya know? Plus, I haven't been following any results this year."

"Ah, me neither, not much. I saw that Emerson Fittipaldi won in Belgium and England. And that Mario Andretti started a few races at the beginning of the season."

"Bored of Indy."

"Guess so."

Suzy hears a new engine rev in the concealed pit lane. She's surprised to see so much action on a weekday morning. She used to run in the evenings, once Wayne was home from the glassworks. He wouldn't even head into the house. He'd pull up to the curb and throw open the door and tease her by pulling away ever so slowly so that she'd have to chase after him and hop into the moving car like a double-0 agent. Palmer would follow her to the curb, obedient to the property line, and they would play out the scene on repeat every weeknight from June to September.

That new car appears at the end of the pit lane and merges onto the course where turn one dumps out, a little shaky shifting, from what Suzy can hear. The red 3 and the blue 6 whip wide onto the outside lane of the homestretch and hit the line moving even better than before.

"They're in a nice fight, too," Wayne says as Red clips the inside and retains the lead out of turn one. "That little guy that just went out better keep close eyes on his mirrors."

"Hey," Suzy says, "there's something I want to let you guys know about, not 'cause it's a big deal, but just 'cause it's a thing, and I feel like I've been bad about keeping you up."

"Oh yeah?"

"We had a close call last week," she says. "Almost had one of those hijackings."

"You're kidding me."

"I mean, I guess when you do the math, it shouldn't be that surprising, there've been so many this year, but it took me by surprise a little. I just sort of figured that thing would fade out."

"Christ, what happened?"

"Guy on the flight back from Hawaii. As soon as we were off the ground, he gave one of the other stews a note. Note said he wanted to talk to the pilot and that he had a gun and that he'd shoot up the plane if the message wasn't relayed and the demands weren't met. So Marion, the stew, took it to the pilot, and the pilot waved the guy up, and when the guy knocked at the door, the pilot opened it and punched him in the face. Knocked him flat. First-class passengers screaming. Pilot on top of him, punched him again, knocked him out. Took his pistol. Cleared out the back row and tied him to the seat. Flew to L.A. just like that."

"Good Lord. What a maniac. Both of them, sounds like."

"I read a bunch about hijackings afterward—I mean, more than I had already. Went to the library, read some papers from a couple years back. Guess the guy made some classic mistakes: said he had a gun instead of a bomb, said he was acting alone instead of with partners on the plane, didn't even make his demands real clear up front."

"What did he want?"

"He didn't say at the time, but they got it afterward: wanted to go to Vietnam."

"Why didn't he just enlist?"

"I think he had something wrong mentally. Younger guy. Actually from Hawaii. Hadn't been on an airplane before. Wanted to go and try to help get people out or something. Very unclear, not the best-laid plans."

"He didn't want money?"

"Never got that far. But apparently, he'd had plans for a while to start a church-gym combo thing."

"That makes sense."

"The captain—this was his third this year. He was fed up. Took it real personally. Looks like he might actually face discipline, though. You're not supposed to take things into your own hands."

"The captain really might get in trouble?"

"Hard to say. I have to give a statement. He kinda broke down with me in the back after it happened. Said that they'd be out for him. I don't know, but the more I read, I'm guessing he won't catch flak for the first punch. Maybe not even the second. But he gave the guy an elbow to the face as he walked back to the cockpit, after the guy was tied up."

"You don't have to mention that one."

"He winked at me after he did it."

"Good," Wayne says.

"Dad, I'm kidding."

"I woulda been okay with that. What do you know about him? He fly in the war?"

"He said something about Korea. He's a little younger than you. Mulaney. Jack Mulaney."

"He an ace?"

"Guessing maybe not, considering he's flying Grand Pacific."

"What I woulda given."

"You wanted to be a fighter pilot and an astronaut. Not a lifer on the Phoenix to Dallas."

"No, but I'll take Honolulu to Los Angeles."

Suzy's not sure why she's always made an effort to make her father feel better about it. It's not like he tried and failed; he didn't even beat the eye exam. He doesn't need her, she knows, to reframe the short-comings of Wayne Whitman, nineteen-year-old.

"Well, thanks for telling me. Upsets the hell out of me that you went through that."

"Yeah, just a little unsettling." Suzy has thought about it on and off since it happened—why it hasn't affected her more. It was contained, but it was cool. No rerouting. No deboarding. All over in fifteen minutes. It made her want to start her flight lessons all the sooner. Plus, the way even Ruth and Marion handled it—not quite business as usual, but devoid of frayed nerves. They just carried on afterward, taking orders and pouring drinks, deaf to the peril. "But it also adds a little gravity to the work, ya know? They'd told us all about it in training, but I'd never really thought it was a real possibility. Makes me respect the girls more. Plus, I'm not opposed to a little buzz."

"Be that as it may, I don't like it for you. And I especially don't like it for your sister. Jesus, I don't know if I can even tell Mom."

"I'll tell her. If Grace hasn't already by the time we get back. I'll tell her minus some details."

Blue has overtaken Red and nips him by a couple lengths as they move across the line. This time they wind down the engines, signaling the end of the ride. They corner into turn one at half speed and settle into a cool-down lap. After Green powers through the homestretch again, he loses his grip in one and jars a wheel loose on the turn's exit. Suzy and Wayne grimace at each other, and then there's a vacuum of sound on the track. No danger, but no action, either.

Suzy fixes her eyes on the careless growth of grasses and shrubs at the fringe of the track, the spotty forest that's been cut down so often it fails to grow properly, like overplucked eyebrows. The circuit rests on top of a hill, perched there around the edges of the crown in the manner of a monk's haircut. It has always been such a spectacular space for her—the site of such pleasure. But now, as a quilt of fog slips between the sun and the hilltop, the color is drained from the scene and she begins to regard the optics as pretty beat. A shiver seizes her. In the onset of gray, Suzy feels summer ending prematurely, death in the trees, Wayne's cool edge to the heat. It's a terrible sensation in July. For thousands of years the mightiest empire in North American history made living here seem easy. And for three generations of Whitmans and Rochelles, it was easy enough, too. But in the instant of a cloud crossing between the sun and Suzy—the instant of the shadow—Suzy knows she'll never live here again.

On the way home the mood carries over. They make stops at the model-train shop and the liquor store, where Wayne picks up refreshers of Macallan and Beefeater.

"While we're at it," he says as they exit the highway, drawing up a conversation that ended an hour ago, "I mean, while we're talking about things like airplane hijackings and stuff the other might not love to hear, there's something I've been meaning to mention, and I'm starting to feel guilty about spending the day with you and not saying it. Even though I'd rather tell you and your sister at the same—"

"Dad."

"There's been some bad news."

"Worse than Palmer?"

Suzy's turned her body a full ninety, so that she sees the sad grin split his face. "That's up to you, but I'd say worse than Palmer."

"Dad?" Suzy's voice cracks like a little girl's. It disgusts her. Her distaste for the sound she makes crowds out the acid she feels beneath her skin in anticipation. She knows already, it seems, and now she's already trying to defeat it, to play offense against the news that still isn't spoken.

"Last couple months I've had some back pain. No-big-deal soreness. The kind of sore you get from a weekend of yard work. Chopping wood, overhead painting, and what have you. But I hadn't been doing anything like that. Nothing but glass. Some sailing, like I said. And so I went and got it checked out. Doc thinks it's a little strange, wants to do some tests. Does a *bunch* of tests. They take a picture of my back, the whole thing. And turns out I've got a tumor wrapped up around my spine. And evidently that tumor is cancerous."

"What...does that even mean?"

"I have a tumor, on my spine, that is malignant. I have cancer on my spine."

"I don't even...what are they going to do about it?"

"Well, listen, hon, the thing is four inches, and it's gripping my spine the way a fighter pilot puts his hand on the stick." And here he holds a tightly coiled fist in the space between them. "It's wrapped around my vertebrae and it's wrapped around my spinal cord and it's kinda seeping out and putting pressure on my ribs, that's really why I hurt. It's like someone dripped some pig iron down my back and it cooled into a little steel clamp right here," and he reaches over his shoulder and waves behind his wings, right behind his heart.

Suzy accepts that they are in motion and that they are passing the oak trees and mailboxes and root-veined sidewalks of a block she's covered thousands of times, on foot and on bike and in car, and yet she feels inexactly displaced, dropped in a current, an unfamiliar soup of colors and lines sweeping around her and through her without moving her along with it, like she's a rock on a river bottom.

"But what will they do to *fix* it?" she says.

"There aren't good options."

"What are you talking about? What are you saying?"

"They can't operate. The risk of severing the spine is too high. They can try radiation. The risk of frying my spinal cord could leave me paralyzed from the middle of my back down. Might affect my heart and lungs and other organs. Plus, all that stuff is expensive. Too expensive. Too expensive to really even comprehend. Other option is to just let it go. It's early. It's apparently a weird kind of cancer that's not terribly aggressive. They could try radiating it down so that it's smaller without a ton of pain. But it's not a real solution. It just sort of prolongs the inevitable. It's slow, that's the only good news."

"But you can survive this."

"The odds are quite low."

"Dad."

"There is a path to surviving this that leaves me without cancer and without grave consequences, but the odds are damned near nothing. I don't totally know what I want to do yet. Mom and I have been working it out for a few weeks, and I'm seeing the doctor Friday."

"Oh my God, I'm sorry." Her voice cracks again.

"I'm sorry, too, sweetie."

"I just—"

"I'm sorry I didn't tell you sooner. Mom tried calling a few times...."

Wayne passes their house and takes another loop through the neighborhood.

"I think you should do the thing that keeps you alive."

"It's complicated. I hear what you're saying, but there are many factors."

"I just don't understand how it can be any more complicated than trying to live."

"There's money, there's pain, there's quality of life."

"But you're good with pain. You burn your hands at work all the time. You cut off a finger and practically sewed it back on yourself. You broke a leg in a car crash."

"I appreciate the vote of confidence, I really do. But I'm just thinking on it still. Really, it's like this: I'm a B guy. I've always been a B-level guy. That's the life I was given and the life I led. I tried to make two A girls, but I'm a B guy with B luck, B options, and B means, you understand?"

"What the fuck are you talking about?"

"We don't get to have all the things at our disposal."

"It's money."

"Money is a factor that can't be ignored."

"What if money wasn't a factor?" Suzy says.

"It's never been a thought exercise your mother and I could really indulge."

"But what if you could do anything here?"

"I suppose I'd try surgery. The best surgeon, the one who might give me better than five percent odds. I'd try radiation. I'd hope that the radiation would eradicate the tumor and that I could still breathe and that my heart could still pump blood and that I'd be back to work on Monday after a weekend of R and R."

"That's why Mom was weird when you talked about coming to California for Christmas...."

Suzy has been distracting herself with the interrogation, forcing the issue in order to win a confession that there is indeed a solution that can be enacted. But when she shifts her attention, even just this much, to recall her parents' soft commitment to Christmas at the beach—it's what unzips her. She begins convulsing. She collapses into a pile and bobs with the timing of her sobs. She slams her hands onto the dashboard and then slams her forehead onto her hands. She *uh-huh-huh-huh*s. Real crying like she hasn't cried ever really. And then it's Palmer, and Grace not knowing, and Mom all alone in the house during a blizzard, a split bough kicking out the power for a week with no one around to light the lanterns on the back porch. Most of all, though, there's the thought of a life that continues on without her father, a life that hasn't even really gotten going, so far as Suzy's concerned, a life that's currently missing hard progress toward the things she's meant to do. He would miss all that stuff and never even know.

"It's okay, sweetie, it's okay, really. I'm not going anywhere. Not for a while, you hear me?"

"You're not allowed to go yet."

"Nothing's happened. I'm the same as I was twenty minutes ago. I'm good. Things could get worse, but they might get better. I'm gonna try it."

"You're gonna fucking *try*."

"C'mon now."

"That wasn't a question," she says, sniffling. "That was me being relieved to hear you say it. Thank you for trying. Thank you, thank you, thank you, thank you..." And they pull to the curb just a little late for dinner.

The girls planned to leave early, to get to the city around noon, to dip in at Macy's and log some hours at Grace's old spots in the Village, before crashing at a friend's apartment. But Wayne is taking his time making pancakes, says he's going to be a little late to work today. Even when they've had two, three, four each, he keeps pouring batter into the pan. He's making breakfast so that it doesn't end. It's a scene that played out twice a week every week for the duration of their childhood—pancakes in the kitchen, juice and coffee on the table, the slips and collisions and other nonnatural sounds of *The Pink Panther Show* or *The Flintstones* skipping from the living room like shimmering foil at the edges of the say-nothing breakfast patter.

Edith gestures toward the stack of papers near the window and mentions a story about the first Stones concert in New York—the first of four in three days—that took place Monday. "'Jagger and Stones Whip 20,000 Into Frenzy at Garden,'" she says, pointing to the front-page headline with the arch of her eyebrow. "Just...be careful."

"Mom," Grace says.

"I came to terms with it years ago," Edith says. "I'm okay with what I don't know. It's just when it's right in front of me—on the *front page.* That's when I get worked up."

"Seems like everyone survived," Grace says.

"You I'm not worried about. You're the survivor. It's...," and she thumbs.

"Me?" Suzy says.

"I'm not prejudiced against the Rolling Stones, if that's what you're thinking," Edith says. "I'm an equal-opportunity worrier. Every day of yours at the racetrack—and every night of your sister's in New York City. It's really one and the same to me."

"We raised an adventurous pair," Wayne says from across the counter in the kitchen. "Who are, it's important to come to terms with, well past the turn-back point."

"We really don't need any more," Edith says, meaning the pancakes, "unless you're making them for later."

"I'm making them for now, and later, and we'll throw out whatever's left, but I'm not done yet."

He places a new batch in the center of the table and then takes a couple steps back to fit all three women in a frame.

"We did a good job," he says. Grace bites the edge of her glass of orange juice. "It's all been good when you think about it."

"Jesus Christ! *Dad!* Please stop fucking talking in the past tense!"

"Gracie!" Edith says.

"He's talking like this is the last time we're ever going to be here together!"

Wayne told Grace last night.

"I'm just taking a good long look at you guys and feeling proud."

"Okay, but *please.* Just, like, quit it with the pancakes! We all know what's going on. Please can we just treat today like we always do? We're here, great! We'll be back when we're back! We'll see you next time! It's normal!" She rises to her feet and makes her way toward the living room. "Suzy, we're going. Just like we always go. At the time that we planned to go. And we'll see you soon. Same old same old."

"C'mon, Grace," Suzy says. "We'll head out in a minute. Just take a seat."

"I'm gonna go pack."

"Gracie, sit down," Edith says.

Grace stands in the doorframe and presses her arms out to both sides, the posture—the girls have learned in California—of earthquake safety. "I just don't understand why there isn't anything we can do."

"We're going to do something," Wayne says. "We're going to give it our best shot."

"We're going to do our best," Edith says.

"We're going to figure out the options, figure out the money, and you two will be part of every conversation."

"So long as you pick up our calls…," Edith says, raising her coffee mug to her lips.

Grace stares at her mother vacantly, energy too low to take the bait. "This just can't be it," she says in a whisper. "None of these things can be it. Let's just please not treat anything like it's the final time."

"We're not doing anything," Wayne says. "We're eating breakfast."

"Okay," Grace says. "Then let's get out of here. Thirty minutes tops. We always leave early 'cause you're always off to work."

"You're right, I'll get ready for work, and then you can follow me into town."

Suzy strategically returns to the article about the show: "'Jagger,'" she reads aloud, "'a strutting, swaggering Nureyev of a singer, tiptoed up to the edge of the stage and back, suddenly flinging himself into wild leaps and graceful spins as he sang.' Mom, you love Nureyev. Are you sure you don't want to come?"

"It does not say that," Edith says.

"Right here," Suzy says, handing it over. "Paper of record. It'll be just like *Swan Lake*."

Wayne insists, as he always has, on leading them to the highway, a tugboat to his daughters' rental car. He pulls to the shoulder at his turnoff, smiles, and salutes them as they roll on southeast. The minute that follows is long, nothing but rubber on blacktop and the metronome of highway seams. *Shoomp. Shoomp. Shoomp. Shoomp.*

"What the *fuck?*" Grace says softly.

"He's gonna be okay."

"But what if this doesn't work?"

"Then he dies."

"How can you say it like that?"

"Because you're asking sucky questions."

"What the hell is your problem?"

"You're not the only one hurting right now," Suzy says. "This isn't just your thing."

"Well, what am I *supposed* to do? Sweep it under the rug like Mom? Roll over like Dad? I don't even know what you're doing, but you're acting like the news was that the mail might not come today."

"Just 'cause I had my cry in the car before dinner doesn't mean I'm feeling less than you. I'm just... still thinking about it. There's gotta be some other option."

Suzy's done it for years now—positioned herself as the elder sister emotionally. Matched every tear of Grace's with a stoic dry eye. It's a point of pride that no one else cares for. But it's always been important to her. Especially after a broken levee like last night—a steady return to calm and clear, to the rational position. Suzy doesn't know shit about dealing with death, but she knows how to piss off her sister with her stoniness.

"You aren't gonna think yourself... into a better... place with this one," Grace says, tripping over the reproach because of a clogged throat. "He's sick and there's only one thing to do."

"But what are *we* supposed to do?"

"Maybe we can move back," Grace says.

"You don't want to move back."

"I could help Mom. We could help with the hospital. He's not gonna be able to work after surgery or radiation or whatever they decide to do."

"You're not moving back," Suzy says. "Mike won't live here. You don't even *like* it here."

"Then, what about you?"

"You're volunteering me?"

"What's your problem?" Grace says. "We could rotate. Ask to fly out, trade off weeks. Try to do all our off days out here, drive up and back."

"They didn't ask for our help."

"Well, what if I *want* to help? What if I *want* to be there?"

"Grace, no offense, but you've gone home, like, twice a year since high school—at least, when you're not getting married and I'm not graduating. It's not like you've spent all that much time there."

"Well, *Suzy*, the circumstances have fucking changed!"

The scenery out the window is the scenery that will be outside in five minutes and in thirty minutes and in three hours.

"I'm sorry, you're right," Suzy says. "You should do what you want. We should help. We should plan to be here, if that's useful to them. All I'm saying is, they seem to have it under control for now."

"They have literally *nothing* under control. They are in the worst position I can imagine."

"There's just…there's nothing we can do today. Coming home, sitting around there, it'll mean four sad people instead of two. Four people who suddenly aren't really working. Five if you include Mike. And until someone knows how we can help, we just have to keep at it as planned, you know? Just like you said."

"Mike said he'd move here. On the phone last night, when I told him, he said he'd move."

"He's a noble guy. You're very fortunate. I just don't know how right that is for you two."

"I thought it was sweet. It was the right thing."

"Do you think we should've stayed longer?" Suzy says.

"Dad wasn't gonna allow it. He's even more concerned than you are about missing out on things."

"We should've dragged him to the concert."

"We're not too far yet."

"Nah, you're right, stick to it," Suzy says. "That's Dad: Fidelity to the game plan, that's what wins races."

They crash in the Village, across the street from the park. It's an old roommate of Grace's, Rose, red lipstick and black hair and an

Alabama accent so much itself it sounds like bad acting. They met on an Allman Brothers tour, ended up in New York around the same time. Rose said it was 'cause she wanted to follow the culture, but Grace explained to Suzy on the way in that it was really because her husband was black. The place is smaller than Grace and Mike's. There's a pullout bed in the couch that comfortably sleeps one but that's capable of squeezing in two sisters who grew up sharing a room.

The windows look out onto the northwest corner of the park, and they've been open since June, Rose tells them, on account of the blackouts and air conditioner bans. Suzy stretches her head out and around the corner and glimpses the arch through the trees. She feels a heightening tide of interest in her sister, the contrasting awareness that someone she's known without gaps these last few days—and whom she knew without gaps growing up—could have come here in a huff of certitude and lived in all manner for *years* without Suzy really hearing much about it. Though Grace hardly spoke of her New York period to Suzy, it all just seemed to have transpired so naturally, so inevitably, that it had gone just as it would ever go. For Grace—and this is the point, the differentiation—there is never an anxiety of mislocation. The only place she could ever be is where she is.

Here now, there is this scene out the window. The corner of Waverly and Macdougal, sidewalk, trees, brownstones, park. Suzy feels a familiarity with it—not the precision of this vantage point, but a sort of cubist collage of all vantages onto the park. She begins to imagine the occupation of the frame out the window by everyone who's ever passed through it before. Everybody who's crossed that intersection, every kiss on the corner, every trumpet solo at the benches along the walking path—all layering in composite. That interconnectedness, the density and overlap, the city's suggestion of constancy, of relatedness, of infinity. And Gracie amidst it all, carving out her existence. Or whatever she did here. It's a lot to process—every body in all of time all at once. And for a little while the exercise crowds out the beacon at the edge of the frame, that bright light Suzy's spent the car ride attempting to ignore. But now that it's been invoked—explicitly ignoring it only brings it forward—it shows itself in full, a marquee in neon:

DAD IS DYING
DAD IS HALFWAY DEAD

Rose is home now and she's animated about market produce—strawberries, blueberries, peaches. But she quickly pivots to the concert. Rose heard about the tour on the radio in the spring. The terms were clear: there would be a postcard lottery, and those who won the lottery had the opportunity to stand in line to buy tickets. She sent in a few postcards with her name, address, and number—and then several dozen others with her friends' and family's names and addresses, but her phone number still. In the end the Garden received over a half million postcard requests, and Rose, she wound up with three winners, twelve tickets scattered throughout the arena and spread across the last two dates. She went the night before and earmarked this pair for Grace. Which is how Grace and Suzy wind up dusting makeup across their faces and heading out the door, a door so wet with heat Suzy has to dig her heels into the mat to pull it shut. They hit the street a little after seven.

In order to avoid the congealing cab traffic around MSG and the furnace of the subway, they walk from Waverly Place. It takes a half hour, passing over to Sixth Avenue and up into the edge of the West Village and Chelsea and finally Herald Square. Every glimpse south, the two towers, nearly complete, leering twins. Grace says she'd watched them grow from stumps. At almost every corner there is a direction—north or west—with a blinking walk sign, and even when there's not, there is a gap in the traffic, such that it's possible to eat up blocks without stopping even once. Grace leads Suzy into the street as though all accumulated habits from the past seven months—all that Sela-brand behavior—had simply been borrowed on short lease, had had no effect on her bearings in New York. At the busier intersections a battalion from their curb meets a battalion from the opposite side, and without stutter-stepping or even meeting eyes, one slips past the other with zero contact.

As they inject themselves into a capillary off Herald Square, the foot traffic has trouble passing unmoving cabs on their way to the beating heart at Seventh Avenue, cabs and town cars with transmissions in neutral, a sense of the imminent failure of blood-pumping Penn Plaza. It's a half hour before Stevie Wonder is due on and it's still light out. There are shirtless men, some in body paint and frosted sparkles, someone in a loincloth and top hat, colored bandanas and sleeveless tees with The Tongue, necks and arms and stomachs with a half summer's tan, girls on the shoulders of boys, looking the police horses in the eye.

The crowds gathered in the plaza fail to find lanes to the checkpoints—past the drug dealers and the scalpers selling six-dollar tickets for fifty. The flow is slow, and in frustration fights erupt and arrests are made. Though it feels like movement is futile, Grace is convinced it's gonna work out—this is the fourth show in three days, it's worked out before. Only in faith of slow certain progress do they find their way to the first security checkpoint, and then the second, third, and fourth—where staff collect wineskins and champagne bottles—before funneling at last into the mouth of the arena. Dante's fifth circle, Suzy says. There wasn't much cool air to breathe on the outside, but it's altogether absent as they press deeper.

Grace had shoved the flask she brought down the front of her underwear, right beneath the zipper of her jeans, a spot security elected not to frisk. And so Grace and Suzy head to the bathroom to take swigs. It's lazy on the floor, thick and anxious, the uncomfortable hum of a hometown crowd after a visiting slugger's grand slam. It's a distended anticipation before Stevie, whose set is only the signal that it'll be that much longer until the main draw. And yet in that time distance before the show, most of the men are still walking around—to get malt balls, to buy beers—with Jagger hips thrust forward and Jagger mouths pursed. Everywhere the strut and the pout.

In the bathroom the sinks are for blow and the stalls are for smack. Finishing a flask, it seems, is meant to be done in the white light of the concourse.

"We can just drink at our seats," Suzy says.

Grace shakes her head like Suzy's missed the point and pulls a tightly wound plastic sandwich bag of cocaine from her bra.

"Where'd you get that?" Suzy says, and Grace says Rose had leftovers from the night before. *We've never done this together,* Grace intimates with a look, *and time is, as we've learned this week, rather precious.* Suzy keys enough to satisfy Grace and wonders if any of the people here are using the blow she brought from Sela. As the bump hits her brain, she seizes on the thought: it's empowering, her magnitude, her capacity to affect a big thing. She rolls into the arena, her feet like racing wheels, her brain holding a new thought, a thought she's had before, the same thought she had the first time she tried coke at Vassar, which is, *Oh right, this stuff really does work.*

Their seats are stage left, at the preliminary ascent of the lower bowl. They're pretty good seats for a concert, but they'd be even better for a Knicks game. All Suzy can really make out are the sunglasses and the shirt at the piano, rainbow scales like a freshwater fish. The memory of the set, Suzy knows in the moment, will be stripped down to that shirt and Stevie's Clavinet. Rainbow scales and the *wah-wah* of that electric piano, left hand on the Clav like a bullhorn of rhythm. Each time Wonderlove moves into a new song, she forgets the previous one, all except for "Superstition" because it's the last.

Stevie bows, with an allusion to possibly being back later, and as the lights come up, the crowd continues to dance, stomping the seats to no beat but the memory of that *wah-wah*. No music but the effortful rhythm from the clap-and-stomp of the section across the court.

"I need to pee," Grace says, the meaning of which is ambiguous to Suzy, who follows her. No point coming down in the middle of a Stones concert, and so Suzy digs in with her painted pinkie nail, hits both nostrils. The way Grace smiles—wide enough to hurt—and the way she just hangs there watching Suzy, failing to dial that smile back to sane, convince Suzy that Grace has not ever loved her quite as much as now. *"This is fun!"* Grace says twice without space for a response, and then they chase out when some ladies in headdresses demand they share.

"This is good, this is fun," Grace says again at their seats, swigging from the flask and rolling her hand in a soft demand for Suzy to do the same.

Grace is dancing to some memory of a beat, hands above her head, hair shaken out into her face, lips and hips clicking to a four-four.

"What song is that?" Suzy says, joking.

"I don't know. All of them."

Suzy closes her eyes and moves to the same thump, and soon, somewhere in that black moment when she's not seeing, the sound in her head becomes the sound of twenty thousand attempting to will a beginning with its rhythm. An unflinching beat—hands clapping above heads, and feet on concrete steps; the punching of an uncountable number of beach balls like a Drunk 'n' Draw rally that has no shot at ending. Two minutes, three minutes of antici—

And then the lights drop on the upbeat, and the plinkings in minor of a Halloween sound track prompt the "Ladies and Gentle-men…"—and then they appear—"the Rolling Stones!" Some shad-ows stumble into position, followed by this little streak of white skipping across the backdrop like the reflected light off a watch face. And so the band is playing without any buildup—enough's been had—and they're thirty seconds in, and then they're a minute into "Brown Sugar," and it's a Bobby Keys solo, which is about when Suzy stops thinking about the fact that she's seeing the Rolling Stones for the first time and starts experiencing it, a distinction that only makes it more difficult not to sit above herself in row 16 and watch her-self watching, watch herself watching herself drunk and high, in all ways elevated an inch or two out of her skin, a feedback loop of self-consciousness that's exitable only when she starts watching Grace, who, she supposes, has never had trouble experiencing an experience before.

There really is a moment—right between "All Down the Line" and "Midnight Rambler"—when she is listening, having stepped up and onto her seat, off the ground like Grace and everyone around them, dancing on her two-by-two-foot cushion stage, and fully inside her-self, a pipeline between the guitar solos and the liquid slink of her body, when it is being processed as a personal thing, twenty thousand people each with their personal things, too. And then white lights, arranged like cannons on the stage, slam the ceiling, where more white lights come raining down. Suzy fixates on the white above, which turns out not to be lights at all, but Mylar mirrors reflecting the audience. No one seems to notice, but deeper, a half hour later, it happens again, white light into the space-paper reflectors, which begin rotating slowly and showing the crowd back to itself. The audi-ence screams in response, as if fully realizing its size and its presence in this place, before that stage and those men, proof, more or less, that they, the twenty thousand, exist.

The rest feels like being sprayed by a fire hose, maybe four or five more songs, with a communal "Happy Birthday" to Mick, cake and all with twenty-nine candles, a food fight with custard pies. During "Jumpin' Jack Flash," Mick shovels rose petals onto the fans in the front row, blowing kisses, whipping his arms in windmills. When the light catches him right, it's possible to make out the nubs of his ribs, even from a distance, accented by the plunge of his blouse. Eventually a version of "Street Fighting Man" that fails to end — this collective will, it seems, of the crowd, pushing the bouncing ball on the sheet music along, run after run, in order that it not resolve in the Keef-and-Charlie wind-down and Mick bow. And though it's over, they come back. They play one of Stevie's songs. They play "Satisfaction." And then the stage is cleared, and because she read about it in the paper this morning, Suzy knows what happens next: the band members ride the waves of the sealing Keef chord off the stage and into the concrete corridors to the town cars underground, each of the seven onstage dripping sweat, none more than Mick, wrapped in whatever costume has been appropriate for the encore, and in less time than it would take to perform one more song, they're out on the street, off to Mick's birthday party, rolling through illuminated darkness, as though anything that just transpired might not have happened at all. And back inside, with the lights high and the mirrors still swirling, Suzy finds herself, a white grub in a pointillist garden, and she asks Grace for one more bump before facing the exit, where they'll stand without patience, pushing out as they pushed in, but with nothing to look forward to on the other side.

They debate skipping the subway again but decide to funnel down and wait for the D at Herald Square, one long express stop to the apartment. The platform is crowded, as hot as the arena and smelling a little worse. Suzy insists that wherever they end up next — they accept the reality that neither of them is falling asleep for hours—should have more favorable light than this station to hide their streaky mascara and the sweat stains in their halter tops. Then they hang there quietly, waiting, privately yet simultaneously accepting the new reality that there is nowhere deeper they can escape to and there is nothing left to keep them from considering it head-on. When it comes to Wayne's news, they are in the place beyond deferment.

They stand at the edge of the tracks, peering into the tunnel every couple minutes, looking for the first faint suggestion of headlights. When it comes, theirs is a graffiti train, tagged from nose to tail. "The D originates in the Bronx," Grace says by way of explanation. Once aboard, they stand against the doors and Grace sticks her hand out the open window, trying to touch the wind without touching the wall.

They sit together in the park, near the arch and the fountain, near the frame Suzy imagined all of New York passing through while she watched from Rose's apartment window. They recap the entirety of the show, once and then again and again. And as they wind down, as there is less to say, Wayne creeps in once more. Wayne center stage. *The place beyond deferment.*

And it is awash in the acceptance of his presence there that Suzy is seized by the beginning of an idea—something she knows she could do, because she's already proven herself capable of doing it. Something she could do to solve the problem. But for now, with earliest light threading into the sky, she explores the idea without consigning herself to it, the way she can sing along to the Rolling Stones without meaning the words. The idea will be considered more fully once she sobers up, banks some sleep, gets back west.

They're in California the next day. And the first moment she's alone, when Grace and Mike head out for lunch together, Suzy calls Billy from the airline phone. She asks him what he's doing and he says, "A lot of the usual," which she takes to mean he's free. She asks to meet up with him, and he suggests a bench at Twelfth, right on the Strand.

"No," Suzy says. "Let's meet inside."

"There's nothing you can do inside that ain't better outside."

"Jesus," Suzy says. "Let's at least meet on the sand, then."

Thirty minutes later they're sitting near a bank of ice plant, facing the water, matching skateboards spiked side by side.

"What's up?" Billy says. "Why down here?"

"There's too many people walking up there. You know half of them, and I need to actually talk about something."

"Are you following the Stones to Europe and inviting me along?"

"Are you still . . . is the opportunity still available?"

"Hmm?"

"Are you still doing what you were doing? Do you still need someone to do the thing?"

"The flight to New York just didn't have the same bounce without it, huh?"

"The question's really simple."

"Yeah, there's a backlog, in fact."

"Okay, so."

"What changed your mind?"

"I just need the money."

"You're not working for a cop or something, are you?"

"Nah. I need to help someone out and I need money."

"You'd have to say if you are—that's a real thing. You'd have to tell me."

She pats her sides, stomach, and tits—presses through her T-shirt to prove there's no tape recorder.

"C'mon," she says.

"Well, like I said, there's a little bit of buildup here. Need someone to get two to New York in the next ten days. And one more a couple weeks after that."

"I'm talking about one or two. No more than that—that's it, really."

"You buying a car?"

"I just need it—a little bit, is all."

"It doesn't make a ton of sense, businesswise, for us to only have you do one or two."

"Do you need my help or not?"

"Listen, I'm on the line, just like you. It's just not making sense to me what's causing the big change."

"You offered it up."

"And you stormed away like I'd kicked your dog."

Despite the reddest stretches of that first flight to New York—the parts that were flooded with revenge plots—she's realizing hers has been a put-on indignation with Billy, a grimace papering over a real warmth. She cycles forward and back through their hours together and can't come up with a reason not to share what's going on. Especially if it's the only way he'll let her in.

"We went home, me and my sister, we drove home before the concert, and we saw our folks. My dad told us he's sick."

"What kind of sick?"

"He has a tumor on his spine."

"That's very bad."

"He needs better doctors, he needs better treatment, he needs surgery—and they need money. They don't have money."

Billy is silent and his mouth is small. His face is free of expression, and it looks to Suzy as though he's attempting to slow his heart, his brain, his blood beat. It's a commitment to half speed.

"What?" she says.

"That's terrible. I don't know what to say."

Billy, who has something to say to everyone. It's a generous response—honest, unselfish. It isn't cluttered up with the whipped air of overblown sympathy. It's not wet with remorse. It's about all she could want, even though she didn't know it.

"Yeah," she says. "I do this thing whenever I get bad news. . . . I play this mental defense and I immediately rationalize it, give it context: *This is bad, but at least it's not that other thing. . . . It's nothing compared to if that other thing happened. . . .* And what I think I've always compared the medium-bad things to, what 'that other thing' is, is my dad dying. My mom dying. Grace dying. *You're gonna be okay about this dumb thing because it's not Dad Cancer.*"

"So you have to accept that it's just as bad as it seems."

"It is the max-bad thing."

"What is it you think the money can do? Or that you want it to do?" he says.

"My dad was ready to just let it ride—that was the plan before Grace and I came home. Just, nothing. I hate that."

"He'd already given up on it."

"I think they were seeing the impossibility that even the best effort, the best circumstances, could bring. And decided it wasn't worth spending a bunch of money and time and pain on those long odds."

"But you think it's worth trying? Or at least you think you can help them try with money?"

"I know that what he was saying is a thing. That sometimes, for some people, it's just better to let it come, face it head-on, instead of fighting it and making it worse. I just didn't think my dad was like that—I figured he'd fight it till the fighting killed him. I can't face the alternative. I can't accept him, or me, or anyone, I guess, not wanting to live."

"It's probably not 'not wanting,' right?"

She brushes the hair from her face. "I can't let him not have the opportunity to live if he wants to try."

"So, runs and money."

"Just money. Money by some means. And even though it's the last thing I want to do, the circumstances require that certain efforts be made. And I heard of a way to make some scratch...."

"Well, okay," Billy says. "What's the next time you're going?"

"I'm gonna call the airline today. I'm gonna tell them what's going on, that my dad's sick, and that I'd like to try to get out there once every two weeks and spend most of my days off at home. I think that so long as it doesn't affect the airline all that much—that I can still do other routes just the same—they should be okay with it. Fly-in—two-days-at-home–fly-back sort of thing."

"That's pretty ideal if you really do want to be involved with this," he says.

"I'm talking two or three times max," she says.

"You said one or two before."

"Then two."

"Well, all I mean is it doesn't have to be. If you need more or whatever."

"My sister's gonna try to go out when I'm not there, to help at the house and in the hospital, too—we talked about it."

"Does she want in?" Billy says.

Suzy looks at him to make sure he's kidding, and he lifts the corner of his mouth.

"You want to eat something?" Billy says.

She shakes her head without really checking with her body.

"C'mon, you can tell me about the concert."

"It was good," she says. "It was really, really good."

"Thanks, Robert Christgau, I feel like I was there."

"What do you want, what would you want to eat?"

"Let's get some soup at the diner."

"It's eighty fucking degrees."

"'It wasn't nothing but some water and potatos,'" he says, stomping a big beat with his heel, building in animation, "'and the wonderful, wonderful soup*stone*!'"

"I don't know that song...."

They hang around and the sun passes behind a mountain range of clouds, so that it turns to winter, an optic threat of rain. Sand-sea-sky in a chrome gradient. Neither makes a move to leave. Without the sun there's no shadow to tip off Suzy that Billy's leaning over to kiss her on the cheek. "That's all very fucked up, seriously," he says. "I'm sorry."

Suzy nods but doesn't move, and then says, "Okay, let's eat."

The first one's an afternoon flight, weekday, half businessmen, some empty seats. It's the same package: the five-pound sack of Gold Medal flour inside the sealed Ziploc inside the brown paper bag. This time Suzy packs it herself, in a lunch pail with measured proportions of brown sugar, chocolate chips, and vanilla extract. A container of ready-made ingredients, just like Billy said—dry mix for the fledgling bakery business in Manhattan.

Of course they don't check her bag. They've never checked her bag. Cocktail dress, jeans, shirt, and underwear. A pair of comfortable flip-flops. A couple books and a lunch pail with the dry mix. That's about as domesticated as it gets. In the mirror: the reflection of the high-femme stewardess image she's never quite pulled together naturally. The painted nails, the three-dimensional hair, the hundred-and-fifty percent eye shadow—it's always been effortful, a necessary performance. And now she's a girl whose greatest charge against her is just loving baking *too* much.

By the time there are tall mountains out the windows, Suzy's feeling confident there's nothing left to complicate the run. Just three more hours of happy-hour cocktails, cigarettes, and headsets, and it's off the plane and into the bathroom, just like before. But there's a pair of eyes in a first-class aisle seat that won't drop from her body. She sees them as she passes facing forward and she feels them trailing her as she moves back into the forward compartment—eyes peering out of a face that's been quickly sketched, a loose bag of shaved lines, a head with a countable number of hairs. She's beginning to wonder whether he's some sort of monitor, if it's some sort of trap. It's about then, over Colorado, that he asks for a drink: "Something whiskeyish with something sour."

"So a whiskey sour," Suzy says.

"Well, anything but that, but the same basic idea."

He seems amused with the complication, that it's made him memorable.

Suzy mixes the drink—Johnnie Walker with some concentrate out of a plastic lime squeeze bottle. She doesn't have real options. She places it on his tray.

"Well, what'd you do?" the man says.

"Something whiskeyish with something sour."

"What do you call it?"

"I don't know. Whiskey lime."

"Give it a good name."

She thinks on it. "Indecision's Remorse."

"I don't know if I'd remember that one. I like when they're named after famous people. Or pretty ladies."

"How 'bout *my* name, then?" Suzy says with exaggeration. "Beverly Hills."

"That's not your name."

"You got me. And though I'd love to chat, I've gotta run back and get this food service started."

"Well, hold up, before you go, what do you say you and me go out tonight."

"I appreciate the offer, genuinely, but I'm turning around and heading straight back."

"Well, how 'bout I jump on that plane and we get drinks tonight in Los Angeles?"

"That's . . . that's very sweet of you, but I'm probably gonna be busy then, too."

"Well, consider it. Maybe we'll get grounded in New York or something. Just know it's an option."

"Will do," she says.

He asks her again over Missouri and a third time on final approach, the last cabin check. Suzy smiles through the advances but starts to sweat his lingering eyes as she gets closer to the handoff. At the gate the cabin clears, and the pilots thank the girls for their service—the sort of five hours that passed without incident, five hours that will fade from recollection for the pilots and the stews by next week, no-memory memories that will last forever. For everyone but Suzy, at least, whose trip glows a little more on account of her elevated ordinary.

At the end of the jet bridge, the man is waiting. She's fairly certain he's not involved, only that he's distracting from the task at hand.

"Hey, lemme at least buy you dinner in the terminal, since it looks like it's blue skies for the return flight."

"Oh, thanks again, really, but I'm just gonna go nibble on something at the lounge and freshen up. We've only got about forty minutes."

"Well, how 'bout I join you there?" he says. Suzy's walking now, in the direction of the Union News and the bathroom. She's scanning the terminal for Cassidy and her friends.

"I don't know, I don't think they'd let you in there."

"I just don't see what the big deal is, why you can't eat with me if you're eating in there?"

She strains to grin and shakes her head in subtle yaws. "I don't know...," she says, preparing to let him down less easily. And then she spots Cassidy. Cassidy's keeping her distance, on the edge of aborting on account of the stranger, who's not part of the plan.

Suzy perks up and her eyes widen and she says, "Oh my God, this is my friend! She came all the way out to surprise me!" Suzy raises her hand and waves, and Cassidy has no choice but to approach, her face tight with reluctance. "Cassidy! See," she says to the man, "I haven't seen her in forever."

They close the gap and Suzy says, "Are you here to surprise me for dinner?" Cassidy's face doesn't move, but Suzy says, "Thank you *so* much."

"Listen," Suzy says to the man, "I need to run to the bathroom, and I need to catch up with my friend. It was nice meeting you, nice talking." And Suzy grabs Cassidy by the arm, hooks her in the crook of her elbow, and vanishes with her into the bathroom before Cassidy can protest in full.

"What the *fuck* was that?" Cassidy says in the empty bathroom.

"That was a passenger who wasn't going to leave me alone. He was going to fuck up everything."

"Don't ever, *ever* say my name out there again."

"Sorry, sorry," Suzy says. "I'll make something up next time."

Suzy carries her bag into the stall, unzips, pops the lunch pail, pulls out the sack, and waves Cassidy over impatiently.

"Look who's an old pro," Cassidy says.

Cassidy is such a Broadway tough when she's barking instructions, but there's a luminescence when she smiles, especially coyly like now. Crooked lips into a noncommitted grin, words out of just one side of her mouth. Suzy kinda likes her just then. But Cassidy doesn't break role for long—takes the sack and puts it in her bag.

"Who has the money?" Suzy says.

"Same as last time."

Suzy zips up and walks out of the bathroom with Cassidy left behind. She looks for the men, and when she finds them in a newsstand, she clops in a direct line, approaches without pretending to browse, and says, "Thanks for holding my purse." The man squints at her and looks for a signal over Suzy's shoulder, a sign from Cassidy. When it comes, he hands her the bag, and Suzy leaves him, too, without another word. Three minutes on she's in the lounge, and her appetite is expansive. She asks the chef at the carving station for some slices of roast beef and a scoop of mashed potatoes. She pops a Coke and sits near the window, where the sun is coming in flat. She reaches into the bottom of her bag and lifts the purse, unfastens the brass, thumbs the cash.

One done. She can handle another. If she's honest, she feels herself looking forward to it. The same scenario, a beeline from the plane to the bathroom, only next time maybe they trust her enough so it's Cassidy with the money herself. Cassidy softening even further. Cassidy and Suzy alone.

"Are you sure I can't be a stew?" Cassidy might ask.

And Suzy would have the opportunity to purse her lips in mock assessment and say, "Still too short."

Suzy's first lesson at Zamperini is on a Monday evening. It's not the class with J.P.—you can't hook up with a course midstream, turns out—but rather another one at the airfield. The instructor's a young pilot named Millikan. He doesn't even say his first name. Or maybe that is his first name. There's no Mr., no initial. Just Millikan. Former military, he says, but he looks jarringly young. Narrow face, long nose, tight skinned if a little baggy eyed. The first night in the classroom is introductions. Suzy and seven middle-aged men—most of whom, sounds like, have money set aside to buy their own planes. Though she's come into some discretionary funds herself, Suzy's an aberration, the only one without military experience or facial hair. When Millikan asks why she's there, she says she wants to learn how to dogfight. That's a long way off, he says, and Suzy says, "Four months, right?"

It'll be two months before they even get inside a real plane, he says. It's all reading, props in the hangar, then on to the simulator—this new box hooked up to a yoke and pedals that Millikan's a little wary of. He didn't learn on one, figures they might be a waste of time. But they're fun to play with, he says, even if they're not fully effective for certification. Once they're through with the prep, they'll get up in the planes with Millikan—feel their way around a cockpit, put hands on the equipment, and fly side by side with their instructor, he says, like fifteen-year-olds do in driver's ed. Suzy smiles at this. She remembers her own driving lessons—lessons required by the state, even though she'd been fudging her way into racing via a tractor license for a few years. The driving instructor moved her through the typical motions and lifted his clipboard to make notations only when Suzy started downshifting into high-speed turns.

All this, though, Millikan says, is logistics. The real reason to be here is for the wonder.

"Think of it…," he says. "Flying is still, in 1972, an underrated achievement. Getting up in the air and winding up somewhere else because I or you choose to—that is some *crazy bullshit!*" He describes flying's capacity to make us more aware of the bigness of the world and the smallness of man, but also man's ("and lady's, I suppose") ability to push back against nature. Our ability to eat up impossible distances—journeys that had taken us months—in the space of an evening. "Flying," he says, "is about our collapsing of the distances that have divided us since the Garden. About seeing, from way up high, how parts form a whole, the ways we interconnect. Or at least have the *opportunity* to connect. This is about celebrating *that*. Appreciating *that*—right?"

At the end of class Millikan reminds them that it's important to study. That they could be the best natural pilots since Yeager, or more-articulate humanists about the poetics of flight than even he, Millikan—but that they won't even get a shot if they fail the written exams at the end of the month.

On her way out of the hangar, Suzy passes Millikan as he's lighting a cigarette. She smiles, and he smiles back and says: "Don't forget to hit the books, sweetie."

She worries her face: "Hope I can find someone to help me read."

Grace flies an up-and-back to Seattle the day of a Howlers show, and Suzy and Mike go for a drive. Suzy's been itching to get behind the wheel since the visit to the Glen and the promise of the first flight class. So Mike hands over the keys. Suzy pushes the Karmann Ghia into testy revolutions in low gear, swishing around cars from the shoulder to the centerline like a fish navigating a reef—upshifting through the McClure Tunnel and bumping up to a strained fourth in a cleared-out stretch of PCH, low on the water, past the Jonathan Club, below the Palisades and the Getty, and finally into a big left-leaner to Malibu, where the beaches are narrow and the houses live restless, trembling at the suggestion of the next mudslide.

Mike likes to drive when he's not reading or writing or scheming about his magazine. He hadn't spent any time in L.A. before the move. Grace bounced out after the wedding, and Mike wrapped things up in New York, ran out the last couple of months of his apartment lease. When he arrived, he bought the Karmann Ghia, mostly so he could go on "fact-finding" missions. He liked to drive out to the edges and work his way back in—south to Long Beach and way out east to Pomona. Up to the mountains in Pasadena and Burbank. Up the gut of the Valley—Van Nuys, Reseda, Canoga Park. He'd take notes, find people in gas stations and diners, wait for shoppers in parking lots. He didn't have an especially clear sense of what he'd make of it all, but at the very least he was growing familiar with the map. Today they're riding the western edge.

On the way out Mike does most of the talking, all of which has to do with his magazine. It's a chicken-and-egg sort of thing with the writers and the money, he says. Nobody's gonna commit to a publication that doesn't have funding, but financial backers aren't interested in a new mag without at least a few marquee names. Mike's spent the last couple months writing fan letters: high praise followed by deferent requests. "Should this thing get off the ground, could we count on you, Mr. Vidal, to write this *kind* of piece for a fall issue?" Sneak into Bohemian Grove with Governor Reagan. Follow a drop of water from a lake in the Sierras to a faucet in Brentwood. Shadow a retired and reclusive Sandy Koufax. Sit with Angela Davis and her team of lawyers to debrief them in the wake of her trial. Embed with a team building the first space shuttle in El Segundo. That sort of stuff.

"I know someone who could help with that."

"Someone working on the shuttle?"

"That guy from the Fourth—did you overlap at all? His dad worked on the X-15 and Saturn V."

"What parts?"

"Dunno. 'Airframe'?"

"Can he get me an interview with Yeager?"

"I'll ask Dad Zar."

"This is good progress."

Suzy passes a brand-new Pontiac Ventura, and its driver speeds up to trap her in the left lane.

"What an idiot," she says, peeling into position. "I think I want to fly an X-15. That's what it takes to get into Apollo, right?"

"That and some other things." He smiles. "You should probably join the navy first."

"But I have stewardess experience."

"No more moon program anyway."

"Mars, then. Test pilot. Mars. Then retire into flying the L.A.-to-Acapulco on Glam Air."

"Sounds like a plan."

"Or you could make me Aviation Editor of the magazine." She's struggled these last few days to think of much else besides flying. "That's what Amelia Earhart was for *Cosmo* in the thirties."

"All right, Aviation Editor, first task: who should write about the defense industry in L.A.?" Mike says.

"A woman."

The music has been fading to static, and as the road breaks away north at Point Dume, onto the far side of Malibu—the hills severing the line between the hood's antenna and the radio towers in Burbank—the car goes silent and Suzy starts swinging out into the empty oncoming lane. Quick slip wide, then slowing things way down to a near stop, before slapping the gear shift up in a single gulpless breath—*bah, BaH, BAH, BAAAH.*

"What's my zero to sixty?" she says.

"I dunno, twenty seconds?"

"I think I'm quicker than that. Time it."

"On my watch?"

"When I say go."

She brakes to a standstill right in the middle of the highway, where PCH points north toward the naval air station. A black sedan's gaining fast and Mike's glued to the side mirror, looking nervous but playing it cool.

"Go," she says, and upshifts like a stone skipping across the surface of a lake. Fifty, fifty-four, fifty-eight, sixty. "Now."

"Halfway between eighteen and nineteen."

"That's okay."

"This car will do?"

"I like this car," Suzy says. "And I'm ever so grateful you let me screw around with it."

On the far side, near Zuma Beach, the terrestrial vibe of the undeveloped flatlands further removes them from the time and the trends and the politics of the east, a physical space with its back turned on the news. It's also pretty clear out, sight lines up to Santa Barbara's Channel Islands, air filtered of smoke, Suzy and Mike and the Karmann Ghia like a nearly drowned bug who's crawled its way out of the milky cereal bowl of the L.A. basin. Fresh air and invisible light.

"Maybe I should get me one of these."

"Yeah, you saving up?"

"If I put twenty bucks away per paycheck *and* stop paying rent to you and Grace, I should have enough for a new car by the time I turn thirty."

"Speaking of which, we should head back soon to pick her up. Friday rush. If we get stuck in a little traffic in Santa Monica or Venice, we can probably hit the airport just as she's landing."

"Fingers crossed for a Sig-Alert," Suzy says.

The following week there's a day when none of them are working. It's the first time since the Fourth that both girls are home with hours to kill. After running through the standard shower cycle and hoarding sections of the *Times* into separate rooms, the three make impassive attempts to figure out what to spend their day doing. The same options as always: Mexican food, the beach, the bars. Anything else involves the car. Mike suggests seeing something new—maybe checking out the homes of an architect named Gehry the *Times* wrote about last weekend—but the girls don't feel like being on their way to anywhere on their day off, much less crawling through traffic.

Grace has a way of sitting on the couch, two feet planted ten feet from the edge of the sofa, endless legs at full extension leading up into a body that's flattened against the horizontal cushion, head and shoulders wedged into the L where a normal sitter hinges at the hips. It's a position it is impossible to get up and out of. It's how she reads. It's how she watches television. It's often how she naps. And she's doing it now, barely listening, picking through the crossword.

It's hot, no fog this morning, what Suzy imagines to be an everyday Valley heat. The small room feels squeezed, the oxygen's scarce, the roof and walls and floor pinched at each edge. There's a lot of yawning.

"Well, listen," Mike says, "I'm gonna go to the market because we're all out of food, and I might as well pick up something to cook a real dinner with. I just went Tuesday...." He pauses. "We're going through food too quickly. We're burning through everything faster than we should."

Suzy looks up at him with a forehead like open window shutters. It's not the sentiment, it's the passive aggression. Especially after they got along so easily on the drive the other day. She knows she needs to find her own place, but what a way to say it. Mike busies himself at the kitchen island, acts as though he can't feel her looking his way.

"Hmm?" Grace says after a slack silence.

"I'm gonna cook some steaks tonight. That okay?"

"Oh, that's a great idea. What can we do?"

"I don't care."

"Cool," Grace says, refusing to engage him. "We'll go to the beach and pick up some wine on the way back."

It takes them a while to get going, Mike clattering in the kitchen, Grace dictating a shopping list and handing him some cash. He says he's heading way downtown to see a new part of the city in the meantime, at least. He's been reading a book called *Los Angeles: The Architecture of Four Ecologies*—it encourages that sort of thing. He told Suzy all about it in the car when explaining his little adventures.

Suzy tidies up. She packs her dirty clothes into her overnight bag, refolds her clean shirts and shorts in her allocated drawer. There, on the drafting table: five or six legal pads flipped a couple pages deep. New idea, new legal pad—each in a shallower state of abandonment. The *Playboy* investors had just declined involvement in the magazine. How long, Suzy wonders, will he give himself? How long, without editing a magazine, can he call himself a magazine editor? How long without publishing writing can he call himself a writer? It has become this inert enterprise, but anytime a new person asks—at a party, at a brunch, on a fact-finding mission in Koreatown—the answer comes without complication: Mike says he is a writer and an editor, making a new California magazine. Suzy knows that her knowledge of the real state of things—or rather, his knowledge of her knowing—is bittering him toward her.

"I think it's time to get my own place," Suzy says when she and Grace settle down by the water.

"Oh please, we've adopted you. Makes it so we don't have to have kids yet."

"No, seriously, it's time. It's been two-and-a-half months. I need a real room, but more importantly I need to get out of your guys' hair."

"I hardly notice you."

"Yeah...but you don't work in the house. You're on the road. You're in hotels. I get the sense that I'm stepping on toes."

"Mike's just in a funk. He's crushed about the lack of financing."

"It *is* his house, though. And it's his office. And he spends more time there than the two of us combined."

"I'll talk to him."

"Please don't. It'll be a good thing to get out, I've got a little money now, I can—"

"Not enough money."

"I can find a place, I'm sure. Or I can move into a stew zoo."

"You're not living with those girls. And you're not moving out. Suz, I know how much you make and I know how much it costs to live alone here."

"I'll move to Westchester."

"You will *not.*"

"All right, well, listen, how 'bout this, then: *I* feel a little uncomfortable. *I* feel like I'm walking on eggshells. I don't want to spoil things with Mike. I'm sure as soon as I start even looking, things will get better."

"Okay, but you don't sign anything without talking to me first."

Suzy is so very susceptible to her big sister playing a big sister. It's a glaring weakness she recognizes in herself, but one she willingly indulges. In many ways she used to relish the worst injuries and illnesses for the sympathy Grace would show her. Grace wasn't always there and she wasn't often around for the second Suzy mistake. But Grace happened to be present and capable when it mattered most, and her sugar cut the pain every time. Suzy never sought to rely on Grace, but she always curled herself into the smaller shape when her sister actually made an effort to big-spoon her emotionally.

The sand is hot—the top layer seems to caramelize. And yet it's as crowded as Suzy has seen it since the Fourth. Mothers and children and a few dads who cut out after a slow August morning at work. The inland temperatures must be excruciating, triple digits in Riverside. Grace is mouthing something in a delicate register. Suzy's ear narrows on it, but it takes a verse to find the melody and fill in the words: "Readin' *Rolling Stone,* readin' *Vogue*...California I'm comin' home."

Suzy is somehow still working on *Fear and Loathing.* Oil tankers dock in the C-clamp of the bay, more tankers than Suzy has seen at any one time. They're nearly identical and vertically stacked on the water. It's like looking at physical frames of film, perfs and all, for a movie of a lone boat—one frame on top of another. The glut of tankers helps explain why there's so much tar in the sand, the petrochemical link to the beach cities. Grace turns over and rubs some baby oil on her shoulders.

The sun is covered by a pair of heads. Two women, one black and one white. The white woman asks Suzy and Grace how they're feeling, and Grace shrugs apologetically, feigning deafness and signing, *My name is Grace and I'm ten years old*—a phrase she learned in elementary school.

"Oh, I see. We love deaf people," the woman says. "How about you? How do you feel?"

"Hot," Suzy says.

"You know what else is hot?"

Suzy doesn't recognize these two, but she's seen others like them around. Born-agains from that church on PCH, the one that's run out of a strip mall.

"Hell?" Suzy says.

"Eternal damnation."

"So I got it right?"

"I'd like to invite you to something," the woman says, handing Suzy a flyer. "It's tonight and I think you'd like it."

Suzy's eyes locate the date and time and place—tonight, downtown L.A. That seems like a long way for people to go for a church that's right in town.

"I've actually got a dinner," Suzy says.

"Bring them along afterward."

"I'll…I'll float the idea to the table."

"It's changed my life."

"That's great to hear."

"I think it could change yours."

"I admire your conviction," Suzy says. The woman's partner is with another sunbather now.

"What's that you're reading?"

Suzy glances at the cover of the book—the demons in the convertible, the cacti and skull. "An account about…Christ's forty days in the desert."

"That warms my heart."

"Yeah, well, I'm glad," Suzy says. "Looks like you have a lot of flyers left to hand out before sunset?"

"I hope to see you again sometime," the woman says.

The woman catches up with her partner, and Suzy watches them approach another pair on the sand. Suzy lies back and lifts the flyer to her face, shading herself from the sun. She reads from the top.

REVEREND JIM JONES

THE MOST UNIQUE

PROPHETIC HEALING SERVICE

YOU'VE EVER WITNESSED!

BEHOLD THE WORD MADE INCARNATE IN YOUR MIDST!

AUGUST 17 & 18

8 P.M.

EMBASSY AUDITORIUM

9TH & GRAND

LOS ANGELES

She reads the small type, too. Reverend Jim Jones. The Peoples Temple. Started in Indiana, coming permanently to Los Angeles next month. So it's not the local church, but out-of-towners. A congregation of four thousand and a mother temple on sixty acres in Redwood Valley. Salvation with an indifference toward race.

There's a photo in the corner of the flyer, darkly exposed, badly copied. Reverend Jones stands taller than the rest, a blocky head and a genial swoop of hair. He looks a little like Elvis. There's his wife, older looking, plus "three of their seven adopted children"—each of a different ethnicity. She hasn't heard of this man or this church, which doesn't surprise her. But there's something sticky about the picture. Something grand and utopian, warm and beneficent.

Her eyes track to the very bottom, the smallest print she didn't even notice. "Reverend Jones, with members of the large interracial youth choir and orchestra, will be traveling in some of our modern fleet of air-conditioned Greyhound-type busses." She imagines the motorcade rolling down the 101 now—the reverend, like the president, concealed in the automobile with the thickest windows and doors. She folds the flyer twice and pins it to her hip with her bikini bottom.

Once Suzy can make out the pink on her stomach through the tint in her shades, she knows she's past burned. They hoof it up and over the hill and back to the house. Mike's in the side yard dumping briquettes into the Weber. He looks like he knows what he's doing, and he tends to look better when he knows what he's doing.

"Good timing," he says.

Grace asks to borrow his lighter fluid so she and Suzy can clean the tar off their feet. Mike grills three filets mignons, green beans, and some cobs of white corn. But the coup de plate, to Suzy at least, is the handmade pierogi. She's never eaten any before, but this is a Mike family recipe. The simplest, Mike says, of the sixty or seventy his grandmother brought with her from Poland in the twenties. He makes enough to last a week. Onion, sauerkraut, diced pork, and potato.

"They had all this at the market downtown?" Grace says.

"I didn't go that far. The traffic was incomprehensible. I went to that place in Gardena instead."

"Not officially a new place, then."

"Well, figured it'd be better than baked potatoes."

The pierogi are good—everything is good. It's probably the best meal any of them have eaten in weeks, not because the food is exceptional, but because Suzy knows homemade things of equal quality taste better than they do in restaurants, or on airplanes.

Mike is visibly buoyed by the win. The girls forgot to buy wine, so they crack open a bottle of Jack, empty the ice bin into their glasses, and ease into the heavy, uncut syrup—the warm and heavy proof growing wetter and cooler by the second.

Grace offers to do the dishes and ends up cleaning most of the kitchen in the process. Mike finds the flyer, and Suzy describes the encounter on the beach. Mike hates being approached by the born-agains, but he has a different reaction to the language these folks use. The from-scratch-ness of it. The race dynamic. He asks Suzy if he can keep the flyer and she says sure, laughing a big, low laugh like Grace's.

Mike skates to the record player and drops the needle on *Ziggy Stardust,* and the three of them sing the chorus and first verse at each turnover. Mike helps clarify some mondegreens by consulting the printed lyrics on the liner notes: the pink monkey bird, the tigers on vaseline—the animal lines. Mike and Grace dance together in the kitchen, and Suzy—hot in the chest and cheeks and shoulders, physically radiating heat from her burns but also puffed up with a sense of domestic harmony—announces over the music that she's going to get some MoonPies. And in the darkness of the side yard, she retrieves her skateboard and hits the alley. When her board runs out of steam, she drops her bare foot to the road and rows her way onward toward dessert.

Millikan holds the results of the first flight exam till the end of class, and keeps Suzy's for last. He squints as he hands her the blue book. She hasn't missed a single question.

"I didn't even get all these," Millikan says.

"You should've studied harder."

"You were kidding about the not-being-able-to-read thing, I guess."

"I guess."

"I wish I could give you a real prize."

"Let me sit in the cockpit."

"You want to sit in the plane?"

"Sneak peek."

"Um..."

"Fine, nice offer."

"No," he says, "hang on. Stick around a sec till things clear out. Nobody else needs to see."

Ten minutes later he's helping Suzy into the cockpit. The glove fits. She knows what everything means now, but from a faintly reproduced diagram——a faded mimeo with basic descriptions. She hasn't put her hands on the yoke before, hasn't even sat at the simulator. She slides down in the seat and places her sandaled feet on the pedals. She eyes the throttle. What if she just rolled onto the runway and tried taking off? She knows the ground speed at which she's supposed to pull up, the angle of ascent. She could probably do it. And she could climb to a couple thousand feet, tool around pretty easily. She just might not be able to get back down. That's how it was in the trees in the yard growing up—she could always get high and then would have to call out for Wayne to provide a couple of arms to leap into.

She imagines herself taking off and failing to land. She plays the whole thing out, just sitting there, dreaming with her eyes open—Suzy up in sunlight with a register like a piccolo, so bright it might make a sound like a dog whistle.

Millikan looks around, a little anxious, and asks her to step down, but she's still midflight in her mind, plenty of fuel left for the tour over the South Bay, and the thing she thinks when his voice comes into clarity, when she returns to earth, is a simple thought but one that touches her body the way the only thoughts worth having do: *This will not be boring.*

August is almost gone when she makes a third run, a run that's weirdly smooth, devoid of the heat. Takeoff and land and swap and takeoff and land. And suddenly she has cash enough not just to move out, but to pay a whole year's rent if she so desires, with plenty left over for lessons and concerts and beer and pretty much anything else she wants. She keeps the money in an envelope shoved down the leg of a pair of maroon hose she'll never wear in warm weather. Balled up in the back of her clothing drawer in Mike's office, looking as though they conceal a severed foot.

Suzy sees an apartment on Twenty-Ninth Street, ten blocks from Mike and Grace, up the hill, in the shadow of the oil refinery. It's even closer to the airport, in and out with ease, off in a notch of Sela that wedges itself between the beach and the refinery and the butterfly sanctuaries beneath the flight path. It's a small apartment, but an apartment with a view. There's a wooden staircase that's twice as tall as would seem permitted, rickety like an Escher, that leads to the top apartment, a bedroom and bathroom, living room and kitchen, with a long look out over the water, about as high as the hill at Nineteenth, the same view she got on the Fourth before bombing the descent on her skateboard. The thickness of the stroke of neon blue on the horizon is the same weight, and the peninsulas, both visible from this height, are still bookends on the bay. There's sand in the carpet when she drags a flip-flop from one room into another, but it will never not be there, the agent says. Two hundred bucks a month. More than Grace would ever let her spend. But given the new reality it's more than affordable. She gives the woman cash and they agree to sign something later. Suzy moves in the next day. And that first night, when the sun goes down, it's rose gold through the big window without drapes, the sky and the water reflecting each other, blurring their opposition.

"He spent the last few days on the beach thinking they might just stroll up to him," Grace says.

Suzy's invited Grace and Mike to dinner at her apartment. She hasn't bought much furniture yet, but she has a card table and folding chairs and a radio hooked up in the corner.

"He'd heard an interview with Reverend Jones about the new temple downtown and thought he could just sit there in the sand and they'd flock to him to spill the secrets."

"Suzy made it look so easy...," Mike says, numb to the ribbing.

"No luck?" Suzy says.

"They're obviously only ever around when you don't want them to be," Grace says.

As Suzy waits for the potatoes to boil, Mike and Grace debate the merits of a vacation to Hawaii, and Suzy finds herself lost in the river of the baseball game on the radio. During an endless at-bat, Vin Scully slips in a Bobby Fischer update. Suzy's taken interest in the Fischer thing since reading the article about him in *Rolling Stone*. She follows along in the *Times* sports section each day, the strange code—almost a Cyrillic-numeric—of the scoreboard: 1.e4 c5 2.Nf3 d6 3.d4 cxd4 4.Nxd4 Nf6, etc. After seven weeks, Scully says, Fischer has clinched—the first American world chess champion. Reykjavík on the dateline in every newspaper on Earth. A place where American accents are banking some cachet. Reykjavík, a place for Suzy to go. A place to escape to should she ever need it—should she accept a desire to go on vacation with one of those full-$50K envelopes of cash.

After dinner Suzy meets Billy at his house to pick up a payout, and she ends up staying to watch Mark Spitz swim the 100-meter butterfly. Two lengths of the pool, he wins by nearly a second and a half, sets a new world record, his fourth gold and fourth world record of the Olympics. Suzy makes a joke about Owen, Los Sandcrabs' manager, the one who lost his girl to the fantasy of a world-class athlete. Billy says it's not funny—he's still banged up about his ex-lady.

"I wonder," Suzy says, *"if she's there."*

While Suzy's on a flight a few days later, the story breaks: eleven Israeli Olympic team members have been taken hostage. That's what the captain says to the passengers, a move Suzy rules a mistake. She and the girls spend the rest of the flight struggling to answer the questions being asked of them. When they land and she watches the television in the Grand Pacific lounge, she learns she's not the only person in a bind. There are Cronkite and Brokaw and Nixon and Golda Meir. They're not answering the questions, either, and she feels a little lifted by the company.

She'd been thickly adding to her stash those first few runs, her cut, two grand each go. But before the flight to New York in September, her fourth, she makes a deal with Billy—trusts him to hold her money as collateral. She's gonna take the entirety of the new payment up with her to Schuyler Glen and give her father whatever he needs. Billy doesn't like it, says she should just deal with what's hers, not theirs. Suzy still hasn't met anyone above Billy. He insists they're not so bad themselves, but they deal with guys who it's better not to know. Just regard them the way they regard you, he says—as an idea. No name, no face. It's better that way.

Up in the air, as they're settling into the speed chute over Pennsylvania, Suzy sits for the first time all flight. She's up front, facing the passengers, and the time off her feet, the proximity to the luggage compartment, draws her mind back to Billy's opaque warnings, the resistance to her heading home with the haul. *The way they regard you,* he said. *No name, no face.* But she can't help but wonder if they know more. Especially as her eyes move along the aisle to the back of the cabin, passenger after passenger who know something about Suzy, who know this stew, know just enough about her without knowing what she's got stuffed away in her bag. She presses herself back up to her feet and moves to the rear of the cabin, looking over each occupant of each seat in each row, checking their faces and dismissing their threat to her. Near the back, though, there are two men in suits, hair product and neckties, tan enough that they shade toward vague ethnicity, large enough that they seem to spill over the armrest and into each other's space like the circles of a Venn diagram. *The pair of suited men,* Suzy thinks. The pair of suited men from the Fourth of July. The pair of suited men following Billy from the beach to the parties at night. Maybe? She passes them slowly, waits for them to react, to turn up. But they are lost in the stock index of their shared business section. They seem to pay no attention to Suzy.

The handoff is frictionless. Cassidy seems in a rush. The purse and the envelope are Suzy's before she traces her anxiety back to the suited men again. But even they're off the plane and out of sight before she can really track them. This time, clear, she heads not for the lounge but for the exit, rents a car, and points it toward Schuyler Glen.

She spends the first night at home catching Wayne and Edith up on her new apartment and the soon-to-be-announced Grand Pacific routes to Mexico. They tell her that a new doctor they visited in New York says they can try to nuke the tumor. Intensive chemotherapy, with an aim toward reduction to an easily operable size. *Easily* in quotes—at the very least upping the odds of success. It's expensive, but they're talking about it.

When Edith heads upstairs to read in bed, Suzy pours two glasses of Macallan. Wayne is slumped in his chair, watching golf on *Wide*

World of Sports. Wayne called Suzy "a Masters baby," born as she was in early April during the first major of 1950, and Suzy has always associated the game's whispered commentary with the comfort of home. But she's happy to see the programming switch over to the Olympics, a replay of the gold-medal basketball match between the US and the Soviet Union, a game Wayne's already heard the Americans lost.

There's been a lot of nice normal all evening, so she cuts to it:

"How much, all told?"

"What's that?" he says.

"I said I could help with the money."

"I remember that." He straightens up in his chair and grimaces. "And I appreciated you saying it. But we're gonna do this on our own and not lean in any way on you and your sister. I think we're talking about money that is much greater than any of us could scrounge up anyway."

"How much did they say?"

He pushes air through pursed lips. "Five, ten, fifteen grand, I don't know. It depends on a bunch of factors. But insurance covers only so much. And then we're looking at measuring the benefit versus liquidating the house, you know?"

"You promised me you'd try."

"I did—and we drove way down into the city and we saw a specialist and all that. It's just, there are insurmountable elements that are still factoring into all this."

Suzy has been alert for this cue. She walks to the foyer and picks up her carry-on, thumbs out ten grand in twenties and hundreds, and tucks the wad into her waistband. It's more than she's earned—she's dipping into what's not yet hers.

She sits back down in the living room and waits for Wayne to say something. He watches her and then, bored, sips his drink. That's when she places the money on the table, four short stacks. He still doesn't say anything, so she straightens the edges and the stacks are like a low-lying skyline.

"What is this?"

"I told you I could help with the money."

"Whose is it?"

"It's mine."

"What do you mean it's yours?"

"I found a way to make some more money."

"I don't..." He rubs his face. His body fell asleep sometime in the last hour, and now his head's been called to response. "What are we talking about here?"

"I'm flying extra legs and I'm racing again on the side."

"Please don't lie to me."

"I'm not lying. I've been saving up, plus I've borrowed a little from people I can pay back no problem. It's all very under control, and it gives us options."

"Suzy Ames Whitman: I know you're lying to me."

Suzy leans back. Her eyes drift across the table to the walls behind Wayne's chair where the gallery of family photos begins. She can't make them out in the dark, but she's aware, keenly, painfully, that the fate of those photos has everything to do with tonight. Either her father dies and there's nothing left to add to that wall. Or he lives and they're forced to sell the house to cover the cost, nothing physical left of the life Suzy lived before college. Racing is gone. School is gone. Now, without an intervention, the house might vanish, too. She leans forward and speaks before she's worked through the thought.

"You promised me you'd try. And part of that meant letting me help. I'm not going to tell you any more about where the money came from. And you're not going to tell anyone about it, either. The glassworks found some funds for you—they found a loophole in your insurance. Whatever you want to say. There's more money available than they anticipated. Enough for you to get through chemo and get through surgery. However much that takes."

"I'm not taking the money."

"Then you lied to me. Because this—this here—is trying to live."

Suzy gets up to move to her bedroom.

"I want you to stop whatever this is. I'm not gonna ask you about it again. I don't want to know. But you're gonna get rid of this money and you're gonna go back to your regular routes doing your regular work."

"You can't just get rid of ten thousand dollars."

"Is that really how much is here?"

She holds still and makes her mouth small. There's forty more in the envelope.

"Suzy, I didn't ask for this."

"But it's here—you don't have to *ask*."

"Promise me you'll stop."

"Think of it as payback for things growing up."

"This *must end.*"

"I'm going to keep bringing you cash until you spend every bit of it and start to get better."

"I'm demanding that you stop."

Suzy shakes her head and sniffles.

"I'll stop if you take this and do all the things you said you'd do," she says.

"I'm not taking the money."

"You can either take the money and get better, or I'm gonna pay the doctors up front in New York."

"You can't spend this money on me."

"You can either take the money and get better, or I'm gonna buy the '54 Maserati from that calendar in the garage."

"You can't spend this money."

"Either way, by the end of the day tomorrow it's gonna be gone. You can either take it yourself, or I'm doing something stupid with it for you."

Suzy sees his jaw pulsing and she prepares herself for the breaking of the dam. She steps back. But instead he sips the rest of the whiskey water and whispers, defeated: "You have to listen to me."

"That's not the case anymore."

"*You* are not the daughter who doesn't listen."

"There's nothing for me to do except try and help."

"You're not helping, you're making things worse."

They hang their slack in the room, with the basketball commentators working through halftime analysis.

"Take the money and I'll quit," she says.

Wayne is silent and Suzy is unconvinced she's made a dent. But he rocks out of his chair and gets to his feet. He gathers the cash off the table, searches the room, moves toward the bookshelf. He takes short stacks, ten or fifteen bills each, and places them between the covers and the flyleaves of the uncracked Penguin classics.

"You're taking this with you tomorrow," he says without looking up. "I just need to get it out of my sight for now."

"No more," Suzy says, answering to the bargain.

"Don't forget to collect it all before you leave."

"Don't forget," Suzy says to herself, tapping the memory center of her brain.

At flight school, at Zamperini, they work on the simulators. The eggplant backdrop and the lime-green vectors of the runway and the horizon. A contour drawing of the edges of flight. It's a silent simulation, yoke in hands, foot pedals plugged into the computer in the wall. Suzy has a display of altitude and airspeed. Millikan moves them through a basic series of motions, of pitch and yaw. It's the second session on the simulators, and the ease with which she's taken to the dynamics has made her confident, maybe overly so. She knows it's another month until they're up in the air, but after class Suzy asks Millikan if there's any chance that she can get another preview with him. Hers is a posture she rarely deploys. It wasn't taught in stew school, but any target might assume it was: a reversal of spine curvature, hips open and chest high, one hand on her waist—a teapot-shaped Suzy. Millikan says no without acknowledging the effort.

"How 'bout this, then," Suzy says, and Millikan turns to her, rubbing his temples. He's looked like shit all evening. "Let's move this off the books: you take me up in the air, and I'll take you for a spin around that racetrack in Ontario. I'll show you how to drive a race car."

"I've driven race cars."

"Not like this, you haven't, no way."

"You seriously think you can show me something?"

"It's a dumb trade considering how easy it'll be for you to fly me out there in your plane. You're going up later anyway. You said so yourself."

He watches the room empty and then looks closer at Suzy's face. Rather than desperate, she's made herself look bored, as though she's already moved on from her own proposal. She leans over to pick up her bag.

"Look," Millikan says, "I can't do it today, I'm...under the weather. But how 'bout next week? Later in the week. We can fly out. I'll show you some things in the air. But if *you* don't show *me* anything..."

"Nah—what do I get if I *do?*"

"A lift back to Zamperini," he says. "Otherwise it's a two-hour hitchhike."

Suzy smiles wide. "I feel motivated."

*   *   *

Mike calls Suzy in the afternoon on a hot September Saturday when Grace is in the air and out of town.

"Wanna take a field trip with me downtown?"

"What do you mean?" Suzy says.

"I finally bumped into some of those recruiters on the beach. Got invited to an information session at the newly blessed temple. I'm on the books for a meeting. Wanna tag along?"

"Sure, I guess," Suzy says. "I was just gonna spend the afternoon on the beach."

"I need someone to make sure I don't walk into the building and disappear forever," he says. "And besides, it's your fault I'm wrapped up in this thing anyway."

They shoot up the Harbor in zero time and find a parking space across the street from the temple in a lot wrapped in chain link and razor wire. The temple sits at a forty-five on the corner of Hoover and Alvarado. It's an old synagogue, probably half a century old. Romanesque Revival, ringed by palms. Tan bricks with a red tile roof and a semidramatic entry between Roman Composite columns. It seems clean to the touch, but the shadows give a cobwebby feel to the place. When they pass beneath the central arch, Suzy pinches Mike's arm.

In the narthex a pretty black woman in a sky-blue dress and glasses smiles at them. She's younger than Suzy, barely seems old enough for college. Mike checks in and confirms his guest. They're led to an antechamber that was likely used until recently for standard Bible instruction. A man is waiting for them there. He is from what's called the Planning Commission. He has jeans on and a denim work shirt and what looks to be a priest's collar. He offers a hand to Mike and then to Suzy. His hand is cool and damp, like the walls of a crypt.

The man welcomes them to the Peoples Church. He describes the basic tenets, which sound very much like those of any other church, but with bonus material—in-house social and medical programs, outpatient clinics, a drug program for addicts, a legal program for criminals, a dining hall for the indigent. The man has just moved here from San Francisco. He's been called on to develop Sunday services at the new location. Until they're up and operating at full steam, he says, buses from Ukiah and San Francisco bring members through each weekend. "The members are out milling around now," he says, "but you won't believe it if you come back tomorrow."

Mike crosses and uncrosses his legs beneath the table. Suzy can sense his mind fidgeting, too.

"Is Reverend Jones here, then?" Mike says.

"No, no. He's in Ukiah," the man says.

"Will he be returning anytime soon?"

"I suppose he'll be in and out. He's a very busy man, always on the move. We're all over the state now."

"So he won't necessarily be here anytime soon, though?"

"I suppose before the end of the month. We blessed the church just a couple weeks ago. He was here for a week leading up to it. He did radio. He's quite a speaker."

"I've heard him," Mike says. "I'd very much like to meet him."

Suzy still isn't totally sure what they're doing here, what Mike's up to. If he's genuinely moved by the mission of the church. If it's a combative, dialectical itch he's looking to scratch. Or if he's searching for something for his magazine—a cover story for the debut issue.

"And he'd very much like to meet you, Michael. He loves nothing more than meeting new men and women and sharing his vision. His articulation of The Cause."

The man spends the next forty-five minutes surfacing some of what he means. The utopian vision that Suzy gleaned in that first flyer on the beach. A world of mixed race. (Eighty percent of the organization is black, the man says.) A world, too, of compassion for the elderly and tenderness toward children. A world with the sort of free services on offer here—medicine and drug treatment and food. An institution financed internally, without any help from the government. An institution of healing. The man tells stories about Jones's propensity for healing. His capacity to rid church members of cancer, sickness, and pain. He tells a story about Jones being shot one evening while leaving his home in Ukiah. An assassination attempt. Blood everywhere. Jones crawled back into the house, the man says, and emerged shortly thereafter in full health.

The man then shifts and asks Mike and Suzy a therapist's litany of questions.

When Mike mentions that he is a journalist, the man sits up straighter. Suzy can't believe Mike's said it right out—that he insists on establishing himself that way. She's certain they'll be asked to leave.

"Reverend Jones will be very interested in this," the man says. "The Prophet cares very much how his word is disseminated. He contributes a large percentage of our funding to newspapers. We're always in search of men and women who've worked in the press to help us with our message."

Suzy's shoulders relax. The man just wants Mike to do their PR.

"So there's really no clear sense of when Reverend Jones might be back?" Mike says again, when the questioning is over.

"There's no telling. He is a man moved by the spirit. There are just so many others elsewhere who've yet to be exposed."

Once their orientation session is deemed complete, the man leads them back toward the narthex and reiterates his desire for them to attend the service tomorrow. The woman with the glasses asks Mike and Suzy for their phone number and address. Mike fills out the form for both of them. Lies, Suzy hopes. When he finishes, the woman asks

Mike for a contribution. The church relies on The Commitment, she says. Mike meets Suzy's eyes over the forms and then reaches for his wallet and a pair of tens.

When they exit together, it's the same sensation as leaving a summer matinee—bright on the way in, brighter on the way out. Mike and Suzy each have sunglasses over their eyes before they reach the car.

"What was that about?" Suzy says when they buckle in.

"I'm looking for some healing in my life."

"Seriously—is it for the magazine? Do you want to write about them?"

"I don't totally know," Mike says. "I mean, there's something incredibly odd about Jones, obviously. You don't just build a new religion in this country, not this easily. That's a thing you could do last century, not this one."

"I didn't like the lady on the beach and I didn't like that guy. Are they even *allowed* to wear collars like that?"

"I just...I want to meet the main man."

"But that's what I mean—what's it for?"

Mike pulls out of the lot and has a necklace of green traffic lights before him.

"Did Grace ever tell you about my mom?" he says.

Suzy knows she left when Mike was a kid, but she doesn't know any of the circumstances. It was a thing that Grace left alone, with Suzy and even with her parents.

"Just the most basic..."

"She left me and my dad when I was ten," Mike says. "She made me lunch in the morning and walked me to school, and then I waited till dark for her to pick me up. That night I walked home alone for the first time. There was no note, no sign of anything. Her car was in the driveway. Her house keys were on the kitchen counter. My dad was freaking out. He was sure she'd been kidnapped. He called the cops. They came over, started prowling around the house. Separated me and my dad. Interviewed him in the kitchen. Interviewed me in my bedroom. I don't remember the questions. But I remember throwing up at one point. I haven't been able to eat peanut butter and jelly since. My dad was crying, yelling—I could hear from the second floor. Meanwhile, one of the cops noticed that a bunch of the hangers in the closet were bare. Most of her underwear and socks and pants were gone, too. She'd packed a bag."

Suzy has her eyes on the hot lane lines of the Harbor.

"My grandparents got involved. My dad was still convinced that she couldn't have left on her own. She loved him too much, he said. And she loved me too much, too. Once the search went wider, once extended family and friends were called and messages were left with everyone in her address book, that's when we got the letter. Wrong word—not a letter. The plea: 'I'm okay. Please stop looking for me.'"

Suzy is silent.

"So, you know, she never came back. And this guy here reminds me of what happened to her."

"You think it was something like this?"

"It wasn't an affair. At least not *only* an affair. She'd met a woman in line at the supermarket, it turned out. She'd started going to some meetings at the rec center. She'd told one of her friends about it. Her friend didn't think anything of it at the time. I don't know what sort of organization it was. You know much about that Hubbard guy? Mega best-selling author—that's the craziest part to me. But he's the one with the center on Hollywood or Sunset or whatever. I got a wild hair while I was in college that it was his organization. I tracked him down once when he was speaking in New York. I brought a photo, I told him her name. He claimed he'd never met her before. At least not in his present life."

"I know it doesn't mean much at this point," Suzy says, "but I'm so incredibly sorry."

"There's just this much of me that still wonders, counter to my best interest, whether she might turn up at a place like this, you know? Walk in for the orientation and—oh, it's Angie Singer."

"You think this might be some sort of cult?"

"Every religion, right?"

"But I mean—"

"I don't know. I really don't know anything about it. But that was weird, wasn't it? I think I need to come back."

Suzy meets Billy on the beach to share a burrito. She'd delivered the balance of cash when she returned from Schuyler, and she's worked out a plan to pay him back the extra amount she lent her father. Business aside, she hasn't had an opportunity to tell him how it really went with Wayne, to share the whole thing in full. Suzy breaks it to him that she promised Wayne she'd quit.

"Well," Billy says, "I understand your situation, but I'd recommend against that."

"I didn't say I was doing it," Suzy says. "I just said that's what I promised."

"Besides what you owe me, you could use some money to sit on. With the new apartment, too."

"New apartment, flight school. Plus enough to put something away. I'm talking one more, basically, two max."

Billy nods. She knows he's just letting her say what she needs to say without believing it.

"What'll you do when you're through stewing?" Billy says. "You said a year, right? That's the mark?"

"If that. Make a little money while I can. I do like flying."

"Female pilot," Billy says incredulously.

"The way you just said that makes me want it more than ever."

"It just sounds like a tough road."

"In that case, I'll go to law school and work on becoming a senator. Take an easier path."

"I didn't mean anything. Though law school would be a pretty funny move."

"That's what I'll tell 'em I'm saving the money for. I mean, if anyone comes across it, if anyone asks."

"'SC law school's pretty good."

"You're like a Trojan booster."

"Just stating facts."

"I still don't get why you didn't just go."

"Didn't need anyone to make a plan for me. Had a pretty nice thing. Plus, get to go to all the games anyway."

"They win today?" Suzy says.

"That's what I hear. Another blowout. 55–20, or something like that. Three and oh now. I haven't seen a team like this one before."

"Well, maybe we can watch sometime."

"Maybe we *go* sometime. I better take you soon, before you clip your wings."

"Why's that?"

"No use to me after that."

"Ah, right. Cash in while you can."

They eat in silence and then Billy reaches for an oversize seashell. He inspects the inner ear of the shell and then holds it at arm's length. "'Alas! poor Yorick. I knew him, Horatio,'" he says, turning to Suzy with great commitment, "'a fellow of infinite jest, of most excellent fancy; he hath borne me on his back a thousand times'!"

Suzy shakes her head. "You are filled with many, many surprises."

He grins without opening his mouth. "Eighth grade. I forget the rest."

"Still impressive. I barely remember what I ate for breakfast."

"Hey," he says, "speaking of clipped wings, are you gonna be one of those girls who hang out with all the former stews down at Howlers or whatever? I saw them the other night."

"My sister always jokes about it. She's appalled by the thought. I think she's just worried it's gonna be her one day."

"They seem to have fun."

"Ever talk to the older ones? Who did it in the forties or fifties? Best year of their lives—every one of them. European vacations. Magazine spreads. *High glamour.* After a couple drinks they start in; sounds like it's been all downhill since then."

"What about the husband and children?" Billy says.

"Guess it's not the same as trips with the girls to Rome."

"Whatever, that's the case for a lot of people."

"Spend their whole lives reminiscing about being twenty-two?"

"I get it."

"Not me," Suzy says.

"Maybe you get your 'SC law degree and become queen of the stews, then. Make it so they don't have to quit when they get hitched and knocked up."

"Hearing you describe that future is an effective strategy to keep me in *your* business," Suzy says, burrito in her mouth. "Now I'm never gonna stop making runs."

Suzy shows at the airfield in the morning, wearing tight jeans and a canvas shirt, all business. She isn't even convinced yet that it's not a prank. But there he is leaning against the door of the classroom, sipping coffee and squinting at the prop plane that's coming in wobbly over her shoulder. She expects a warm welcome, but Millikan waves her unsmilingly toward the plane, a single-engine Cessna 172, postured with high shoulders like a tiny, proud Olympic gymnast. He hunches over as he opens the door and corrals her into the cockpit. They're buckled in, with matching headsets, locked and loaded, and the engine's up before he even asks her how she's doing. Suzy has an anchor in her gut, the uncomplex feeling that this is a mistake, that she shouldn't have pushed it on him, that he's only doing this because he worships at the altar of keeping his word.

They're first for takeoff and then the wheels separate from the concrete, and she's reminded immediately of the sensation she'd get in gym class all those years ago, practicing the long jump, speeding, leaping, basking in the lift but suffering for the inevitable arc toward the pit. Only, of course, they're pulling higher here, and it's at those heights, with Millikan one-eightying back toward the Inland Empire, that he seems to grow comfortable with where he's going, the rules he's breaking. "Just fifteen minutes," is what he says, and Suzy drops her eyes out the window to where the land looks just like it should, the Thomas Guide index pages she's been studying at home writ real, natural tones and highest resolution.

At the track Suzy admires the cars Millikan has reserved. A pair—it's only fair that they're the same—of Shelby GT350 Mustangs. A half hour is all they're signed up for. They initial on the liability line.

The infield course—the street course—is closed, so they're stuck, to Suzy's side-eyed dismay, with the oval. At the starting grid, buckled in but engines dead, they set the terms—ten laps around the oval, a little sprint. Suzy upgrades the deal. If she wins, she says, she gets to fly some on the way home. She lets Millikan move off the line and hangs on his bumper for the first eight laps, right there in his rearview, drafting three lengths back. She'd always loathed racing ovals, the long left turn. But she watched the cyclists in Munich, the practiced tactics on the velodrome, observed and took note. And in the ninth lap she moves high on the track, just to get him dancing a little, before dropping back down into a drafting position. A bogey on his six. She goes high again, and he moves with her. She makes it look as though she's trying to pass, but that she's dispossessed of the power to pull it off. Finally, when she's sufficiently bored and ready to start racing, she slings out of the stream and presses the car into the higher gear she's been pretending not to have. And for the final lap it's as though his car has decided not to take chase, to let her just go instead.

By the time he pulls into the pit, Suzy has already jumped out of the Mustang and is assessing the gunk on the windshield.

"Where'd the extra juice come from?" he says.

"See," she says, "I told you you were gonna learn something."

On the way back he lets her put her hands on the equipment. Her hands look small compared with his. She watched them on the way out—thick, strong, broken-looking like a boxer's. He asks her to change altitude, to tinker with speed—sticking to his word all over again. He asks for readings on the heading, attitude, VSI.

Then Suzy asks a question.

"How'd you end up teaching? You've gotta be so much younger than most instructors, yeah?"

"Just talked to some people at Zamperini." He pauses and the volume of their cruising speed seems dialed up in the cockpit. "Pretty straightforward."

"But you flew in Vietnam. Is that a normal thing? To end up doing something like this?"

"Not terribly normal."

"But you like it. . . ."

"You teach, you get paid, you make new pilots out of people who might be willing to rent your plane at a decent hourly." Suzy purses her lips and bobs, semisatisfied. He turns and considers her face, the bait of her lingering skepticism. "I had some trouble, if that's what you're asking. Flunked some tests you're not allowed to flunk if you want to work your way up the ranks. When you do that, you sorta limit your options. If you want to keep flying, there aren't a whole lot of opportunities."

"Even though you're good at what you do, specialized—that's what you said that first class, right? They don't have a use for you?"

"You're not supposed to do what I did."

"What—booze, blow? Drunk driving?"

He flips in his seat and flashes two mirrored aviator lenses in her direction. "How 'bout we get back to me asking the questions." Suzy squinches her nose and smiles to herself. Her hands are still on the yoke. She starts to think about him being "under the weather" a couple classes in a row, wonders what life's really like for Millikan during the 166 hours a week they're not together.

"Yes, sir."

"What about that there, that's a good one to know," he says. "What's that telling you—the flight recorder?"

Suzy scans the dash and finds the instrument. She doesn't know what he's getting at.

"It tells you how long you've been flying...."

"More importantly," he says, "it tells you how much you owe the owner of the plane for your joyride. It's a good one to keep an eye on."

On the first leg of the out-and-back to New York, the pilot comes on to say they may need to make an unexpected landing. They've already been squeezed onto a southern route by weather over the Rockies, but this is more severe, more urgent. *My God,* Suzy thinks, *it's happening again.* She's in the back of the plane brewing coffee when the announcement splits the silence of the cabin. At once there's the flare-up of a collective murmur, the sound of a lit stove top. None of the passengers in the back seem to be seeking her attention, but she can't quite see all the way to the front. The other three girls are near the cockpit, and she makes a line forward, cautiously, pacifically.

"Miss, what is it?" says a woman in a yellow dress. Suzy can tell she's shaped like a papaya.

"I'm heading up to check. It's all under control."

Each row she passes, though, she scans for signs that would suggest otherwise: bags with explosives, overstuffed shirts, shaky hands, sweaty eyes. And yet nothing presents itself ringed in red. There's an empty seat just before she reaches business class, a window seat she's sure was occupied. She closes her eyes tightly in an attempt to visualize the manifest, as though the darker she can make her mind, the better the odds of developing an image of the list of names and their associated faces.

But she comes up blank. And so she moves deeper toward the front of the cabin, watches the doors of the cockpit carefully. She doesn't want to startle anyone should the doors open suddenly. She passes the compartment with her bag. What happens if she fails to make a delivery? She can't be held responsible under these circumstances, can she?

She's nearly to the front of the plane, eyeing the compartment, wondering if the hijackers could possibly know about the haul. The run to pay back Billy. There's quiet up front—the three stews are seated. This confuses Suzy. But her confusion is cut off by the giant whoosh beside her, an imbalance of pressure, the cabin door unsealing, or some such equivalent. It springs her stomach. But then it settles, fizzy still but blushing, too. Someone's flushed the toilet. Suzy steps aside, out of the way, and the elderly woman belonging to the missing seat returns to her window.

Suzy presses in to the head stew and whispers softly so that the first-class passengers don't overhear.

"Is everything okay?"

"What?" Marcy shouts.

"Is everything...," Suzy says at the same unhelpful volume. Then: "What's going on?"

"Weather," Marcy says.

"Weather?"

"Gulf storm," Marcy says, shouting still.

"Nothing else, no other problems..."

"Don't look so spooked."

"Ladies and Gentlemen, this is your captain...." And he proceeds to explain. A late-season gulf hurricane has slowed its metabolic rate and turned into a mean, doughy central-Texas mess of shit that's forcing all planes in the area down to the ground for at least an hour.

That's it. Suzy's relief is rapidly overwhelmed by her distaste for her own paranoia. Here she was certain that they'd be flying to Cuba to drop off another radical in Havana, like she'd been reading about all summer. A favorite destination. She even heard from a pair of pilots that the government had considered building a fake Havana airport near the Everglades so that planes wouldn't even have to leave American airspace. A Hollywood Potemkin village for hijackers.

But instead: just standard Texas weather. An hour on the ground in Dallas becomes two. The storm turns out to be so bad, winds so significant, that they clear the runways entirely, rush all planes to hangars. It reminds Suzy of *The Wizard of Oz,* and she wonders if that one was the first "It was only a dream" in movie history.

From the gate she watches out the windows as a pair of fighter jets taxi right there between the commercial birds. She feels the familiar wistfulness for the claustrophobia of the cockpit. She can make out the red smudge of the pilot's helmet and finds it to be a shade she might like for herself if she ever races regularly again. After three hours the airline calls it—no one's getting out until the morning.

Suzy's put up in a room downtown with the rest of the crew. It's still light out and not even raining by the time they get to the hotel, and so she walks down by the Book Depository and trudges through mud on the grassy knoll, mud that dries bone-light on her boots. Some of the other girls go out to dinner, but Suzy heads to the bar with another something Mike gave her—a fat one, a weird one, Doctorow's *The Book of Daniel*—and orders a rib eye and a glass of Johnnie Walker Blue. And because it's the same bottle the cowboy at the end of the bar is drinking from, he says it's on him, a gesture Suzy waves off halfheartedly until he insists, and she gives him an over-cooked smile and a double thumbs-up.

When she asks the bartender for another, the bartender says the same guy's got this one, and the following one, too. They're already paid for. And so Suzy waves and mouths a thank-you again but returns to her book all the same. She moves through her meal slowly so that she's not left alone with just the drink. When she re-ups again, the man at the end of the bar stands and ticks off the number of seats between them until there's just one left. He gives her the space of a single stool.

"You're eating in a hotel and so I'm gonna assume you're not from here."

"You assume right."

"Tupperware sales?"

"Ouch."

"No, no, wait.... Replacement-cheerleader tryouts for the Cowboys."

"Thank you for the drinks, seriously, but—"

"Don't do that. Gimme a clue."

Suzy throws her shoulders back in mock posture and says "Can I get you anything else?" in an accent with big Texas hair.

"A stew?" he says, puzzled. "You sure don't remind me of a stew."

"Because I'm reading a book?"

"Oh boy, you aren't making this easy."

"I'm sorry, why don't I look like a stew?"

"I guess I've just never met one out of uniform, is all. It's like seeing your schoolteacher out on a date or something."

"Well, voilà," Suzy says.

He's tall, with a thick head of close-cropped dark hair, mussed flat by the Stetson that's resting on the stool beside him. His ears stick out a little and he's got the nose of a prey bird. His eyes are a blue that seems plugged into a wall, and they're roofed by a pair of bushy brows. Wranglers and double-pocketed powder-pink shirt and a bolo tie with the regal profile of a Cherokee chief.

"That's something," she says, nodding at it.

"This old Dallas wildcatter, this energy man, listed it for real cheap in the *Chronicle,* over where I'm at, in Houston. Clearing out the estate. Had that hat there and a pair of boots, too. Best I've seen. Came over yesterday. Guess how much."

"How much for what?" she says.

"The boots!"

"Couldn't guess."

"Guess."

"A thousand bucks."

"*A hundred and twenty* bucks," he says, slapping the bar. "Can you believe that?"

"Those there?" Suzy says.

"Nah, not wearing 'em. For my poppy. He took a new job in New York and he's missing the Texas stuff."

"Mazel."

"Pardon?"

"Congrats to your dad," she says. "And thanks again for this."

"Don't mention it. We're all stuck here together."

"Didn't you just drive over, though?"

"You ever driven through east Texas during a storm like this?"

"I have not."

"Well."

"I bet it's not that bad," Suzy says.

"Oh yeah?"

"I bet I could make the drive."

He narrows his eyes. "Stuck's fine with me."

Reports on the Cowboys-Packers game in Milwaukee have been coming in low on the radio, but it spikes now, awash in a debate over injuries, and Suzy's barmate leans into the news.

When his attention drifts back, he says, "So you're a stew and I'm a pilot. Bet you didn't realize how much we had in common."

"Oh yeah?"

"Texas National Guard."

"You fly in the war?"

"Just Texas Guard. Kept it close to home. Over at Ellington."

"You gonna go commercial?"

He looks puzzled. "Figuring it out. Taking a break, working on a political campaign in Alabama."

"Politics, too?"

"Not my primary interest."

"You'd rather be flying."

"I'd rather be pitching for the Astros."

"Wow, you're all over the place."

"Astros. Convair F-102s. Alabama senate campaigns."

"State senate?"

"C'mon."

"The big show?" she says. "That's a diverse portfolio."

"Thinking about business school after that."

"Keep 'em coming...what else?"

"Nah, that's enough from me. How 'bout one from you?"

"Well, believe it or not, I'm gonna be a pilot, too."

"They move a lot of the girls into the cockpit?"

"Not as often as they should. I'm in training now."

"Nothing to it once you're off the ground."

"That's what the boys say."

She doesn't even see him order another whiskey, but there it is. He lowers the waterline of his drink with the hand sleight of a pickpocket.

"Say, what's your favorite stew joke?" he says.

She smiles without her teeth and turns in her seat: "They're all pretty lame."

"Wanna know mine?"

"You bought the drinks...."

"So the stew goes up to the cabin and asks the pilot, 'Coffee, tea, or me?'" He pauses for effect. "And the pilot goes: 'Which one's easiest to make?'"

"I really didn't think that was gonna be the one," Suzy says.

"Lame, huh?"

"That's the joke even the shrews at stew school feel okay giggling at."

"Yeah, I like it."

"How 'bout this one," Suzy says. "Which do you prefer, sir? TWA coffee or TWA tea?"

"I've never flown TWA."

"Ah, it wouldn't make sense, then," she says, chewing a cube so it squeaks.

The man mouths the riddle to the ice in his tumbler. And then he shifts in his seat and smiles, like it's all gone to plan, like it's working out just right for him.

"Ha!" he says. "I hadn't heard that one. T-W-A-T, I like that....I prefer... *TWA tea*."

She sizes him up all over again.

"You don't look much like a horses-and-lassos cowboy."

"You're picking up on my time back east." He flashes a gold university class ring, and in the instant she thinks she recognizes the familiar Hebrew letters of the Yale crest. But his hands tuck back beneath his elbows on the bar before she can see for sure. "Odessa, Midland, Houston, before that. Poppy worked in oil. I went away and now I'm back. I've gotta say, I missed the clothes."

"Don't take this the wrong way, but when you're dressed up like it, you kinda have the Jon Voight thing going on, when he steps off the bus in Times Square."

"Still haven't seen it," he says. "But I know the Nilsson tune."

Suzy smiles and finishes her drink and drops it loudly on the bar. She scrapes the last of her zucchini around with a fork and presses her plate in the bartender's direction.

"Can I get you another drink or something?" the cowboy says.

Suzy's got an early call time and she's the kind of lit that's one drink too many for a good night's sleep and one drink short of a sure hangover. She's making a hard break of the twenty-four-hour rule either way. And here, after thirty minutes with this traveler—this thing before her that's hogging her field of vision, this shape that the camera in her mind has irised in on, this creature with whom she's collided and intertwined and that she's come to regard as the sole protagonist of her recent memory—Suzy's growing susceptible to the idea that he might very well be the only man left in the whole world.

"I'm good," she says, lifting herself and subtly falling forward toward him. "But listen: you get something else for yourself and put it on *my* bill. To pay you back. The airline's got it anyway, you know?"

He looks a little hurt, since things seemed to be going so well—but he has a nice mouth. And the longer he keeps that ring tucked under his arms, the greater Suzy's conviction grows to see it again.

"Room 325."

"Yes, ma'am."

Suzy slides what's left of the last ice cube into her mouth and cracks it in half. She steps closer and wraps her painted nails around his bolo tie. For whatever reason, that's the moment she remembers that there's freight glowing undelivered in her carry-on, and she feels a fuzzy heat beneath her skin.

"You understand what I'm saying? Room 325, 'kay?"

Suzy's over for a Sunday dinner and the energy's high. Mike had stayed on Reverend Jones. Went back to the downtown temple. Found out enough to know there was something worth doing. But he couldn't pursue it with the present revenue stream. He needed someone else's advance. He'd called an editor at *Rolling Stone,* a guy who used to throw Mike lines when he was living and writing in New York. Mike was dismayed to find that the magazine already had someone on Jones, but just this afternoon he received a call—the original writer had begged off, hadn't been able to get anywhere accesswise. Did Mike think he could do better? They gave him three months.

It's a good assignment. It's important and it's money. But Suzy knows it kills his new magazine, maybe for good.

After eating, while Mike and Grace do the dishes, Suzy picks up a recent *Saturday Review,* sees a new piece by Susan Sontag teased on the cover, flips to the opening spread: "To be a woman is to be an actress," it says. "Being feminine is a kind of theater, with its appropriate costumes, *décor,* lighting, and stylized gestures." It's not just the stews, then, Suzy is reminded, who are forced to play for the audience. It's a piece of writing that reminds her of the sort of stuff she read every day while studying with Camille. Those exercises, that routine, already feel so distant. Trapped behind a curtain, almost belonging to a different life.

It's still early, and so Suzy, Grace, and Mike hop in the car and head up to Hollywood together to a special movie thing Mike heard about. *Last Tango in Paris* is showing, fresh off the US premiere at the New York Film Festival. Traffic's nonsensically bad and they arrive between screenings. They have an hour to kill, so they park and buy cheeseburgers and walk over to Hollywood High, sit on the concrete barriers out front, on the corner of Sunset and Highland, where teenage skateboarders attempt and fail to grind on the edge of a bench. Suzy's been holding her breath for the moment that Grace says she wishes she could just see *Cabaret* again. But instead Grace pulls a joint out of her pocket and, under the showers of streetlights, convinces both of them to smoke with her.

"Where'd you get that?" Mike asks. And Grace says, "A friend at the beach," before specifying that she means J.P. Mike squints searchingly as he inhales, and Grace ribs him for having fun only when a high-snob Italian film is on deck.

It's a shitty thing for Grace to do, Suzy thinks—he's damned if he does or doesn't.

A teenager who's a head shorter than his friends, curly brown hair and tube socks pulled up to his knees, rolls over and asks if he can have some. Grace laughs and Mike smiles shiftily, but Suzy says, "If you land that"—meaning the trick they've all been failing again and again—"then you can keep the rest." The boy smiles and turns back to the starting line. "But if you miss," Suzy says, "I get to keep your board." The boy stops and turns back over his shoulder, pausing to weigh his options, and then he shakes his head, *No thanks*. He waits to see if she'll change her mind, but all she says is, "Bitchin' board." And so he returns to his friends and waits till Suzy and Grace and Mike get up and leave before he tries the trick again. Suzy resists the urge to turn back and watch, but listens and smiles at the sound of a clean landing.

*   *   *

Suzy wakes up the next morning to the sound of the airline phone, a call in predawn darkness. She'd passed out on the couch at Grace and Mike's after getting home late, and she lifts herself foggily to cut the alarm. She catches it on the fourth ring, and the man on the line is speaking with such distance that she wonders if his message is prerecorded.

"Whitman," he says.

"Yes, Suzy Whitman," she says.

"Grace Whitman."

"This is Suzy Whitman."

"Oh, Yahtzee, you're on my list, too. Two Pan Am girls got in a fender bender and landed in the hospital this morning, so we're short a stew on a double to London and Paris. Thing is, they're taking off soon and would need you at LAX in an hour. I understand you live close, which is why you're on my list. Whatdya say?"

"France."

"Need an answer in five, four, three—"

"Yes."

"Yes?"

"I can be there in an hour. But I'm supposed to fly to Denver this afternoon."

"You'll be covered."

"Okay, yes, then."

"They'll give you a uniform when you arrive. But bring your own in case nothing fits."

Suzy calls a cab to meet her at her apartment in half an hour.

"What's going on?" Grace says. She's in a red-and-white checked nightgown that cuts off in the middle of her thigh like a tailored picnic blanket. "Who was that?"

"Grand Pacific. They were looking for a last-minute sub to do a Pan Am flight to London and then to Paris."

"London and Paris."

"That's what he said."

"We don't go to Europe."

"Apparently, they're helping out Pan Am, like I said. Two Pan Am girls got in an accident and they just found out, and they're looking around for subs who are close."

"So you're going?"

"I'm going."

"How long are you gonna be there?"

"I didn't ask."

"You didn't ask?"

"He started counting down from five. A day? I don't know."

Grace uses her fingers to brush some tangles out of her hair and then pulls a shock of it to her nose.

"What are you supposed to do about your uniform?"

"They said just to bring it. I guess they have extras of theirs, but bring mine just in case."

"Is this even *real?*"

"I'm gonna show up," Suzy says.

"Why were they calling for *you* here?"

"They must've had the old number."

"Are you sure it wasn't for *me?* What happened to seniority?"

"Don't know."

"How 'bout I go instead and you take my St. Louis."

"Don't think you'd make it in time."

"I'm going back to bed."

"I'll put some coffee on for you."

Grace pauses. "Do you even have a passport?"

"As of just last week! In training they asked us to fill out the form if we didn't have one already. Said they'd cover the fee."

"This is weird, dude."

"But thank you for reminding me. I would've left it in my sock drawer."

"This is so totally weird." Grace disappears slowly. "Maybe you'll still be here when I wake up."

"I'll bring back some *macarons*."

Suzy arrives under the gun and they find a uniform that's her size. It's blue and white, a five-button jacket and a wide-spread collar that rests like sleeping wings. The skirt falls to her knees. Suzy is giggling as she fastens the fifth of five buttons all the way to the top, but she falls into full peals of laughter as she places the hat on her head. She considers it from several angles: a horse saddle, a fortune cookie, an inner ear. In any case, it's very foldy and it's the color of the constant California sky. By comparison, Grand Pacific uniforms are disarmingly casual. Shorter, slimmer, fewer *components*. Suzy is dressed like her mother dressing up like Suzy dressing up like her mother.

The girls on board are as amused by the pinch-hitting as Suzy is. Stewardesses aren't traded to other airlines. You come up training and playing for one team and stay put till you're married, pregnant, or dead. They have a fun time comparing notes, sharing secret lingo. Pan Am, it turns out, draws a more conservative line for booze cutoffs than Grand Pacific, even though the beer is free. While they're a little keyed up, the other stews are also concerned about the girls in the hospital. Apparently, one was driving and both were drunk. That's grounds for at least the driver to be laid off and possibly even the passenger. That's assuming their faces aren't roughed up too bad and their return is even up for debate. Nobody knows much, but there's plenty of gossip, dressed-up facts in a hat.

Suzy is mesmerized by the plane. Grand Pacific runs a fleet of 707s from the early '60s, so this is her first flight on a 747. She finds herself checking the window to make sure this place exists in real space and not on a soundstage. The preflight time has been less crunched than the man on the phone led on—they needed her when they needed her, but that's because of the full hour it takes to board the plane. Four hundred and fifty passengers, three-by-four-by-three in the body, and spread out like a hotel lobby bar up on the second floor. Burnt-orange and goldenrod seats borrowing from van der Rohe's Barcelona chairs; knockoffs of Saarinen's tulip tables; service stations that humble Grace and Mike's home kitchen. Four hundred tons of skeletons and steel and blood and fuel. Everyone boarding seems to vibrate in face of the boldness—boldness of color, boldness of design, boldness of furry stairs to the upper deck. Even the business-class passengers, who have surely flown the route to London before, seem to regard their clubroom-in-transport with an innocence of spirit.

The Pan Am international service runs like a Grand Pacific bicoastal, only with scheduled naps (the girls have the sort of reclining leather chairs each of their fathers occupies in the evenings) and just enough differences to trip Suzy up. The brands of soda. The temperature at which the desserts are heated. The generous commitment to replacing broken headsets and keeping the cabin smelling like orange groves. Suzy sleeps for all of thirty minutes; otherwise, she's pacing the dimly lit midnight aisles checking on passengers, replacing one headset and then another.

After eleven hours she can hardly account for, they arrive in London in the darkness of a new morning. When they exit the plane, the girls lead Suzy through the terminal to the Pan Am service lounge. It's close by, and in the short walking distance Suzy is on high alert for evidence of non-American signals—the cheese sandwiches for sale, the holes in the outlets in the walls, the shapeliness of the pound sign. The next one's an early flight to Paris that'll arrive around eleven. It turns out she'll have the day and the night, and then it's back the following morning, retracing the bread crumbs.

She eats with the other stewardesses—four of whom will be join-ing her on to Paris—and they get word about the accident. The girls were driving a dune buggy on the beach in Laguna. Middle of the night, bonfire. Got up to speed, hit the ramp of a lifeguard shack and spun like a bullet. Somehow, though, both girls are being released from the hospital. The one riding shotgun wasn't wearing her seat belt, got ejected, landed in a tumbling ball. (She was, someone tells the group, a gymnast at SMU.) The driver was buckled in but got knocked out. They weren't going fast enough to get too beat up, turns out, but they brutalized the lifeguard shack and rode in an ambulance anyway.

Suzy reads for a while in a corner near the window as the sky bright-ens. It is her first look at Europe. She strains to detect an accent in the line and color of the trees at the edge of the tarmac. When she feels her-self flagging, she pours herself some tea, but it fails to cool to drinking temp by the time the intercom requests her presence at the gate.

On board, the pilot introduces himself over the PA: Thibaux, a Shreveport fighter pilot who sounds like Beemans and Lucky Strike and Levon Helm's singing voice. Everything in English first, followed by a thirty-second ribbon of indecipherable French. Everything but "Pan Am" and "Paris" is round-edged noise to Suzy. Upon takeoff Suzy leans over her seat partner to get a look at the countryside. It is *Europe*. She's imagined this moment—not clearly, but con-sistently—since she started racing, since the possibility of Europe presented itself even faintly. And all she sees is the green. The endless Jane Austen of growing up, and here it is looking just as she said it would. How has this scenery failed, in this modern moment, to defy the centuries of played-out description? How could it really look so much like itself?

The green is socked in by a fat, ailing gray that has no intention of lifting—not like it does in Sela. Boundless Sela! So pleased with its one great trick. Dumb to literature, deaf to history, unconvinced of its unexceptional existence in the greater context of civilization. These are Suzy's thoughts as they rise—much too quickly, as the ceiling is so low—above the clouds: What power can Sela possibly hold over her compared with the place she's headed now? Where everything that could have been spoken and imagined, built and broken, won and lost, has been accounted for already. What, in contrast, is there for Sela to live for in its time?

It is too young to know better. That's basically it. An adolescent for whom all knowledge and experience is novel, original, singular. It conceives of itself as the first and only—and is quite relaxed about the fact. The very topography mimics a body in recline, a coastal hill range propped up on a beach towel, gazing at the water, back turned with stern indifference to the east. It is a place that behaves as though it's living out all there is to experience with little regard for anything that is not there. Suzy recalls a sunset last Friday. An ordinary sunset on an evening like thirty others she's seen in four-plus months. The sky went blue and orange and red and black, and then it was as though the sun had never existed—but for twenty minutes, right there on the edge, they stopped, up and down the Strand, on balconies, on bikes, surfers and stews and bassists and acolytes, they all stopped and looked and it was as though nobody had ever lived anytime or anywhere ever before.

Over the Channel they serve bread and cheese and red wine. They are things that are meant to project Frenchness. And yet they are meant not just for the British and the Americans, but for the French fliers alike—they are the actual things that are actually consumed by the actual French. Though the ovens are a step down from those of the transatlantic suite Suzy worked on the way over, she's happy to spend the jumper warming baguette after baguette, meeting an unceasing demand for hot bread.

Soon they're over land again: The Continent. In this case it's not Madame Bovary or Candide or Gigi, but rather images of the countryside from ABC that file forward in her mind. When she was a teen, *Wide World of Sports* brought one or two Formula One races to television, but what she's seeing out her window now is reminiscent of the steeples and farms and Alpine weigh stations of Eddy Merckx's Tour de France. It possesses the quaint stillness of a budget establishing shot. The helicopter flybys of *Mister Rogers' Neighborhood.* The artificial earth tones of a model train set. It looks nothing like she doesn't expect it to. It is the color of a continental European countryside. Not the golden grid of the US middle, not the overgrown forests of the mid-Atlantic and Northeast, not the crag of the Rockies, nor the feverish cultivation of L.A.'s eastern, inverse frontier. Rather what she sees is a precise visual reproduction of the projector slides in school (they themselves reproductions of reproductions) that had primed all of them, anyone born in America after the war, for their first encounter with the Old Country. It is so familiar seeming that Suzy feels almost unaffected by the momentousness. How can she be so incapable of a fresh metaphor?

The feeling only intensifies when she's dropped off in the center of Paris, at the curb of their hotel at the base of the Second. On the way to London she studied a map in the in-flight magazine—prep work she felt good about at the time but finds useless now. Still, she senses some markers. Around the corner, the convergence of several streets and what looks to be an ornamental epaulet of l'Opéra. Down their street in the other direction, a plaza with an obelisk wrapped in oxidized copper. She retrieves her key, nods through the advisements of the concierge, and drops her bags in her room. There is a gilded telephone receiver cradled flat. The phone forces her to consider the distance traveled—not just milewise, but the nine hours she's advanced the needle on the record of her life. She considers making a long-distance call home, to Grace or Mike, but gets consumed by the fantasy of *Suzy* picking up the phone on the other end instead. Suzy in the Parisian afternoon, from nine hours in the future, speaking to Suzy of the morning in Sela—Sela Suzy with a fresh day before her, all the time in the world to get it right.

It is an afternoon of solitary roaming. It is an afternoon beneath the invisibility cloak. She speaks with no one, buys nothing, enters not a single shop, café, or boulangerie. And yet she suspects she has experienced very few things in her life so completely. Never has so little been required of her to feel so animated.

She follows a well-worn route, perhaps the most well-worn route. Why, she reasons, with just eighteen hours, would you attempt to carve out a personal path in a place of such confident cliché? Just suck it up and surrender yourself to the spoked boulevards and grand city planning of the democratic despot. Connect the dots from one over-size monument to the next. Find ways into the breathless frames of Godard and Truffaut.

As the light begins to slip off the edge of Paris and the city joins the darkness of its neighbors to the east—those places where she'd gladly surrender her cool, as she has here, in order to see things with the full heart of a transient—she acknowledges a sensation she's been ignoring for hours. She is hungry and she will be forced to speak with someone. She leaves the Musée Rodin—where she spent half an hour reading the labels, as she imagined Camille might—and makes her way to her hotel's side of the river. At the markets men and women buy food for this evening only and pack it into bags brought from home. Even this! Just like they said it'd be. Suzy picks up enough for a picnic for one—a baguette, a starfish of Camembert, a carton of raspberries, a bottle of Bordeaux—and doesn't come close to spending the hundred francs the airline gave her as a per diem.

She passes over the Seine again and sits to sip straight from the bottle of wine. She notices the riverbank filling up with couples. Could they really all be tourists? Or could this be a legit ritual of third- and fourth-generation Parisians? She flashes again on the sunset in Sela last week—the locals in awe. Even here Sela slips into the frame. The way sand gets into Suzy's carpeting. Not a day gone and she can't help but wonder what's happening there.

Billy—the new zipper for Suzy, the thought that opens her up to all those raw, unasked-for feelings. What would Billy be doing on a night like this one, anyway? Lurking, surely, somewhere right around the corner from wherever Suzy was, ready to pinch her elbow and involve her in the evening's game. But just look at that river and those bridges and those bell towers of Notre Dame. Here she is, physically in this place she's long desired to be. And yet mentally she's in another. Fully possessed in neither. Content to exist in no place all at once. It's impossible, Suzy reasons, to determine whether she's more concerned about leaving behind what she knows or missing out on what she doesn't know, what's just over the edge. Is it a life meant to be lived in Schuyler Glen and Sela del Mar, or should she pack up her bag in the morning and thumb her way across the rest of the Continent? It's an even simpler question than that, though. It's fundamental, binary: does Suzy Whitman head home or keep on going?

Her stomach makes an audible sound, as if to remind her that the little mental things will always pale in comparison with the physical ones. Suzy is bored by the nuzzlings of the couples down below and wanders her way into the lawns deviating the Louvre from the Tuileries. Unleashed dogs scatter into the hedges and emerge at new entry points. She dumps her spread in the shadow of a small bronze sculpture of a naked woman fleeing something off-pedestal. Think, Suzy reasons, about how this thing—judged against its contemporaries to be not even good enough to be *inside* the museum—would be lauded were it unveiled from a sculptor's workshop today. How the average of one era is better than the best of another. Is there a single person alive who can make something this indelible? While tucking into her dinner and inspecting the other sculptures, Suzy comes to realize that the fleeing woman possesses one of the most frightening poses in the garden. Suzy pulls directly from her wine bottle and an unexpected burst of light files beneath a nearby arch. The head of the sculpture catches the light, and in the new weird shadows it suddenly shows more of her face to Suzy and appears to smile. *It's just a game we're playing,* the look seems to assure her. *Running for your life is nothing,* it says, *even if it lasts forever.*

From there it's a series of windings down. Suzy's hungry, so she eats; she's thirsty, so she drinks; she's drunk and full and running on practically no sleep in twenty-seven hours, and so she leans back and collapses on the grass, and in the instant before her brain shuts, she acts the wiser, picks herself up, and wanders home, half-conscious—moving in a line that's just more jagged than straight, through the dark gardens of the museum and the streets lit like memories of sleep.

After returning home and running Grand Pacific routes to Seattle, Salt Lake City, and San Francisco, she finally has a day off, a wet day, which she spends inside listening to the early radio broadcast of Game 7 of the World Series. It's an afternoon game, a Sunday matinee at Riverfront Stadium in Cincinnati, a game that started at 10:00 Sela Standard Time. The sound of the game is so sticky in its suggestion of the garage in Schuyler Glen, of summer and early fall with Wayne, that she moves to the phone, lifts the receiver, and dials. She should've called days ago, but she hasn't wanted to welcome bad news.

He's in front of the television, just as she suspected, tuned in to the NBC telecast. He hits her with the sorts of questions about her trip to Europe that she should've known to prepare for. The precise exchange rate with the franc. The range of pricing on the hotel. How well they seemed to preserve the ornamentation on this monument and that church. Then Wayne tells Suzy he's been cleared for surgery. It'll still be some time — they're thinking six weeks — but the chemo has reduced the size of the tumor and they're feeling better about their chances of operating effectively. Twenty percent up from ten. They can afford to take the chance. Wayne says he's lost more of his hair. What hair he has left, he says, seems to have given up on his body.

For stretches Suzy and Wayne are silent. They let the baseball in on both ends but choose not to sever the line. She opens her mail and dumps some chicken and vegetables into stove water for soup stock. The A's go up in the top of the sixth and don't look back. Suzy twists herself up in the phone cord, spinning herself in and out as though in the arm of a dance partner. Blue Moon Odom, Catfish Hunter, and Rollie Fingers close out Rose and Morgan and Bench. It's the first World Series for the A's since moving to California. It's a sign that has something to do with Suzy and Grace, Wayne says. Suzy wonders if a better collective of names has ever won a title in any sport before.

Speaking of names, Wayne wants to make sure Suzy knows Emerson Fittipaldi ended up winning the Formula One season, the youngest-ever champion, Grace's age more or less. He wants to make sure Suzy's still okay working flights — that she doesn't feel shaky after the summer and fall of terror in the skies. (This, Suzy knows, is not the time to mention her lessons.) He wants to make sure she knows that he's not so worried about her as much as he is about her sister. The dying man wants to make sure Suzy and her sister know that flying is still the most dangerous thing there is.

It's a day of training when everyone's up in the air. Thirty-minute sessions, Suzy's scheduled second to last. She and Millikan mime their way through the motions within eyeshot of the others, as though they haven't been in a cockpit together before. It's been a month, but they pick up where they left off. He's moving her through a checklist. Change heading fifteen degrees south, tap the air brakes, pitch and drop five hundred feet.

It has been foggy all day on the ground near the beach, a sewer lid of smog that dims the world. Above the cloud line, though, it's radiant. The sky: Genesis blue. Original blue. This cockpit, Suzy realizes, is a guaranteed exposure to sunlight, certain escape from the gray. A way to subvert the claustrophobia of low clouds. Up here is the exception, the cheat. The escape from the squeeze of weather. As though she needs a new reason to want it.

It's getting dark earlier, and on their way back, farther east where it's clearer, they're cruising over the liquid streams of scarlet and cream on the Santa Ana, the Long Beach, and the Harbor. As they circle back to wrap up their half hour, Millikan asks Suzy out to dinner.

"What makes you think I'd say yes to *this* pilot when I say no to all the pilots at work?"

"Well, for one, it's wise to give at least some hope to the guy at the controls."

He can't be all that much older than she is, but the lines at the corners of his eyes are like rake gratings. Each class since their last time in the air, she's run through options for what he could've done to get discharged. And she's convinced herself it has to do with drinking. Now she can't help but see the cracks in his face as belonging to someone who's worked his way through a garbage dump of booze bottles. That face, entirely his, utterly unique, like the revolutionary "bar codes" she just read about them trying at a grocery store in Cincinnati.

"I could land it if I needed to," Suzy says.

"I'll take that as a maybe, then."

He smiles, a little goofy. She wonders if he's ever been drunk in class, if he's drunk now. It's unfathomable, that sort of carelessness. But she imagines that the kind of demotion he suffered, to the classroom after war, doesn't get you any closer to sobriety.

"How 'bout this," Suzy says, "I'll get dinner with you if you let me land."

She wonders if it had to do with drugs, too. She wonders who his dealer might be now. She considers just saying his name, just testing the water . . . "Billy Zar?" But it's just in her head.

"That still sounds like a strong maybe," he says. "And to be clear: you do not get to land. It's socked in."

"Give me ten more minutes, then."

"We've got one more person to go today and it's already getting dark."

"Ten more minutes and I'll get a drink with you. I'll stick around for the last one and get a beer."

"Five more minutes," he says.

"Half a beer, in that case."

"Okay, ten," he says. "Jesus."

"And a landing," she says.

"And *I'll* be landing."

On Halloween morning Suzy stops by the house to borrow a shirt from Grace, but Grace isn't there, it's just Mike. He's sitting in the office, her old room, and he's staring at a sketch of a trumpet. Suzy recognizes it from somewhere, but it's in Mike's handwriting, on one of Mike's yellow legal pads. He has a book on his lap, well worn, yellow but not ancient yellow, modern yellow, and it's open to the last page, the author biography. Suzy recognizes the book, too — *The Crying of Lot 49*. The trumpet, the secret symbol of their mail society, or whatever it was. She never read it, but she met lots of boys during her semester at Yale who had. Who were talking about even getting the trumpet as a tattoo.

Mike's face is erased of its color. He looks only half-full of necessary body fluids. Someone has died, it's the only explanation.

"Are you okay?" Suzy says.

"Did you know that he *lives* here?" Mike says.

"Who?"

He shows her the last page, the photoless author bio. "But it doesn't even say it here. I just heard from my editor today, he asked if I ever saw Pynchon around. And he explained the whole thing. Said he has a book coming out in the spring. A big one. 'A rocket book.'" He does scare quotes with his fingers.

Suzy stands in the doorway, silent. "So?"

"I just...can't believe he lives here."

"Maybe we'll run into him at Howlers tonight."

Mike doesn't smile. Mike is spooked—the effect of having heard the clarion call that his turf has been infiltrated without his knowing. It's a look that says Mike Singer can taste another writer's blood in his mouth.

The after-lesson drink with Millikan turned into two, which turned into dinner TBD. And so the first Friday in November, he offers to cook for her at his place. It's the sort of bad idea Suzy regularly wonders how the women in the papers could make. Offering up one's body to be tied and taken, sliced and diced. Or even just adding a complication to the training—wrapping up the fate of her pilot's license in the satisfaction of a dinner date. It's not like her to take the bait so readily, but, basic as it sounds, there's something about the way Millikan *smells,* an effect to which she submits. It's his aftershave, she's pretty sure. She didn't really notice it before the last lesson. But the richness of that eucalyptus head-cloud, it's the smell she now most associates with the cockpit. A scent that reminds her of air and light and lift, but also the bone planes of Millikan's well-shaped skull. That double association gets her like a hook in the gills.

His house is an actual grown-up house—not an apartment, not a condo, not a beach pit, but the sort of place people with children might live in. There's a freshly mown lawn and hedges that appear tended to. There's a concrete drive that looks poured over recently, crack-free. There's a porch with a rubber tree in a plastic bucket and a two-person seat suspended from the overhang. There's even a red door—an upstate door—with a brass knocker and everything.

The door opens. It startles her. He dries his hands on his shirt and waves her in. He leans forward and kisses her cheek. It surprises her. It's not a gesture she receives often out here, and it's certainly not something he's done before. Not at the airfield, not at the racetrack, not when she left him hanging at the bar. The whole thing has the scent of that eucalyptus—the kiss, but also the room, the house. She promised herself to check the house for emergency exits, first thing. But she finds her resolve melting away already. She's brought a six-pack of Coors and he takes it from her, leads her to the kitchen, and she follows without reluctance.

The kitchen overwhelms with a new smell—straightforward, everlasting: butter, potatoes, greens. Two fat steaks sit on a flowered plate, oiled and seasoned and ready for the grill. He offers her a drink, and Suzy says whatever he's having, and so he pours her two fingers of Jim Beam over ice. He moves through the kitchen in tight lines. The efficiency makes the kitchen seem larger than it is, but really it's quite small. An undersized table, a slim counter, a stove with four burners, a fridge, and, near the side door, a washer and dryer. It's through the door that she smells the coals burning. He can practically tend to the grill and the stove top at the same time.

Millikan. *Mitch. Mitchell.* He is the same but different. He looks fresher than he has on other occasions, lit up like a watered plant. Jeans and white shirtsleeves rolled up to the elbows, showing off the hairy wrists, the boxer's hands. It's a version of what he wears to the airfield, only made softer by the smells in the kitchen. Made softer by the streetlights that spill into the house and the fact that it's too dark out for aviators. The tight toasted skin, the casual lift of the frequent haircut, the peninsulas of the forehead on the hairline—firmly established, but with no plan to press deeper toward the crown. He never touches his hair, a sign he's not worried about it going anywhere. There's the squint, even in low light. The beady eyes and the crinkles. Signs of the quiet type, signs of the thinker. Narrow face, tall face, tapered to the mouth and its down-turned corners, and a chin that announces itself as neither prominent nor obscure. *God,* Suzy thinks, *this pilot.*

He hasn't spoken since pouring the drink, but he's making no effort to scramble for conversation. He's comfortable at the stove, he's comfortable with this woman in his place. Suzy, resting her hands on the back of a tall wood-and-wicker chair, imagines all the other women stacked up in that kitchen: one leaning on the counter, another twirling the phone cord around her finger, a few more plumping their asses up onto the windowsill to watch him work. She can't fantasize about the others and speak at the same time, and so she opens her mouth and starts.

"Thanks for having me," Suzy says.

"Thanks for coming."

"This your standard move? For the promising students, I mean?"

"Yeah, I love cooking for older men who are desperately seeking a new hobby."

"But, I mean, you seem to be at ease with me here. You seem to know what you're doing."

"This is not the first time I've prepared this meal for a guest, if that's what you're getting at."

She sips once and then twice and stands her ground, comfortable as he is. Without announcing it, he takes the steaks out the side door to the grill. She hears the sizzle as they hit the grate.

"You hear about the hijacking last weekend?" Suzy says.

"The, what was it, Algeria?"

"Same terrorist group from Munich. Demanding the release of the killers who were caught."

"How'd it wind up?"

"Dumped the plane, I think."

"Jesus," he says. "Barely notice anymore, there's been so many lately."

"The crashes in the past few weeks, God."

"You keep a list?" he says.

"Our newsletter from the airline has this little Bad News box. We hear about every one."

"What were the latest?"

"There was that Uruguayan plane."

"Oh, never mind, right, the rugby team."

"Flew into a mountain? I mean, how does that happen?"

"Clouds, carelessness. Flying by wire and switching over too late."

"And then the congressman," Suzy says. "Alabama...Mississippi...Louisiana?"

"Louisiana," Millikan says. "I guess this stuff does register somewhere."

"Disappeared. No wreckage, no sign."

"What about the rugby team?"

"According to the box, no sign of any survivors there, either."

"Does it make you nervous about flying?" he says.

It touches Suzy cold. Not because she hasn't considered it, but because she hasn't engaged the question with another person before. She was lying there on the beach just this week, reading words, magazines, newsletters, and she came across the deaths of these dozens, and she felt the illogical urge to get up into the air, to run straight into the burning building. It was an impulse that was both her present and her past—a thing she'd felt previously only on the racetrack. The more difficult the course, the more frequent the accidents, the more convinced she grew that she was the exception, that she was the one meant to make it out. Now she's ready to put her hands on the yoke for days and days and be the kind of pilot who doesn't ever crash.

"Honestly," she says, "it makes me want it more."

Millikan smiles. "Thata girl."

"If you're good, you're good," Suzy says. "If the plane's gonna go down, it's gonna go down. But you can do some things. Preparation, practice, skill..."

"A little luck," he says. "You can only control what you can control. But there's a lot you can't control."

"So how do you do it? Why aren't you afraid?"

"I've been close to going down, and when you don't, it's sort of like house money. Who's afraid with house money?"

"I don't know how to play craps."

He smiles again. She can tell that he can tell that she's kidding, that she gets it. It's a comfortable wavelength to operate on. A slick compatibility.

He slips out the door to flip the steaks and she excuses herself to the bathroom.

The house is comprised of five small rooms that reveal themselves off a coiling hall. The living room is sparse—a worn leather couch, a spare coffee table, a television, and an overstuffed bookcase. The bookcase surprises her, distracts her from her line to the toilet. The books are all for adolescents. Stuff she remembers male classmates carrying around in elementary school and junior high. Hardy Boys. Narnia. Slim paperbacks about sports and war and wilderness survival. The shelves filled edge to edge. They look hastily distributed, not necessarily collected and organized one by one. Like he's inherited them recently, his childhood cache, maybe. Rescued from the junk pile during a paring down. Suzy can imagine her parents doing that sort of thing. Sounding an untelegraphed alarm of *Everything must go*. The race home to salvage things she hasn't thought of in years. A bookcase of her own with all the nostalgic crap she might not even ever look at again. Here is that for him: Mitch Millikan, Boy Detective, adventures K–12.

Next is the bedroom, dark, lit at the windows by a streetlamp, just enough for Suzy to make out an uncluttered floor and a bed crisply made. Then, a second bedroom, an office that leads into a yard via a sliding glass door. In the office are a single chair and a single lamp. A reading room, perhaps. But on the floor—brown boxes with black glass faces. First one, then a few, then at least a dozen sharpening into view. She steps into the room, looks closer. Television sets. Each like the other. Newish-model Sony Trinitrons, sitting quiet. In a pile in the corner, pairs of antennae, rabbit ears separate from their heads. Suzy can't begin to guess what this is, but it boomerangs her back to the animal fear, the porch thought—she doesn't know this person, not even a little.

She still has to pee, though, and so finds the last room off the hall, the last room of the house. The bathroom is petite and peach colored. She sits and inspects the walls—white, bright white. Fresh paint, no mildew. She stands and flushes and draws the shower curtain. It smells like new plastic. The tub is spotless. She peers out the mail-slot-shaped window above the tub and finds a view of the neighbor's kitchen. A man with a mustache is doing the dishes. He stares directly at Suzy. His eyes catch light like the blade of a knife.

She pulls the curtain back quickly and washes her hands. The sink is scrubbed porcelain; the mirror is smudge-free; there's nothing in the trash bin besides a few strands of floss. Everything is military spick-and-span.

She dries her hands—freshly laundered towel—and returns to the mirror. She's even more translucent than usual, spooked by the neighbor's unobstructed view into the shower. There are freckles, there are light eyes, even some lines beneath them. Her hair looks as lightly and thinly drawn as a pencil sketch. Her mouth, though, stacks up full, her lips a pair of pinkie fingers. She notices that the mirror doubles as a cabinet. She opens it. Finds the usual things. Every new detail comes as a small relief. Beside the tube of toothpaste is a jar of Proraso shave cream. *That's it,* she thinks. She unscrews the top, finds herself overwhelmed by a higher concentration of the scent she most associates with him. The eucalyptus. The way it clears the head like horseradish. She fingers some excess from the cap and touches the lines beneath her eyes. She rubs it in, coolly, a shot at reducing the swelling. When she opens her eyes again and the picture of Suzy comes back to her in the mirror, she inspects herself and is satisfied. There's nowhere to go but back in there. "Okay," she says.

Dinner goes quickly. She feels badly that she's eaten in minutes what took an hour to prepare. They talk about growing up. Suzy's Schuyler Glen and Millikan's Omaha. Mom at home, Dad in the stockyards—there's a reason this steak tastes as good as it does. Three brothers, three sisters, Millikan in the dead middle, the easy-to-overlook centerpiece. He joined the air force after high school, ended up in California. Got into the test-pilot business. This has never come up before. Suzy can't believe he was one of that maniacal strain. The one-in-four-dead odds that made it the most dangerous job in America. The backstory is beginning to touch the edges of things she's heard about. She knew he'd been at Edwards at some point, but didn't put together that it'd been with that gang. Somewhere along the way he wound up in Vietnam, she knows, but she hasn't quite pieced that part together yet. She has a second Jim Beam and then stands up to pop the top off a first beer. She's through eating, doesn't need seconds. Doesn't know how long she really has to get to the heart of it, anyway, and so wastes no more time.

"I have some questions," she says.

"Oh yeah?"

"What's up with the TVs?"

"You found the TVs?"

"It's weird."

"It's a side thing."

"You sell them?"

"It's only a dozen at a time. TVs, repairs, installation. We get 'em from somewhere, the buyer gets a discount, we make a little something."

"A man with two jobs."

"I take what I'm given."

"But what does a pilot like you...I don't totally get it. What are you really doing here?"

"I wanted to cook you dinner."

"But what *happened?*" she says. "What did you *do?*"

He smiles at her—she's proud of her directness, like a child who's smug about the first check of a chess game.

"I killed somebody I wasn't authorized to kill."

Suzy is cold all over again. These sudden, extreme temperature changes—in a sink they would break a glass.

"You killed somebody?"

"I hit somebody while I was driving a car, a farmer near Edwards. We'd been out at the bar near the base and we were racing home—

that's what we did—and he was on the side of the road, the edge of his property. I didn't even see him."

"And he *died?*"

"You ever hit an animal?"

"We grew up with deer."

"So you ever hit one?"

"Just once," Suzy says. "But it was glancing, a clip. All we had to do was knock the dent out."

"Well, lemme tell you what happens when it's square. It's not a thud. It's like, I dunno, it's like a trampoline. The car launched him. The body was thrown over the property fence and into a field. Eighty feet."

"Oh my God. Was it instant?"

"I know people only die one way, but this guy looked like he died a hundred ways. All the bones, all the bleeding."

"But it was an accident."

"Sure, but I'd been drinking."

"They arrested you."

"If they'd've arrested me, I'd probably be in prison."

"So, what then?"

"The air force guys showed up first. They got me back to base. They called the cops, dealt with them directly. Said they'd take care of the discipline. They wanted to handle me themselves."

"Is that a good thing or a bad thing?"

"I thought it had to be a good thing. A protective thing. But the short of it is they needed better pilots overseas, and they weren't gonna get any of the guys they really wanted to volunteer. They gave me one option, pretty much, and so I went."

"So you did a tour."

"They made me stay three years."

"Jesus."

"Same deal each time—another go or they'd court-martial me for the drunk driving or turn me over for manslaughter. They let me out after three. But I knew I wouldn't fly with the air force again. If they make it so you can't get where you want, why stick around? And with the way information moves with those guys, it's tough to even get a shot at flying commercial."

"And so: Zamperini Field. Mitch Millikan meets Suzy Whitman."

"And so."

"That's a tough story," Suzy says.

"I've grown pretty used to it."

"Do you like the teaching, at least?"

"Not...not especially. It's what I can do until there's something better."

"Guess they didn't take it all away," Suzy says.

"You mean I'm still allowed to rent a car at the racetrack?"

"Sure, but also—"

"The Cessna?"

"I guess? You can still get up and go."

"That's right: I can still get up in the clouds," he says, smiling sadly. "Glad to see you've been paying attention to the whole point of this stuff."

They don't know each other—that's the thing. That's the thing with a dinner like this one, with an innocent entry point but no discernible way out. Which is why, with the food gone, Suzy drinks more, meeting Millikan at his dark pace—one for one, and quick. The act does the work of longtime acquaintanceship. And it's how, by the time they're out of things to say to each other, there's been a bridge built, a natural little path to the other side and the next stretch of uncharted wilderness, where their faces can meet across a kitchen table.

*　　*　　*

The night of the election, bartenders at Howlers are giving out free beers if you can prove you didn't vote. Suzy and Billy can prove they didn't vote, though Suzy did. She snuck in early to a booth at the lifeguard office on the Strand, when there was no one around besides blue-haired volunteers. The California polls are still open, but news organizations are close to calling the thing for Nixon. The televisions are off in the bar and the speakers are blasting the new Genesis album in full, and the sense is that this day feels less than even every other day like an election day. There's a vacuum of consequence. Especially in Sela, the farthest point possible from meaningful democracy.

Suzy and Billy drink beers, and because her flight was canceled while he was at her apartment in the afternoon, she can't get away with the excuse that she has to be at the airport in the morning. The twenty-four-hour rule, never in great effect under ordinary circumstances, need no longer apply. They really drink so many beers, and on their way out Billy pats his pockets and realizes he's left his keys at Suzy's apartment. So they hike up the hill and take the seemingly hundreds of stairs to Suzy's front door, stairs through which Billy loses a flip-flop, and as she moves through the door and turns on the lights, he taunts Suzy with the presence of his keys in his hand—he's had them all along. Her indifference is a win for Billy.

She closes her eyes and scuffs her feet toward the bedroom door, and when she slowly reaches toward the knob, she waits, expectantly, for the bolt of lightning to jump from brass to fingertip. By then, she figures, if Billy doesn't know he's in—which maybe he doesn't, he's still standing by the front door—she doesn't totally care anyway. She has a hot hand. The more she gets, the more she wants. But whether she's sleeping in her bed alone or not is up to him, and so she moves to her room so that whatever's gonna happen can get on happening.

*   *   *

On the second Monday in November, Suzy reports to the private-jet terminal in the middle of the morning. It's a press flight, her first one. Two dozen newspaper, magazine, and catalog writers from "the West" are gathered at the private check-in gate, drinking coffee and eating little muffins. The plan is to show off Grand Pacific's first 747. It'll be used primarily for the L.A.–New York route, but today they're just gonna take it to San Francisco. It's the sort of junket that would've been happy to host a writer from Mike's California magazine. Suzy knows about the press flights—that you're meant to turn your standard High Bubble even higher. That while there are only twenty-five passengers on the 747, the crew is meant to work as though it's full. It goes by in a snap, and they've landed before Suzy's even paying much mind to the fact that they're in the air.

At SFO there's a hot lunch of chowder and sourdough while one of the Grand Pacific executives gives a lengthy presentation on the new 747 service, due to launch in the early part of next year. The journalists are served bottomless lunchtime martinis, and they stop taking notes ten minutes into the talk. There are a few obligatory questions, and then it's more drinking. Suzy hangs around the back of the presentation room, watching the planes on the runway and counting down the minutes till they reboard. It's a waste of a day, but it's double flight credit. While watching a Pan Am plane taxi to its gate—imagining what international location it's most likely to have slept in last night—she receives a light brush on the shoulder.

"I promise not to take it too personally, but you seem more interested in what's going on out there."

It's the executive from the front of the room. He introduces himself and Suzy says hello. He's younger than he looked with the microphone—probably the oldest-looking young person Suzy's seen. Thick hair and a smooth face, but a dark-gray suit that fits him like a garbage bag. He asks about her time with the company, and Suzy answers all his questions politely. When he finishes his drink, he stays hovering in the back, looking for a new angle. He asks Suzy if she's auditioned for the latest ad campaign.

"I hadn't heard of one," she says.

"It's quite good, I think. And I suspect you'd have a very good chance of being selected."

"Selected for what?"

"We're picking ten girls to be the faces of the campaign. These new advertisements in magazines and newspapers, on billboards. TV, too."

"What do you have to do?"

"Oh, not much, really. It's just a picture of a pretty, caring, hardworking stewardess such as yourself, and the words say: 'I'm...' Remind me your name again?"

"Suzy."

"And so it says: 'I'm Suzy, Fly Me.' And then the next line would be: 'Fly Suzy. Fly Grand Pacific.'"

Her face is a soup of uncertain lines.

"You like it that much, huh?"

"Maybe not for me," she says. "I mean, it's clever. I just—maybe not for me."

"We don't have a light red yet."

"My hair."

"It's tougher than any of the others to find."

"Gotta have one," she says.

"I think we do."

"We're always the last."

"Just think about it," he says. "If you change your mind, give me a call direct. I've got a good bit of the say-so." He hands her a business card.

"If you're still short a light red...," Suzy says.

"Then call and I'll have somebody make it happen."

"'Fly Me…'"

"See, it's pretty good, right?"

"I'd vote for them to just print a portrait of the 747 instead."

"See, I like that attitude—selling for the brand even when the writers are all over there."

"You wouldn't even have to change the copy."

"I like the enthusiasm."

"That 747's the sexiest girl we've got."

The weekend before Thanksgiving, Suzy meets Rachel at the base of the trail to the Observatory. Suzy and Rachel were roommates in stew school, twenty four hours a day together for three weeks. They slept in twin beds on metal frames on carpetless linoleum, like *Madeline*. Suzy and Rachel locked without effort, not because they were exceptionally well matched, but because you could never be odd woman out as a pair. Rachel was from Chicago. She'd grown up on the South Side and moved to Wilmette before high school. She happened to know the only girl Suzy knew from the North Shore—they'd met at church and then again at New Trier and then again at Loyola in the city for college.

As graduation grew nearer at stew school—as it became clearer that they would not be kicked out for infractions or a lack of competency, like half of their class—Suzy and Rachel were given the pick of their home base and both selected Los Angeles. Though they'd live in different corners of the sprawl—Suzy in Sela and Rachel in Pasadena—they learned that it wasn't *that* far, really, during light traffic, and so seeing each other wouldn't be an issue. But they hadn't seen each other. Except on the occasional flight, maybe two or three times, which was always great. Still, Rachel did this thing that bugged Suzy where she always had to acknowledge it, call it by a name: "We've just *got* to find a way to do this outside the airport!" she'd say, and Suzy would agree each time, meaning it but knowing that she probably wasn't going to leave Sela on most nights. It was an odd conviction of Suzy's—in spite of the fact that she had no great obligations keeping her wrapped up, just Mike and Grace and the occasional thing with Billy. But after their last encounter at LAX, that latest "Absolutely, you're right, we must," Suzy realized that failing to follow through one more time might end their friendship for good, and so proposed a hike in Griffith Park.

Rachel is freckle faced, a freckles-on-the-lips sort of density. But even she's browned out in L.A. compared with Suzy. She's wearing Nike-swoosh running shoes and dolphin shorts and a T-shirt without a bra. It rained the day before, and the heavy shower pruned the trees, the green leaves of the live oaks mixing with the golden sycamores' to give the impression of a true autumn. The lower part of the trail is a canopy of trees and is sopping with damp shadows. They talk about flight plans. They talk about passengers. They talk about the Bad News box in this week's newsletter.

"Have you seen the latest?" Rachel says.

"Not yet—another hijacking?"

"The newsletter said there's gonna be security changes."

"Really? Finally? What set them off?"

"Three dozen passengers on that plane for thirty hours."

"This is the one that went to Cuba?"

"Right—on Southern. *Thirty hours.* Can you imagine?"

"So, what, the new rules are…"

"Don't bring knives, don't bring guns. Major airports. And then pat-downs, bag checks, metal detector."

Suzy's legs go weak and she falls a step behind. She imagines at once how Billy will take it.

"Bag checks?" Suzy says. "Metal detector?"

"Yeah, starting first week of January."

"Wow, soon..."

Even if she wanted to keep going, it wouldn't be possible. She counts on her hand the max number of runs she'd be able to do in that time.

"But obviously doesn't affect us," Rachel says.

"What do you mean?"

"Pilots, stewardesses, and airport staff are exempt."

Suzy can't tell if she's relieved or not.

"We're still only subject to the hens in flight ops."

They step out from beneath the canopy and into direct sunlight, the dirt path casting above them like a fly-fishing line loose on the water. It's a steady ascent but with curves to cut the grade, the Griffith Observatory like Oz at its end. Suzy lays down asphalt with her eyes, imagines racing a car to the top.

Rachel mentions that she's been seeing a captain. They wound up in a crew that works together on the regular—a pair of pilots, and a quad of stewardesses who went in for Midwestern flights out of L.A. Not the most sought-after routes—Chicago, Minneapolis, Kansas City—but routes Grand Pacific is happy to let them run together. Rachel and the captain had been sharing a room on the road for three months.

"And he's married?" Suzy says.

"He is."

"Welp."

"And get this: his wife is a former stew. That's how they met."

"So she knows what's up, then."

"I'm proceeding as though each time is the last time."

"It can't last, Rachel."

"That's okay."

"So why do it?"

"C'mon," Rachel says. "Ace in Korea."

"Ha. You sound like my dad."

"How's that?"

"Doesn't matter. But wait, how old is he?"

"Midforties."

"Jesus."

"No kids, though."

"Yeah right."

"No, no. Shoots blanks. That's part of what makes it okay."

"Maybe it's her problem," Suzy says.

"Maybe. But I'm not pregnant yet."

"Do I know him?"

"Oh, probably."

Suzy thinks hard, really wants to nail it. "Mulaney?"

"Ew…God…no."

"What?"

"He's *old*," Rachel says.

"He's gotta be the same age as whoever you're talking about!"

"But Mulaney's going bald. Plus he's got those weird intense eyes."

"Manson eyes."

"Right, yes. He's just…*hard-core.*"

"It's true. We had a hijacker on a flight with him."

"*What?!* You were on that flight?"

"I was, but I'll tell you about it later. What's important now: *who is it?*"

"Do you know Bill Mackenzie?"

"So I really wasn't far off."

"You do know him, then," Rachel says.

"He's Mulaney with thicker hair. If Mulaney's Aldrin, Mackenzie's Armstrong."

"If Mulaney's Aldrin, Mackenzie's *Gordo Cooper.*"

"That's right, you've always been with Gordo," Suzy says. "You finally got your Gordo."

"We'll see. It's been a couple weeks. It might be over now and I wouldn't even know it."

Suzy's reminded of Grace's veteran—the temporal distance between a death and learning about it.

"When do you fly again with him?" Suzy says.

"Tomorrow to Detroit."

"So you'll know soon, then."

"I just don't want his wife to call again. It happened in the summer, only once. But I can't deal with that again. I like these guys, but I don't like them *that* much. I'm on her side in the end."

"Well, maybe tomorrow you just do your job, do the work, and pretend like you've never done it any other way before. When he tries to talk to you at the hotel, just say you're going to the pool with the other girls. He'll get it."

"But what if he wants to marry me?"

"I can see you've really figured this out," Suzy says.

"*Me?* What about *you?* You haven't said a thing! Never a story, never a word about anything!"

"I've been flying a lot."

"Who have you been going on dates with, though? Where have you been going out?"

"No dates to speak of. I just kick around Sela. Really."

"How are you *this* uninterested in meeting men?"

It's a question that hits right as they roll into the steepest incline, and the sun seems to have pulled in like a camera for a close-up, right at shoulder height, right in their faces, and she's searching for some shade or the next flat, and it's just not coming. The thought of spending evenings with strangers regularly—it had, even in high school, never much interested her, just another thing that had made her feel like less of a normal young woman. Out of the groove with her female friends. And though she hasn't had to muster up many explanations recently—Grace and Mike stopped asking, maybe because they'd assumed something about Billy—she just shores up her heavy breathing and tells Rachel about the cowboy in Dallas. A brief story and an isolated incident, but it cuts the edge off the appetite nonetheless.

At the top of the hill, after one last big push up the final sloppy incline, they turn over their shoulders and behold the Southland, certainly not the filthiest day they've seen, but not clear, either. The basin's like a bathtub, edges at the peninsulas of the bay, filled up with old water that won't drain.

"There's you," Rachel says, pointing toward Sela through the smog.

"And there's you," Suzy says, pointing at an opaque wall farther to the east.

"How could you even tell?"

"Blind faith," Suzy says. And they debate going inside the observatory to look at the stars.

Rachel smokes a joint she brought along, and they end up watching the show, stretched way back in their seats. Afterward they hike back down to their cars, red and sweaty, and they hug tightly anyway. Rachel holds Suzy's head close, so that Suzy sees all the freckles rearranging in the patterns of the star show, and Rachel says, "We *have* to do this again soon," and Suzy says, "I know, we do." And she really means it this time, until the car door's shut and she's on the Harbor and the world is erasing itself behind her, so that all that truly exists for Suzy is what's in front of her, on the other side of the traffic.

Suzy brings the booze to Thanksgiving, whiskey and wine. It's raining—a miserable, freezing (that's the word Grace uses now to mean fifty), flooding afternoon. Suzy didn't know until today, but two storm drains let out near Mike and Grace's place, Yellowstone geysers that flood all the way back down Nineteenth to the beach, where the water Vs a path through the sand to the ocean like a snowplow.

"This is good," Mike keeps saying throughout the prep, to more thunder and lightning, and the louder rushing of water out the window. There's been a drought and this should at least pull the crisis back from red to orange.

"Not if the water's just dumping straight back into the ocean," Grace says.

"It'll do enough," Mike says. "It'll make it just enough not-bad."

"I miss *summer*," Grace says. "I miss the November that it was last week."

"What a couple of fantastic brats you've both become," Mike says.

"Don't wrap me up in this," Suzy says, flipping through the magazines. On top, that issue of *New York* that has been sitting around for months, the one with the first look at Gloria Steinem's *Ms.* magazine.

"I've seen your face when you've gotten back from New York recently," Mike says.

"You're right. When I get off the plane here, I feel loaded," Suzy says with a put-on smile. "I feel rich—with good fortune."

The turkey's ready just when Mike said it would be. And after a day of prep they're finished eating in fifteen minutes.

"Did Dad seem ready?" Suzy says as she clears her plate. Grace just flew back from New York last night.

"I guess," Grace says. "I mean, he looks and feels like shit, but I guess he's more confident than he was."

"That's good."

"Still a chance the date gets pushed. But he seems pretty fixated on the surgery."

"And ready for the trip out here?"

Wayne and Edith had decided to come for Christmas after all, pending complications with the procedure.

"Seems like it," Grace says. "I mean, it's hard to feel solid about anything...."

"It's all gonna be good," Suzy says. "Seriously."

Mike starts to pile up the dishes, when Grace waves him back to the table: "C'mon, just sit for two minutes. Leave some dirty dishes in the sink, one day of the year."

"You know I'm gonna be gone all week for the story. I just don't want them to be there when I get back."

"I baked a pie!" Grace says, ignoring him.

Suzy checks the clock.

"I'll have a slice, but then I have to split."

"It's still pouring out," Grace says.

"I said I'd stop by Billy's."

"Billy Zar's Thanksgiving," Grace says.

"Right," Suzy says. "He invited me to Thanksgiving, in case I didn't have anything going on."

"Even though he knew you would."

"And so I said I'd come for dessert," Suzy says.

"Even though I baked a pie."

"I'll go over for dessert, say hello, say thanks for inviting me, and then skate back."

"That's a lot of back and forth."

"Well, what the fuck, Grace? Just say I'm not allowed to go if that's what you're getting at."

"You do what you want. You can come over for leftovers tomorrow or something."

"Here, take my car," Mike says, moving for the keys.

Grace levels a shard of incredulity his way.

With the car it takes five minutes instead of twenty. Suzy sits in the driver's seat outside Billy's house and plays back through the decision she's made. She told them she'd be back in an hour but regrets having left. There are infinite days of not-Grace in the future—separate lives in separate houses, separate cities maybe—and she knows she should stick around when it means something to her. Suzy knocks on the front door—she's never been in the big house—and Billy greets her in a collared shirt and a tie, the first she's ever seen on him. He's shaved and combed his hair back with some matte goop.

"You're here," he says. The din of a large group can be heard in another room.

"Hey, look," she says, "I'm sorry, but I've gotta head back. I didn't think ditching out would be such a big deal, but I was wrong. I wanted to come over in person so you didn't think I was full of shit. Just wanted to say hello and Happy Thanksgiving and all that."

"You're not coming in?" Billy says, fingering the seam of his shirt.

"Nah, just wanted to say hey and that I'll see you tomorrow or this weekend."

"Sure you don't want pie?"

"Grace made a pie, that's what this is sort of about, actually."

"Say no more, *guapa*. I get it."

"All right, well."

Billy checks over his shoulder to make sure no one's getting too expectant. He knuckles the screen door, a little contact with Suzy's hand, and then he winks.

"Did you just wink?" Suzy says.

"I'm throwing everything I've got at you," he says, and smiles kinda sadly and closes the door.

She drives back, running it through her head—*has* he been throwing everything he's got at her?

Suzy pulls up to the curb and splashes to the stucco overhang of the front porch. As she reaches for her keys, she hears panicked breathing—the sort of breathing you can identify even if you haven't heard the voice breathe that way before. The way you can tell someone from their cough, the *voice* of the cough, she can tell the voice of this breathing. And then it grows rhythmic and constant, a little louder, and Suzy covers the distance to the car in a fraction of the time it took her going the other way. She slams the door and shuts her eyes and makes earmuffs with her hands, tensing her body all over, trying to expel the sound from her brain, a deliberate exercise that only makes her laugh herself to tears in the steam-shrouded cab of the Karmann Ghia.

At least, she thinks, they're doing better.

At the outset of an hour-long session, with the Zamperini airfield growing postage-stamp-size beneath them, Suzy asks Millikan if he's ever crossed paths with J.P. J.P. did his lessons with the other instructor, but Suzy is still surprised she hasn't seen him around even once.

"Don't know him," Millikan says. "But Foley seems to run through an enormous number of students."

"What do you mean? He fails them?"

"Even if you pass the exams, he finds ways to weed people out. He and I tend to stay in our own lanes, but the little I know him, I don't love the guy. It's like he does the job in order to keep the skies clear for himself. To make sure there aren't too many new licenses. Bad luck this guy you know landed with him instead of me."

Suzy hadn't realized it was that easy to cut a student. Her hands grow tense on the yoke.

"I hardly even know him," Suzy says. "But I do give him credit for planting the idea in my head. I didn't realize I could just sign up."

"Well, then, I'm appreciative, too...."

It's the sort of thing he's said each time they've been alone since their dinner together. Each lesson—floating the sentiment to gauge the response. But Suzy hasn't given much, certainly hasn't opened the window wide for another invitation.

She enjoyed herself at his house, but after the fact, alone, she drifted back to the nagging concern that she might gum up her certification with a false move, interpersonal-relationship-wise. She crossed the line going to his house, but she knows it might've been an even greater risk to refuse. Now she simply keeps the idea alive, nurses it, neither explicitly indulging in his affection nor rejecting it outright.

She likes this just how they are. Side by side, working together toward greater comprehension, the control column before each of them moving in unison. It's the sort of charge she hopes to live in for as long as it will last. After today she will be one hour closer. And Suzy knows that's all that matters.

Two weeks before Wayne and Edith are due to fly out for Christmas, a United 737, on its most well-worn route, crashes on approach to Chicago. Noses down after an incident-free two hours and seventeen minutes from National to Midway, four hundred feet short of the runway. Kills forty-three of the sixty-one on board and two on the ground.

Though she's spending the wet afternoon in Seattle and no one outside Grand Pacific knows where she's been put up, Suzy receives notice from the front desk that there's a caller on the line. Before she can get a hello out, he's off. Wayne says he just spoke to Grace, too. Says he's not feeling good about flying. Says they might back out of their trip altogether.

Suzy catches a glimpse of her face in the mirror. A face that's speaking no words but is twisted, roiling, edging up to disgust. The weakness in her father's voice is poisoning. Hearing the man who told her, at fourteen, to accelerate into turns at the go-kart track, who told her, at sixteen, to pass the boys on the inside, to pound the gaps, to live in racing's underexploited odds—it turns her mind into a blender.

"What are we talking about here? You're just not gonna come because you're afraid? You're gonna stop because of an outside threat of dying? You, of all people, should have *less* fear—now more than ever. You have next to *nothing* to fear at this point." There is silence and Suzy fills it. "Dad, what's really going on?"

He takes a few breaths before starting again.

"I just sit here all day watching the mess. *This* mess, or whatever mess. Day in and out. The coverage on the television especially, they break in every hour with news of the mission." He means Apollo 17. Eugene Cernan and Harrison Schmitt—the last crew NASA plans to send to the moon. "It's the end of the biggest thing that's happened for mankind in your lifetime."

Suzy's face is fixed in disbelief. This is what life without work reduces you to. Lines like that one. A living room humid with schmaltz. She hears a sniffle and imagines his eyes running like the storm drains on Thanksgiving, his face shining dull in the weak Schuyler light. She feels herself growing stuck to the bed, drying like concrete, and so she springs herself to her feet to pierce him with a pin through the phone.

"Sorry, were you asking for my opinion or just saying that you'd already made up your mind that you're too afraid to come to California for Christmas?"

There is a break, which means it's worked.

"I'm not saying that. I'm just...," he says. "We're still coming."

It's a packed flight from L.A. to Denver, preholiday traffic, and the pilots are worried but not too worried about the snowstorm hammering the Rockies. When she can, Suzy asks to work up front—first-class full service, which requires a touch more effort but puts her closer to the cockpit. She likes to pop in more often than necessary to ask questions, even though she knows how it looks, knows some of the other girls suspect she's digging for a pilot.

The pilots tell her how to adjust for the storms, the prep they can do, the elements they can control. She brings coffee with her, lingers like any stew trying to make a play. But they recognize her aptitude, the right questions, the fluency with the instrumentation.

"Come on, get your hands on here," the copilot says. He's got a voice like so many of them, the up—outta—West Virginia voice, the sugary scratch and gravel, all calm conviction.

Suzy hesitates, knowing how it looks to be leaning in over the pilots. She scoots her skirt down and moves into position. It's black and white out the windshield, no use whatsoever. So she keeps her eyes on the attitude indicator, the artificial horizon. They're level, there's nothing much to do. She feels a nudge on the right side of the plane, some heavy winds.

"No sweat, right?"

"No sweat," she says.

She leans back up and thanks them, asks if they need anything else.

"Once you've got everybody tucked in on approach, come on up for landing and we'll walk you through it. You can sit on the booster there. Gail won't mind, will she?"

"Not if y'all insist." She notices that she's leaning into the drawl, twanging a little, mimicking without meaning to, like it'll maybe contribute to her faculties at the controls.

"Well, then, it's required. There'll be a little action. It'll be a good look for you, especially if we can actually settle this thing down on the runway."

Suzy laughs. She loves this kind of joke more than she even realizes. She loves this kind of talk. She wants to talk like it forever.

She sits behind them on approach, once all the trash is cleared and the drunks in first are passed out. (Suzy had handed out a tranquilizing "holiday surprise" courtesy of Grand Pacific.) She pulls down the booster and crosses her legs, and the two pilots walk her through the steps. They dive through the clouds that are too high for precipitation, and then submerge into the storm, fat, newly conceived snowflakes slipping off the windshield. They still don't have eyes on the runway, but the tower's given them a go-ahead and they're on the right line. *The right line,* Suzy thinks. She's silent, a little tense. Extraordinarily alert. The snow has given a point of context for the speed and they're moving fast. They're at three thousand feet when she finally makes out some lights on the ground and the plane starts rattling with winds, a heavy, two-handed shake of the body, a rattle that tests the seat belts. The pilots speak to the tower with a disaffected clip, flipping some switches she doesn't recognize from the Cessna and barreling on down toward a snow-covered Stapleton. The landing gear drops and the runway lights align like rails on a bobsled shoot, and suddenly they're leveling and touching down eventlessly. There's a sense of ultimate control. It's the closest she's felt to touching, by proxy of the landing gear, a physical inevitability—the right line. The captain keeps up the low chatter with his man in the tower, and the copilot turns over his shoulder, as if to say, *Welp?*

And Suzy says, "Piece of cake."

Wayne and Edith book a place with an ocean view, halfway between Suzy and Grace, short walking distance to each of the girls. But after helping Wayne and Edith check in, Suzy hesitates even to place their bags on the floor—the carpet faintly damp and the walls dusted in mildew. Suzy insists that they stay at her place. She'll just go back to bunking with Grace and Mike, she says, but plans to crash at Billy's most of the time.

Ten days. Ten whole days. Once they're settled, Suzy walks Wayne and Edith down the hill to the Strand and they pick a bench, where they sit and watch the water without saying much for several still minutes. It's not exactly sunny, but the sky is filled with a bright white fog, like if you dropped dry ice into a fishbowl. It's a rich, almost three-dimensional light. It's not hot, but it's warm, high sixties. And this is the thing Wayne keeps doing: walking up to one of the houses on the Strand that has a thermometer hooked up to its fence. He says it over and over, "halfway between sixty-eight and sixty-nine degrees." He's not looking great—bald, pale, and thin—but he's moving all right, walking straight-backed between the bench and the fence to verify the findings.

"Halfway between sixty-eight and sixty-nine," he says again. "On December twenty-first."

"And it's always like that," Suzy says.

"It's something," Wayne says.

"And a birthright to all of them," Suzy says, gesturing down the Strand.

"Aren't *you* a little expert," Edith says, watching the locals close by.

"I guess I'm still smitten," Suzy says. "Same as everyone else here."

"Well," Wayne says, "I get it."

And then they scheme about what they'll do now that they're finally here, the trip having been a node of the future they never seemed to have fully projected themselves into.

A couple days before Christmas, Suzy's flying to New York, there and back, and she's planning to go empty-handed. But before she leaves for the airport in the morning, Billy surprises her with the prospect of a package. Suzy resists. It'll be no problem, he says, same routine as ever. But she's trying her hardest to cut back to zero, to at least attempt to keep her pact with Wayne. Billy says he'll give her part of his cut.

She doesn't quite know how, but she leaves his house with a heavier bag.

The psychic pulse that cased the freight, in Suzy's mind, those first several trips is reduced to a weak quiver now, ordinary, just another bag among the bags. The conversation and activity—the regular work of serving a planeful of passengers—that she encountered during the first runs no longer rearrange themselves into the searing colors and shapes of memory-making associations. Just the feel of the aisle carpeting beneath her feet, the calm pitch of the heavy plane, the sense that as she moves back and forth through the cabin, she is moving with a moving thing.

It goes just as it should, except Cassidy isn't even covered. They've grown as used to Suzy as she has to them. It makes her uncomfortable, that comfort. She and Cassidy are alone in the bathroom, and Cassidy looks a little beat, like she hasn't slept much. Suzy asks if she'd like to get refreshed in the stew lounge. Cassidy seems turned up, as if by a dial, at the suggestion.

"Can you do that?" she says.

"They finally gave me a guest pass," Suzy lies.

Together they pick out croissants and pour coffees and sit in plush chairs by the window. She's alone today, Cassidy says, because the two guys—Frank and Paul, their names for the first time—had to buy gifts for their kids. Suzy asks about Cassidy—where she lives (Forest Hills), where she grew up (Elmhurst), where she's been and where she's going: "Home after this."

"But I mean, how long have you been doing this?"

"A couple years."

"And what do you think you'll do after that?"

"I don't know—save money, buy a house, get another job."

"Are you married? Do you have any kids?"

"Not yet." Cassidy begins to curl in on herself, quills out.

"I don't mean anything by it—I'm single, too. I guess I just meant: Is this good for a while? Or are you, I dunno, trying to do something else?"

"I don't have a *date,* if that's what you mean. I probably won't do this for the rest of my life. How 'bout you, what's the deal?"

"No plans, either," Suzy lies again. "Just keeping on with this until I stop stewing, I guess."

Cassidy seems not to believe her.

"It don't matter to me either way," Cassidy says, Queens in her voice.

"But I really don't have plans to quit," Suzy says. "Not now."

"Well, all right, then."

"So, no husband, no kids," Suzy says. "Do you have a boyfriend?" Cassidy smiles at Suzy's persistence—stuffed lips that stay weighted and red even when they're stretched wide. Cassidy rewards her with the story of the married man she's been seeing, the man from Glen Cove, with the Thunderbird and the chain of Laundromats. Who doesn't know anything about any of *this,* who thinks he's doing her favors by giving her money for groceries and wheelbarrowing quarters up to her door. Which she's perfectly happy to let him keep believing, she can certainly still use the thousands of quarters. She lets him believe she's just the barely paid travel agent–in–training everyone else thinks she is.

"Travel agent–in–training?" Suzy says. "So there's something."

"Sure, I guess. Three months I'll be full-time," she says.

"That's a good job."

"Too short to stew, right?"

"It's a dumb rule."

Cassidy has a large, light croissant flake hanging off the corner of her mouth. And Suzy, piggybacking on a force greater than self-control, finds her hand drifting across the space between them, plucking the flake from Cassidy's face, and grazing her lower lip.

Cassidy's eyes drift to the armrest.

"I got it...," Suzy says.

"So, travel agent's the next-best thing," Cassidy says, doubling back and lifting her eyes again. "I still get to do something related to flying. Still get to look at the map. We've got a great big one with every city in the world on it, runs floor to ceiling right along the main wall of the office. I like looking at the map."

"Me too," Suzy says.

When the coffee's gone, Cassidy says she's gotta make her drop-off, that she doesn't want to overstay her guest pass. They say "Merry Christmas" and hug uncertainly, and then on her way out Cassidy offers a little sack of quarters she's been hauling around, maybe ten bucks, that she has an idea about.

"Christmas bonus," she says.

Suzy smiles and takes the sack, weighing it in her palm like they're jewels.

"See you next year," Suzy says.

Suzy's back to Sela for Christmas Eve—home by lunch to stuff the cash beneath the sink. Wayne and Edith have gotten comfortable at her apartment, but when Suzy asks what they've been up to, she learns they haven't been doing all that much, exactly. They ate breakfast at Huevos. They saw *The Poseidon Adventure*. Mostly, though, they've passed hours standing on the Strand and staring at the water.

The days have this ordinary extraordinariness. That's what Wayne and Edith keep getting at.

Wayne says reading the *New York Times* here is like reading an international edition. Everything is distant, belonging to a different world. Nixon feels as far away as Brezhnev. Schuyler Glen seems buffered in gauze. Things there just don't seem as important, as urgent, as they usually do. They don't ring clearly.

"Get used to it," Suzy says. "The longer you're here, the stronger that feeling grows. Wait till the end of your first week."

Mike is at the Peoples Temple downtown again, so Wayne, Edith, and the girls pile into a rental car. They drive the length of the bay, south, up onto the Peninsula, where Suzy passes, she's certain, the estate where she and Billy dropped the pig on the Fourth. She can't see much, but she makes out the heads of horses bobbing above the hedges. And somewhere on the property, Suzy imagines, there's a lion and a pig, an island of misfit pets.

The views from the Peninsula dwarf those in Sela. There is height, a look back at the entire stained basin of the Southland, all the way out on this clear winter afternoon, to the skyscrapers—and Mike's temple—downtown, straight across the bay to Malibu, and out toward the eastern flatlands that Suzy's never really conceived of as anything but an extension of her runway. The sky is swept clean of clouds. It is, Wayne says, the sort of thing he's failed all his life to recognize as an alternative—a winter sky limitless in height, the whole Christmas thing outdoors. After he says it, Grace points out that you can see the airplanes filing in for miles. Suzy says that pilots claim to see the lights at night stretching east for three states.

Wayne likes it up here. He says this might be the perfect place for post-op recovery, the consummate site for convalescence.

"You hear that, girls?" Wayne says to his three. "This is where I start the next chapter."

Christmas is warm, so warm, so clear, so blue. During the gift exchange Suzy and Grace surprise each other with strand cruisers. Mike knew what was coming and successfully held off tipping either's hand. Wayne and Edith find the whole thing beyond terrific, and while they urge the girls to get out and ride right away so that they can snap some photos, Suzy and Grace push another idea.

They convince Wayne and Edith to spend an hour on the sand. Mike stays home to read, but both girls and Mom and Dad get dressed for the beach. Wayne vomited up coffee cake most of the morning, but by noon he's changed into an aloha shirt he's kept buried in his closet for decades. Suzy and Grace lead him slowly down the hill, through the intersection, and across the busy Strand, where skateboarders, bike riders, and even recreational runners speed up the standard strolling flow. The courts are filled with volleyball games, and the palm trees are tall and frozen without even the flinch of a breeze. The water collects the sunlight and looks, in its bright flicker, the way a TV does when it's turned on but not hooked up to the cable. They spot a surfing Santa Claus—*the* surfing Santa, Grace specifies—paddling out.

Suzy and Grace walk with Wayne the way nonparents do with a toddler. Out in front, uncertain of speed and safety. As they crash into place on the wide acreage—still vast and empty-ish, in spite of heavier numbers, each plot of sand personal seeming—Grace leans into Suzy and says: "I don't think I've ever seen Dad's legs before."

They laugh about the skin and hair beneath his knees, white as the tube socks he's insisted on wearing over his feet. "Guess that's where I get it, huh?" Suzy says.

They read on the beach—books and magazines and newspapers. The wind picks up some, in the wrong direction. It's offshore, blowing the tops of the waves back out toward Asia, creating a light frosting of salt spray every time a new set breaks into the beach. Grace and Edith work on the crossword puzzle together. Suzy dives into the Christmas fiction issue of the *New Yorker,* a thing Edith picked up at Kennedy for the impression it might give. There are stories by writers Suzy's heard of, but the one that catches her attention is by someone she hasn't, a woman named Renata Adler.

There are icy scenes from that bar, Elaine's, and descriptions she reads and rereads of things she's never seen in person, like the Broadway Junction subway station: "It seems to me one of the world's true wonders: nine crisscrossing, overlapping elevated tracks, high in the air, with subway cars screeching, despite uncanny slowness, over thick rusted girders, to distant, sordid places. It might have been created by an architect with an Erector Set and recurrent amnesia, and city ordinances and graft, this senseless ruined monster of all subways, in the air." She loves the sound of it in her brain, the picture made there. There are allusions to stealing "a washcloth once from a motel in Angkor Wat." There are sentences that are just, "A few days after that, there was the war." There are whole sections that comprise fifty words: "Alone in the sports car, speeding through the countryside, I sang along with the radio station, tuned way up. Not the happiest of songs, Janis Joplin, not in any terms; but one of the nicest lines. 'Freedom's just another word for nothing left to lose.' In a way, I guess."

Amidst it all, there is one passage in particular that cuts her open: "I think when you are truly stuck, when you have stood still in the same spot for too long, you throw a grenade in exactly the spot you were standing in, and jump, and pray. It is the momentum of last resort."

Suzy feels a thing on her arms and at her throat. There is a hot branding of recognition. Not of a life or of an eye or of a mind, but of a disposition. A regard for things she's never encountered herself, a regard that feels familiar, like it might be hers, were she in another place, in another name or line of work. It reminds her of stretches during school. That heat of likeness she felt among certain people she admired. She could read stuff like it forever.

This is a voice. This is a voice that widens the frame. That drives her to want to do something she's never done before—to do, maybe even, the sort of thing Mike's trying to do. It's like Camille would say: the reading before writing is a pitch pipe, not to be copied identically but to harmonize with. She wants to do something in this key. Write or fly, et cetera. This is a voice she's never heard, but one that sounds so familiar, like when an adopted child is reacquainted with a mother tongue. She moves through the story with a closing off, with blinders, but no explicit comprehension of those blinders, not until she's through thinking back on where she's just been. Suzy can't typically read without acknowledging that she's reading—considering the length of the sentences, the size of the font, the rate at which she's flipping pages, and, of course, the inescapable calculation of opportunity costs. Everything that could be happening instead of reading. Every bit of life she's missing by pausing her own to slip into someone else's.

But this story—or whatever this thing is in the magazine—doesn't so much show her the opportunity cost of its consumption, but rather articulates one of the possible lives she's missing. Not the life of Cassidy in Queens. Not the life of the Grand Pacific girls who live in the stew zoos of the upper East Eighties. But the life of a woman she could've been, had she maybe, just possibly, stayed the course and followed a boyfriend to New York. "A part-time grant writer, a part-time librarian, a part-time journalist," the story has it—some woman of varied occupation who has "been lucky, in my work, at getting visas to closed places." A journaler, a describer of things, a drinker who "quite often now has a drink before eleven." A professional noticer. It's the thing, she realizes now, she's been reading all her life to find. A new summit with a vista.

She feels crackling with a current but also inexplicably defeated. It's almost like a glimpse of a life she's forfeited already, unrecoverable at twenty-two, sacrificed for the look and sound of the very thing over the edge of the magazine page here: a plain of a billion crushed shells; a body of salt water; a sunny seventy-five that's neutralized by the touch of offshore breezes, of Santa Ana winds, winds that may be frying her ions, charging her body in a manner she might be mistaking for the effect of good writing. She reaches for the brass loop on Grace's purse and watches the blue bolt of microlightning jump from her finger to the metal.

While lost in the turning of pages and the rapid breaks of short-story sections, Suzy doesn't even notice that Wayne has stood and removed his socks. He's walking, barefoot, and Edith calls out his name. He doesn't seem to hear and keeps moving toward the water, and where the sand dips to the surf at a sharper grade, he removes his shirt, with its orange palm trees and orange-plus tropical birds, and leaves it in his wake, moving deeper down the decline, so that all the girls can see is the top of his bright new bald head. It disappears and Suzy stands, only to catch Wayne vanishing beneath the surface of the water—the only others in either direction surfers with full-body wet suits or a Santa costume.

Edith and Grace stand, too, but nobody moves toward him.

"His back," Edith says, but still no movement forward, all but full certainty among the three that there is no threat. He treads out farther—his feet seemingly still touching sand—and lets a wave crash him hard in the chest and face. Once he's past the break line, he flips onto his back and throws his arms wide and rests there like a bobbing gull, catching the blowback froth from the offshore, as though it's the first of a Christmas snow and it's no different for Wayne Whitman than ever.

It is a good day for contrails. Suzy hosts everyone for dinner, and Wayne spends most of the hour leading to sunset sitting in the chair by the window with the view. From here it's less looking out at the ocean than down on it. It's not just the vacuum-cleaner suction of the jets taking off over the roof that makes him say it's like looking out the window of a cockpit—it really does feel like a privileged height. Edith helps Suzy in the kitchen, easy stuff, some prime rib Mike picked up in the afternoon, some potatoes, some green beans, some pie. Before sitting down to official dinner at the tartan-draped card table in Suzy's living room, Wayne surprises them with a treat he's brought from Schuyler. Though they'd long lived in America, Wayne's Whitmans maintained the English tradition of Christmas poppers and paper crowns. The girls put on an enthusiastic show about springing their poppers, wearing the crowns, playing with the crap unplayable games housed in the poppers' stock. The food goes quickly and Wayne and Edith are down early, Wayne worn thin, in spite of denying it to the teeth, by his afternoon polar bear swim.

Mike's ready to head home, too, but Suzy and Grace decide to go for a ride on the new cruisers. The bikes are at Mike and Grace's, so the three walk back together, and the sisters head down to the Strand in darkness. Every block there's a single cone lighting ten feet in each direction, and then it's black, unassisted by a sliver moon and the dim reflection off the water. It's like riding across an endless chessboard. They ride for a mile, then two, and reach a turnaround at the edge of town.

Grace, to Suzy's surprise, is crying.

"What's going on?" Suzy says.

"What if this is it?" Grace says.

"You mean Dad?"

"What if that's the last Christmas, just like that?"

"I'd say it's a good one, then."

"How can you say that so matter-of-factly?"

"Grace, I'm feeling the *exact same thing*. It's just—it's out of our hands. And all we can do is do the most here and at home, and hope for the best with surgery."

"I just have this horrible sense that we're in a position of things getting worse before they get better," Grace says. "Like we're going to look back on today as a relative high point, even though things seem so tough."

The light is low, but there's enough for Suzy to see the shiver in Grace's eyes, the trepidation. It's like she's already skipped over into the place beyond Wayne, speaking to Suzy from across the river.

"That could happen," Suzy says. "But today *was* good. This will always be a high point. Just, he's not going anywhere—not for a while."

"What if the surgery doesn't work?"

Suzy shrugs. She lets Grace ask all the unanswerable questions.

"At least," Suzy says, finally, "I think they've enjoyed the last few days more than if we'd been at home, you and me bitching about visiting, you know?"

"They didn't say it was the last Christmas," Grace says.

"Yeah, they've stopped that 'cause you asked them to. No more suggesting it's the end."

"I like that."

"Me too," Suzy says.

They hang there, straddling their bikes—dark silence, draining hours of Christmas. And then without signaling, Suzy swings her leg over the frame and drops the bike in a tangled clatter. She closes the space between them and wraps her sister up like a blanket, one arm around her shoulders, the other arm across her stomach, squeezing as hard as she can. Grace doesn't say anything but finds Suzy's hands and threads Suzy's fingers with her own.

"C'mon, let's go back," Suzy says.

As they pedal beneath the first light, Suzy catches a glimpse of Grace's bike.

"Are you barefoot?"

"Yeah," Grace says, serious, before laughing through wet eyes, which makes Suzy laugh, too. And then Grace says: "The beach at night."

"Yeah?"

"That's numero uno. There's a lot of things to love, but if you made me pick."

"I'll never make you pick."

"It's cool you came out here."

"All right, no more mush, let's just get goin'."

"Last time I say anything," Grace says, and they ride home across the endless chessboard.

Grace is gone when it's time for Wayne and Edith to head to the airport. It's been a strange few days. The anticlimax of the week after Christmas. The newspapers and magazines—all piling up on the coffee table at Mike and Grace's place—running their tributes to those who died in 1972. Suzy watched the papers for new deaths, those who'd died *after* the deadlines for the year-end specials. Suzy has a pang of special interest in making sure Wayne gets to 1973. The only tragedy greater than death, she reasons, would be to die in that last week of '72, to be practically forgotten, to have the date after the dash on the headstone suggest that you hadn't lived those extra hundreds of days. Like poor Harry Truman: dead the day after Christmas.

That one gets Wayne. He's worse than he was with Apollo 17. All these endings all at once. It's not something Suzy takes seriously, but she listens to him theorize about America cleaving into a new era, a worse moment, Vietnam and Watergate becoming the norm, the afterglow of his war formally extinguished with the death of moon missions and Truman. Wayne was always more titillated than frightened by the transformation of the '60s, but this isn't social change, this isn't hippies and headbands, this is the end of things that mattered.

On their way to the airport there is an announcement on the radio: Eastern Air Lines Flight 401 has crashed into the Everglades, death toll unknown. This is the fifty-fifth commercial airliner crash of the year. They listen in silence. Nothing new needs to be said. But when they get to the curb, and Suzy helps them carry their bags to check-in, Edith kisses her firmly on the cheek—a long hold, longer than Suzy can remember ever—and a "Thank you" possessing just the right number of multiple meanings.

Wayne holds Suzy at her shoulders like he would before a race. He leans in toward her face and says, "You can't fly anymore."

It's straightforward enough. Suzy doesn't nod in consent or shake her head defiantly. She looks into her dying father's eyes and says, "I'm not going anywhere."

He doesn't know what this means and she doesn't really, either, but he decides she probably hasn't heard him right.

"Please: tell me you'll at least start looking for something else."

She doesn't say anything again and just moves in for a hug.

"I promised you I'd try," he says. "*You* promise me *you'll* try."

"I'm not afraid of flying," Suzy says instead.

"I know you're brave, I know you're not afraid of anything," he says. "But you should be."

"*You're* not afraid," Suzy says, "*I'm* not afraid."

Suzy still hasn't mentioned anything to Wayne and Edith about flight school and chooses not to tell them now, as proof of her fearlessness, that she's just thirty hours short of certification. But the fact that she considers it—the bald inappropriateness of it—makes her laugh.

Her father's hands are still on her shoulders and he watches her laugh without emotion.

"You know what?" he says. "I don't give a damn. Do what you want—I mean that. I mean that without animosity. If you like the work and you're good at it, or whatever it is that makes you happy, then that's all a father can ask for, and I know I can't stop you anyway."

Suzy smiles, proud of her father's pride.

"You put me behind the wheel," she says.

"And you were good," he says.

Edith hurries Wayne up to check-in. Suzy watches through the glass as he hands his suitcase to the attendant and it disappears along the conveyor belt. She wrapped up another couple grand in leftover Christmas paper and placed it in his suitcase before they left her apartment. She hadn't wanted to make the Christmas run, but she might as well funnel the spoils toward its primary target—it was all for this purpose, anyway. Two thousand dollars in cash, a card with a snowman, and a little red bow. "Happy New Year," she wrote. "Just another year of many to come." She placed it in his suitcase without him knowing, without him even thinking to look, a move she'd picked up along the way. And that's pretty much it, they're gone, and it's back to the beach, to that life she lives here.

Grace says she's been booked last-minute to Hawaii on New Year's Eve. She's gonna have to stay two nights—the thirty-first and the first. It throws some plans.

Suzy's left to her own designs on New Year's. With Billy busy making house calls, and an afternoon with Billy planned for tomorrow, she gives Mike a ring and they decide to go out for dinner. They meet at El Guincho, which shows no sign of cutting hours for the holiday. They order margaritas, and the first round is gone before they order food. Suzy asks about the magazine story and Mike grimaces. He can't find Reverend Jones anywhere. And since there's been a lot written about him recently without access, his failure to land him is a potential deal breaker.

"The thing about these stories is they're not real until they are, ya know? I could work on this for four months and turn in a bunch of string with no center—it'll just unravel into a mess, and they can cut it for the other hundred stories they have waiting in reserve. It's my deal to fuck up."

"Is there any lead you think could potentially work out?"

"I'm going to Ukiah next week—I've been talking to a couple people who think he's there. I'm just gonna knock on the door and hope somebody doesn't kidnap me. Even if he lets me in and makes me coffee or whatever, it still doesn't matter if he doesn't agree to let me run tape, ya know? That's one of the last things I can try."

"Do you still get paid?"

Mike closes his eyes and seems to be searching the backs of his eyelids for a line.

"I get some money, but not enough to do anything with," he says.

"Could you go back to trying the magazine?"

"You're hittin' all the sore spots, huh?"

Suzy smiles. "Just asking the questions my parents avoided over Christmas."

"I love that thing about people like them—that maintenance of other folks' dignity in the face of obvious failure. It's nice."

"And a little unfeeling."

"Guess it wasn't necessarily passed down."

"Grace lost it when she moved out. It was like, 'Now I feel free to say whatever enters my brain.'"

"Which is one of the first things that attracted me to her," Mike says.

"Despite what I just said, I think it's maybe rubbed off on my parents a little, too. Because of all that's going on. They're learning how to ask questions. My mom knows how my dad's *really* feeling. Probably for the first time ever."

The burritos come wet on porcelain plates, and Billy's buddy Pablo refills the plastic basket with hot chips from the chip drawer. They order a third round of margaritas.

"The answer to your question is there's a new clock on the magazine," Mike says. "I was talking to a friend in New York a couple days ago, and he mentioned that the folks at *Esquire* and the editor of *New York* have been batting around ideas for a California magazine. If it's gonna happen, I've gotta at least try to be first—sell off some of the groundwork to them or something."

"So it *is* still on the table?" Suzy says, chasing her own directness. "It's still something you have time for, I mean."

"If I had the funding, it'd still be the number one plan."

"You could work for *their* magazine."

"A few months ago I would've dismissed the idea, but I'm a little fucked here. I just *need money.* I'm ready to answer the bartender ad at Howlers."

"You've never bartended."

"See, not good enough for that, even."

"I mean, you could *learn.* But why don't you finally write a book or something?"

"Grace may not have mentioned it to you, but we're really, truly in a pinch. She knows she's not gonna fly forever, maybe another year or something—if they don't find out about us. But I need something else. I'm burning through my inheritance. I'm not as comfortable with hanging out and doing nothing as it sometimes seems. I just need to sit at a desk in an office and rot away for a little while."

"Carpets without sand," Suzy says.

"Not even—I just need something fast or else I'm afraid she's gonna get a little pushy."

"Pushy how?"

"We've been fine lately, but you know how it is, things change and you want to change together."

"What are you actually saying?"

"I mean, it's no shock to you that we're not always a hundred percent. It can be fine for little runs, but still. And so we're thinking about maybe starting a family, patch some of it back together."

"*Thinking* about it?"

"Well, yeah, I mean, we think it could be a good idea. Or at least we're beginning to all of a sudden."

"Is she pregnant again or something?"

Mike is chewing and chasing his burrito with a swig of his drink, so it comes out a little delayed: "Pregnant again?"

It's not until Mike says it that Suzy recognizes her mistake. "Pregnant, pregnant again, whatever, I just mean is she actually pregnant?"

Mike squints. "What was that?"

"That wasn't anything, I was thinking about something else and my mouth's full."

Mike is silent, then says, "Not that I know of."

"Well, whenever it happens, I'm sure it'll work out."

There's a crack now between them, and Suzy tries not to acknowledge that it's lengthening. The physical context of their situation is the same as it was a minute ago—the plastic palm fronds, the surf stickers on the fryer, the four-month countdown calendar to Cinco de Mayo—but new information, the way the camera has swung around, has changed the way all of it looks.

"You could write newspaper stories," she says, "you could write grants, you could write art catalogs or technical manuals for one of the defense companies, Hughes or whatever." She lists more jobs like the woman had in the story in the *New Yorker*. "You get in somewhere, and then you can get me a job."

"All that stuff you said, that's the stuff you do *before* you get to where I am. Or at least before you get to where I was. Where I was in New York, that's the level when you get to stop writing crap in order to pursue the real thing."

"Well, I'll take the crap."

"If I find anything, it's all yours."

"Thanks for looking out," Suzy says.

"Before I forget, I have a belated Christmas present. I didn't really think of it till it was too late, so I can't take full credit, but whatever, we're still within the twelve days, right?"

He reaches for his jacket, which is hung on a hook beneath the counter, and pulls a paperback from an inside pocket. *The Hunters,* by James Salter. It's yellow and it's read.

"Is this your copy?"

"No, no. But I couldn't find it new. They didn't print a ton. I like this writer, though. Liked the most recent book he did, too—this American and this woman driving around France having sex. But this one's about fighter pilots in Korea. People say he's the best writing pilot—or pilot-writer, guess it depends—since Saint-Ex. I read it a few years ago but was flipping through yesterday in the bookstore, skimming the first few pages."

He thumbs to the dog-ear and begins to read: "'Friends on the outside were always asking why he stayed in'—in the air force, after his duty is up—'or telling him he was wasting himself. He had never been able to give an answer. With the fresh shirt on his shoulders still cold as ice, chilled from an hour in an unheated radar compartment at forty thousand feet between Long Beach and Albuquerque, the marks from the oxygen mask still on his face, and on his hands the microscopic grit of a thousand-mile journey, he had tried to find an answer sitting alone at dinner in the club filled with administrative majors and mothers talking about their children, but he never could. In his mind he carried Saturdays of flying, with the autumnal roar of crowds on the radio compass and the important stadiums thirty minutes apart and button-small, the wingmen like metallic arrows poised in the air above a continent, the last sunlight slanting through the ground haze, and cities of concrete moss; . . .'" She watches his finger skim to the last line of the paragraph. "'It was all a secret life, lived alone.'"

He looks up from the book and raises his eyebrows.

"Whoa," Suzy says.

"Consider it a Christmas-slash-congrats-on-flight-school sort of thing."

"Still got quite a bit left."

"But this'll be a motivator. Might stoke the fire. Not that you need the encouragement."

It is a good gift, Suzy thinks. It's nice that she and Mike can do stuff like this without a fuss. That they can spend time together with ease, but also that they can connect on the level they do. Share in a thing, share in thoughts.

Suzy suggests they take one more shot of tequila before they go. Mike cinches his lips into a tight purse and shakes his head. But Pablo overhears and insists. Tequila on the house, Happy New Year. "'Sela Vie,'" Suzy says, biting her lip and pointing her eyebrow at the bumper sticker on the fryer, and they clink with him and it goes down badly. They beg with their hands for some lime wedges. It is as it always is, the hot roll down the throat and over the stomach lining, the image of a coated cartoon digestive track like in a magazine ad for antacid. Suzy is warm and Suzy smiles, holding up her book triumphantly. Mike Singer is handsome in the sticky light of El Guincho. An even match for Grace, as much as Grace likes to act like she's the catch. An even match even though he chased her out here and into this predicament. Suzy is exceptionally warm, and she does something she's never done—she reaches both hands toward Mike and touches his cheeks with her fingers and palms, lightly, just a little framing. And she says, "Thank you, seriously." And then she drops her hands and he laughs and looks away so as not to embarrass her by acknowledging the embarrassing thing she's done.

*   *   *

It's a weird parting: neither has plans and each knows it, but Mike's in a focused mood, wants to go home and sulk in the magazine pile even though he's drunk. And so Suzy hops on her bike and goes for a ride in the opposite direction of home.

While coasting along the Strand, under another winter sky of edgeless darkness, she acknowledges a simple order that has arranged itself in front of her face—a clarity, a paring down of interests for the day and the year to come. In this blank evening, with no one else really applying much pressure, there are two people she misses—two people she would feel a full swell of contentment to run into right now, to follow into more of the night. If she's honest with herself, she's never really felt that way about Grace at any point in her life. But now the prospect: passing hours talking about other girls at Grand Pacific, flight plans, bid sheets, hotels in Dallas and Denver and Honolulu, bands and books, family and money and babies. She looks forward to a lifetime of turning Grace on to the stuff she discovers, and being turned on in return. They are still separate spheres, but in recent months, really since that trip home together, there's been this easy overlap, a tangent plane, that has aligned their whole program. Suzy loves her parents, but that love, made manifest in time together, always stresses an upper limit—two weeks over Christmas during college was that upper limit, the last ten days in Sela was, too. She'll see them again soon, back to visit after the surgery, hopefully without a run to cloud things up. But there is no longer a constraint, really, with Grace. Suzy inadvertently spilled Grace's secret to Mike, and though Suzy has convinced herself Mike let it go, Suzy feels like she owes her sister something for the slipup. More than owes. She wants to tell Grace about the runs. She wants to tell her the truth about Billy Zar, whatever that is. *God,* Suzy thinks, *I need a true friend like I haven't had in years, and maybe that's my sister, maybe that's happened.*

She cuts off the thought train there—it's life sustaining, propulsive, to know there's plenty more to talk about with her sister tomorrow.

Tomorrow she's going to the Rose Bowl with Billy. That USC team he's been propping up all year rolled undefeated through the Pac-8, won the season-ending rivalry games with Notre Dame and UCLA, and cruised into a Rose Bowl tilt with Ohio State—a New Year's national championship game. Billy's parents had an extra pair of tickets, off on their own in the corner of the bowl, and Billy asked if she wanted to come along. She didn't jump at first—they'd kept things pretty low-key, not much time in public together still. But he tried hard to be convincing. He went on about the quality of the football and the historical potential of the team—all of which was fine though not much of a deal sealer. But when he said that the Rose Bowl was the only place in L.A. he liked as much as Sela, she figured it was worth a few hours of her day off. Billy championed almost everyone and everything, but he didn't deploy loose superlatives when it came to equating things to his hometown.

Still, in spite of the fact that they've got tomorrow, she can't deny the bright desire to see him tonight. She knows where some of the parties are and she's done it before—filed out into the dark grid, as on the Fourth, followed the shrieks and squeals and melodies to find the party maker in the middle of it all. As she rides along, there's a sudden onset of a countdown that strings together from balcony to balcony like telephone lines—"nine, eight, seven..."—though it must be for something else, since it's hours to go still. At "one" there's an explosion of noisemakers and fireworks, children on the Strand banging pots with wooden spoons, wet kisses consuming couples on balconies that look as though they might slip banisters and tumble to the concrete. Suzy pulls to the side, and through a ground-floor window notices a large television screen displaying the confetti raining over Times Square. The New York New Year, celebrated as though it's their own—the first time she's noticed a critical mass of Sela del Mar paying attention to the other coast.

Moms and dads pick up extinguished sparklers and file back up the hill to homes on the back side. Pairs move in off the balconies like performers in cuckoo clocks and shut the sliding doors until the hour of the next countdown, the hour of Rachel's Midwest, of Chicago Minneapolis Detroit.

There're just too many parties tonight. Not three or four, but uncountable gatherings in need of a bump. From here, near the pier, to the north end, where Suzy's apartment sits quiet and dark, she rides her bike back slowly, wondering how Grace's flight has gone and who Billy's got on the hook. She slows her pedaling so that it's just one single push, a long coast, followed by another, like when she rows her skateboard. The north part of town is darker, the number of Strand-front parties dropping off. And when she gets to her turn-up, she tilts her face west toward the fissure where she imagines the black sky and the black water meeting. She can't really distinguish it. She sends out this weird thought to the whole scene, something she's never done before—a sort of general gratitude and an appeal to the next year, a year she is certain will be filled with a shift. This thing she's looking at will never ever change, but she's gonna maybe change around it—that's the idea, that's the vibe she's putting out there. *Keep your eyes on the constant, keep the center fixed, and then maybe you can let yourself take a ride on the outer reach of the wheel.*

She doesn't want to start sweating on the final steep climb to her apartment, so she walks her bike to her stairs, rests it against the rail, and finds her way through the front door. Inside it's cold—a broken heater maybe. There's so much to do and so many people in the periphery. But right this instant—9:37 is what the clock says—it's the old anxiety, all the places she's not, all the people who are with

everyone but her. Right now—9:37, New Year's Eve 1972—she is
here, and she is so so alone. But then the spell passes, and the facts
and memories and perceptions realign into high contentment, maybe
even *highest* contentment, because who is Suzy kidding, where else
could she be?

Suzy drives. Up from the beach towns, through downtown, snaking
along the Pasadena Freeway ("a former street course," Billy tells her),
and then they're over the Arroyo Seco and filing slowly onto the golf
course, which spreads out from the Rose Bowl. They park on the golf
course, practically in a green-side bunker, catching shade from a walnut tree and the tailgate tent of the USC fans beside them. Before
she's got the ignition off—it's Billy's parents' Volvo, and she's careful
to make sure everything's where it needs to be—Billy's out the back
and has the tops popped on two Coors cans.

The golf course is settled right down in a little valley at the foot
of those omnipresent San Gabriels. The mountains are modest in
a wider context of all geology but made marketable by the relative dullness of most stadium settings. The cars file in behind them,
parking in rows that cut across the fairways. They sit on the back
bumper and watch the makeshift lot fill up. Billy's wearing an aloha
shirt with a rep pattern of the interlocking *S* and *C,* the pair of
tickets peeking over the edge of his pocket. He's wearing corduroy
shorts that hit him in the middle of his thigh, dark legs with blond
leg fuzz. He sips his beer and quietly marvels at the cardinal and
gold spilling out in all directions. Suzy watches him watch the fans:
he's laughing about something pleasant, a memory that he doesn't
share with her.

"I still don't get why you just didn't *go* there," she says.

He shrugs—he's answered the question before.

"And I guess you couldn't be more connected to all this anyway."

"I mean, don't get me wrong: there's a difference. And I am definitely not in the *real* club. I think about it sometimes."

"Go now, then."

"Twenty-five-year-old freshman?"

"They'll just think you're in law school."

"It's too late."

"That's such a stupid thing to say. *Twenty-five.*"

"I *have* thought about it."

"And?"

"Then I get busy, don't know what I'd do it for."

"I heard you graduated top of your class in high school."

"That's not true."

"Just a rumor that's out there? That's a pretty weird rumor."

"Number two. Catherine Engelbert."

"Sounds like a nerd."

"Totally," Billy says. "She went to 'SC. Got cool."

"Got rid of her glasses or something?"

"Right roommate in the lottery, I guess. Right sorority. In med school there, too, last I saw her. Commuting from Sela. Sold her some blow."

"Nice."

"I guess that's the moment that sometimes catches me. Just being on the other side of that one. Selling versus buying."

"You think about college with the fantasy that one day you'll be buying instead of selling?"

"But then I wonder what the point is anyway—I mean, what do you get after all that time and money? What's the life it leads to that's inaccessible now?"

"I'm not the best one to speak on this," Suzy says.

"What do you mean, you're gonna be a pilot-senator."

"I think I'm gonna give myself till June. Five more months, a full year with Grand Pacific. Give myself till then to figure it out—to get my license, to see where my dad's at, I don't know. I just don't think I can be a girl who's flying more than a year unless I need the free flights."

"Not like your sister."

"Not like my sister."

"And it doesn't bother you, all the news or whatever lately?"

On the way out they heard another one—that Roberto Clemente had died in a plane crash the night before, just after takeoff near the coast of Puerto Rico. They hadn't found his body yet.

"It's all the same odds. At least, that's how I'm thinking of it. The same number of crashes."

"That can't possibly be the case."

"It's just been some famous people recently, is all," Suzy says.

"It'd make me nervous."

"But you've never been on an airplane, period."

"I don't know, dude. Or maybe it's the case that the more crashes there are, the less chance there is that anything could happen to you?"

"But that's not really how statistics work. They call that the gambler's fallacy."

"Yale fallacy..."

"The fact that something happened today has zero effect on whether something will happen tomorrow, is all it is. Each flight is built with the same long odds. Each flight's either gonna go down or be fine. Its fate is preprogrammed in the machinery."

"That doesn't factor in pilots," Billy says.

"Or hijackings."

"Or weather."

"True," Suzy says. "I don't know what it is—I just feel like every flight I work, it's preordained. What's gonna happen is gonna happen."

"Like you have no effect."

"Maybe that's why I like learning to fly. So that I can take some control."

Billy pops two more beers and lifts his for a toast.

"So: nineteen seventy-three," he says.

"This is the year it all happens."

"You: pilot's license. Me: college. Gimme another thing that's gonna happen."

"Well, I didn't really mean to mention it till after the game, but, I dunno, I really am done with the other stuff."

"You've said that before."

"And then I did another one. And another one. But it's over."

"I don't know if they're quite ready, you know?"

"I need you to just let them know," Suzy says.

"I'll mention it. But before I do, you should really think about what you're saying."

"I kind of said my good-bye to Cassidy. I made my last moves out there."

"You told Cassidy that you're through?"

"No. No, no. I just wrapped things up for my own sake. You're the only person who knows. So you can handle it for me."

"Let's just talk about it later. Figure it out for sure tomorrow, cool? They're going to want to keep you going. Hundred percent. And they're gonna fight it. But we'll find a solution."

"It's simple: I don't want it anymore, they can't force me."

"I'll talk to them later this week. Next time they ask, I'll make something up."

Suzy smiles even though it's a weak assurance.

Across the golf course there's a balancing going on—the scarlet and gray of Ohio State evening out the proportions with the USC fans. Bent old men raise their hands in mock fisticuffs. Kids in both sets of colors draw up sides of a scrimmage to settle things ahead of time. Score predictions and turkey sandwiches and Bloody Marys. Kick's at two, and so after finishing the six-pack, they start the pilgrimage to the stadium.

They fall in behind a family split in their matching home jerseys—a pair of nameless cardinal-and-gold 22s and a competing pair of 28s. Lynn Swann and Anthony Davis, Billy explains; Davis scored six touchdowns against Notre Dame a month ago, including two full-field kickoff returns. Billy knows the numbers of all sixty-five Trojans dressed for today's game, even though their names aren't on the backs. They walk along a concrete river that bisects the golf course, and the bowl grows larger. USC fans in jackets to shell from the wind. Buckeye fans in Midwestern sweaters and Midwestern driving caps. Suzy thinks about Mike and his Big Ten town. They clop from the fairway to the rough to the meandering cart path back toward the clubhouse, directly adjacent to the stadium. It takes a while to file in, but they're at their seats by the time the Trojan marching band is running through its routine of fight songs and formations. Suzy and Billy are halfway up the wall of the bowl, in a corner of the visitors' end zone, a view up the gut of the field, the end zone letters appearing, from their seats, to be on their heads: *OIHO.* They have a view across the field of the seats filled with Buckeye fans, singing their song without the lead of the band.

Suzy hasn't seen anything like it before. The interior of the bowl is covered in a pointillist wallpaper—half cardinal and gold, half scarlet and gray—pierced only by the black eyes of the tunnels. Four colors tracking down to the emerald field that's faintly crowned. The canary of the goalposts. The chalk a sharp-edged white. The field framed by the hundred and six thousand, which is some sort of record, Billy says. The First Lady is greeted with a shrug, but the parade's grand marshal, John Wayne, pulls people to their feet. The national anthem is performed by *the* Ohio State University Marching Band. Flags are hoisted up flagpoles. A flight of four Thunderbirds buzzes the stadium in a diamond formation. Kickoff teams in motion and then there's a brown bug of a ball tumbling end over end, high and short, to the far side of the oval, reaching the heights of the bowl's upper lip, where it draws Suzy's eyes to the Charlie Brown squiggle of a mountain range with pointed peaks at steady intervals.

It's warm and windy and the first quarter slips by quickly. Ohio State hardly attempts a pass—the "three yards and a cloud of dust" offense of Woody Hayes. They're here for rushing and defense, the Trojans for flash scoring records. Billy had smuggled in a flask and nips at the intervals of the television time-outs. He doesn't speak much, keeps his eyes leveled at the play—rarely involving himself in the hand motions of the fight songs or the roar of a third-down stop.

The bands play at halftime after an evening-up: USC 7–Ohio State 7. This is part of the game as much as anything else. The PA announcer introduces each marching band with résumés attached—national championships, competitions claimed, unofficial accolades. Billy thumbs at the long list of important-sounding things and nods in suggestion that Suzy be impressed. The 'SC band plays the Doobie Brothers' "Listen to the Music," Chicago's "Dialogue," Isaac Hayes's theme from *The Men*. They accompany Diana Ross on the title track from *Lady Sings the Blues*. The song girls' legs spill like water from their wool minis. The hometown fans cheer as loud as they do for a stop on third-and-short.

By the middle of the second half, the game has broken wide and Billy has gotten drunk. Three rushing touchdowns—from Anthony Davis and fullback Sam "Bam" Cunningham—to Ohio State's one. It's like someone's decided to stop sitting on Billy's chest. The second half also begins to take the sun out of play. The klieg lights turn up the color on the field and in the stands, but what's hap-

pening outside the stadium is the thing Suzy's been promised. It's
that winter rose gold, the sunset she's grown to rely on. It's slapping
the mountains over the lip of the bowl with a dumb lavender, a
non-natural-seeming color. All those shades in the sky and the hills,
they're all for football. It's just not the football Suzy knew on fall
Fridays in Schuyler Glen.

When Cunningham scores for a third and a fourth time, the colors
are gone, the field and players darkened to muddy versions of their
afternoon selves, and then the game is in the books. Billy stands at
attention as the fans in the lower flats of the bowl storm the field
and the players lift Cunningham and the band plays to the faithful
home corner. Billy replays highlights on the walk back to the Volvo.
He hands out high fives and loops around the golf course, looking for
his parents. But it's no use: the course is so dark it's incredible they're
able to find their own car, let alone anyone else's. It takes an hour to
get going—a hundred and six thousand fans—but there are a couple
beers left, and the radio's celebrating. National Champions.

When they're back out of the mountains, back off the canyon
roads and into the cream stream of the Harbor, they're not far from
home, but no way Billy's letting her off yet. It's too early. The waves
of relief seem to compound.

Billy wants to head to Howlers. Suzy could probably do without,
but she feels like she owes him at least a ride. Owes him for the ticket.
And besides, it really isn't late. There's a horde on the sidewalk out
front that looks to have just left, smoke drifting from their numbers
up into the neon. There's no concert, but it's crowded, holiday Monday out of the three-day weekend.

"I'm surprised more people didn't take it easy after last night," Suzy
says.

"Are you really *that* surprised?" Billy says.

Billy's greeted by strangers to Suzy. She always forgets. She lets herself forget. She doesn't repress it—it's just not the Billy she seems to know, the one with whom she spent hours alone today. But these are the people who know him for the other thing. They seem to recognize that he's playing a different role, that he's not on tonight. He high-fives and shakes hands, shows the victory-*V* fingers. It's halfway to a real party. A new band's turning over and Suzy wonders if it'll be J.P. and The Cover Band. She hasn't seen him in forever and she wants to ask him about his training status. If he didn't get booted, he should be close now. For Suzy: just thirty more hours. The thought makes her antsy—though it's been a good day, it's been a day without flying.

They drink so much more. After the drive she was gassed out and ready to call it, but she's riding higher with each beer. The band isn't J.P.'s, but it might as well be. Allman Brothers, CCR, Eagles and Stones. There's some method to the set of covers that's turning the space, by gradual ticks, to a dancier place. Southwest stews on tabletops. An 'SC girl Billy knows climbs on the bar. Then the big Clavinet intro to "Superstition," just like at the Garden in July. A big, heavy funk beat and a spot-on Stevie voice. When it hits, Billy grabs Suzy's hand and leads her to the strip between the tables and the stage. It's as crowded with dancing as she's seen it. Billy has a strangely proficient rhythm. His slinky frame seems to drift all over the small space, but it hits on the beats, a lot of head swiveling, like a sidewinder in sand. He has Suzy laughing and he has Suzy spinning. Just the right amount to keep her on her feet. "Superstition" pushes toward a little countdown in Suzy's head, the last round on the chorus, and she's hoping by some fold in musical time that it's only the first chorus so that they can keep going. Billy's eyes are closed now and he's standing taller than usual, supremely light. And when the song ends and the band announces the turnover, Billy smiles and leans down to whisper: *"We won."* He opens his mouth and eyes wide, like how a child shows glee, and Suzy cracks up all over again.

Suzy drives to Billy's by zigging through side streets, hoping to avoid any other headlights along the way. She feels the Volvo rocking beneath her some, like she's guiding a sailboat back to its slip. At a stoplight they pass a VW Bus that Billy recognizes, and he flashes a *V* out the window.

"Peace or Victory?" Suzy says.

"He's like me," Billy says. "Two 'SC parents but didn't go himself."

They park out front and Billy doesn't struggle to convince Suzy to follow him down the side yard and through the side gate. The lights are out in the big house. It's gotten late all of a sudden. Billy takes a minute to search his pockets for his keys, before shouldering the door open.

"I always forget to lock it anyway," he says.

He's quick to pour some warm whiskey into two glasses and he's quick to put the needle down into the Bowie. BWAH— "Pushing through the market square…"—BWAH— "So many mothers sighing…" He reaches for her hand again, and they do some soft swirling around the center of the room, spinning for spinning's sake, overly dramatic hits on the big strums, Billy pulling her into a sort of slow dance, one hand on her hip, the other with her freckled arm stretched out to full extension, a modified waltz. Suzy left her shoes at the door, and the tightly coiled rug feels slippery on her soles. They start spinning a little faster than the music again, dizzy all over. It's a soft ending but they're still moving, left foot to right foot, waiting for the layered percussion of the next song.

In the quiet gap the phone rings. Billy makes a disgusted face. Ring and ring and ring. The music's going again and they both stand there wound up, waiting to hear if the phone will ring again, if he's gonna be forced to answer. But the phone holds so still it's as though it maybe didn't ring at all a moment before. Billy grabs a scarf off the dresser and tosses it across the room toward his bedside lamp. It falls well short and he excuses himself with an exaggerated *One minute* index finger, and he pulls the scarf wide like a parachute and lays it over the lamp, dimming the light. They make slow little circles in the rug in the center of the room as they dance through the A side.

At some point somebody kisses somebody else. There's kissing in the middle of the room, Suzy catching a glimpse of their height difference in the mirror. It kinda snaps her out and she finishes her drink. He takes the breather to finish his, too. But then they don't move, they just keep hovering there to the weird waltz beat of the last song on the side. And then someone kisses someone again, but this time they outpace the music, and shirts and belts and socks come off. They've been here before, but before it always felt impulsive. Satisfying on the surface but uncertain. This is something else—built-up, earned, inevitable. She felt their bodies moving for hours toward this squeezing together, as though guided from a deeper place. Suzy senses his fingers on the fly of her jeans, and she can feel the individual teeth of the zipper uncouple, it's happening that slow. He's left the button hooked, and as his hand slips the eye over the brass, and her pants *V* and she feels his thumb snap the exposed elastic playfully, she can't tell, really, whether it's a kick drum on the track or something else that's beating. An explosion or just music. Which is when she feels Billy leap back from her, and catches his eyes as they dart toward the door and the heavy knock that's happening there.

"What the fuck...?" Billy says, moving toward the door. He looks out the crack in the window and says to the center of the room, "It's my dad."

"It's twelve thirty," Suzy says.

"He never comes back here," Billy says, waiting as Suzy pulls her shirt back on and zips her pants back up.

He opens the door slightly but keeps the screen where it's at.

"What is it?" Billy says.

Suzy can only hear the voice.

"Do you have a friend over?" he says.

"What?" Billy says.

"Are you by chance with a woman named Suzy Whitman?"

Billy looks at Suzy and she begins walking toward him.

"There's a man who called our house phone looking for her. Says it's an emergency."

"What?" Suzy says.

She steps to the door. Billy's dad is in a robe. He's slight for a man and missing most of his hair. He has glasses and the purposeful look of someone on a military graveyard shift.

"Who was it?" Suzy says.

"A man named Mike Singer. Says he's your brother-in-law. Asked if I could check to see if you were here, 'cause he's been trying all over for you. He didn't stay on the line, he wanted to keep trying other numbers. Just told me to have you call him if you were here."

Without saying another word, she moves through the screen door. But Billy grabs her arm and points toward the phone in his room. "Suzy, just...we'll stay out here while you call."

On her way to the phone in Billy's room, she imagines it just as it must've gone. Dad's died in the night. Right on the eve of surgery. Or it's suddenly inoperable and he has only days to live. Maybe not even a matter of days, but merely hours.

All the things she could possibly think about, and her mind goes to an afternoon in the garage when she was nine or ten, a winter lesson in engine repairs. Suzy riding the dolly around the perimeter of the garage, as though it were a racetrack. Sliding on her back beneath the Alfa Romeo and emerging on the other side, beneath the I AM SUZY! sign, her father's face registering upside down, eyes and nose and mouth, discernible but uncanny, like the letters in the end zone: *OIHO.* That inverted smiling face is what her mind holds fixed as she dials Mike and Grace's number.

"Mike, it's Suzy."

It's so quiet. She presses the receiver hard against her ear.

"Mike," she says.

"Grace. Crashed."

"Mike, I can barely hear—"

"Grace's...plane." There's a sticky click of a swallow. "Grace is dead....Her plane crashed."

"What are you talking about?"

"There's..."

She waits and then waits some more and then screams: *"MIKE!"*

She runs through what she's said, to make sure she has indeed said something. To make sure it's not her fault there's only silence on the other end. But when what she hears next is Mike choking on his own breath, she drops the phone, grabs the skateboard in the corner that's the twin of her own, and blows past Billy and his father, quick to get the wheels on the asphalt in the alley, to get rolling toward home. And even as Billy shouts "Suzy" over and over, all Suzy can manage to whisper in the wrong direction is "Grace."

Part III

Fly Me;
or, The Momentum
of Last Resort

uzy makes the drive alone. It is identical to other drives in all ways but one. A set of familiar stretches and signposts, the unchanging sequence of billboards for tire repairs and cheeseburgers, so much as they should be that they articulate the edges around what's absent, who's absent. In early February there's an absence of color in the pavement and the trees and the snow, and there's an absence of Grace in the car. It's a familiar context with a Grace-shaped hole at the center.

Suzy passes sixty-five cars on the four-hour drive. She counts to mark the distance. She drives most of the way with the radio off, counting cars, hunting, like a race from the back of the starting grid. She used to prefer it that way, a girl starting at the back, an opportunity to doubly defy her competitors' expectations. Some kids would carry over the sting of a grid penalty from qualifying, let it corrode their confidence. Suzy would relish the challenge, just pick them off one by one, as she does now. Suzy is a good driver in the snow.

It happened so fast. Five weeks gone, as though snipped. The phone call straight through to here, experienced with the speed of a daydream, a mind's projection into the future. A phone call, followed by a weightless ride to Mike and Grace's. The details of the plane crash—over and over from a thousand vantage points. Grace in Hawaii, Grace in the prop plane. Just Grace and the pilot and, of course, J.P.

It was a revelation at first, an aftershock, what would've been the leading surprise were it not for the deaths. Grace in Hawaii with J.P.—the first Mike or Suzy had heard of it. Grace and J.P. in Hawaii at the same time, coincidentally or not. They wouldn't know that first night and still don't really know now. But the three of them—Grace, J.P., and a local pilot. On a private little tour of the west coast of Maui. Out from Ka'anapali, down the S curve to Wailea and Makena, and then back again. Low is how their plane ride would be described by witnesses, low and unassuming. And then suddenly, just below Ka'anapali, not low at all, but high. Higher, and in short space, getting greedily high. So that when the engines cut, when the engines stalled out and all went quiet, they fell into the bay as an inevitable body with no force acting on it but the original force, the apple force. Thirty-two feet per second per second—it was the first thing Suzy thought when she heard they'd stalled. Her miserable physics retention, but this was the first-day-of-class equation. There were witnesses, but there was nothing much to do. Witnesses driving on the road watched the plane fragment upon impact and disappear beneath the surface. But the cliff at the edge of the water was steep—fifty, sixty feet, sounded like—and nobody was getting down there fast enough to do much. The plane was just off the edge of the island.

There was one man in a boat. A little fishing boat with an engine and a till. He got to the wreckage first. He dove. The cabin floated just beneath the surface. He dove again—found the door, clean lines and smooth rivets, nothing to grab hold of. He dove again, and this time he approached a window. Not to the cockpit, but to the little cabin. And there he saw the two—young woman and young man, their heads hanging from their bodies the way flowers hang when their stems have been snapped. The fisherman surfaced, caught his breath, nothing to be done. But he dove one final time, and by then water had filled the cabin. The entire thing was filled and it was beginning to sink, slowly, the way a party balloon falls from the ceiling when its helium has thinned. The fisherman made it to the same window for one last look—the same woman and the same man, buckled in side by side. But this time their heads were lifted off their chests, almost upright, buoyed by the slow-motion descent. He saw it then. The one thing through that window that cut the other way, that cut in an impossible direction of beauty, the thing he kept saying over and over, to police and reporters and eventually to Wayne and Edith and Suzy and Mike: the image of Grace's head held tall, her long blond hair reaching toward the surface, extending itself up in all directions.

They learned only the basic facts that first night. It was the trip they took the next day that brought the details. Mike and Suzy on the first plane out in the morning. Wayne and Edith the day after that, meaning another postponed surgery. By the time they arrived, the pieces of the plane on the surface had been cleared and the three bodies had been pulled from the cabin. But the rest of the plane was still on the ocean floor, to be retrieved with less urgency. Wayne and Mike IDed the body at the morgue and arranged for it to be shipped back, in an expedient three weeks, to Schuyler. Boat to San Francisco, train to Reno and Salt Lake and Omaha and Chicago. Truck from Chicago to Detroit to Cleveland and Erie and Syracuse, where Wayne could wait with the owners of Schuyler Glen's Gibson and Sons Funeral Home to pick up the package and prepare her for burial at the Painted Post cemetery, where Grandpa and Grandma Whitman had been for a while.

On Maui, Wayne spent an hour with the fisherman, working out the details, pressing him for all the sensations, all the images, he could recall. When Wayne told the three of them about her hair in the water, the way her head rose up, Edith attributed this to sweet Gracie's soul ascending to heaven, and Suzy said it sounded like a made-up memory.

It was not a good few days. It was different from Suzy's last time in Hawaii. There was not much to do besides fill out paperwork and sit still and uncomprehending, careful just to keep breathing. It reminded her of when Grace used to sit on Suzy's head. Pin Suzy down on the bed or the couch and just sort of rest there, heavier than Suzy by twice, at least earlier on, and how Suzy would just stay still with Grace's weight, scared at first that she might suffocate and break something, until she'd ward off that fear by breathing slowly from the little gap near her mouth where there was light. That's what it was like—Grace sitting on her brain. Suzy couldn't think of anything to do or say, except take one breath at a time.

Edith spent thirty-five of the first thirty-six hours on Maui crying—as much for Grace, Suzy figured, as for Wayne, the potential halving of her family. Wayne spent it being sick. Mike stayed in his hotel room, mourning in private, undoubtedly wondering, beneath all the immediate grief, what the fuck Grace was doing in Hawaii with J.P. Suzy wondered, too. It made plenty of sense—at least, as far as surprising things go. They had such an easy compatibility. Suzy didn't plan to talk about it with Mike, but it was forced in their face when J.P.'s parents called from their hotel and asked to meet with the four of them. It happened on the third day, after J.P.'s parents' trip to the morgue. There was a round of hugs, but they had nothing to say to one another, really. In her mission to eliminate awkwardness, Edith treated the situation as though they'd all just met at a wedding. She asked about their lives in California, smiled, said sweet things. Edith and J.P.'s mother played along together, and Mike left for his room without acknowledging them.

It went like that for a couple more days and then everyone headed home. The doctors were able to fit Wayne in the very next week on account of a cancellation. Mike and Suzy flew to L.A. on the same flight, in separate rows. They shared a cab home with a slighted cab-driver. They got dropped off in between their houses and then started in opposite directions. But before separating, Suzy asked Mike if he wanted her to be there with him when he walked into the house. Mike said it was fine. And that was the last they spoke. Or at least the last they'd spoken in a month.

The airline canceled Suzy's flights that first week. She said she was good to go, that she wanted to keep flying, but they insisted. One week and then a second and third. She spent her days on her back in her bed watching the ceiling fan. She did some other mean-ingless things, too, but it didn't really matter, 'cause it just floated away with the rest of the film that had been scissored out. LBJ died—that's something she remembers. She read a lot of newspaper stories, watched a lot of television reports: the death of another ex-president. Billy came by every couple days. And you know what? He didn't say a word about runs. She admired that about him. Or ad-mired the idea of a Billy that understood the order of significances in the universe, a Billy that granted space, that exercised restraint.

Wayne had surgery and he woke up from it—that happened, too. He was in the hospital for a week and then he went home. It was an all-world terrible January in Schuyler Glen, but Wayne was home, and he wasn't dead. Consider it a win. Before she went back to work, Suzy got in a couple hours with Millikan. She got in a small plane and flew around the southern edge of the county. When they landed, she said it was nice it had gone like that, since her sister had just died in one. Millikan didn't get the joke and then recognized that it wasn't a joke at all. Suzy smiled sweetly and scheduled more time for the fol-lowing week.

And then, finally, early February, here she is, heading home. She makes the drive alone. It is so cold.

It's the kind of cold that memory refuses to bank. She lived this cold, months without a break, each of her first twenty-two years. And yet when she steps out of the car to fill up in Owego, the sensation is all new, impossible seeming. It's not just below freezing—it's not that gradual dip into discomfort, the relief of a reasonable twenty when she's bundled up for ten... this is much worse. This is zero. Zero plus or minus a couple. This is a shotgun blast to the face and body from northernmost Canada. The parts that are practically Greenland and Norway and Russia—the convergence. That's how it feels. Her boots crunch on muddy ice, ice that's resigned to holding tight to the blacktop until May. She shuffles to the white light of the service center, the only light for miles, a star around which a weakly populated system might orbit. Leftover sleigh bells clatter lazily when she passes through the door. Long shelving units line the floor like rows of corn, but they're sparse, fallow, quarter stocked. Near the register the goods are bunched: candy bars and motor oil and ROAD WARRIOR trucking T-shirts.

"Five on two," Suzy says.

The man behind the counter moves with heavy hips. He is thinner than she is but carries himself like he's fat. He's young, not much older than Suzy, but his skin falls off his face, a wet sag around the eyes, muddy stubble, a mouth that's cracked and stained by tobacco spit. It's that stained lower lip, that stained corner of the mouth, that dominoes her toward the realization that it is in fact late, that it is desolate. That she hasn't been careful enough. That she's had her guard down. That though Suzy used to not worry about men, it was because those men were boys in literature seminars, boys at rock concerts, boys on footpaths on the New Haven Green. This winter is different.

In part it's Sela's fault. Sela has felt so safe. When did she last fear for cracked lips and loose skin and a lack of advantage? To calm her nerve, she assures herself that she is—in heavy pants and snow boots and a giant, shapeless tube of an overcoat—hardly a woman just now, except at the hole where her eyes and nose and mouth ask for gas. But when she catches a quick glimpse of herself in the mirror behind the attendant, she sees that the strangest accident has transpired: the wind outside has torn her hair out from under her jacket and whipped it up and over the fur of her hood, strands of long light-red hair folded back over the mane, almost like eyelashes. Big, luscious pink hair-lashes framing her face as this single, giant, beautiful batting eye.

She ruffles her hood and tightens it around her face again, casts her eyes downward, reaches for the five in her pocket, places the five on the counter. She waits with a lowered head for some acknowledgment of payment, of services rendered.

"Cold one," the man says.

Suzy smiles and nods to herself.

"Anything else?" he says.

Suzy lifts her face and catches his eyes for the first time. She sees Mike eyes, not Manson eyes. Isn't it strange how the Manson eyes have absolved all the other eyes from posing a threat? The hungry, the blameless, the searching.... These are closer to those, and she feels better. Suzy tries to say "No" and it comes out like a cough, so she tries again and says "No thanks" like a stew, and the man smiles and turns back to the pot of coffee he was brewing when she walked in. Out the door she crunches through the snow with a little trot, some speed to get out of the wind. It is so cold.

The rest of the drive is elating. Or rather it's the relative high of normal after her mind had drifted to kidnapping—to kidnapping, rape, murder. Normal—even a supercold normal—feels good after a glimpse of the very worst. Wayne and Edith have one daughter left—that's all. It is important for Suzy, she realizes now, more important than it was five weeks ago, not to die.

She hasn't been home since the accident. The first flowers are still out, the winter whites and pale pinks of the daphnes and camellias. They're all dead now, but they're still on the table in the dining room. Edith has soup in a pot on the stove top, soup that was dinner a few hours ago, that's been reducing into a paste during the double-digit evening hours. Suzy fixes a bowl anyway. Edith leads Suzy to the bedroom to see Wayne.

"We've been waiting to tell you," he says.

"What's that?" Suzy says.

"We went to the doctor today, the local doctor," he says. "To take some pictures. To see where we stand after three weeks."

"What do they really expect?"

"We're in a place of no expectations," Wayne says. "But I thought you should know that we'll have a better sense this weekend. We should know the score, is all I mean."

"And what's your body telling you?"

"It's silent."

"Okay, then," Suzy says.

"Can I get you anything else?" Edith says. "You look not yourself."

"Weird," Suzy says, gesturing her eyes toward her father.

"I just meant you look exhausted."

"I'm gonna head to my room. I'll see you guys in the morning."

"I love you, Suzy," Edith says.

"Me too," Suzy says, on her way out the door. "I mean: same."

The next morning, moving up the stairs from breakfast and along the hallway, in the psychic shadows of the family portraits and the heat pulsing from the room that was Grace's, Suzy feels her feet and ankles grow heavier, as though she's walking over flypaper. She opens the door to the bedroom and closes it behind her, closes her eyes, too, and collapses on Grace's bed, on the quilt Edith pulled out each year when the clocks changed in fall. She rolls herself into a ball, sniffing

Grace's shampoo on the pillow, waiting for the tears to come, Suzy willing the tears to come.

It has been over a month and she's failed to cry a real cry: a heaving meltdown, a sob with cut brake lines. The scent on the pillow isn't of Grace in California, but of Grace in middle and high school. Edith has been buying Johnson's baby shampoo since they were toddlers and still keeps it in stock in their old bathroom. Grace evidently put it to use on recent trips. So it isn't just the picture of Grace that the shampoo summons, but the picture of Suzy, too—sisters sharing sonically porous walls, a filthy sink clogged with honey-blond hair, half redder than the rest. Suzy has spent a life defining herself as distinct from Grace. A three-year gap in even middle school was practically the difference between child and adult. And that single year of high school together, they barely spoke a word—Suzy reading and racing, Grace plotting her exit with the folk crowd in Ithaca. Suzy sharing in her sister only insomuch as she was forced to wear her hand-me-down dresses, listen along to her music, wash her hair with the stuff that defined her sister's smell. But there was no avoiding it, Suzy realizes now on Grace's bed, gazing at the posters and the records that never made their way to New York or L.A. There was no avoiding the ways in which her sister, even when Suzy most resisted, infused herself.

Suzy's head is pressed flat on the bed, half on a pillow and half on the stitched edge of the quilt. She contracts the ceiling-facing muscles of her neck to press her face into the bed, making her eyelids stretch and her vision go fuzzy. She's going to draw out some tears even if it requires physical force. She presses her head deeper into the springs of the mattress, deeper like a dive beneath a wave, eyes thin and sealed, diving below the surface of the bed, breaststroking through the secrets Grace stashed there—cash and grass and raunchy magazine clippings about sex—and then she comes up breathing. Breathing hard, in the real present, from burying her face, holding her breath, exerting the muscles of her arms and shoulders and neck.

In the light lift of heavy breathing her mind floats to the ceiling and glimpses Grace at the beach that day with J.P., when the idea of flight lessons was first introduced, Grace in a sunray-colored bikini with the thick, sugary pleasure of grass on her eyes and lips, a little sweat on the cilia between her mouth and her nose, and the way she said it about flying like she'd always said it about racing: "Just *do* it, Suz. Just be so, so good." And how she'd probably have said it about anything—about a desire of Suzy's to dive into the ocean that instant, or to see a show at Howlers, or to order a turkey sub. But in that moment it meant something, it carried weight, and it pushed her off the edge of the diving board and out into the air. That look, that shove, made Suzy act. The months since have been such a series of shocks, a life beyond her control, a life lived in unwitting submission to forces greater than her own. But who is she kidding, it was that line—"Just *do* it, Suz"—that's led her to here. And it's that line, that iceberg tip that stands for all the support she provided for Suzy all along, that sits on her chest now, the bed pressing up and the memory pressing down, so that it's difficult for Suzy to breathe again.

She remembers what happened next that afternoon on the beach. The look on Grace's face. As clear to her now as a classic family photograph she's walked past all her life: that sweat on her lip, the sun breaking in a thousand directions off the lenses of her shades, a tickle on the end of her nose that made her sniffle, and then the pretty cracked lips, fighting off a giggle that came with the tickle, failing to hold it back a moment longer, and breaking into a floodgates grin and a low-throated laugh at no joke, her tongue and teeth and lips and skin dancing at a cellular level, uncomplicated joy, a plain disinterest in anything that had ever happened anywhere or anytime that was not there in that moment, which—like all moments—died the same instant it was born.

The service is on Friday afternoon. It's silver and cold, and Suzy spends the prep before the service worrying about the conditions at the cemetery, the snow, the extra effort it will take to get the body in the ground. She doesn't understand why they didn't just cremate her in Hawaii. How much easier it would've been. It was in part for Nana and Pop Rochelle, sure, but think about the money, the logistics. They're at the big brick church on Fox Street, Saint John's. Wayne's in a wheelchair, with Edith greeting people as they come in. Mike's at their side, silently shaking hands of strangers. He asked that they consider having a service out in Sela so that more of her friends from Grand Pacific might be able to make it. But after Wayne's surgery, it was impossible. It would be a Schuyler affair. Nuclear family, cousins within driving distance, leftover acquaintances from high school. It's not many people—not like you'd get if you died at fifty-five (a third of the town and half the glassworks might show up for Wayne) or seventeen (Suzy had one of those—drunk-driving accident involving a classmate and a gorge). There are good times to die, turnout-wise, and twenty-five—on the road, living away from home—is not one of them. The rector, Father Degan, confirmed Grace and Suzy, knew them both as younger girls, but has little to add besides referring to her love of life and music and her passion for flying. Suzy is embarrassed that stewing is all they can really talk about. It's all there is and ever will be.

Edith bawls through some remarks about Grace as a little girl, and then Mike reads what he clearly intends to be the last word on the matter, a short piece of writing he's worked over. It's about selfishness. About how unselfish Grace could be, but how hungrily she pursued the things she loved. That by skipping out on college, she was able to pack more living into those borrowed years than anyone else he knew. That while twenty-five is tragically, impossibly young, it wasn't your typical twenty-five years. Et cetera, et cetera. That if there's anything to take away from this, it's that all of us need to be *more* selfish, not less. That there will suddenly come a day when deferring life is no longer possible because it's just ended. "Fuck everyone and everything else," he says. "And live for you."

There's a hurt confusion that moves through the pews, an Episcopalian murmur. Suzy gives three crisp, reverie-shattering claps. Just: *thwack thwack thwack.* Father Degan hustles to the microphone to steer the service back toward the intended conclusion. He urges the organ player into action. Suzy considers standing and following Mike with comments of her own, even though it hasn't been planned. She hasn't written anything but has thought about what she might say if she absolutely had to speak. She's thinking all this even as Degan moves toward the lectern, even as the organ begins to play "Amazing Grace," and then the window is shut and there will be no speaking on behalf of the sister who can't speak anymore. Suzy regrets it immediately but starts warming toward the reality of what she hasn't done: she's kept the thing she most wanted to say about Grace all to herself, a secret she whispers to her hands as though in prayer.

Suzy has a full extra day at home after Mike's gone. She makes Wayne and Edith pancakes and eggs. Today is a big day. They try to busy themselves around the house, cleaning out the wicker food baskets and picking up the dying petals that have dropped from the flowers. Suzy asks Edith how long you're supposed to keep the flowers, and Edith says she'll keep them until they've turned to dust.

Just after noon, as Wayne's lifting a bologna sandwich to his mouth, the kitchen phone rings. He's in his chair, no way of jumping to his feet, and Edith lifts it on the second ring.

"Yes, he's right here, just a minute."

She pulls the phone toward his seat at the kitchen table, uncoiling the cord so that it's extended in full without its curls.

"Hi, Doctor," he says, and then he listens. There are some indiscernible reactions: "Mm-hmm," "I see," "And what does...," "I see," "Mm-hmm." And then a long pause, longer than any other. Suzy stands at an opposite corner of the kitchen from her mother. Suzy has the scars of a frown on her face. "Well, thank you, Doctor," he says. "Speak soon, you bet." And he gestures for Edith to hang up.

There are no words and no one presses.

"They think it's gone," he says.

"What?" It's Edith.

"They don't see it at all. None on the spine and not at its edges, not spreading."

"Oh my God," Edith says.

Wayne looks disinterested, distrusting.

"How are you just... reacting like that?!"

"I feel the same as I did before they told me what it looks like, before they told me what they *think*. They could be wrong."

"Or they could be right. Dr. Bard has no reason to give you that news unless he's feeling good about it. He always has three others look at it—that's what he said. And they concur? *Nobody sees a thing?*"

"That's what he said."

Edith's cheeks are wet all over again. Her face hasn't had an opportunity to dry out.

Suzy is at the table and bends down to hug her father and kiss his cheek. She doesn't say anything, doesn't know what she'd say anyway. She just holds him another second and then another, and she feels Wayne's breath in her hair, smells the juniper from the gin he snuck into his orange juice. And then she feels his face shift, about to say something, and before Edith joins the embrace, he whispers it to Suzy's ear only:

"But what about Grace?"

The shadow waiting at the base of her stairs surprises her badly, kicking up the little bird in her chest, but she approaches it with high shoulders and a bored, flat face.

"What do you *do* while you're waiting?" she says.

"I haven't been waiting that long."

"You eat a burrito, you read a magazine." She gestures to the ball of foil on the ground and the large-format, folded-over *Rolling Stone* tucked under his arm.

"I wanted to see how you were doing," Billy says. "I haven't seen you in weeks."

"You could've called."

"I have called. You have a stalker's worth of messages."

"I went home. I told you I was going."

"You know I mean before that. I understand what's been going on—I mean, I *don't* understand—but I just wanted to check in."

"How did you know I'd be back tonight, anyway?"

"Called the airline."

"I wasn't even on duty."

"They skimmed the manifests."

"What the fuck."

"I sell to Janice. I cut her a deal."

"You could've been a serial killer."

"Yeah, well. Like I said, I haven't been waiting that long. Good information."

"I'm pretty beat," she says.

"Just, let's talk for two minutes upstairs."

"I really don't feel like watching you smoke."

"Just let me come up. I promise I won't stay long."

Suzy doesn't like this, doesn't like that he cares about something enough to be pathetic about it. This was always the appeal, the insouciant remove. Her eyes track up the long ascent and she hands him her suitcase.

"How are you feeling?" he says when the door clicks shut.

"The funeral was pretty horrible," she says. "But my dad's doing okay."

"That's great. That's really great." He seizes on the uplift. He's being careful—his enthusiasm is tiptoeing. She doesn't like it, but she can't react badly.

"Better than expected," she says. "Knock on wood."

"That's great, Z."

"Don't call me that."

"That's great, Su-Z."

"You came here not to just ask me about my trip."

"What do you mean?"

"Come on, spit it out—I wasn't just putting you off, I want to go to bed."

Billy stands in the center of the living room, hands in the pockets of his dungarees, shoulders slumped like a marionette with slack strings.

"I wanted to know…in addition to how you're doing…whether you'd thought much about the near future with regard to your work."

Suzy wonders if it looks as though she's smiling because of the upticks of her lips, the tonally inappropriate one-note repose of her well-shaped mouth.

"I haven't really thought about it beyond what I said at the football game," she says. "I'm still out, I guess."

"Just so you know, it's not me asking," he says.

"Oh yeah?"

"I know all the reasons why this is a horrible thing to have to talk about. But fact of the matter is, we still technically work for people, and they have questions and interests that are more important to them than the space I wish they'd give you. They need someone to make a run this week."

"I haven't thought about whether I'm going to keep flying even generally."

"They want to know if they should hold out or find someone else."

"Tell them to find someone else. I was done anyway."

"They're not going to want to find someone else, though."

"Then why did you just suggest that as an option?"

"Look, I'm trying my best here to buy us a little space—"

"Thank you so much."

"Right. And they were cool with some weeks, a month."

"Why didn't you just tell them I was done when I told you to?"

"Because we hadn't settled on it *officially*. And besides, that's a big deal to them, it's not as easy as just—"

"It *is*, though! All you had to say was 'Don't wait around for this one.'"

"Look, they're actually open to the idea of you walking away eventually. Soon, even. But they need you to do this run to New York ASAP."

"I was just in New York."

"You weren't working. And, frankly, they don't know that. I lied and said you've been somewhere else."

"I really don't owe them anything."

"It doesn't—look, Suzy, it doesn't matter. Don't act like you don't understand what I'm saying. It's what they feel. How *they* perceive things. They feel like they've let you hang pretty loose on the line. They've lost stews before, that's all part of it, but so long as you can physically do it, so long as you're still working for the airline, they're gonna put the screws to you to make runs."

"I'm not gonna fucking do it! Just tell them that."

"My whole position here," he says, shifting up to a higher plane of conviction, "has been, all along, to protect you from these guys and what they're really saying."

"*Protect* me? *All along?* Are you fucking *kidding* me?"

"After the first time...I put it all on the table, and it was your choice."

"Get the fuck out of my apartment."

"Suzy: *listen to me.* If you don't make this run, they're going to turn you in."

"That's bullshit. They'd be implicated."

"It doesn't really work like that. They have cops on payroll. You're just a runner. You're just a stewardess. They'll point them to the surveillance tapes in New York. They have all sorts of records. It's easy."

Suzy wonders what this conversation would feel like during the day. With the light sloshing through the blinds, with the boring constancy of the waves rolling in off the horizon on the pace of a dialed-down metronome. But instead it's just a single naked bulb, the ceiling fan sprouting like a fern. The only light in a dark world, tar at the edges of the frame, all the threats and volleys caroming off the walls and settling around her in a whirlpool of distortion. What is he even saying?

"I really think we can convince them," Billy says, "to let you walk away, but not until after this last one."

"I don't want to do it," Suzy says.

"It's just...not really one of the options. They have this way of doing things, they're not—"

"Don't say 'they' again."

"What?"

"You've been talking about 'them' and 'they' for seven fucking months. I'm not working for 'they' anymore."

"One run."

"Do you get turned in, too? Is that why you're so concerned?"

"I will be turned in, almost certainly, but that's more of an implicit threat. What is being said about you is less vague."

"I want to meet 'they.' I want to say things to 'they' in person."

"I don't think that's really possible."

"Of course it's possible."

"It's just not gonna happen. The whole point is to stay a couple layers removed. That's the whole point of me."

"Well, that broke down tonight," Suzy says. "'They' want something that only I can provide. If 'they' want it bad enough, tell them we're gonna meet in person to discuss formally. I don't want anyone coming after me. I don't want any threats lingering over my head. If I agree to do this one, then I want to get an assurance from 'they.' I want to get on with things and never hear about it again. Everybody else gets something out of this, but I'm the only one really putting my ass on the line."

Billy's body hasn't moved, has it? Did they begin in the same physical relation to each other that they're in right now—Suzy close to the kitchenette and Billy near the door? Or did they swap positions at some point? Suzy can hear the filament in the lightbulb buzzing like a low E string. Has it been ten minutes or an hour?

"I'll ask him," Billy says, breaking the silence.

"What?"

"I said, I'll ask him."

"Him?"

"You said no more 'they.' And it's just one guy. You know that."

"I most certainly don't."

"I've told you all along."

"Seriously don't patronize me. All along it's been this army of drug spooks, hidden in plain sight. *Don't take the wrong breath, or, Suzy, they'll…*"

"I think I can go to him with this. He might balk entirely, but I think he wants whatever it takes to get this one done. He's mentioned maybe meeting you before anyway. Not as *El Jefe*, you know, but, like, as a normal person. Thought about taking one of your flights."

"One guy."

"Maybe he *has* taken your flights. Maybe he's a regular. I wouldn't know."

The movie plays in reverse—seven months of passengers' faces in rewind. From that suited pair she thought she recognized from Sela, back to the man who dug his wedding ring into her hand on that return from the very first run. She's been monitored this whole time, hasn't she? Every step on every flight. Strangers watching her ass tock between the aisle seats. A South American drug lord keeping proximate tabs on his cargo.

How is she not dead yet? That's what Suzy's thinking as Billy moves to the door. How—with all these men in the world ready to slit her throat, silent and solitary at the gas station convenience store and the foot of her apartment stairs—is she still breathing?

"I'll ask him tomorrow," Billy says with his back turned to the room. And before the door snaps into the frame, he adds: "Happy Valentine's Day."

Suzy wakes up in darkness. It's the next day or the day after. The same tar at the edges of the frame. She checks the clock and it's not yet six. Since forcing her tears at home, she hasn't been able to stop. A wet pillow and a gummy mouth. She lies there quaking until she detects the neon through the blinds, the first sign of the east's faithful imposition on the west.

It is so cold. Forty degrees at the beach, the thermometer on the landing says. Balmy by comparison with Schuyler, but somehow chillier in context, against expectation. She's not flying today, but she's up and anxious. She brews some coffee, swallows a handful of uncooked oatmeal. She notices a stack of books at the edge of the sofa, Mike's books. Mike left Schuyler early because he'd heard Reverend Jones was supposed to make an appearance at the L.A. temple. Though Suzy and Mike haven't made any plans to see each other, Suzy figures he should be around. She gathers up the books. Updike: *Rabbit Redux.* Stegner: *Angle of Repose.* Brautigan: *The Abortion.* She hasn't cracked the latter pair, but she feels guilty about not having finished the Rabbit book. When is the last time she finished anything? Actually brought it over the line? Hers was a life of finish lines for so long, and then it wasn't.

She sits on the couch in the reflection of the foil-colored fog. The light attaches itself to objects in its immediate presence—the coffee table, the lamp, the stack of books. A blanket of light wrapping her up roundly like the orb of a perfume cloud. It's enough light to read by, and she picks up *Rabbit* and thumbs open at the dog-ear. Skeeter. She remembers the name. Skeeter, Jill, Nelson, Rabbit. Sharing a home, Rabbit's home. Skeeter, young black Vietnam vet; Jill, young white runaway; Rabbit, oafy former athlete whose wife, Janice, stepped out on him; Nelson, Rabbit's middle schooler. Rabbit, who lets himself get caught up in it all, who lets the '60s into his living room, literally. The four under one roof together—Rabbit sleeping with Jill, Jill sleeping with Skeeter. Why did Suzy put it down? It had grown soft in the middle. Overuse of the word *cunt.* It had all grown redundant. She finishes a second mug of coffee and promises herself she won't lift her eyes until it's through, until she finishes *something.* And then the house catches fire. The white girl gets burned alive, the black boy gets framed,

Janice gets traded up on, comes back through again. A story at its end right where it started.

Suzy feels happy to have turned over the last page, feels excitable, caffeine and proximity to someone else's life. It is the fourth book she's read of Updike's—the earlier Rabbit; the mythical *Centaur;* the one that came with the *Time* cover, *Couples*—and she feels like she understands the basic rap: once-in-a-century stylist, convinced that fucking is the only point to life. She remembers the way Janice's mouth was described in *Rabbit, Run,* a book she read as a junior in high school, too young really to form a stamped opinion, except toward a phrase she's never forgotten: Janice's mouth described as a "slot." When she first read it, the word cooled the fluid in her spinal column, and it does so again now.

What does Mike even mean when he recommends new books to her? What does he intend to say to her through them? She used to love opening a new book and racing through the pre-story pages behind the cover—the title page, the Library of Congress filing codes, the table of contents, and the dedication—and then accelerating through the first few paragraphs, playing like a skeptical book editor. Judging. Assessing, critically. Even if she hasn't enjoyed reading as much lately, she's at least enjoying *having read* this one. She considers the two other books but can't muster the interest. She picks up her skateboard and rolls herself over to Mike's.

He's home, she can tell by the lights. Because she's walked in on Mike alone countless times, it doesn't feel as impactful when only he comes to the door, when there's all Mike and no Grace. He cracks the door and it catches on a chain.

"Oh, hey, Suz, gimme a second."

As he opens the door, it's made clear he's wearing boxers and tube socks and no shirt, and she realizes she's somehow seen him shirtless only on the beach. He's moved the papers from his office out onto the living room table. The dishes are piled up in the sink, and there's a pot of water on the stove top. He doesn't act surprised to see her.

"Heeyyy...," she says, an elongated note, as she takes in the mess. "How have you been doing?"

"Uh, okay. Okay. Listen to this. Listen to this from the Pynchon, the one I was telling you about a while ago, the one that was written here in Sela. It's rockets and probably a hundred characters so far, but he's got a *glassblower*. How 'bout that." He spends half a minute in silence, flipping, scanning, flipping, scanning. Suzy stands in the center of the room, and the whole thing takes long enough for her to become aware of her posture, aware of the force of gravity on her neck and shoulders.

"Okay, the glassblower. 'Darkness invades the dreams of the glassblower,'" he reads. "'Of all the unpleasantries his dreams grab in out of the night air, an extinguished light is the worst. Light, in his dreams, was always hope: the basic, mortal hope. As the contacts break helically away, hope turns to darkness, and the glassblower wakes sharply tonight crying, "Who? *Who?*"'"

"Hmm," she says.

"Right?"

"I don't totally follow, I guess, but that's cool there's glass stuff."

"Don't go all Grace on me—you get it."

"Okay..." She stands taller. "What about your other things, then? How's Jones?"

"I, uh, I still haven't found him. He didn't show. But I'm gonna spend a bunch of time with his congregation in Bakersfield now. He might not be there still, but there are people who are closer to him than these folks in L.A. People who have been with him longer. It'll be good for the story either way."

"Have they converted you yet?"

"Some of it makes sense."

"Please."

"I just…need him for this thing. I'm…I'm out of time."

Suzy takes a couple cautious steps toward him.

"You okay otherwise?" she says.

"I mean, I guess I'm trying to stay busy. What have you got?" He gestures to the books under her arm.

"Just returning these," she says.

"You like 'em?"

"I only read the Updike."

"You can keep them as long as you want."

"Just…before I forget, I guess. Before I lose them or something."

"What'd you think?"

"I liked it more than the first one, the first Rabbit one."

"Me too. He's fast, man. He just gets it all down. Nails what it's like to be living now. When was that set—summer and fall of '69, right? And it's out in '71?"

"What it's like to be living now, as a *man*," Suzy clarifies.

"I guess. But everything else, too."

"Do you really relate to what's in there?"

"Are you kidding?"

"I just mean, it doesn't much resemble this here," she says, a thumb over her shoulder to the ocean.

"It's high-order literature."

Slot, Suzy thinks. *Janice, you dumb cunt with that stupid slot of a mouth.*

"He's who Updike would've been if he hadn't gone to Harvard," Mike says.

"Fat, sad, war hawk. Deserter of child and wife," Suzy says.

"He came home, and then she left him."

"Keeper of an underage concubine. Teenage runaway dies 'cause of him."

"Look, this is one of the best we've got. It's only degrees of agreeing. There's a hierarchy of taste, ya know? You don't have to love it, but you have to recognize it's genius, you have to..." Suzy stops listening. She actually kind of likes Rabbit. Soft spot, he's so pathetic. Rabbit's so far from right he can't even find a full wrong, either. The more she thinks about it just now, the more she realizes she has no problem with the book. She pities Rabbit, but she's growing to despise Mike. Mike and his stumbly, self-asserted "hierarchy of taste"; at least Rabbit lives in the lift of Updike's language.

"And besides," Mike is still talking, "just trust me, he *does* get what it's like to be a man."

She smiles and imagines Mike back in the Midwest. Working the Linotype. Falling in with a teenager. Who Mike would've been if he hadn't gone to Columbia. That's certainly what he's getting at, isn't it? *You tragic man,* she thinks. *What was my sister doing?*

"Well, here are these, too." She places the books on the table.

"You really didn't even read the Brautigan?"

This is getting to be a waste of time.

"No," she says, "I've been a little busy. My dad got some good news, by the way."

"This book is basically made out of stuff you like. Books and libraries, a reasonably realistic affair."

"Cut the tumor right out, no sign of spread, at least nothing they can't get with more chemo. Might even walk again one day."

"Know what just occurred to me? As I said that about books and libraries—know what's different about books and libraries than any other kind of twentieth-century culture consumption? You put out a film, right? The only other films you're competing with for business are the other films in the theater that night, right? The other films that opened that weekend, or that have been kicking around for the last month, or maybe that are showing at some special midnight thing. In a bookstore, though, you put out a new book, it has to compete with not just every other book that came out that week, and month, and year—but with every book that's ever been published. It's Updike versus Tolstoy. It's Brautigan versus Kafka and Hemingway. I mean, those are stacked odds. I guess that's why I try to be such a champion of these guys, why I find it so impressive. You can't just be better than the other guy publishing this month, right? I think that's what I like about Jones, too. He understands this idea. It's him versus John the Baptist. It's him versus Henry the Eighth. He'll take the Bible and throw it on the floor. He'll do it almost every time he preaches, he'll say: 'This black book has held down you people for two thousand years. It has no power.' Men in the contemporary moment taking on the received wisdom of the ages. Asking of it whether this is as good as we can do. You dig?"

"'*You dig?*'"

"You shoulda read *The Abortion*. It bums me out that you didn't. You sure you don't want to keep it?"

"Haven't read *The Hunters* yet, either." She says it to be cruel.

"Well, that's a major bummer, too. Just read them both. Keep *The Abortion*."

"Feel like I can learn something from it?"

"Can't hurt to read another book. Can't hurt to keep the education going. There's a Tijuana abortion that'll make anyone think twice about getting that kind of work done."

"TJ, huh?"

"I can't really believe girls your age—girls your age and younger— go down there sometimes. What a fucked-up business."

She wants him to say something. Just one more thing, one more push. She's got the high swell in her throat, the other night with Billy all over again, but different, the room sucking in toward its principals, heating her cheeks, little bends that might lead to a break.

"What?" he says. "Why are you looking at me like that? You never got one, did you?"

She can't believe he's obliged her request. She can't believe he's taken it there.

"It's none of your business whether I have or haven't, but I'm relieved that it's an option."

"That's some dangerous bullshit. I'd never let anyone come near my girl with a fucking coat hanger."

Slot, she thinks.

"What if I told you—"

"Don't," he says, plugging his fingers into his ears, "I actually don't want to hear it, seriously."

"What if I told you I knew someone who went to Tijuana for an abortion within the last year? And that it worked out pretty all right for her."

He drops his hands to his hips. "Are you serious? With who?"

"You think it's *me?*"

His eyes hold unblinking on her. Her view of him binoculars and she sees his face, really sees it, for the first time since the plane crash, broken and irretrievable. The whole thing has passed over him and slashed his face in half. It's broken his cheekbones and his jaw, flattened his nose. His eyes fall out of his skull, attached only to the vines of the optic nerves—that's what it looks like to Suzy. It's what it looked like when he found out Grace had been with J.P. Over the past month and a half his face has stitched back up, healed over, but it's incapable of reconstructing itself back to where it was before the news. The lights in his eyes had gone out.

A lump rides his throat from his collarbone to his chin. He still hasn't blinked; he's waiting for her to tell him about Grace.

"With Billy," she says. "I went with Billy."

"Oh, Suzy," he says, his face soft with relief. "Did Grace go with you?"

"No," she says. "Grace knew but only Billy went with."

"She didn't tell me. No offense, but I kind of can't believe she didn't tell me."

"Grace was good at keeping secrets," Suzy says.

The water's boiling now and Mike moves to the kitchen to crack some pasta into the pot. Breakfast spaghetti. The world is happening again in the apartment. She hates Mike for making her lie, and for most of what's come out of his mouth in the last five minutes.

She moves to the door with an "All right" and doesn't turn back at first to say anything else.

"'Our history,'" Mike says, "'is an aggregate of last moments.'" Suzy stops at the door and looks over her shoulder. He has a wooden spoon in one hand and *Gravity's Rainbow* in the other, book hand stretched to cradle the width of the reclining spine. He waves the novel at her. "That's another one from in here."

Her feet carry her through the door. She doesn't want to be read to anymore, doesn't want to wonder about meaning in meaningless places. She should get home to wait by the phone anyway—to see if today's the day of the meeting. She hates Billy for making her wait by the phone. She hates Billy for trapping her between another run and a prison sentence. She hates Grace for dying.

Billy picks her up at noon on Sunday, just as the fog's burning off. He's still without his license, but he's borrowed his mom's Bug. It has a hundred thousand miles on it and requires a push start. Suzy in the driver's seat, Billy shoving at the passenger door. A little nudge until they hit the slope and she kicks it into second gear. They brake at the stop sign and the engine holds, then they turn onto PCH and off toward the center of town, off without trouble. Small satisfactions, each required, before she asks what she's needed to ask since before she stepped into the car: "So, what did he say?"

"He said it seemed like something he could do."

"Is that exactly what he said?"

"He said, after not being open to it at all, 'That seems like something I could do.'"

"Those are carefully chosen words. 'Seems.' 'Could.'"

"Look, there's nothing for us to do but go."

"Do I even have us pointed in the right direction?"

"Yeah, just stick on this. We're headed south."

"Am I getting on the 405?"

"Just listen to me: stay on PCH until I say to turn."

"'Cause this would *not* handle the freeway."

"It's been driving freeways for twelve years. It's fine."

"You can hear the grit in the oil. The engine's gonna fall out of the fucking bottom of this thing if I push it above forty."

"Listen, Suzy, just shut the fuck up about the car, please. I'm putting my neck out here. I'm trying to do what you want. This is a bad situation and I got us a car."

"Just tell me where we're going. I can't stand driving like I'm blindfolded in the trunk."

"We're going up on the hill. We're going up to the Peninsula."

They stick on PCH, just as Billy said they would, down through the beach cities, and when the highway narrows, they turn onto the twelve-mile rim that circumnavigates the Peninsula. They take a long, heavy right through a bamboo forest that leans Billy across the gearshift and into her. They move past the Spanish-tiled shopping center and through the uniform colors of the township's homes—white stucco, green trim, orange roofs. They push through to the edge—two-hundred-foot cliffs, gilded in high light, wiry brush tickling the sculpted sheer walls of cliff face like hair on an athlete's abdomen. A pair of bobbing wet suits and boards trickle down the cliff at a low angle, the gradual descent of the surf trail like a long escalator.

The two-lane road follows the notches of the cliff line, winding out with the points and in with the bow of each cove, back out and in, dangling at relative intervals, sagging in low curves. The road is old in the straightaways and more recently paved at the curves. Previous iterations of the road can be seen discarded farther down the slope, having broken off and ridden mudslides toward the water. Elbows of older road that give the effect of cartoon motion lines. They're more than halfway around the Peninsula when Billy tells her to turn up, to climb. They follow a series of switchbacks that draws them higher, from the cliffs up to the summit. It all feels vaguely familiar to Suzy, as though she's done it before. As they rise, the world itself seems to rise with them. The island offshore, typically shrouded in haze, shows itself and climbs the wall of water.

"You'll tell me when to turn?" Suzy says.

"The road ends at his house."

"This isn't what I expected."

"I would've guessed you wouldn't have guessed."

"I was thinking maybe Gardena. Chino. Long Beach," she says.

"Racist."

She starts to grin but stuffs it back in her face.

"We're basically there," Billy says, and then they are. She registers the familiar property fence, and the months collapse like a badly baked cake. She's right back where she was on the Fourth.

"Hamlet. Hamlet, Mr. Honeywell," she says.

"Wow, good memory. He would not be stoked to know you had his name on the tip of your tongue all along."

"*This* is the guy."

"Is that clock right?" he says, meaning the hands on the dashboard. "What's your watch say?"

"Twelve twenty-five."

"So this thing's fast. We're early." He sits silently. He bites his nails.

"You wanna just wait?" Suzy says.

"We agreed to twelve thirty. He keeps a tight schedule."

Suzy lets the Bug idle. They can't afford to shut it off while they wait at the gate, or else it won't start back up. She listens to the texture of the oil, and she counts a minute measured in the clicks of Billy biting his fingernails.

Then an intercom in the bushes comes to life, a swarm of static. "You just gonna sit there?" it says. And the gate opens inward.

The paved named road does end at the gate, and then it shifts from blacktop to dirt, a redder dirt than she's seen at the beach, redder, she reasons, because of proximity to the sun. They follow the road slowly up to the front of the house. The property spills down the side of the hill, and the fence vanishes into a cypress farm. Animal cages sprout like capped mushrooms from the vast lawn.

"That's what I was talking about," Billy says. "Way back."

"Larry the Lion," Suzy says.

"Lion, panther, tiger, pig. Who knows what else."

She takes the path slowly to the front of the house and feels a vestigial rush of embarrassment on account of the crappiness of the car. There's a Porsche parked off the front steps—the Bug is all wrong here.

The house is white, low and boxy, a ranch stacked on a ranch, two stories, with bright-white wooden siding and square wooden columns, a series of long boxes like the modern homes of Wright and van der Rohe, but skeined with warm white wood, white window boxes, green shutters and trim. A porch wraps itself around, all flats and corners and right angles. The first floor wears a visor, the rim of a roof that wraps the house as well, one home squatting atop another. The front door is green, and as Suzy cuts the engine, a man appears in its frame. *El Jefe.*

It's so warm, the sun so unobstructed at this height, that the heat scratches at her skin like wool. She feels her pulse in her throat, but it's slow and heavy, the tempo of a fading record. She and Billy step out of the car and shut their doors simultaneously. And before she even has a chance to approach, the man waves the two of them along the porch and out toward the back.

He doesn't speak, but they follow close behind. He's barefoot and in khakis and a green Lacoste polo, and all she really sees is his height. A basketball player at a New England prep school is the impression. Even without seeing his face, Suzy knows he's handsome. The rich hair makes it certain. The pool is lined with paving stones, and there are three seats around a table beneath an unpopped canvas umbrella. He works it open, cranks its wings wide so that they provide a canopy of shade. He sits and crosses his legs tight at the thighs and knees and calves, gummy legged like Cary Grant. He's got an actor's tan and golden hair, parted without product. His eyes are fixed on Suzy—he's staring at her, blank in expression, squinting into the bright blue. Suzy stands with her hands on her hips, feeling every impulse in her blood to turn away, to look at the pool or the side of the house or something, but she goes on looking right back at him, squinting like he does, snapping one eye shut and then the other, so that she doesn't blink with both, wetting one eyeball at a time, and overselling it, one big stew wink after another.

"Well, Mr. Honeywell," Billy says, "thanks for doing this. I think it'll make everyone feel better." Billy moves toward an empty chair. Honeywell holds steady, patient as geology. Which is when Suzy cracks up. A big, low, throaty giggle that sounds to her own ears like Grace's. That makes her fold at the waist and laugh at her knees, a toppling weight of funny. She's never laughed like this, but the whole thing makes Honeywell break, too. And when he starts laughing, it comes out lower, rocks rolling around in a dryer. Suzy grabs the seat and sits, matches his crossed legs, reaches over the glass table and offers her hand. "Suzy Whitman," she says. "Pleased to meet you finally."

Honeywell takes her hand and crushes it. He says, "Jack Honeywell. But you already knew that."

Billy hangs dumbly at the edges, and Honeywell snaps to him and says, "Billy, sit the fuck down."

"This is Suzy," Billy says, slipping back into the scene.

"Are you fucking deaf?" Honeywell says.

"I don't think so, sir."

"Let's get at it, I need this to be quick. My wife and girls will be back from church in thirty minutes."

Suzy and Billy wait for him to go on.

"Well, you asked for the meeting. What do you want?"

"Suzy and I were—"

"I'm out," Suzy says, cutting him off. "I never wanted in in the first place. But I did what you guys asked—"

"And you were paid for your services."

"It's really pretty straight, the way I'm thinking of it. I know there's one more thing you want me to do. But then after that I want your guarantee that that's the end of it."

"Your two weeks' notice?"

"Is that when this is? Two weeks?"

"No, it's next weekend. But I'm wondering if you're thinking about it the way I need you to be thinking about it. This is a business, and businesses have rules, standards of practice. I just want to formalize this conversation. A guy leaves my company, he gives his two weeks. That's within his right, and it's within the business's. He's not technically obligated to do anything, but he does it anyway because that's the social contract, the professional courtesy. He does everything in his power to tie up the loose ends of his accounts. To make the handoff, the transition, as seamless as possible. To find a replacement. What are you doing to make this work?"

"It's not my responsibility any longer," Suzy says. "I walk away and Billy can find someone new."

"Look, I don't want this to be a problem. I just want you to think about those who've treated you well these last many months. I need you to keep some skin in the game. Otherwise, what's gonna keep you from getting greedy with the information you have? You know where I live. You know where I work."

"I don't know where you work. I didn't even know your name until five minutes ago."

He turns to Billy, and Billy shrugs, like, *I don't say shit.* Honeywell looks at her harder. "That surprises me," he says, and Suzy expects him to latch the door on the matter. But instead he starts in: "I'm a twenty-five-year veteran of IBM. I was transferred here eight years ago, on my own accord. Know why I moved out? I was on a flight to L.A. with a pair of pretty young stews, just like yourself. And we were lowering in over the Southland and I was on the left side of the plane. 'Bout an hour out of sunset, and the golden light was coming in as it does. And out the window I see this big old hook of land, swinging out into the ocean, and I asked one of the stews—she was based in Sela just like you—what I was looking at, and she told me, 'That's the Peninsula, Mr. Honeywell.' And I watched it out my window for the last five minutes of the descent, getting closer to the ground all the while the top of the Peninsula stayed up in the clouds. Know what I mean? You've seen it like that, I'm sure. So I drove up here my day off, bought this hunk of land practically sight unseen. Worked out the transfer to the L.A. office after I flew back to White Plains. Divorced my wife. Married that stew. Chained her up in the basement, and the rest is history."

Suzy shifts in her chair, scoots her ass up closer to the vertical of the backrest. Straightens her spine, but holds her squint. Honeywell dabs his mouth with his wrist like he's whisking away blood.

"That's sweet," Suzy says.

"Company man," he says. "Sixty-minute drive each day and night. Work during the week, the girls on the weekends. Take 'em sailing. Take 'em golfing at the club down the hill. Just put in the hard court out by the cottage, right around back. Leveled out the grounds, the girls are getting pretty good. You play tennis?"

Suzy shakes her head. Billy does, too, but the question's not for him.

"The court's been a good thing. A lotta the local cops have been coming over to break it in. Free is cheaper than joining the club, you know? A bunch of feds live up here, too. Office is way up in Westwood, doesn't make much sense. But it is what it is. And it's funny, those guys can't get enough of the new court. They just learned to play, caught the bug. Plus, I think it's the shading from those cypresses—see 'em? From our cypress farm on the low end of the property. Planted a few and they give this nice elegant shade to the court. A lot of those fed guys, some have been to Europe. And they've taken their wives to places like Spain and France and Italy, you know? And they say the reason they moved up here was 'cause it reminds them of this little stretch of Italy on the Amalfi Coast. This little thumb called the Sorrentine Peninsula. The thing they go on and on about is how my property reminds them, more than any other thing they've seen in America—and these feds have seen a lot of America—of the grounds of the little hotels along the Amalfi Drive. The honeymoon they spent there. The best days of their lives. They love it." He's frowning and he holds a moment, and then he says with marked disdain, mocking some idea, some thing: *"You dig?"*

There's not much left for Suzy to say, except to spit it out, to mow over the subtext of the monologue. "So we're good, then? We're on the same page?"

"You tell me," he says.

"I do your run. I get on with it."

"I know everything there is to know about you," he says. "And now you know everything there is to know about me. That's a partnership. That's trust. I hope you really, truly understand."

It is so warm. She shuts her eyes and watches the red veins in her eyelids shape themselves into a cooling picture, a picture of her father and mother shoveling snow. It's a strange, impossible image—Wayne may never shovel again. But he just might live. And so should she—she should do what it takes not to die.

"I'm glad we're in agreement," Suzy says, and rises from the table. Her legs are rewaking. They feel like the television looks on a broken channel. Suzy worries that a step might buckle her knees, might drop her to the ground. So she stands there, sort of lording it over him. And it's his turn to start laughing. He laughs until he's coughing, and she hears a thousand cartons of cigarettes in his throat.

"Come with me," he says, standing. "Before you go. We've got a small amount of time."

They don't have a choice. They both get it. Billy inserts himself between them, and the three work as a train around the kidney of the pool and along the side of the house, where Suzy catches a first view of the tennis court, way up on the slope, but also a view of a path that leads seemingly straight up. There're steps in the side of the hill—stone and dirt, leveled off ploddingly. What must be a hundred, a hundred fifty steps into the sky.

"Come on," he says. "From what I know about you. About you and Schuyler Glen and Vassar and Yale, about Grace and Edith and Wayne, and just, you know, generally how you feel about Sela del Mar"—Suzy watches Billy's head droop—"I just think you'll be happy to have seen the view."

The steps are stone and red clay. They're lined by olive trees and oleander bushes. The steps are of awkward design. They're too large to be taken one stride at a time, and they're too tall for Suzy to ascend without lunging. One-two-UP. One-two-UP. She presses on her knee at each big push. She feels a heat in her hair, the strands growing redder like toaster coils. She feels a cool proclamation of sweat on her neck.

They pull even with the tennis court, shaded by the ring of cypresses. It looks just as she imagined. But there are so many steps left, and they take them quietly, mostly. Billy's and her sandals crunching the sand, Honeywell's bare feet turning the red of unfired ceramics. The more steps they take, the more steps seem to emerge. As it did in the car on the drive up, the island at their backs rises on the ocean along with them. Soon the court is well below, the same view she had that summer in high school when Wayne took her and Grace to see a tennis exhibition at the Aud in Buffalo. They sat in the last row, and theirs was the view of hawks trapped in the arena. They're way up above the house and the court now, and the steps are finally eroding in number, reducing, so that Suzy can count them all in a single glimpse, twelve, and then seven, and then three two one.

The flat up top is laid out with the same paving stones as the pool. And as with the tennis court, the flat is circled by cypress trees. They're splayed in an arc, like a womb, but open at the entry, spread like legs. There's a plain granite bench before them, and a little pediment of stone with a bowl on its top, and the bowl is filled with water.

Honeywell moves toward the water and says, "Have some." He

cups his hand and pulls the liquid to his mouth. "Natural spring. Way up here. I built the path and then the pump to pull it out of the ground." Suzy and Billy stand catching their breath, don't move any closer. "Come on, there's no fucking LSD in it, promise." Billy takes a handful first, and when he stays alive, Suzy dips her hand in. It's warm—cool out of the ground, but heated all this closer to the sun. The water tingles her tongue and gums like mouthwash, and it tastes like pennies, like a split lip. Honeywell moves to the edge of the flat and considers the view—across the dip of the Peninsula, out onto the water, all the way to the island. "I come up here," he says, "to do my thinking. My big thinking. I don't go to church with Gwen and the girls. This is my shit, this is the thing I believe in." Suzy is alone in her sensations. Her heart is still pumping down through her stomach, out toward her fingers. A puff of breeze freezes the sweat on her arms and back. That lingering sting in her mouth, someone else's blood. But still, she finds herself following along with what he's saying.

"This is the one belief system I buy into," he says. "The one for which I can be God and Gabriel. I make the rules and I deliver the message. Do you understand what I'm saying?"

Suzy does her best to ignore the sound of his voice, imagines herself trickling down the stairs, down toward the court and the house, toward the cliffs and out to sea. She wants to run.

"While I like to be in control, I don't fuck with the universe. I don't tempt her. I don't tempt Mami. I control what I can control. This is a stacked game and I try to keep her on my side. I make sure I'm doing all I can, just to cover myself. Give it back to the water and the clouds and the cliffs, give it back to Mami when I can, you know?"

Christ, she wants to run.

"I sacrificed a pig up here a couple months ago. One that Mami had presented to me without my asking. It came with a message. Popped up out of nowhere. And I knew its purpose. The girls fell pretty hard for it, but on New Year's I did the trick, knew it had to be done. I love that Aztec stuff, you know? Cut its heart out with a garden trowel."

Suzy sniffs the wind, senses her cool, wet head growing lighter not heavier, as though buoyed by her proximity to the clouds. Is that the line they're allowed to leave on?

"Don't ever think about it," he says.

She can't make full sense of what he's saying anymore, but the words are out before she hears them, her own: "Don't ever think about what?"

He turns and catches both of them square, but it's all for Suzy: "Don't ever think about *anything* with me on your mind. No thoughts, no action, no words. You know all there is to know about me now—but as far as you're concerned, I don't exist. This is what I mean about an understanding, about trust. I hear you so much as mention my name to anyone, including this piece of shit here, and I'll fucking gut you."

And he's to the stairs, the soft padding of hard footsteps on the finely crushed shells of a half billion years. And she and Billy file behind him like long shadows. One-two-DOWN, one-two-DOWN, one-two-DOWN. *You dig?*

Suzy makes the run. It's a big one. Triple load. Fifteen pounds in her little bag. She feels the same strange heat and colors as she did that first trip back in July. The unflappable focus, eyes on the bag, while taking care of all the normal things, too. As they dip down beneath the clouds in New York, into a freezing platinum rainstorm, she feels as though she's almost there, skims back through the trip to make sure she didn't do anything that could've drawn attention, realizes, in that low coast to the runway, that she needs to find something new to do for so many more reasons than the big one. That she's better than a job she can handle in full even when her mind's occupied with something else entirely.

And within fifteen minutes of the last passenger clearing out, she's off the plane and into the bathroom. Cassidy and the cash. As Cassidy slings her bag over her shoulder and makes a move for the door, Suzy holds her up, sort of sadly. Apparently, no one's told her.

"What?" Cassidy says, and Suzy waits for a sign of recognition that this is the end, the last one.

When it doesn't come, all Suzy says is "Super good seeing you" and awkwardly clops toward her to hug her like she did at Christmas. Only this time she presses her cheek to Cassidy's cheek, and feels Cassidy's body progress from slack to tense to slack again, a freezing and a melting on account of the skin-to-skin. When she lets her go, Cassidy turns, wordlessly, and walks away. That's it.

Suzy heads to the lounge. She strips down, checks her watch to confirm the forty-five minutes she's got before she needs to be back at the gate for the turnaround, and steps into a hot shower, just like that very first time. Everything as it was before, only different. Shower then, shower now, bookends on this defining phase of her life. The selfless, savior, up-to-the-edge phase.

She flies home. She serves drinks with an extra-special smile. She falls asleep somewhere over the middle and has to be roused by a girl she recognizes from one of the new Grand Pacific ads. The blonde. "I'm Mia, Fly Me. Fly Mia. Fly Grand Pacific...to Tokyo!" The airline is expanding. The airline is growing into its name.

She takes a cab from the airport. Shouts down the cabdriver when he starts bitching about her request: two stops in Sela del Mar. The first is a quaint little house with a cream Volvo and a lemon Bug. She sneaks along the side yard, through the fence, and to the screen door to Billy's back house. She pins the envelope between the screen and the door, and runs back to the cab that's idling in the alley. She didn't take her cut—doesn't really care if she ever sees it anyway, the relief is so distracting, to be through.

The cab drops her at home, and she carries her half-packed bag up the stairs and into her bedroom and sleeps for a day—in bed, on the couch, on the floor in the box of light created by the mouth of the window. She sleeps in sunlight. She catches up. The sun's down again, two days come and gone. The phone rings: it's the airline, Janice saying how nice it is to have her back, that's all, just really good to have her back and that she's thinking about her and her sister. Suzy's going to miss parts of stewing. They've been better than she sometimes gives them credit for. She feels the snake of paralysis slipping down her spine, the frozen feet and legs, the tingly fingers. Maybe Grace will visit her here in the night. Slip through the blinds with the moonlight. What would she say, what possible message could she have? *"I'm Grace, Fly Me."*

It's then that the phone rings again, running the ringer out. She imagines a voice—*Pick up pick up pick up.*

The phone rings again.

They don't usually call twice. It scoops her to her feet. She stumbles over, suspended in the in-between. *Pick up pick up.* It is difficult to tell if this voice is a deeper extension of her paralysis, a new room unlocked. But then the real voice announces itself, slicks around the cartilage cast of her ear like cold seawater.

"Hey," it says, "there's a problem with what you left me."

"What kind of problem?"

"They say you're short twenty grand."

"I didn't even open it. It's exactly what they gave me."

"Why didn't you check?" Billy says. "Why didn't you count the money?"

"Because it's none of my fucking business anymore."

"Look, I'm at a pay phone at the bottom of the Peninsula. I just left Honeywell's. He opened the envelope and he said it's twenty grand short. And he says it must be with you."

All things considered—the weird half sleep, the shock of the call—she puts it together pretty quickly.

"He could say that no matter how much money is in there. You never told me what to expect, what the deal was. I'd never delivered this much before. He can say whatever he wants."

Billy is silent on the other end of the line. Billy gets it, too, is what the silence says.

"He said that the people in New York claim it was all there. Whatever amount they agreed on."

"There's absolutely nothing I can do," Suzy says.

She's at the blinds, they're turned flat. Her view is toward the water. She feels her shoulders curling over, her knees bending into a low athletic base. The gradual crumple, it's like collapsing in the cold. It's been years since she's felt that impulse, but she remembers it precisely. Being broken down on the side of the road senior year of high school, caught out on the way between the track and home, flat with no spare, so unlike Wayne. No pay phone, no heat. And a need to cover a mile plus in the snow to the nearest gas station. Arriving after nearly an hour and finding them closed, shut down with frozen pipes, blacked out for the evening. The temperature dropping, the nearest station another two miles. And the inward turn away from panic. No shouts, no screams, no tears. Only a greater resolve to stay solid. To slow her toes and ankles and hips and shoulders. To slow her heartbeat to a record low. To slow her mind to a place of ultimate contentment—*It isn't even that cold.*

She hears Billy's breath. Her mouth is small and she counts her pulse making noise in the fattest artery of her neck.

"There is...," Billy says. "There is something you can do."

He waits for her response. If he could see the glaze in her eyes, he might not expect one.

"Something that was proposed by Honeywell himself..."

Again, waiting for her gratitude.

"He said you can make another run. Make up the difference."

"I didn't take anything...," she says.

"Well, that's not really a position we can take."

"'We.'"

"I'm trying to help."

"You fucking ruined me."

"C'mon, let's figure out one thing to end this, and then you can move on."

"Are you dense?"

"I'm trying to help."

"I have no *real* options."

"I think—if you're interested in my opinion—that you need to do just one more. That we all make the terms even clearer. That you know what's coming. That he can't claim that you did or didn't do whatever."

"He can say *whatever he wants!*"

"But maybe this was just a misunderstanding. Maybe this was bad luck and someone out there really did just give the wrong amount of money, I don't know. All I mean is this is the thing we have to do."

"He said he'd *gut* me."

"He was just trying to scare you. Trying to keep you quiet."

"And what's this, then? Some more harmless rhetoric?"

"I think he's just in a pinch. I think one more and then you're out."

"You don't believe that."

"I've been looking for a replacement. I've met a couple girls I think could be good. He just needs someone reliable, and then we're close."

"I have no leverage whatsoever."

"I need..." He starts again. "What I really need, as much as you don't want to hear it, is a commitment. I just need you to say you're going to do this. I'm at a pay phone, but Honeywell's in the car. I can't really be saying this, but we really...there's nothing we can really do except have you say you're going to do this. Otherwise it's more threats, it's cops, it's I don't know what else. Maybe you figure something out. Maybe we figure something out. But we need the time. We need more than two minutes right this instant to work on it. I have to say yes."

"What can I even say to that?"

"I'm telling him you're in, but that it's the last one for real."

"Billy, fuck. What am I supposed to do?"

"It needs to be sometime in the next week. A slightly different thing. They need you to go to Honolulu."

"I hardly ever fly to Hawaii."

"Say it's for your sister. Say it's a memorial thing."

Her head actually falls forward, the way a fighter jet nods when it hooks up to the slingshot on a carrier. A little bow of incomprehension. Her lower lip cracks the seal from her upper lip, her mouth comes apart. There are no words, just a click in her throat, a click on the line like a bugged phone. And she will think about it for days, how regrettable it is that she can't say what she means to say. How this simple request to get her off the phone—to keep her life moving along, a gesture Billy evidently regards as helpful—is the thing that marks the end of it all with Billy. And instead of saying something real, there's just that fucking click that comes out, a little sound with no meaning, but also, on a bad phone in a hustled moment, an approximation of silence Billy takes to mean *Okay.*

There is nowhere left to go. Midafternoon, Suzy bombs the hill at Nineteenth and pulls up at the edge of the Strand. Suzy carving, Suzy rolling the board with the arches of her feet—all of that. The Strand is crowded. Winter at the beach. The whole town is out for a stroll, but there's no one in the water, no one on the sand. The sand is too cold. She plants herself halfway between the Strand and the ocean. Nearer the water an uncountable number of gulls stand at attention, facing the same direction in evenish rows. Edith had called it "Sunday school" for the birds.

Suzy's due to fly at eleven tomorrow. She feels backed up to the edge of Sela, to the edge of the state, her heels hanging over the precipice. The options have diminished: not Schuyler Glen, not New York, not Paris, London, Rome. Not Gracie, not Billy. She sees a man coming toward her with a stack of flyers, a savior. And she stands quickly to outpace him. He calls after her and she starts laughing scared. They are after her, they're at her door. And there's just one place left for Suzy to go.

Mike is home and he looks crisper than he has since the accident. He looks like he's spent the weekend in the sun. He's had a haircut. His whole head looks as though it's been moisturized. She expects the glow to mean good news, but Mike's quick to say it once she's inside the house.

"I don't have anything," he says. "I can't find him. And they don't want it. They're gonna kill it. Four and a half months for an unpublishable piece and a kill fee."

"They won't give you more time?" Suzy says.

"I'm out of time. I signed—" He pauses to swallow. It's a blurry *s* on the *signed,* the sort he gets when he drinks. The slur Grace would poke at. "I signed a contract and the contract is unfulfilled."

He's shaved, too. That's the big difference. Mike never grew a full-out beard, but he always seemed long-days deep in stubble. The clean, wet cheeks draw greater attention to the stark sideburns, the contrast of their edges. The length of his hair, too, shorter than she's seen it and parted to the other side. Everything is five degrees different.

"I'm in a bad spot," he says, running his right hand through his hair, crossing up the new part, not used to it himself. "I'm gonna sell the car."

"You're gonna sell the car? Is that really the best thing?"

"I'm out of money. I need money."

"But is not having a car really the best idea? That's been the one thing you've liked most out here."

"Well, *you* liked it. I mean, you used it as much as I did."

It's a slap like she hasn't received from him since she moved out. She spots the green bottle of gin on the counter. She wonders how long he's been at it.

"I just mean it's a thing you've needed most," she says, "to just get out and see things when Sela got a little claustrophobic."

"I haven't thought it out fully yet," he says, returning to the kitchen, to the freezer and the ice tray. "But I might as well let you know now: I'm gonna move back to New York. I have a life here and everything, or at least some leftover pieces—I know some people, I know you. But I'm gonna have a better chance back there. I came out here, I tried. And I failed in a lot of ways."

The number of things there are to turn to is now zero. Suzy is silent. She feels exposed—she feels as though her life is threatened by the circumstances. She gets out a "What?"

"I don't mean to drop this on you," he says. "And I don't know how soon it would be or anything, but maybe a couple months, get out of the lease early. One month, two months."

"You're just gonna leave."

"C'mon, Suz, is this really that surprising?" The *s*'s are softened again, like eraser smudges. "I came out here and I fucking failed. It never got me like it got Grace. It never got me like it's gotten you.

You found people, you're doing well enough. You're gonna find your way into a new good thing when you're through with stewing. I dead-ended. I tried a marriage, I tried a magazine, I tried to get back into writing, and I've got nothing to show for it. It's like I've reverted to being twenty-two. To being my younger self. A me who's failed to build up any equity over the last five years."

"Are you suggesting that you *lost your equity* when my sister died?"

"Suzy, relax. I'm not saying anything but what I'm actually saying: I fucked up, I don't have much; bad things happened; I'm going back to where things will be easier for me."

She hardly hears him. She's stuck on the *relax*. "Relaxshh" is what he says. She feels like kicking him in the mouth. But she lets it pass, the red drains. And then the fact fully envelops her: Mike has somewhere to run to. Mike has somewhere to start again, with no baggage, with no threats. He's trading a car in for an apartment and a job. It's wide open. Hanging in the stillness of the house, the still-fresh absence of Grace everywhere, Suzy tries to solve her own problem in a single move. But there's nothing that makes sense, nothing she can work out. She is still backed up to the edge.

"Before you do any of this," she starts. "I just...I really need your help with something." He's still in the kitchen. He's pouring gin into a cocktail shaker. "I'm in trouble."

"What kind of trouble?" he says. He caps the shaker and throws it over his shoulder, the ice clattering so loudly that she's forced to pause her disclosure until he's satisfied with the temperature of his drink. He shakes, hard, for five seconds, ten, fifteen, and Suzy stands in the living room, silent. He uncaps the shaker and pours a martini. She's still silent, and he says, "Well?" She's beginning to despise him all over again. But she has just one opening.

And so she tells him from the beginning. The first run on the Fourth. The runs over the past seven months. The money for Wayne's treatment. Billy's flip on her, the trap. The meeting with Honeywell on the Peninsula. Honeywell's ties to Colombia and the LAPD. The death threat. It comes out in a crooked line, with diversions and asides, but he doesn't interrupt. He sips at his drink, standing at the kitchen counter. And then, finally, she says it, as a capstone clause: "...between you and me."

He has a look on his face that reminds Suzy of when she's watched him read. A small, tight mouth and a wrinkled forehead, eyes focused on the page. He betrays no sense of shock or judgment. He just waits for her to finish.

"Mike," she says finally, "what?"

"What what?" he says.

"What are you thinking? What the fuck do I do?"

He holds steady and then a grin chops his face in half.

"What?" Suzy says, her blood moving quick through her body.

"This is such an amazing story. This is exactly what I need."

She's reverting—her feet clasped to the floor, her mouth open but words quiet. She feels the frigid paralysis at the edges.

"I can do this story instead," he continues. "Sell them this as a swap for Jim Jones. This giant ring, and you're the key to bringing it all down."

"I'm telling you this in *confidence*. This isn't for a *magazine*."

"Look," he says, "you said it yourself—Billy told you the cops won't do anything, that this guy Honeywell has them on payroll or whatever. So you can't go to them. You need an independent party to investigate, to publish and to draw the attention of federal agents or whoever to get everybody all at once."

"What are you talking about? *I'm* implicated. *Billy's* implicated."

"I don't know about Billy, but you'd be protected. You're a confidential source. I'd protect you from everything. It's journalistic privilege. It's Deep Throat." He's projected himself forward to a place in the future she refuses to go herself—when the story's on news-stands, and the culprits are in cuffs, and Mike Singer's on the Sunday news programs blocking out the details of the sting, launching a career, upgrading his apartment in New York.

"This isn't *Watergate*. This isn't *fun*. I just need to get out of this flight tomorrow. I can't go. And I need to figure out an alternative."

"This is what I do," he says. "This is the thing I can do. You give me all the information—all the people involved, the big web, and we trace it all the way from Colombia to New York, with everybody in between."

"Billy would go to jail."

"Billy would likely be arrested. But so would everybody else you're caught up with, everybody who's threatening you. Who's making you do things you don't want to do. That's your out, by the way: if you're not bullshitting me and you've been trying to stop and you've been forced to do this against your will all along—whether that's true or not, that should be the story, and that'll get you doubly off. It'll be an explosion. It'll be a bomb. And we'd just have to be careful about it. To make sure you don't suffer any collateral damage. Or that I don't suffer any collateral damage. I'd have to be careful. It's a tricky piece, it's tricky material."

It is a colossal mistake—she shouldn't have mentioned it. She's already lost her grasp of this thing, has felt it slip, right there in the room, into Mike's control. He's referring to it as his own. Not even as people and actions and consequences. It's already moved in his mind to "material." Meat to be butchered and seasoned and grilled into its most delicious state of existence. She's misjudged him, and if she doesn't speak up now, he'll have it sold to *Rolling Stone* before she leaves the house.

"I don't want that," she says. "I can't have you do it. I can't sell Billy out like that and I can't sell myself out like that."

"Suzy, don't be thick. You'd be *protecting* yourself. And you said it, not me: Billy was the one who brought you into this mess, who's kept you on the line. Acting like he's had your best interest in mind, while he's really just been using you for his own ends. To save his own ass. To make his boss happy. You owe him nothing. This is a potentially enormous piece."

"I shouldn't have said anything. I should've kept it to myself and figured it out on my own. This isn't your 'piece.' This is my life."

"Well," Mike says, running a hand through his hair the wrong way again, "I can't do anything about it now. It's out there. You gave me the information. On background. I can't do this without quoting you, without having you on the record, but now that I know, I'm gonna have to report it out anyway. It's my duty."

"What are you *talking* about? This holier-than-thou bullshit. Are you *listening* to yourself right now? I'm telling you you're not gonna do anything with it. It was a mistake to think you might have some practical advice without making this about you and your career."

"You've been running *cocaine* back and forth to the East Coast! On multiple occasions. That's a federal crime. This isn't some petty stewardess infraction of Grand Pacific alcohol policy. Drug trafficking is a *massively serious broken law,* and the people behind it are threatening to fucking *kill* you. Why are you protecting them?"

"I don't need your help. Just leave it alone."

"I can't do that. Now that I know, I'd be aiding and abetting if I didn't do or say something. I could go to the cops now, but that's not powerful. Cops aren't powerful. *Rolling Stone* is powerful. My piece was supposed to run next month. If they're into it, I can make it a clean swap. Crash the reporting, crash the story. Get it all done and out there by early April. I'm gonna do it with or without your help. I really hope you're on board. We can make this as important a thing as has ever been published about drugs on the West Coast. About coke in California. About the end of the sixties and the dawn of the current moment. I can't imagine how far up this goes—how tall and how wide. I'm giving you an opportunity to be part of something huge."

She's never seen him accelerate like this. This must be what he was like in the very beginning, in the bars in the Village when Grace first met him, hustling for assignments that actually got assigned. When Mike had something to believe in, something to maybe do well. She hates him for it.

"I'll deny it all. It'll never get past your editors. The magazine would never publish it without the primary source."

"I'm a good enough reporter to run it down everywhere else."

"Do you really want to fight me on this? Do you really know what I'm capable of?" She doesn't know what it means, but she knows why she's said it. She's farther out than before. The pebbles are slipping over the edge, down through the brush along the cliff face, into the chop of the Santa Monica Bay. She's run out of space, she's run out of continent.

"I'm gonna fight you if you're gonna fight me," he says. "I'm gonna do it. This is too important. This is the story of your life and it's the story of my life. This is what we need."

It's quiet, a cease-fire. Mike swallows hard and his Adam's apple elevates in his throat.

"Please don't do it."

"I'm gonna do it."

She shakes her head with her eyes cast down and then moves to the door.

"You know," he says, approaching carefully. "I always thought you and I were the better fit."

She can't believe he's just said it, but he takes her silence to mean: *Say more.*

"Didn't you? I mean, it only made sense. It was never destined to work the way she and I had it going. It was a fight I was willing to fight for a while."

"Stop. Seriously." She says it too quietly toward the door.

"I always thought it'd be you and me who made it, who'd get to do things together. Here's a chance. This project. Another project. You can come to New York, even. It just *makes sense,* Suz."

She opens the door and the light rushes in, desperate.

"Just think about it," he says. "This is for you. This is to protect you."

She takes a straight line to the sand. She's back down near the beach, and the birds' Sunday-school session is letting out. At the hard crash of a heavyweight wave, the gulls engage in a little conversation and then, at dismissal, take flight.

That night, before Billy comes over, she does some of her favorite things. She skates along the Strand, to Howlers and back. She devours a Number One from El Guincho. After dinner, even though it's not late, it's dark and the Strand is the chessboard she and Grace rode over on Christmas. It wasn't the last time she saw her sister, but Suzy knows she'll always remember it as having been the last. Chasing her sister's butt and back wheel north along the California coast. At home she waits in the armchair near the door, waits in silence in the lamplight, and in her mind she rides that ride with her sister, pushing the pedals, the long low-gear glide of their matching strand cruisers.

She hears him coming up the stairs. She checks the clock on the wall—he's on time to the minute. She stands at the door with her hands out.

"Can I come in?"

She doesn't say anything but steps aside. He looks around the room, uncomfortable seeming in the low light.

"Just put it on the floor," she says. And after hesitating, trying to read her seriousness, he reaches into his backpack and puts a package, the usual package, on the floor. But then he reaches inside and pulls out another, and then a third. Triple load.

"Are you kidding?"

"It's not my call."

"How do you have so little sway over this?"

"I work for them, they tell me what to do."

"I can't take all three. My bag barely fit those last time *without* any clothes. It was a same-day turnaround."

"Want a bigger bag?" he says.

"They're completely fucking with me. They're trying to get me caught."

"They would never *try* to get you caught."

"I can't do three."

"This is the last one. They really agreed this time—they told me so."

"I'm gonna get caught on the very last one."

"It's gonna be as easy as usual. Someone's gonna meet you in the terminal. Typical handoff."

"Girl or guy? Who is this person?"

"Local girl. She'll have a lei on, looking like hospitality."

"So bathroom thing."

"Whatever she wants. She'll have the money. But yeah, probably bathroom thing."

Suzy shakes her head, a little disbelieving.

"This is really it," he says. "After this, we're out."

"What do you mean *we're* out?"

"I'm out, too. I told them today."

"Jesus Christ, now you're really gonna get me in trouble. What are you fucking thinking?"

"I'm gonna do what you said. I'm gonna try something new. I'm gonna apply to college and everything."

"You couldn't have waited a month? They're gonna take it out on me. They're gonna punish me for you."

"I know I have no ground to stand on, not really, at least. But you have to understand, I've worked with these guys for a while. They haven't always been easy, but they've never done anything self-sabotaging. It would destroy them if something bad happened to you, at least in another state. They don't have the same pull."

She has nowhere to go. She hates him for it.

"I don't have a choice, then," she says. "No options—again."

"I'm sorry, I didn't know this is what it would be. But it's the last one."

"You put me in this position."

"You took it the rest of the way."

"If this is really it," Suzy says, "if it's really the last one, then we have no reason to talk after this."

"I hope you don't mean that. I hope you don't feel that way for real."

"This was all there was. I've got other things here, other things to do now."

"Sela's small."

"Not as small as you think," she says. "And especially not for an outsider. I found you when I wanted to and I can get rid of you just the same."

"I hope you don't mean it."

"Please leave."

At the door he says, "See you when you get back, at least."

And she says: "Nope—I'll give them the money myself."

In the morning she skates. It's the only thing she can do about the nerves. She picks up speed until the trucks wobble. Down at the southern edge of town, near Howlers, she skids through a sand slick and ends up tumbling into a thatch of ice plant. She splits open her knee and skates back home with blood running down to the top of her foot, dried by the offshore. She checks the clock on the pier as she passes it, moving north. She should leave in an hour, call the cab as soon as she gets home.

When she passes through the door, she spots the three packages in the center of the room, untouched from last night. She hasn't decided what to do with them. She either takes them or she doesn't, and both lead to bad things. She's staring out the window at the ocean when the phone rings—the airline, maybe. She picks up on the second ring and catches the speaker exhaling deeply. She can tell Mike's voice through his breath.

"Oh good," he says. "I was hoping you hadn't left for the airport yet."

"But I'm going now."

"Just... one quick thing: I talked to my editor last night and they're in. They want me to report it, they want me to write it. It's not a guarantee, but they want me to pursue it. I'm gonna do it with or without you, but it'd sure be a lot easier and a lot better if you were on board. To set out the full story again with as much detail as you can recall. To open up the doors and connect the dots. I think this could be a really—"

She hangs up on him. It's happening. He'll have trouble getting enough, especially on the tight deadline. But he's desperate enough to carry it through without her blessing. It's the break he needs. And he'll ruin her to get it.

She pulls her suitcase from the bedroom and loads the packages into its base. She covers them with an overnight's worth of skirts (two), blouses (two), jeans (one), sandals (one pair), and an extra bra. She changes into her uniform in the bathroom—hose, skirt, shirt, jacket, hat. She pins her hair to her hat. She applies her lipstick and mascara. She's as pale as ever, but her hair's glowing redder. Aquamarine uniform and a halo of orange. The cab honks from the curb. There's no room left in her bag, but a thought occurs to her and she unpacks it all and quickly starts again. There's something else she's decided to take, and she folds it flat against the base of her bag.

The cab is laying on the horn as she passes through the door. She waves to him for his patience. She turns and takes a long look at the view, the gradient: sky, water, sand. It's a thin strip from here, but it's not *really* what she sees, if she's honest with herself. She knows it's there, off in the distance, through the rest of the visual noise. But what's here in the foreground, bothering the view, is something else entirely. The power lines. The stacks of the oil refinery. A dead pigeon, on the roof of her downhill neighbor, that hasn't budged since she moved in. She looks north and sees an airplane taking off, the blue and white of Pan Am. Heading west without a banked turn, meaning somewhere way out there, any number of places.

They put her on a Honolulu flight when she said she wanted to visit the site of the crash. It goes just as Billy said it would. Their touch is light throughout, too. No scrutiny at operations. No extra requests from the flight leader in precheck. They give her business class, which means she's closer to her carry-on. It's a long flight in the going direction, fighting the wind the whole way. But when they arrive, it's still midafternoon. A low sun skittering in off the water on landing.

Grand Pacific arranges a puddle jumper to Maui, to Ka'anapali, so that she can get to the spot before sunset. Her connection's in thirty minutes and she's on keen lookout for the point person. She takes a seat in the gate area, pretends to fix something with her pumps. There are local-looking women in leis at each gate, none glancing her way. It's been only a few minutes, but it feels like an hour. Her departure gate is just across the concourse. They're already beginning to board. She walks quickly to the Grand Pacific lounge, hoping to draw attention to anyone who might be searching for her. She sticks outside the lounge, and the women she worked the flight with smile sweetly as they pass through the sliding glass doors.

Fifteen minutes until her flight leaves. The woman working the desk cuts into the PA system and announces a final boarding call, with a specific appeal to Ms. Suzy Whitman. She's out of time. It's never happened before. This is exactly the sort of complication she worried she might be walking into. She waits another minute near the lounge. And then the voice again, an urgency: "Ms. Suzy Whitman, this is the last and final boarding call for Two Eight Eight to Ka'anapali."

She can't miss this. She can't blow off the cover for the trip. The thought slaps her—that she's regarding the short flight to Maui as a ploy rather than as an opportunity to receive her sister at the site of her death. She can't dump it, she can't stash it—she has to bring it with her.

The woman at the desk is in the blue-and-yellow plumeria-print dress of the airline. Suzy hands over her boarding pass. The woman has a soft, round face, straight hair, a center part. She has the cheeks of a child, the sort of puff that seals off her eyes as she smiles.

"Fantastic. Now the only other thing I need is a quick look in your bag."

Suzy's heart stutters. "What do you mean?"

"Oh, you know, just a routine check, nothing major."

Suzy considers fleeing. But the woman looks harmless. It's probably just protocol in Hawaii. The packages are disguised anyway, as carefully as ever—just flour for cookies. Suzy hands over her bag.

The woman disappears behind the desk, kneels so that Suzy can't see her. And before long she pops back up and hands Suzy her bag. It's lighter.

The woman holds her left hand out, ushering Suzy aboard. She smiles without opening her mouth. Just cheeks pressuring her eyes into a squint.

Suzy clicks down the stairs to the runway, but just before she moves through the door to the tarmac, she stops and unzips her bag. Fifteen pounds of cocaine missing, but in its place an envelope that's three times thicker than usual. *Hospitality,* she thinks. *No lei, but a dress with plumerias.*

Suzy feels light as her bag as she takes her seat—a small plane, one-by-two, six rows. She has a single on the starboard side of the plane. She didn't sleep much the night before and she certainly didn't sleep on the ride over. But for the forty minutes between takeoff and landing, Suzy drifts, her head pressed against the plastic window, warm from the tropical sun.

She rents a car at the airport in Ka'anapali and makes the thirty-minute drive to the little crescent-moon bay. It looks like every other stretch of coastline on the islands. And like so many of those, too, this one has a turnoff for lookout parking. It's an hour out from sunset, and the bay here faces west. The sun's dropping down right over the scene. She cuts the engine and steps outside, still in her uniform but in flatter shoes. The wind's whipping up, a warm breeze. She feels disoriented from the nap—a heat in her cheek and forehead, like she used an iron as a pillow.

She plays it through her mind again, the way she heard it'd gone: Grace and J.P. and the pilot, up out of Ka'anapali, north first for ten minutes and then back down the coastline, all the way to Makena. And then a high turn, a showboaty turn that was actually reported to ground control at Wailea by another pilot. They steadied out low and started proceeding back to the Ka'anapali airport. But somewhere right about here they stalled out and plummeted with a dead engine. There was no weather that day, about as much wind as now. She was here in January with Wayne and Edith and Mike, but it's different alone—such an ordinary-seeming stretch. And yet it is singular, incomparable: it has rocks that are only rocks here, its fret of coastline cut like a key to a door.

What Suzy wondered at first news was whether J.P. had been at the controls. She could imagine herself having done something like it. Up in a prop plane with a friend (or whatever they were) and a pay-per-hour pilot, and taking the controls herself if the pilot granted the opportunity, pushing it a little. Proving something, maybe, or showing off for Grace. Perhaps J.P. was at the control wheel down in Wailea, too, at the southern tip of the ride, when the plane ballooned a little too much and almost stalled out.

But what the fisherman who found them said, both to the police and to the newspapers as well as to Wayne, was that they were in the back together. He was certain it was J.P., not the pilot, seated with Grace. Plus, there was nothing showboaty, really, about what happened at the cove. Just a little plane that floated up too high and lost its pull. It went silent, like snapping the radio off, and then it free-fell backward, butt first into the water, the view out the windows nothing but sky until it was nothing but water.

Suzy's worked her way down the side of the cliff, and she's walking carefully out onto the rocks as the tide climbs higher. There are pools with urchins and small, bright fish. The perspective from sea level is different. It's more menacing. The water is moving faster than it appears to from up on the cliff. The chop is a little taller, meatier, more three-dimensional. And the water is cold. Her feet get wet from the waves. And at one point, as she tries to find her way to the farthest rock out, her foot slips on some slime and dunks her knee-high into one of the pools. Her right leg is soaked. And it chills in the breeze. She imagines herself accidentally cracking her head, floating out into the same water as Grace. She thinks of Wayne and Edith: she can't die, she reminds herself—it's duty.

She makes it to that farthest rock and she parks herself on her ass. The skirt of her uniform soaks through. The rock's so far out it looks unreachable during a higher tide. And it's from there that she traces the flight in her mind, printing a copy of the reconstructed memory, the fisherman's memory, as though it's her own. A little buzzing bug hovering off the shore, making the sound of the biplanes that tail ads for beer, growing larger as it comes nearer. Growing larger and seemingly preparing to pass, but flying higher, too, at an aggressive angle of ascent. Pulling up and around to take another look at something—Grace wants another look. And then it's not passing, but rather it's overhead and the buzzing cuts out. This is the part she's thought about most, what happens next.

It must've been so quiet. So shamefully silent. It must have been the sort of quiet you don't get in life—the ceasing of forward motion, the falling back without the noise of choices and missings-out and potential lives lived. There is no opportunity in that silence other than to give yourself over to the thing that's happening, to the inevitable conclusion of the afternoon flight and, more generally, to the lives you've happened to live. Suzy counts in her mind. What would it have taken—five seconds? Seven? At first there's the long, ballooning instant at the apex, then the reversal. That might take a couple on its own. And then the acceleration, backward toward the water. How high must they have been to stall going that sort of speed? Four hundred feet? Five hundred feet? This is the physics midterm she failed.

Thirty-two feet per second per second. That's what she remembers. So, *what?* Long enough, she decides. Long enough to count them out: one Mississippi, two Mississippi…What does one think at two Mississippi? With the uncertainty of life remaining? Is it one more second? Is it three or five? Is there the temptation that survival is possible? There must be. Suzy had always known that there were accidents on the track. She was in plenty herself. But *death* was never really a possibility. It was simply a question of preparation: *What would I need to do to survive this? What would be required of me to not end up dead?* As in: *Here comes the water, better get ready to swim.* Maybe that's what Grace was thinking: *Wish I'd swum in high school like Suzy. It's just a little plane, it's just five hundred feet. It's not a plummet from thirty-five thousand. Why wouldn't we make it out of this okay?*

Assuming you're at three Mississippi, and four Mississippi is coming fast, what's the order of people who pass through your mind? Is it immediate proximity first? J.P. and the pilot? Is it chronological, longest known? Mom and Dad and Suzy, *then* Mike? Why does Suzy suspect Mike didn't receive top billing in either case? And why does Suzy suspect her own thoughts would be on the least consequential people in her life—a fixation on Pablo, the waiter at El Guincho, or Queens Cassidy? Know who else would pop up? Dave—Dave's ragged fingernail playing with the elastic of her underwear during the graduation ceremony. A memory with a psychic sear. There'd be a final sign-off and a little signature—*Thank you, Mom, thank you, Dad, thank you, Grace, for this life, for this award, thank you, Bil*—and then just *bang*. No doubt the worst thought would be on her mind as the plane passed underwater. Is that what knocked them out? Did they hit their heads? Did all three snap their necks on impact? She's pretty sure a two-ton plane free-falling from five hundred feet turns the surface of the water into concrete. It'd be like falling from fifty floors out of an office building and onto the street.

All she knows is that by the time the fisherman dove that final time, the cabin had filled with water. But their seat belts were still buckled, and it didn't seem like they'd struggled any to get out. She watches the film the fisherman described: They just fell silently like snow and slapped the surface of the water. Disappearing before he could even start motoring toward the snapped wings and tail on the surface. She watches it happen in her mind over and over and over. Suzy toggles between her sister's final thoughts and her own, the five or seven seconds distending over the course of an hour as the sun lowers as slowly as the memory of a plane. She tries to imagine a way to make it different: *What would be required of me to not end up dead?* She holds it in her mind and then starts speaking the words: "What would be required of me to not end up dead?" The words lose their meaning. They are sounds. They are one sentence, they are just one word: *whatwouldberequiredofmetonotendupdead?*

It is so dark down in the pools, and her rock is growing smaller with the rising tide. It will be difficult for Suzy to find her way back through the pools and up the cliff face without a struggle, without getting wet and scraping a knee. The salt breezes around the cove. Headlights appear to the south and then disappear over her shoulder, out of sight on account of the cliff. The sound of the water moving into the pools, moving in all around her, it is a constant, and something to hold right up in front of her mind, a sound that will never cut out like an airplane engine. It has been here since the beginning and it will be here once Suzy's gone, a thing that will never not be: water and rocks, *kshhhhhhhhh*. In it, all at once, there is the sound of water, the sound of rocks, the deeper sound of the Hawaiian spirits, of Pele the fire goddess, creator of the islands, antidote in spiritual dexterity to the crudeness of Honeywell's Mami. There is sound, but it disappears into its rhythm. Its constancy has defined itself as an absence: it is so present that it is hardly there. Before Suzy and after. But after's not really an option. *Whatwouldberequiredofmetonot-endupdead?* Wayne, Edith, Grace, Mike, Dave, Billy, Honeywell. That would be her order of thinking before she hit the water, wouldn't it? If she could only assure herself enough time to get through the whole list, to have them right up in front, in the fingers of her mind. *Wayneedithgracemikedavebillyhoneywell.* She has no one to turn to. But she feels a shift in her body, a lightening, like hollow bones. There is no one left. But the resignation steadies her, readies her. *Wayneedithgracemikedavebillyhoneywell.* Suzy says it like a prayer and it lifts her.

The flight back to Honolulu seems even shorter than the flight that brought her to Maui. It passes in blackness, and she makes it to her hotel in what feels like a single stride. They've put her up at the Royal Hawaiian again. "The pink cake," Edith called it. Suzy has zero appetite and no desire to navigate the luau hoards on the waterfront. Her last time here seems years ago, the buzz-cut grass, the blunt-edged sunlight of an afternoon burning on the beach.

In her room she pulls the pilot study guide from her bag—a mimeographed textbook they've been using for the flight-hours phase of licensing. She reads through the pages one by one, reviewing the cockpit diagrams and the aeronautical charts she's already been tested on. She spends an hour in the lamplight turning over the materials and assuring herself of her proficiency. Twenty-five hours to go.

She hears the thunder, but it hasn't started raining. She hears the faint scratch of guests moving across the grounds to beat the downpour. The soft footsteps in soft grass of the hundreds on the water. It makes her hungry for some reason, just hungry enough to step out through the sliding door and onto her porch. The grounds are stuck with palms, pricked in clusters at every turn. The nearest has been dropping coconuts, and she trots across the lawn to retrieve one. She compares three, palming them, shaking them. She picks the smallest, near spherical, brown and hairy, and returns to her room.

She's seen them opened before, by street vendors with machetes. She knows she won't have much luck getting to the flesh, even with a borrowed knife. And so she shuts the sliding door and locks it in place, pulls the curtain and positions herself at the edge of the wooden desk. She takes a couple practice strokes and then lowers the coconut into the corner of the desk. It's a good hit, it leaves a nice dent. She does it again and misses the spot. Three, four, and then on five the corner rips a chunk out of the hide. Silty milk spills across the table. She feels a little guilty — it must be what it's like to off a small animal with a rock.

She works the coconut for half an hour — pours out the milk, runs it through a coffee filter, eats the meat like it's corn on the cob. The whole thing only makes her hungrier. But it's full-out dumping rain now, the constant static on the window, the white noise of a tropical storm. She starts to change for bed, but she's nowhere close to exhausted enough. She wishes she could knock herself out. She wishes she could drink or smoke herself into slumber, but she wants to be sharp for tomorrow. Tomorrow is a day for clean thinking.

So instead, she lifts the receiver from its cradle beside the bed and asks the receptionist to connect her to the mainland. All charges accepted, et cetera. The signal takes an eternity to cross the ocean, plus ring after ring. And when she's resigned to hanging up, of course, is when he answers.

"Hello?"

"I'm breaking my promise."

"I hoped you would," he says. "Did everything go okay?"

"I guess so."

"So, yes? That's great news. That's great news to relay."

"You didn't tell me what he said when you told him you were finished," Suzy says.

"He was understanding," Billy says. "Mostly. But wants a couple more things before he's ready to let me go."

"It's going to go like that forever."

"I don't think so. Not this time."

In the gap it occurs to her that she isn't sure why she called.

"Hey," he says, "someone at Howlers told me Mike's been asking about me. Asked if they had a number he could call. Isn't that bizarre? A: that he would want to talk to me at all. And B: that he wouldn't just go through you?"

Suzy is silent. He's really going through with it, then.

"Suzy?"

She's never felt so knotted up, so seized in the lungs and stomach. More than any other spell of paralysis in the past. A failure to speak, caught in the insipid neutral zone between the instinct to protect herself and a desire to protect Billy. But at this point what can she do? Mike is in motion. *I'm gonna do it with or without you,* she hears him say again. All she'd be granting Billy is an opportunity to flee—which is no good to him anyway. For Billy, a life without Sela is worse than being blindsided.

"Don't worry about him," Suzy says. "He probably just wants some grass. But he can find another dealer. Just, no obligation, 'kay? If he pushes, tell him to talk to me."

"It's really no problem."

"Just don't worry about it."

"All right, dude...," he says.

She pivots.

"Just so you know—just so he knows—I'm coming in on the noon, into LAX probably around eight. And then I'm hand delivering."

"You really won't see me?"

"That part I'm sticking to."

"But you called."

"Just tell him so that he knows it's coming. To show that I upheld my end. And that this is really it."

"Well, I guess we can just talk about it later, then."

"No, no—this *is* it."

"C'mon," he says.

"This is costing me a fortune. Just don't call Mike back."

"Suzy, I like you."

"All right," she says. She still isn't sure why she called.

"This is important: I *really* like you," he says.

She presses her eyes together tightly, forcing the sentiment back out her ears.

"It wasn't just by chance that I picked you, you know? It wasn't Shelly at Howlers that pointed me toward you on the beach. I'd seen you there one night, I'd asked your name, and it turned out you were just who I needed you to be. Don't you get it? You were just the girl I needed right then. You showed up at the beach that afternoon and at the party that night—the universe was working in powerful, meaningful ways, Z."

Fucking coconut milk everywhere.

"Just, c'mon, some sort of fresh start," he says, "how 'bout it? Let's just look at this all over again when you're back."

Suzy knows little about what has just transpired—in the preceding minute and in the preceding eight months. But what she does know is that what's coming is so very much the end of something, not the beginning.

"Well, I'll be back tomorrow," she says.

"Okay." And he sounds satisfied enough by the gap left open that Suzy feels fine hanging up.

Daniel Riley

She uses the springs in the mattress to bounce herself to her feet. She lifts her suitcase onto the bed and unzips it. On top, there's a red skirt, a blue blouse, a pair of cotton underwear, and a change of hose. There's also a manila envelope with $150,000. She counts it out onto the bedspread—fifteen hundred hundreds. (Thirty-two feet per second per second...) The first envelope, way back in July, contained the most money she'd ever seen at once, by an order of magnitude. Now this blows that away. She counts a stack of hundreds until she's convinced the rest is all there.

The most interesting thing left in the suitcase, way down at the bottom of the bag, is a stewardess uniform. Her Grand Pacific uniform is hanging over the shower bar in the bathroom, dripping out into the tub from her time at the tide pools. The uniform in the bag is a second uniform, a uniform she's worn only twice before—to a place and back again. Suzy's breathing is rapid, and she feels light like she did on the rocks. It is the sensation, the tickling of skin and blood, she used to feel at the start of a race. It is the sensation she imagines she'll feel taking off in a plane alone for the first time. She runs a sleeve of the sky-blue jacket through her fingers. It has a nice hand to it. She takes a deep breath and exhales in a short report. She picks up the jacket and presses it to her body, regards herself in the mirror. It looks just right. She turns it over in her hands, grips it tightly, admires its capacity for action. She holds it like a loaded gun.

She checks in with the Grand Pacific flight ops the next morning, and, as is often the case, she's asked to redo her makeup. There's always something. But only with the most disheveled stews has she ever seen the check-in women give more than a single piece of advice. "More lipstick." "Straighten your shoulders." "Give the eyebrows a pluck—there should be two of them." Suzy knows that for the girls who are too lovely to be improved by a line of advice, there's a random bag check instead. Just so flight ops can write something down next to the girl's name on the log sheet, evidence of a job having been done.

With her makeup never quite right, though, Suzy hasn't ever brought a bag check upon herself. And so it goes again today. She parks herself in front of a mirror in the bathroom and finds the instruments. Eyelash curler, mascara wand, lipstick tube. She reapplies her foundation. Rubs it in thickly so that her freckles disappear, like stars do over big cities. She steps out into the check-in lounge and waves to the lady in charge, making sure for certain that she's been seen, that she's been accounted for on her way into the airport and her way out to the concourse.

It is a sticky morning—only three hours light, but with the mature heat of late afternoon. The concourse at Honolulu is open air for stretches, and so it's lightly peppered with myna birds and fragrant with plumerias. It occurs to her that there is no airport like it, the outside slipping in thoughtlessly like tongues of surf.

It's eleven o'clock—she has twenty minutes till it's time to report for Grand Pacific's noon nonstop back to LAX. Over the PA a disc jockey offers a taste of the new Zeppelin album, the first song. It's somehow been less than a year since she submitted her thesis. Suzy's footsteps meet the beat.

She passes her gate—the waiting area's only half-full and no one's at the check-in desk quite yet, just a marquee with the flight number and the destination—and walks to the far end of the concourse, where Pan Am runs out of the cluster on the end. There are three empty gates and three gates with departures in queue. At 52: an 11:45 to Auckland. At 54: a 1:00 to Tokyo. At 56: a noon to San Francisco. Three options. Three orders of pursuit, three separate fates cast into the fate beyond this current one. The San Francisco flight is boarding now. It will be a full plane. Auckland should be preparing to depart.

Tokyo would mean waiting around, maybe just the two pilots and a couple of stews aboard at this point. But her decision is really made up already.

Suzy ducks into the nearest bathroom on the concourse. She sets up in a handicap stall and undresses. She hangs the aquamarine Grand Pacific uniform on the back of the door. From her bag she pulls out the blue-and-white Pan Am uniform, the uniform she modeled last night during the rainstorm. The uniform she wore to Paris and back while pinch-hitting for the Laguna girls. The loaner. A life borrowed.

It fits her as it did the night before. Slim in the waist but layered by the jacket and skirt. Conservative by the standards of the smaller domestic lines. The pink-and-orange short shorts and go-go boots of Southwest. The sleeveless sheath in tangerine stripes of Continental. She packs her bag and opens the door and catches herself square in the mirror. White collar and white cravat. The sky-blue jacket — full sleeves, wide collar, and the five brass buttons. The sky-blue skirt — pleated off the hips, spilling to her knees. She affixes the brass wings to her breast pocket and pins her hair up on top of her head. She pulls the hat down over her hair. It clashes — the pale orange of her hair with the pale blue. She shifts her weight from her left side to her right in a rapid toggle. Her breathing skips like a scratched record. She runs each thumb lightly across the pads of her fingers, back and forth, double-time whole-hand snaps. In the mirror Suzy finds a pair of green eyes and sees herself, fairly, as the person she is in this moment. There is no Suzy but the one staring back, talented as she sometimes is at convincing herself Suzy Whitman's is a different kind of life altogether. Her face goes a little haywire. It's a tense grimace. Her mouth heavy angled, her eyes thin and near tears. She pulls on the down of her forearms.

But just as suddenly as her face fell, it snaps back to attention.

She exhales and appears as a picture of professional service, a young woman who's thrilled to be working for you and only you. She turns a quarter and looks back at the mirror over her shoulder, and there's that smile again—wide red lips and white teeth. "I'm Suzy," she says in a mock whisper an octave higher than her own. She says it through the plastic fixture of her grin. "I'm Suzy," she says, and now higher, with disdain creeping in at the edges: "I'm Suzy. Fucking fly me."

A woman in a yellow muumuu, as wide as she is tall, smiles at Suzy on her way to an empty stall. Suzy breathes through her nose, draws it way down into her stomach, and smiles in the mirror. "Hey," she says to herself in a more careful whisper, "they just added me over here. I don't know if it's on the flight log yet or what, but they added me to the crew." She starts again. "Hey, I don't know if they told you yet, but I'm jumping on with you guys.... Yeah, I don't know, guess it can't hurt to have the extra help, right?" Again, quieter: "Hey, might not be on the log yet, but I'm with you now. I'll head down, sure.... No, no need. I'll talk to whoever's in charge on board and see where she wants me."

She leaves the bathroom and walks on a slack line to the agent working gate 52. Flight 117: Honolulu to Auckland. It looks like an enormous flight and boarding will take a while. Suzy waits casually behind a short older man with a paintbrush on his lip. He's asking for an aisle on account of his poor circulation. She can't hear what the agent says, but the man turns, head-shakingly furious, and floats back to the waiting area in a dust cloud. Suzy chests up to the counter and tests it uncertainly.

"Hey," she says with a soft smile. "It might not be on the log yet, but they just sent me down here last minute, and I'm on this one now."

The woman has a brown bob. She's squat and comes up to Suzy's shoulders. She wouldn't weigh in under the stew limit. The woman squints at Suzy and considers her paperwork. "We're all set, full crew," she says, almost like a question. "Are you sure?"

"Oh yeah...," Suzy says, swallowing, sucking the spit down out of her throat. The flight's due to take off in twenty minutes. She can't figure out why they haven't started boarding. "Are you guys behind on boarding?"

"There's a mechanical issue. At least an hour, but we're telling people two."

She can't wait an hour. She can't wait two hours. She starts to hear it the moment the woman finishes: "Suzy Whitman, please report to..." She's not even certain it's what's actually said. She wouldn't bet the money in her bag on it, at least. But she hears it again, faint at the other end of the terminal, words over the PA that's not hooked up to the speakers down here. It sounds like: *Suzy Whitman. Suzy whitman suzy whitman suzy. Whitman suzy whitman.* She imagines the gate agent and the pilots and the passengers scouring the terminal. Dragging her back aboard the plane to L.A. Detaining her for her plans to fly as an imposter. She can still turn around and change back and get there in time. There are only two other planes at the Pan Am gates. And Tokyo's not leaving for over an hour, either. Just gate 56 back to San Francisco. She thinks it fast and says it faster.

"This *is* the flight to San Francisco, right?"

The gate agent looks at her blankly.

"Or is it...?"

The gate agent turns over her shoulder toward the board: AUCK-LAND, 11:45, PAN AM 117.

"Ah, Auckland," Suzy says. "That would've been something! My mistake. Pardon."

The woman squints at her again and then smiles with professional obligation.

Suzy smiles, too, as she turns and inches toward the San Francisco flight. It has just begun boarding. She imagines the woman at the Auckland gate calling her colleague at gate 56. She imagines herself getting apprehended halfway between the two. She navigates the clumped masses of delayed Kiwis, dodges the airport security guards. At 56, first class has just boarded, up top, twenty total. And business class is invited to line up—another fortyish down below. On deck: maybe the first hundred in the rear, packing the back of the big boat first.

She can see it out the window. A Pan Am 747. She's flown a 747 twice since Paris—the PR trip to San Francisco and her last time to New York. The things she admired the first flight are still admirable now. This isn't the lost luster of years of marriage—it's more like a third date, and the eyes and teeth and lips look just as good as they did the first couple times they kissed. It is the rare case of a nice memory not overdistorting the impression. The glorious wing-span—nearly the width of a New York City block. The pretentious posture of the tail. The unending row of windows, lined up along the white plane side like candy dots on wax paper. Stretching so far out toward the runway that the laws of perspective make them disappear. She sees the pilots through the window of the cockpit, two pilots flipping switches and flipping laminated pages in a steel-ringed book of air maps. The ocean is wide and the islands are small.

Suzy does it again. A rerun, five minutes on. The same line practically, but with greater assertion. The belief that she'll need to squelch the doubt expressed by the Auckland gate agent if she's called over.

"Hey," Suzy says with a soft smile, "it might not be on the log yet, but they just sent me down here last minute, and I think I'm on this one now."

"Ohh-kay," the woman says, glancing down at her paperwork and running the tip of her pencil along the names on the printout. "I don't see any mention of an additional crew member here. But I guess that makes sense. They told us a girl called in last-minute sick, that she wouldn't make it. But they said we'd be forced to do without." Suzy can't believe what she's hearing. She's swimming in her disbelief, gasping in her mind for air as she dunks into her marvelous fortune. The gate agent has said something she hasn't heard.

"Hmm?" Suzy says.

"What'd you say your name was?"

"Grace," she says, the first name out. She hasn't even considered. "Grace Schuyler."

It's a mistake. Already a mistake and she hasn't even crossed over into the jet bridge.

"Great," the gate agent says, forcing an exhausted smile and taking her name down in block-letter pencil.

This time it's unmistakable. It's in her ears, out of the speakers, even at this end. "Grand Pacific stewardess Suzy Whitman to gate twenty-eight immediately. Your flight is boarding. Please report to gate twenty-eight, Grand Pacific stewardess Suzy Whitman."

It's real. The flight to L.A. is boarding. But she is on a flight to San Francisco. Or not quite.

"Just head down there and tell them what the deal is," the gate agent says.

Suzy slings her bag over her shoulder and clicks down the jet bridge. It's wide open, the gap in boarding zones. It occurs to her as she takes the jet bridge with strong strides just how much she's improved at walking in heels. The runoff effect of nine months of flying. She pulls her shoulders back and bows her legs inward an extra couple degrees at each step so that her feet find a tighter line. She feels exceptionally tall. She feels she can make her exceptionally tall hat touch the roof of the jet bridge.

There's a backup at the door: a diminutive passenger runs his fingers along the rivets at the entry, the sleek seam there, in the sort of awe Suzy figures only men who work on machines might experience. His wife tugs at his free hand and pulls him aboard.

Suzy steps up and places her fingers on the same cool rivets. She thinks of Wayne. The stew at the door looks up and is blankly indifferent at first, but then flickers into full flame, a little tick of the head and a big, relieved smile.

"Well, hey," she says, "we thought we were gonna be down one."

Suzy reflects the angle of the woman's neck back at her, reflects the smile, too.

"Yeah, they just told me to head on down here, that I'm with you."

"Well, that's great," the woman says. "We're just settin' up shop here, getting drinks going, warming up the coffee."

"Just let me know where I can start."

Suzy knows the routine from the back-and-forth to Paris. She consciously summoned the memory of those flights last night, recalled the differences in service. She drops her bag in the stew cargo compartment and gets to work.

It goes as it goes. The plane fills up. Not quite full capacity—three hundred and sixty is the final count. That's a lot of lives.

Suzy works the rear—coffee, water, towels. Coffee, tea, or me. TWA coffee or TWA tea. She finds herself enjoying it, almost missing it from a future vantage.

They're away from the gate. They're buckled in for takeoff. Last night's rain clouds seem imagined, it's so blue out her porthole. She holds fixed on the picture out the window, blurred by the thick plastic—Vaseline lensed.

There's a lineup on the runway. The girl buckled in next to her is six or seven clues into the Sunday *Times* crossword. Maybe a New York–based crew, Suzy thinks. So many can be so talkative, but these ones are trapped up and into their own thing.

The phone rings in the back cabin. Suzy lifts the receiver and the captain says, "On deck."

The way they're nosed, Suzy can see the plane in front of them make its wide turn onto the runway and fire its engines. The jet-stream logo on the golden tail of Continental. Continental: Seattle or Los Angeles, she bets. Six hours flat, riding the currents. By the time the thought's through, the plane is gone, and they're making the same wide right onto the runway, stopping at the line, a blue 747 race car in the starting grid at the Glen. Just before the plane rocks back to a full stop, the jet engines wind higher than she's ever heard, fuel tonnage and physical force, three hundred and sixty passengers, eight stews, two pilots, jet engines riveted to ninety-foot wings, engines tall enough to accommodate one Suzy standing up. The palm trees start to tick past like eighth and sixteenth notes, speeding toward the inevitable conclusion of a resolved piece of music.

Just as they hadn't been for the history of time, they are now up in the air together—these specific many souls aboard Flight 45 to San Francisco. They're off the earth, each with the other, the wheels of the airplane curling up inside for safekeeping. Fantastic physics settle them out over the immediate water of the Pacific, this particular water tinted green on account of it cuddling up to the only land for two thousand miles.

They're way up, fast.

Suzy's on the plane. They're on their way to San Francisco, California, USA.

They level off at thirty thousand feet. Heading east. Heading home. The floor is flat, and so they wheel the drink cart through the back of the plane, Suzy and the crossword stew, Miriam. The passengers drink so much POG.

It takes thirty minutes, and Suzy finds herself asking passengers to repeat their drink orders, almost every row. Her mind is elsewhere. It has drifted up front, up top.

Suzy's plan wasn't this at all. She's practically heading right back to where she came from. Sure, San Francisco is six or seven hours from Sela by car, four hundred miles. But on the global scale, when you really take a look at a map that lets you see both Russia and the United States in the same picture—from that height San Francisco and Los Angeles are the same. She'd go back and everyone would be waiting. Wayne, Edith, Grace, Mike, Dave, Billy, Honeywell. Police at SFO. Authorities from both Grand Pacific and Pan Am. She's already forfeited the job. It was over an hour ago, when she ignored the announcement, the call that said: *This is it for you, Suzy Whitman.* But flying back into the trap wasn't the plan. The plan was to step aboard, luck into working the flight, and land wherever she might on the other side of the ocean. Tokyo, Seoul, Hong Kong, Bangkok, Auckland, Sydney. Those were really the only options, escape. Wayne Edith Grace Mike Dave Billy Honeywell. Tokyo Seoul Hong Kong Bangkok Auckland Sydney.

San Francisco.

The plan is shot. But high as she feels in the aisle, high as she feels on adrenaline, she also feels herself approaching a sticky inevitability. A fate with gravity. A reckoning with the thing she's known deep down over the last two days she'd really need to do. There is nowhere else to go—no one, no place, certainly not Los Angeles or San Francisco. Certainly not those places most of all. She is a light-boned bird holding patient in the updraft of a skyscraper, floating on the edge of the breeze, that instant before abandoning the comfort of the rail and giving into certain flight.

What happens as Suzy moves from the back of the plane to the front? Once the drink service is wrapped and the passengers unclick to drain their bladders? What does Suzy see? She sees baldness, she sees hair, she sees black and brown and sandy blond. She sees no red but imagines her own. She sees glasses and stripes and blankets and books. She sees babies-to-be in their final month of preexistence. She sees olds with less than a year left on the clock. That's about it, though. It's not a vision of details—it's a vision of breadth. Three hundred sixty passengers and they do their best to cut a wide berth of Americanness. But beyond the vague perceptions, the named attributes, she doesn't see much more.

Her vision narrows on the stairway to the jet's second floor. And in a protracted instant that might be an hour or a minute or a second, her heels are on the stairs, her eyes are on the door to the cockpit, her fingers are on the latch to the door. She feels the eyes of the upstairs stews on her as she knocks.

"We already…," one begins to say. But the door folds open.

"Hey," Suzy says to the cockpit, "I was just wondering if you needed any help up here."

They keep their eyes busy on the instrumentation, on the neon horizon. The copilot lifts a paper cup of coffee and shakes his head, taken care of.

"You sure?" Suzy says.

He turns now, to assure her he's sure. But she's got the prettiest smile she can muster up. It makes him smile, too. As though the follow-up question's a private joke.

"I'm…yeah, I'm pretty good," the copilot says. He looks young. He looks younger than Mike, younger than Billy. Closer to Suzy's age. She's never flown with a pilot this young. He keeps his eyes right on her.

"You know," the captain says without turning, "I could use a warm-up."

"Great," Suzy says, smiling again at the copilot.

She unbends herself out of the doorframe and lengthens herself toward the ceiling. The other stews watch her move to the coffeepot. They're keenly aware that something's going on, but they've seen it before, they all have again and again, a hard play for the pilots. It's just not usually this brazen, this quick out of the gate.

Suzy knocks again. The door opens. The copilot takes the cup for the boss. The crunched space behind their seats, where Suzy stood while taking lessons from pilots on other flights—it's a little roomier on a 747. There's plenty of space to stand and close the door.

Suzy scoots in and latches it shut.

The copilot turns again, a little disbelieving, and just says, "Hey."

Suzy watches the water out the window. Fixes her eyes on the crisp, level DMZ between sky and sea. Two blues all the way home.

"So," Suzy says, a little breathless. "Something's gonna happen."

"What's that?" the copilot says, caffeinated, down to play.

"I'm gonna say something, you're gonna do something, then I'm gonna do another thing."

"Sounds like Simon Says," the copilot says.

The captain shifts in his seat and squints at his partner. She still hasn't seen the captain's face. He's gray at the ears. He's got the kind of hair around his cap that could mean he's bald or not—it's tough to say.

"Hon," the captain says, "we're actually pretty busy right now."

"Oh, right, of course," Suzy says. She's building toward the voice she was using in the bathroom mirror at the airport. "I don't want to bother you. But listen, just to this one thing...."

She doesn't even take a breath. It just goes.

"There's a bomb on the plane. There are twelve members of the American Institute for Social Justice aboard. Twelve men and women. Twelve identical briefcases. One of them is equipped with a bomb that will take this plane out of the air. Don't try to figure out who they are—they're not sitting there in rags with dirty faces and dreadlocks.

You'll never be able to ID all twelve. The minute you make a move for one, the member with the bomb will detonate. Even if you knew who was who, and planned something simultaneous, there are only two pilots and eight stews, seven excluding me. Point is: it'll never work."

"Gimme a fucking break," the captain says. "Stop screwing around and wasting our time."

"There's a bomb on the plane and you'll be discharged if you don't take this information seriously. You don't have a choice."

"You're full of shit and I don't have to listen to it. I'm sick to fucking death of you people. Don't you realize nobody does this anymore? Don't you know it's *over?*"

"Welp, one more time, I guess," Suzy says, turning to the copilot. "Lemme talk to you, then."

"What do you want?" he says, dumb in the face for having been charmed a minute ago. "What's the demand?"

"It's pretty straightforward. Don't want money. Don't want prisoners. Don't want Cuba. Just three very simple things."

"Okay," the copilot says.

"One: you don't let anyone on the plane know. If passengers are made aware, the bomb's going off. If stewardesses are made aware, the bomb's going off."

She hears the captain's voice cut in: "I don't have to fucki—"

"*Two:* you don't radio about what's going on until I say so."

"If you want this bullshit to be taken seriously," the captain says, "we're radioing now."

"No, you're not," Suzy says, her voice growing gravelly. She sounds like Lauren Bacall. She likes it.

"What else?" the copilot says.

"I'm flying the rest of the way."

"Give me a goddamned break!" the captain says. "You'll fucking kill us, you crazy cunt."

"Jeez," Suzy says, "you're pretty miserable. What's wrong, *hon?*"

"I'm not doing another one of these."

"Well, we're only talking one more. I'm gonna make this so easy. You don't need to *do* anything. You don't need to *call* anyone. And you won't need to deal with frantic passengers so long as you keep shut the fuck up."

"You'll drop us in the middle of the ocean. You have no idea what it takes to fly an airplane. You put in a couple years or whatever handing out vodka and orange juice, cleaning up vomit and shit in the bathrooms, and you think you can fly an airplane?"

"I don't like him," Suzy says to the copilot. "He's gonna get three hundred sixty innocent people killed if he doesn't shape up his attitude. Can you straighten him out?"

"I'm just...this is my first...."

"Good answer, kid."

"Listen, boys, I'll give you this: we're not going to San Francisco, we're turning around. If you want to turn it around yourselves, if that'll make you feel better, then go for it. But now is the moment to start. We're talking ASAP, because we need the fuel."

"You really are a dumb cunt, aren't you? If we turn around right now, every person out there will know something's wrong with—"

It happens so fast it takes even Suzy by surprise. The sound is comical, cartoonish. The sound of an empty beer bottle bouncing off a bar. The sound of a quarter colliding with a flagpole. The sound of a half-full fire extinguisher cracking an airplane captain's skull.

His body gives up in the instant. He slumps there like a napping child in a car seat. Hands slipping off the controls and falling to his sides, body propped up by the seat belt alone. The copilot screams. It's a squeaky scream. Then, when Suzy moves to unclip the captain, he shouts, "Hey!"

"I need you to start taking this seriously," she says. "And I need you

383

to turn this plane, gradually, so as not to attract attention, in a large arc until we're facing the other direction."

"I can't...I refuse."

"Dude," Suzy says, "put your fucking hands on the yoke and start turning around, or we're blowing up the plane. This is so easy for you. You have nothing to gain from fighting me on this."

She gets the captain's seat belt undone, but there is so much blood. Way more than she could've expected, and most of it's coming from his right nostril. She checks to make sure he's still breathing, hears him murmur: *You dumb fucking cunt.* Or at least that's what she hears passing through his lips, even though it's just faint breath. *You dumb fucking cunt. Janice, you dumb, slot-mouthed fucking cunt.* She begins to slide him off of the seat. He's incredibly heavy, much heavier than he looks.

"New plan," Suzy says. "You get him out of that seat, and you sit over there."

"Where am I supposed to put him?"

"We come in here all the time and find plenty of room back there," she says. "Squat there in heels and a skirt. You can certainly find a way to lay him down in that space."

"You told me to turn, I started to turn."

"I'll get in your seat. Chinese fire drill."

He obeys and pulls the captain out of his seat, and Suzy takes the yoke in her hands. Kicks her heels off beneath the display and places her feet on the rudder and brake pedals, tests out the feel. Her eyes are distracted by the instrumentation—the radar, nav control, systems information displays, artificial horizon. She's distracted enough to not notice how much trouble he's having with the captain.

"He's bleeding a lot. There's gonna be blood running back into his throat if I lay him down."

"Then prop him against the door. Sit him up so that the blood drains right. Just make sure he's not gonna die on us."

They're turning just the right amount, a big, sweeping, undetectable right turn, a lasso of a turn.

"Do you really know what you're doing with that thing?" he says, still looking after the pilot.

"I do," she says.

"Okay, well, at least let me know if something's not right."

In another couple minutes the captain's positioned upright on the floor. The copilot climbs into the captain's seat and checks the instrumentation. They're flying due south for a moment.

"You ever sat on the left side?" Suzy says.

He juts out a lower lip and shakes his head.

"So that's cool," she says.

"Where are you going with this? I'm not gonna cause problems, I just need to know in order to make sure we don't run out of fuel. There are only so many places we can get."

"I appreciate that. But I know fuel's not gonna be a problem. I know that we're good to go."

"That's just not—I need to know in order to—"

"Don't ask again."

He stares ahead and pulls the turn a little tighter.

"How old are you?" she says.

"Twenty-three."

"Did you fly in the war?"

"Yes."

"And then you got up front with the airline pretty quick."

He nods.

"I'd love to fly bigger planes someday," she says.

He nods again.

"We'll see, right?"

Three minutes of silence and they've completed the long one-eighty. That's about as far as she's got it for certain in her mind.

"Now what?" the copilot says, and Suzy shrugs.

They sit on bearing back to Honolulu, but Suzy doesn't much think that'll take care of what she needs.

There's a knock at the door.

"You boys good?" It's the crew leader, Flo. Checking on Suzy, no doubt.

Suzy nods at the copilot to answer.

"We're good, thanks a lot," he says.

"You betcha," Flo says, and Suzy hears her pad away.

This is pretty much it, right? She's brought it this far and still doesn't have it figured out all the way. *Wayne Edith Grace Mike Dave Billy Honeywell. WayneEdithGraceMikeDaveBillyHoneywell*—the prayer returning like a vestigial heartbeat. Each compromised by a proximity to Suzy, Suzy compromised by her proximity to each of them. Suzy at the center of all that static, the one all the bad business seems to stick to.

"You know what?" Suzy says. "I'm good for a little while."

"What do you mean?"

"I think I don't need you here for a little bit."

"Okay..."

"Here's what I think you should do: Head out like you need to use the bathroom. Stay in there for a little while and then come back. The key, though, is that none of the other stews can know anything's wrong. None of the stews, none of the passengers. The others out there are watching closely. If they detect anything's up, that you guys are plotting, that the stews are even aware there's anything *to* plot, then: *Boom.* Ya know?"

"Okay. Bathroom, then."

"Great," Suzy says.

He unclicks his belt and moves the captain aside so that he can open the door. He gets it open just a crack and steps over the captain's legs. The door clicks behind him.

There's a risk he'll freak out and tell Flo. But Suzy's feeling like he might lie on her behalf, just to play it safe. A bomb's a bomb.

She slides out of her seat and stands in the cockpit. She marvels at the plane as it flies itself on the current bearing. She checks the captain's pulse. He's still breathing, too, so that's good. She locks the cockpit door.

She moves to the left side, sits in the captain's seat. She checks the instrumentation, feels the airplane humming beneath her, the autopilot pulling the plane as if by rope through the air. It's like the ski lifts in the Adirondacks, the lifts of her youth, little Suzy tailing Wayne to the summits of those mountains.

She pulls out the map book, and before opening it to pages with zoomed-in quadrants, she recognizes it to be a skipped step and stares instead at the cover. Just everywhere there is, pretty much.

She runs her eyes along the Pacific coast—the left edge of the Pacific, the right edge of places she's never been, places she's not even ever thought much about. She imagines, in a dreamy flash, the hundreds of planes in the air at this very moment, the millions of planes before that, the little lines they leave behind in the sky, contrails and carvings through space. She imagines those lines stacking up like the lines on the maps of the airline publicity materials and the walls of travel agents, those lines stretching from all points, an inexhaustible cloud-colored yarn wrapping up a life-size globe, all flights ever run, so many that the edges begin to touch, the lines begin to layer—every flight path, every vector, every pilot, passenger, and pretty young stew making contact at the edges, no difference, from the view up here, between yesterday and today and tomorrow or her or him or you or me. Just one simple, interconnected, overlapping, infinite, human-history-size idea in forward motion.

She places her feet on the brake and the rudder. She lowers her hands, both hands, to the yoke. She feels the low vibration in her calluses, a bass string ringing out in perpetuity. She levels up, marvels at the true blue horizon.

She thinks of Wayne, the pilot that never was. The way all this might look through his living, breathing eyes. She thinks of Edith. She thinks of Grace. But she thinks of Wayne, mostly — she thinks of Wayne, she thinks of Wayne, she thinks of Wayne.

There's a hand at the door latch, and when the door fails to open, there's a quiet knock and a soft voice.

"Hey," it says. And then a light knuckle rap again. "Hey, lemme back in."

Suzy carving. Suzy rolling the board with the arches of her feet, all heels to all toes, way out wide and again across the middle. Suzy skimming the yellow centerline and snapping back at the curb, hard rubber and asphalt pinging like a typewriter. Suzy upright but curved, like parentheses, shifting open and closed, tracing even switchbacks, leveling the grade.

"Hey!" He's at the door. They're all at the door. *"Hey, lemme in!"*

Suzy knows it's time to make the call, the time to make the call is right now. And so she toggles the autopilot to the off position and points the airplane away from everything at her back. Away from every force that's squeezed her into this fateful, tailor-made, Suzy-shaped present. A present that is already past now, that is ancient history, history to be justified one day in the future: see it like Suzy sees it, make it make sense. Well?

She begins to hum to herself, a nursery-rhyme cadence. It's not much like anything she's ever done before. Out the window there is sky and there is water and there is a zipper, absolute in its horizontal, running edge to edge and holding together heaven and Earth. The humming keeps coming, but she's finally worked up to parting her lips and placing words in the slipstream of the sound.

Su-zy, Su-zy, Su-zy, so...

she whispers with a swelling breath and all the curiosity in the world

...where is it you wanna go?

Acknowledgments

Not many kids get to grow up in the shadow of the flight path or amidst a sorority of former stewardesses, but I had the great good fortune of being raised with both advantages. That's where this book begins—countless days and nights watching planes take off over the water, like Suzy does on the Fourth of July, and countless days and nights with women like Ethel Pattison, founding director of the Flight Path Learning Center at LAX, a museum off the edge of Runway 7R-25L devoted to the history of flight in Southern California. It was there that I first flipped through the poster-size airline advertisements, interviewed volunteers (and former stews) about the glamorous days they seemed to recall as faultless, and—perhaps most significantly—ran my fingers across the bright wool sleeve of a uniform that once belonged to a Suzy or a Grace who'd flown in the early seventies. *Fly Me* began with that uniform, and I owe a disproportionate amount to Ethel and the Flight Path Center for that fact. It's right off Imperial—go there if you get a chance.

This book does not exist without the sure-handed guidance, support, availability, and straight-up *rightness* of Kirby Kim and Joshua Kendall. I am perpetually blown away by the generosity and care of all book agents and editors, but especially these two. It should've surprised me not at all that they come with terrific colleagues: Thanks to everyone at Janklow & Nesbit and Little, Brown, especially Brenna English-Loeb, Nicky Guerreiro, Ben Allen, Maggie Southard, Erica Stahler, and Reagan Arthur.

To the *GQ* folks. Too many of you to name, past and present, but especially: Jim Nelson, Devin Friedman, Brendan Vaughan, Andy Ward, Joel Lovell, Lauren Bans, Fred Woodward, Mike Benoist, Geoff Gagnon, Jon Wilde, Catherine Gundersen, Devin Gordon, Mark Byrne, Mark Anthony Green, Benjy Hansen-Bundy, Michael Hainey, Sean Flynn, Michael Paterniti, and John Jeremiah Sullivan.

To old friends on both coasts, especially the originals from the real-deal Sela del Mar.

To English teachers who are forced to read an unfathomable tonnage of bad writing, and yet still encourage students who want to be writers to "keep going."

To extra-special readers: Sarah Ball, Dan Goldstein, Sarah Goldstein, Alice Gregory, Jeff Hobbs, and Charlie Waln.

To Alyssa Reichardt, best brah and first reader. Without you there's not much *Fly Me,* because without AZR there's not much SW.

To all the Rileys and Patons and Pattisons. Some families fuck you up so badly that you write about them. You've made it so good that I'll never have to.

To Sarah Goulet. You're it, man. Wanna do this?

To Neil Riley. You taught me most things. I miss you every day. I hope you got a good seat—how's the view?

To Patti, Penny, Peggy, and June Paton. Gran, in 1946, you left upstate New York, caught a steamer to Hawaii for a teaching gig, and then stopped short on your way home in a town you'd never heard of called Manhattan Beach, California. You had three daughters with alliterative names—one who was twenty-two in 1972, one who died in a plane crash in Hawaii, and one who wound up living her whole life at the beach with her husband and son. This book belongs to you four, because your lives gave it all the life it asked for. Thank you, Gran, for moving to California, and thank you, Mom, for never leaving.

About the Author

Daniel Riley is a senior editor at *GQ* magazine. He grew up in Manhattan Beach, California, and lives in New York City. This is his first novel.